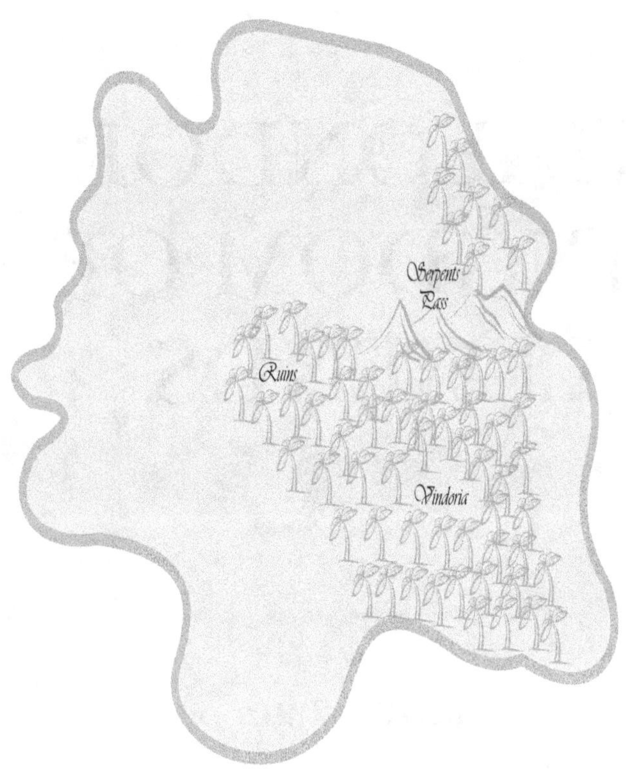
Serpents
Pass
Ruins
Vindoria

# THALONDOR: KINGDOM OF LEGENDS

Shane Lege

Check out our other great books at:
https://legeindustriesllc.com
Or by scanning the QR code below

TikTok: @shanelege

Twitter: @ShaneLege

Instagram: LegeIndustriesLLC

Facebook: Lege Industries LLC

Good Reads: Shane Lege

Thank You for taking the time to read this book. This book will always be special to me as this is my very first novel.

All of this and future editions would not be possible without the support of my friends and family. Thank you most of all.

Thanks for the assist Jim Bacon

# Table of Contents

*Prologue*

Centuries had slipped away, burying the memories of ancient battles beneath the layers of time. The once-besieged land now stood as a testament to resilience and renewal. Where once rivers of blood had stained the earth, now bloomed lush fields and vibrant forests. It appeared peace had settled, and the wounds inflicted by the horrors of the past had slowly healed.

Yet, as the cycle of time completed its thousandth turn, whispers of forgotten legends stirred once more. For the enchantment that had bound the forces of darkness for a millennium was nearing its end. The people, generations removed from the atrocities that had plagued their ancestors, had grown complacent in their peaceful existence.

The echoes of ancient prophecies remained, passed down through the annals of time. They spoke of a chosen hero, one who would rise from humble beginnings and confront the malevolence that had been imprisoned for so long. The burden of salvation would weigh heavily upon the chosen hero's back.

The day arrived, casting a shadow of anticipation across the land. The evil that had been suppressed, held captive within the depths of a timeless prison, sensed its moment of release drawing near. Dark whispers carried on the winds, reaching the ears of those sensitive to the ancient magic that coursed through their veins.

Whispers about this upcoming darkness spread like a spooky song on the wind. People who could feel the ancient magic in their veins heard these whispers. This magic wasn't just a skill learned—it was a part of their family story, passed down through generations. The essence that linked them to their ancestors now felt strange and unstable, as if a big change was coming.

As the last remnants of the enchantment faded away, the prison walls crumbled, releasing the festering evil that had lain dormant for a thousand years. It surged forth like a tempest unleashed, rekindling fears that had long been dormant. Evil creatures would soon roam the lands again, causing death and destruction in their wake. The land, once again, would be tested in the crucible of darkness and despair.

The heroes of old, spoken of in hushed tones and immortalized in legends, were not forgotten. Their spirit, passed down through the generations, found resonance in the hearts of the brave and the righteous. A new generation of heroes emerged, bearing the weight of their forefathers' legacy, ready to face the trials and tribulations that awaited them.

The need for brave individuals to rise is clear during these tough times. They had to use their family's old magic, but their journey would be full of danger. They must fight the problems caused by evil forces that took over the land. The battle for survival and hope was about to begin once more.

The brave champions from the olden times remained in people's thoughts. They had passed their tales down through many years and inspired those with bravery. A group of unknown heroes emerged, ready to face future challenges and carry on their legacy. The new heroes were prepared to maintain noble traditions and overcome challenges.

It was time to face the truth and confront the land's fears. Everyone was together in their goal, strengthened by the toughness of their ancestors. They promised to take back their land from the control of darkness. Evil's thousand-year imprisonment had ended, bringing forth an era that would create genuine heroes and revive legends.

## *Chapter 1 The Landing*

I regained consciousness as I found myself in a disoriented state, memories devoid of what had happened and my whereabouts uncertain. The only thing I remembered is that my name is Valaric, and I was out on an adventure. My body was filled with aching and a sense of being battered, as if a fierce battle had been engaged in. The pounding in my head was relentless, reminiscent of the aftermath of consuming a barrel of wine. I attempted to open one eye, only to be met with a blinding brightness, causing squinting against the harsh sun rays.

A dry sensation invaded my mouth, leaving a lingering salty taste. Lying face down, I attempted to figure out what may be around my immediate area by feeling around with my right hand. I explored the surrounding area, encountering a hot and gritty texture that lacked firmness or solidity. Determined to gather more information, I lifted my head, willing both of my eyes to open and survey the surroundings.

To my right, I saw an expanse of sand stretching as far as the eye could see, giving the impression of extending for miles. As my gaze turned to the left, I observed a similar scene, revealing a vast desert of grains beneath the scorching sun.

"How in the world did I get here? Where is here? Why is there so much sand around me and why am I in so much pain?"

Pain and fatigue relentlessly battered my body, making it protest loudly. It seemed like I was in an uneven battle, where my arms, legs, and back were taking a severe beating. Even though my body was under immense strain, my determination to figure out the situation stayed strong.

Summoning all my inner strength, I began a slow and challenging effort to change my position. It took painstaking work, but I managed to roll onto my back, though this movement sent waves of pain radiating throughout my body. It felt like this action only made the torment I was already enduring even worse, intensifying the agony.

To compound matters, the discomfort was further exacerbated by my trusty sword and shield affixed to my back. These loyal companions, a source of strength and protection, now imposed an unwelcome burden on my already strained body. Each movement served as a painful reminder of the weight I carried, adding to the physical pain I endured.

Now that I was turned over onto my back, the brightness of the sun's scorching rays greeted my eyes, casting a blinding and intense glare that obscured my vision. Squinting and shielding my eyes from the searing brightness, I strained to perceive the details of the immediate surroundings.

Through the hazy veil of light, a shimmering expanse of water emerged, stretching out before me like a mirage. Its glistening surface seemed to extend, reaching as far as my eyes could discern. The allure of the watery oasis beckoned promising relief from the arid and unforgiving desert that surrounded me.

My throbbing forehead prompted me to pause and massage it, seeking some respite from the piercing pain. Gritting my teeth, I mustered the strength to sit up, assuming the same area where I was laying. With a cautious glance around, I surveyed the landscape, taking in the details of my immediate surroundings.

To the left of my position, I noticed a weathered wooden trunk, its worn exterior bearing the marks of time and exposure to the elements. It stood silent, harboring its own secrets and tales of the past. Curiosity piqued, I cast my gaze further afield, where scattered fragments of weathered wood lay strewn about, scattered like forgotten remnants of a long-lost vessel.

The pieces of wood, once sturdy and resilient, had succumbed to the relentless tides and the merciless forces of nature. They now bore the unmistakable signs of decay, their smooth surfaces marred by cracks and fissures. They were relics of a forgotten fate, remnants of a ship that had encountered a mysterious end.

A sense of intrigue enveloped me as I pondered the story behind these discarded remnants. What had transpired in this desolate corner of the world? Were these the remains of a shipwreck, a haunting reminder of a fateful voyage? Or did they hold the key to a hidden treasure, long coveted and sought after?

Seizing the opportunity to ease the discomfort coursing through my back, I unfastened my sword and shield. With a sigh of relief, I set them down beside me, their weight no longer burdening my weary frame.

As I placed my sword and shield on the ground, a surge of gratitude washed over me. For at this moment, I realized my waterskin remained fastened to my belt on the left side. The familiar presence of the waterskin reassured me, for it held the promise of quenching my parched throat and offering a respite from the desert's relentless heat.

With practiced ease, I removed the stopper, eager to quench my parched throat. The first sip, though modest, revitalized me as the cool liquid trickled down my throat, assuring me of its potability.

Happy with the taste and purity of the water, I did it again, taking another sip to clear the lingering sandiness from my mouth. The refreshing feeling spread through my mouth, giving me a brief break from the dry surroundings. Feeling the water's revitalizing effects, I took a few more substantial sips, letting the coolness revive my tired body.

Filled with a newfound sense of determination, I seized the moment to explore further and uncover any other hidden items that might assist me in this enigmatic realm. As I rummaged through the pockets of my pants, my fingers stumbled upon a familiar and indispensable tool: a trusty flint and steel. The weight of the compact yet potent combination brought a surge of confidence, for I knew it held the power to ignite the transformative flame.

During my exploration, my gaze fell upon a familiar object--an crafted dagger. My hand reached out, feeling the cool touch of the hilt as I grasped it. With a smooth motion, I drew the blade from its sheath, reveling in the sight of its honed edge glinting in the light. Its presence filled me with a sense of reassurance and purpose, for the dagger had been a steadfast companion, a symbol of both protection and utility.

The dagger had accompanied me on countless adventures, its presence serving as a constant reminder of its resourcefulness. Its keen edge had sliced through obstacles and enemies alike, a versatile tool that could be wielded for both defense and practical tasks. The weight of the dagger in my hand infused me with a renewed sense of confidence, as I knew it would aid me in the challenges that lay ahead.

The idea of cleansing the gritty sand from my body grew more appealing with each step towards the sparkling water's edge. As I moved forward, I maintained a vigilant gaze, scanning the surroundings for any signs of hidden resources that could assist me in this mysterious predicament. My eyes darted from one spot to another, searching for any glimmers of hope amidst the unknown.

Passing by the weathered trunk that had caught my attention earlier, I made a mental note to return and explore its contents later. There was an unmistakable allure about it, hinting at potential treasures or tools that could hold immense value in this unfamiliar landscape. But for now, my immediate priority was to rid myself of the sand that clung to my skin and clothes, obscuring my senses, and weighing me down.

With purposeful strides, I approached the water's edge, its crystal-clear surface reflecting the radiant sun above. The gentle lapping of waves provided a soothing soundtrack as I dipped my hands into the refreshing liquid, cupping handfuls and splashing them over my body. The cool water offered solace, washing away the gritty residue.

Once cleansed, I straightened my posture and directed my gaze towards the horizon, surveying the expanse in both directions. To the left, a faint silhouette emerged, materializing into the majestic form of mountains or cliffs. Their imposing peaks stood tall and resolute. The sight awakened a potent blend of awe and curiosity within me, igniting a yearning for exploration and the allure of untrodden paths.

To the right, my gaze fell upon an endless expanse of untouched shoreline, stretching as far as the eye could see. The vastness of the shoreline mesmerized me, its emptiness carrying an aura of intrigue and anticipation. Though it appeared devoid of human presence, I sensed that there was more to this expanse than met the eye. It beckoned me to venture forth, to tread upon its sandy tapestry and unearth the secrets it held within.

As I stood there, the rhythmic crashing of waves against the shore filled the air, creating a symphony of nature's music. The salty breeze caressed my skin, carrying with it the whispers of distant lands and untamed adventures. With every gust, it whispered tales of undiscovered treasures and unexplored realms that lay just beyond the visible horizon.

Upon turning around, my gaze fell upon a sprawling expanse of forest, stretching out before me as far as the eye could behold. The sight of it evoked a whirlwind of emotions within me, a captivating blend of awe and trepidation. The forest stood as a formidable stronghold, its verdant foliage concealing the wonders that awaited within its depths.

The towering trees, reaching skyward with unwavering determination, commanded attention, and respect. Their majestic forms seemed to touch the heavens, while their outstretched branches formed a lush canopy, creating a sanctuary of untamed wilderness beneath. The air was thick with the scent of earth and foliage, a heady mixture that stirred the senses and heightened my anticipation.

The sky drew my attention, and my gaze lifted to behold the descending sun, its radiant beams casting a warm and golden glow over the landscape. A subtle urgency stirred within me, a reminder of the need to find shelter before the impending arrival of nightfall, when darkness would enshroud the land.

Pausing for a moment, I allowed myself to soak in the breathtaking vista that stretched out before me. The world, even in the face of uncertainty, possessed a remarkable beauty that couldn't be denied. From the majestic terrain to the vibrant colors painted across the sky, nature's artistry was on full display. A true testament to the wonders that existed in every corner of this realm.

Diverting my gaze from the vast landscape, I redirected my attention to the intriguing trunk that had caught my eye earlier. With a growing curiosity and a glimmer of hope, I set my sights on uncovering the secrets hidden within its weathered exterior.

However, as I planted my foot down to take the first step, a sudden and unexpected force seized hold of my leg, causing my heart to skip a beat. With a sudden jolt of panic coursing through my veins, I attempted to free myself from the grip that had ensnared my leg. Desperation fueled my every movement as I thrashed and pulled, trying to escape the clutches of the mysterious hand emerging from the water. Fear surged within me, intertwining with a sense of dread as I realized the danger lurking just beneath the surface.

My heart pounded in my chest, its rhythm matching the frantic rhythm of my attempts to break free. Adrenaline surged through my body, lending me a surge of strength as I struggled against the relentless grip. But the hand remained steadfast, its hold unyielding, as if determined to drag me down into the depths.

Consumed by panic and a mounting sense of desperation, I fought against the unyielding hold that enveloped me. The icy coldness of the water sent shivers down my spine, intensifying my sense of fear and helplessness. My mind raced, trying to comprehend the origin of this mysterious grip, but clarity eluded me during my panicked state.

In a state of sheer panic, my survival instincts surged through me, guiding my actions in the face of imminent danger. With adrenaline coursing through my veins, I surveyed my surroundings, searching for a means of escape. My gaze darted towards the spot where I had been sitting, fixating on the distant glimmer of my sword, just out of reach.

Summoning every ounce of strength within me, I focused on finding a solution, but the creature's grip on my leg was unyielding, suffocating any hope of escape. Desperation fueled my determination as I sought a way to break free from its clutches. And then, like a bolt of lightning, it hit me - my trusty dagger, secured to my belt at my back.

With trembling hands, I grasped the hilt of the dagger and positioned it for a swift and forceful strike. Summoning every ounce of courage, I launched a relentless attack, driving the blade into the hand that held me captive. With each desperate stab, I twisted my leg, intensifying the damage inflicted upon the creature. The creatures grip weakened, granting me a fleeting opportunity.

Seizing the moment, I yanked my leg free, feeling a mixture of relief and agony surge through me. My body stumbled backward, putting distance between myself and the treacherous waters.

Breathing and trembling with adrenaline, I assessed my surroundings, wary of any further threats, expecting another attempt from whatever had grabbed me with a heightened sense of caution. I realized I needed to be prepared for anything that might come next.

## *Chapter 2 The Setup*

I moved away from the water and took a moment to check the aftermath of the scary encounter. I looked at the place on my leg where the unseen attacker had grabbed me, and I didn't see any cuts or open wounds. However, there was a clear mark left, like a lasting imprint on my skin, reminding me of the creature's firm grip.

The imprints on my leg drew my fingers like a magnet, and I traced their outline, feeling the heated and swollen skin beneath my touch. A sharp pang of discomfort shot through me, as if the area was sensitive to any contact. Upon closer inspection, I discerned an unusual pattern etched upon my flesh, resembling the marks left by scorching heat. They seared the distinct impressions of five fingers into my skin, a testament to the sheer force and ferocity of the creature's attack.

The need to safeguard my health became paramount when I realized the potential dangers linked to the marked spot on my leg. Recognizing the hidden threats that could be lurking, I understood the importance of observing it to prevent any infection. It was not rare for harmless injuries to hide unseen risks, their actual seriousness remaining hidden until it was too late.

While unsure about the identity or motives of my attacker, I felt the need to defend myself from potential harm. I contemplated the significance of the burn-like marks, considering if they might be linked to venom or magic used by the mysterious creature. To stay safe and guard against hidden dangers, I monitored the area for signs of infection, increasing redness, or growing discomfort. It's essential to remain watchful and take action in the face of these unfamiliar threats as I explore this unknown world.

With a heightened sense of caution, I retraced my steps, my gaze locked on the spot where my sword and shield rested on the ground. Every rustle of leaves and whisper of wind seemed to echo in my ears, reminding me of the invisible danger that lurked in this realm. As I passed by the weathered trunk, its contents forgotten for the moment, my sole focus was on arming myself against any unforeseen adversaries. I approached my weapons with a steady hand, feeling a surge of reassurance as I grabbed the familiar weight of my sword in one hand. I secured the protective shield to my arm. With my defenses in place, I stood ready to face whatever challenges awaited me, prepared to defend myself in this mysterious and treacherous land.

Understanding the need to be ready for anything, I bent down and picked up my waterskin from where I'd left it earlier. I made sure it was fastened to my belt, and the familiar weight gave me a comforting feeling. Having the waterskin with me boosted my confidence, knowing I had an essential resource to depend on as I continued exploring this unfamiliar territory.

Looking around, I kept a watchful eye on my surroundings, staying alert for any hidden dangers or signs of movement. Holding my weapon and having my supplies nearby gave me a feeling of readiness. I was no longer vulnerable, and I had faced the upcoming challenges with determination, refusing to let fear or uncertainty hold me back.

Motivated by the pressing need for survival, I secured my shield and sword on my back, their presence a reminder of protection and readiness. With purposeful strides, I approached the scattered remains of the weathered wood, its worn texture and faded memories resonating with the trials it had endured. Each piece held the potential to become the kindling that would ignite a fire amidst the enigmatic uncertainties that shrouded my surroundings.

With deliberate movements, I gathered the salvaged timber, feeling the weight of each piece in my hands. They carried the stories of the ship's journey and its eventual fate, and now they would serve a new purpose in my quest for survival. As I cradled the wood, I couldn't help but envision the dance of flames that would soon come to life, casting a warm and protective glow in the darkness.

I arranged the timber, creating a structure that would facilitate the ignition and steady burn of the fire. I positioned each piece with intention, as if it held the key to warding off the unknown and providing a semblance of security in this unfamiliar realm.

Retrieving the flint and steel from my pack, I prepared myself for the delicate yet essential task of sparking the fire into existence. The steel struck against the flint, creating a shower of sparks that landed upon the waiting woodpile. With each successive strike, the sparks grew brighter, igniting tiny embers that grew into flames.

As the fire took hold, its warmth spread through the air, offering a comforting embrace during the dark and unknown. The crackling of the flames resonated with a sense of determination. Reminding me that even in the face of uncertainty, I possessed the power to create light and warmth.

As the sun sank below the horizon, I found solace in the flickering flames. Those same flames would soon become my sole source of light and warmth. With each crackle and dance, the fire would push back the encroaching chill of the night, revealing the hidden secrets that lay in the darkness. I knew that fire held an inherent power, both as a symbol of safety and a deterrent to any curious or malevolent entities that might prowl the vicinity.

With careful attention, I stoked the fire, coaxing it to grow stronger and brighter. The flames leapt and swirled, casting a warm glow that painted the surrounding landscape in hues of amber and gold. The crackling sound, like a chorus of reassurance, echoed in my ears, reminding me that within this circle of light, I held a measure of protection and comfort.

I watched as the shadows danced along the edges of the fire, their shapes twisting and shifting with an air of mystery. But the fire stood steadfast, its radiant glow pushing back the darkness, warding off the unseen threats that lingered beyond its reach. In its flickering light, I found both solace and courage, knowing that if the flames burned, I was not alone in this unfamiliar and treacherous realm.

With the weight of anticipation hanging in the air, I directed my gaze towards the intriguing trunk that had captured my curiosity. Its weathered exterior spoke volumes of untold stories and concealed wonders. As if guided by an invisible force, my steps quickened, each stride bringing me closer to the treasure chest.

As time went by, my heart beat faster with a blend of enthusiasm and care. What mysteries were hidden here? What treasures and ancient wisdom could I find? The potential filled me with a strong sense of purpose, motivating me forward with an unwavering determination.

As I reached the trunk, I paused, taking a moment to observe its worn surface, tracing my fingers along the grooves and scratches that adorned its exterior. It bore the marks of time and countless journeys, a silent testament to its resilience.

With unwavering resolve, I devised a plan to bring the trunk closer to my campsite, where I could unravel its secrets at my leisure. I assessed the weight of the trunk, gauging the effort required to move it across the sandy terrain. Determined to uncover its hidden treasures, I positioned myself, readying my muscles for the task at hand.

Taking a deep breath, I planted my feet in the sand, gripping the edges of the trunk with a firm resolve. With a steady exertion of force, I dragged the trunk, feeling the resistance of the terrain beneath me. The grains of sand shifted and shuffled as the trunk budged, inch by inch, closer to its intended destination.

Every ounce of strength and determination surged through my veins, propelling me forward despite the strain and fatigue. The weight of the trunk challenged me, but my determination remained unyielding. I envisioned the satisfaction that would come from bringing this mysterious artifact within reach, igniting my spirit with renewed vigor.

As the trunk inched closer to the campsite, beads of sweat formed on my brow, evidence of the physical exertion. The shifting sands beneath my feet added an extra challenge, demanding careful balance and unwavering focus. But I pressed on, driven by the promise of discovery and the allure of uncovering the hidden treasures that awaited me within.

Step by step, the trunk journeyed closer to its destination, the sound of its scraping against the sand echoing in my ears. With each movement, my anticipation grew, as if the trunk itself beckoned me to reveal its long-guarded secrets. The terrain may have tested my resolve, but it only fueled my determination.

With a last surge of effort, the trunk came to rest at my campsite. Beads of perspiration clung to my forehead as I released my grip, standing back to admire the fruits of my labor. A sense of accomplishment washed over me, mingling with the excitement that pulsed through my veins. I had brought the mysterious trunk within my reach, ready to embark on the next chapter of this enthralling journey.

I approached the trunk, anticipation coursing through my veins. With cautious hands, I ran my fingers along its weathered surface, feeling a tingling sense of possibility and adventure. It was here, in this moment, that I knew I was on the brink of uncovering secrets that could change everything.

As I ran my fingers along the trunk's exterior, I couldn't help but marvel at the intricate craftsmanship that had gone into its creation. The smooth texture of the wood beneath my touch hinted at the strength of oak or the alluring fragrance of cedar. This trunk was not just a simple storage container; it was a work of art.

Inspecting it, I noticed the careful placement of iron or steel fittings, adding an extra layer of durability and security. The hinges were attached, allowing the lid to open and close with ease, while the locks and corner reinforcements spoke of a trunk built to withstand the tests of time. They had taken great care in every detail, from the selection of materials to the precision of the craftsmanship.

As I continued to explore the trunk's exterior, my mind raced with anticipation. What secrets lie within its solid confines? What treasures or artifacts had been safeguarded within this constructed vessel? The trunk's robust design and the attention to detail hinted at the possibility of something remarkable concealed inside.

I examined the trunk's exterior, my eyes scanning every inch of its weathered surface, searching for any clue or mechanism that would grant me entry into its hidden contents. The lock, robust and unyielding, stood as a formidable barrier to my curiosity. I turned the trunk around, inspecting it from various angles, hoping to uncover any vulnerabilities or weak points that might grant me access, but my search proved to be in vain.

Frustration welled within me as I contemplated the trunk's impenetrable facade. It seemed to taunt me, withholding its secrets behind a barrier I couldn't breach. I wondered if there was a key or a hidden mechanism that would unlock its treasures, but there was no visible sign of such a solution.

As the flickering flames of the fire cast dancing shadows upon the trunk, I grappled with the challenges posed by the surrounding darkness. Despite the warmth and glow provided by the fire, its illumination did not discern the subtle details that might unlock the trunk's secrets. I realized that persisting in my attempts to solve this mystery under the cover of nightfall would prove unproductive.

With a heavy sigh, I set the trunk aside for the time being. I recognized the wisdom in deferring my exploration until daylight, when the sun's rays would grant me a clearer view and a better chance of discovering the key to unlocking its mysteries. It was a moment of acceptance, a reminder that some challenges require patience and the right conditions for success.

Resigned to my current circumstances, I found solace in the crackling fire. Its comforting warmth embraced me, providing a temporary respite from the burning curiosity that consumed me. With each flickering flame, my mind wandered, venturing into the realm of possibilities that lay concealed within the mysterious trunk.

As I reclined, my thoughts became untamed, weaving intricate tales of what could be hidden within its confines. Would it hold ancient artifacts, long-forgotten treasures, or perhaps the key to unlocking the secrets of this realm? The anticipation gnawed at me, fueling my eagerness to witness the unveiling of its mysteries.

Immersed in the dance of the flames, I allowed my imagination to roam. In my mind's eye, I envisioned when the first rays of sunlight would cast their illuminating touch upon the trunk, revealing its hidden wonders. It was a moment that filled me with a mixture of excitement and apprehension, as the unknown held both the allure of discovery and the potential for unforeseen challenges.

With a sigh of anticipation, I embraced the temporary respite by the fire, knowing that when dawn arrived, a new chapter would unfold. The trunk would no longer be a mere enigma, but a gateway to a world of possibilities waiting to be explored.

## *Chapter 3 Memories*

As I relaxed by the crackling fire, feeling its warmth soothe my tired body, memories came back to me like puzzle pieces fitting together. I remembered when I joined the crew of the Silver Serpent, a choice that changed my life forever. The thrill of adventure and the excitement of the unknown had called out to me, pushing me into new lands and endless opportunities.

Aurelia, my hometown, had forever been a place of comfort and things I knew well, but I longed for something more. The excitement of heading into uncharted territories, where wild nature was waiting, filled me with anticipation. In those distant lands, I would come across strange and magnificent creatures, each one different and challenging, a chance to prove my abilities as a warrior.

As I stepped into the bustling pub in Aurelia, the lively ambiance enveloped me, filling the air with laughter, clinking glasses, and the melodious sound of music. The warm glow of lanterns cast a cozy and inviting atmosphere, drawing on patrons seeking refuge from the outside world. It was in this vibrant setting that I stumbled upon a corner of the pub, where a group of seasoned sailors gathered, their voices resonating with tales of grand adventures.

As the departure date drew near, the excited crew of the Silver Serpent bustled with excitement, getting ready to embark from the lively docks of Aurelia. Situated right in the city's center, Aurelia was a thriving hub for adventurers, traders, and those seeking wealth. Its renown as a trading center and the launchpad for grand journeys drew many individuals eager to join thrilling adventures.

With my curiosity piqued, I found myself drawn to their spirited conversation, captivated by their tales of the open sea and the thrill of exploration. Their voices carried a contagious enthusiasm that ignited my longing for adventure. With each word they spoke, the passion in their eyes and the excitement in their gestures became more clear. These were individuals who had faced the perils of the deep, embraced the unknown, and returned with stories that captured the imagination.

"Hey mates, where bouts are you headed?" I asked, with curiosity in my eyes.

"We are bound for uncharted territories, where the allure of mysterious lands awaited discovery," stated one of the crew members with a glint of adventure in his voice.

"How could I get on such an adventure?" I inquired.

The crew members exchanged knowing glances before one of them spoke up, sharing the key to embarking on this thrilling journey.

"If you seek to join the crew and set sail on this adventure," they began, "make your way to the docks and seek Captain Orion Stormrider, the esteemed captain of the renowned vessel, the Silver Serpent."

"Captain Stormrider!" I exclaimed upon hearing his name, instantly recognizing it. "The stories of the captain's incredible adventures have reached even the remotest corners of Aurelia. He's renowned for discovering uncharted lands and returning with rare treasures and one-of-a-kind items. These tales have enchanted the hearts and minds of adventurers and dreamers everywhere. Thanks for sharing this, and perhaps I'll see you at the docks tomorrow."

The crew members gave me a simple head nod and said, "Maybe so and good luck."

"By the way, my name is Valaric and how about you?"

"My name is Johnny, and that there is Finnegan," said Johnny

"Well, it was nice meeting you, and thanks again for the information."

"You are welcome," Johnny stated as both crew members gave another head nod.

As I left the pub, I was ecstatic about the possibility of embarking on a voyage alongside Captain Stormrider and the crew of the silver serpent. Opportunities like this didn't come often, so I wanted to take a chance to request to join the crew on their next grand adventure.

The next day, filled with excitement and resolve, I made my way to the busy docks where the impressive Silver Serpent was docked. With each step, I felt a fresh determination, and as I neared the towering ship with its massive masts reaching into the sky, I sensed a new purpose within me. The sails, fluttering in the breeze, called me closer, hinting at the potential for greatness and boundless opportunities.

As I drew nearer, the bustling activity on the docks filled my senses. The sound of creaking ropes, the smell of saltwater mingling with the bustling energy of sailors preparing for the voyage—all contributed to the atmosphere of excitement that enveloped the scene. I fixed my eyes on the mighty ship before me, its sleek form exuding power and grace.

The sunlight danced upon the polished wood, casting a warm glow that stressed the ship's intricate details. Every line and curve spoke of skilled craftsmanship, a testament to the countless hands that had poured their expertise into its creation. The Silver Serpent stood as a symbol of adventure and resilience, a vessel ready to navigate the uncharted waters of the world.

As I made my way closer, the anticipation within me grew, mingling with a touch of nervous energy. Spotting a crew member engrossed in their duties on the bustling deck, I mustered a friendly smile and approached, my voice filled with a mix of anticipation and determination.

"Excuse me," I began, my words carrying a sense of urgency. "Is Captain Stormrider on board? I have a matter of utmost importance to discuss with him."

The crew member paused from his tasks. "Aye, Captain Stormrider is up in the captain's quarters, mapping out our next course." Sensing Valaric's eagerness, the crew member continued, "I can send word to the captain if you'd like. What's your name, lad?"

"Thanks, my name is Valaric."

Understanding the significance of this moment, the crew member nodded. "Aye, I'll fetch Johnny to relay your request to Captain Stormrider. Wait right here," the crew member said before hurrying off.

"Johnny, I wonder if that is the same Johnny I had met last night," I muttered to myself.

I stood on the docks, looking around at everyone going this way and that way, carrying stuff onto the ship. The surrounding air was filled with sounds of rigging creaking in the wind, with the distant cries of seabirds. Time seemed to stretch as I contemplated the unknown possibilities that awaited me aboard the Silver Serpent.

The Silver Serpent, an impressive ship, demanded notice with its grand size and powerful characteristics. It was built to house a busy crew and a lot of cargo, featuring many decks, each filled with activity. From the main deck, where hardworking sailors managed the ship's workings to the lower decks packed with supplies and valuable goods, the ship made the most of its space.

A clear sign of its preparedness for any situation, the Silver Serpent displayed a set of twelve cannons lined up on its sides. These powerful cannons, backed by the alert crew armed with different weapons, guaranteed the ship's ability to protect itself from dangers and discourage enemies.

For what seemed like a long time, but in reality was only a few moments, I could hear someone yelling my name. I looked up in the direction to see if I could spot the person yelling at me. It was the same guy I had met in the pub last night.

He motioned me to come aboard the ship. I walked across the docks until I found the entrance to board the ship. I boarded the ship and could not believe my eyes. The ship was even more majestic up close that what it had appeared from the docks. I hurried to where Johnny was located.

"Hey Johnny, good to see you again."

"You as well Valaric. The Captain will see you now," Johnny said, as he motioned for me to come aboard the ship and follow him.

With anticipation coursing through my veins, I followed Johnny through the bustling corridors of the ship, the steady rhythm of our footsteps echoing in the wooden passageways. As we ascended the stairs leading to the Captain's quarters, my heart pounded in sync with the sound of my own footsteps. We arrived at the entrance to the Captain's quarters.

"Captain, I have a Valaric here to see you," Johnny said as he knocked on the Captain's door.

A little while later, the door slowly opened, and there stood a distinguished figure dressed in sailor's clothing. It was none other than the famous Captain Orion Stormrider. He was a tall man with a rugged and well-traveled look, a testament to the many journeys and challenges he had encountered at sea. A full beard outlined his strong features, its mix of gray and black suggesting his wisdom and years of experience.

He had piercing blue eyes that mirrored the vastness of the ocean, reflecting the determination and a depth of knowledge gained through years of maritime exploration. Time and the harsh elements had etched lines upon his face, each one telling a story of battles fought and victories won.

"Hey Captain, Finnegan and I met him last night. He seemed interested in joining the crew for our next adventure. So we told him if he was interested, he ought to come speak with you," Johnny exclaimed.

"So you think you have what it takes to join the crew of the Silver Serpent, do you?" Captain Stormrider asked in a raspy voice.

"Yes," I stuttered.

"Was that a question, or was that a statement?" Captain Stormrider asked.

"That was a statement," I said in a firm voice.

"Very well," Captain Stormrider said, a hint of intrigue in his voice. "If you possess the mettle and courage to face the perils that lie ahead, you may find a place amongst our crew. But know this, lad, the path we tread is one of danger and discovery."

I nodded with unwavering determination. I knew and understood the risks and challenges that lay ahead as I had adventured with other groups to foreign places, but the places were tame. The stories that had surfaced about Captain Stormrider were legendary and always ended up with people injured, but the rewards were always grand.

"Assemble your belongings and prepare to embark," Captain Stormrider instructed, his tone filled with a mix of authority and excitement. "The Silver Serpent sets sail at dawn, and you shall be part of our crew. Welcome aboard, Valaric."

I remembered the thrill of embarking on that grand adventure; the excitement pulsating through my veins as I stepped aboard the majestic ship. The sails billowed, propelled by the whispers of a promising future, while the crew, a diverse assembly of individuals driven by curiosity and ambition, prepared to chart new horizons.

## *Chapter 4 The Shove Off*

As the first rays of the morning sun embraced the docks, casting a warm golden hue upon the scene, I stood with a sense of purpose and anticipation. Despite the early hour, my determination led me to arrive well before the appointed time for the voyage. Without warning, the air crackled with an electric energy, mirroring the excitement that coursed through my veins.

The allure of uncharted lands and untamed adventures enticed me like a captivating melody, drawing me closer to the edge of the unknown. The promise of discovery, the thrill of overcoming challenges, and the chance to leave an indelible mark upon the map of the world filled my thoughts.

I stood there, my gaze fixed on the horizon, reminiscing about the countless encounters with the unfamiliar that had shaped my journey. Through trials and tribulations, I had forged my path, evolving from a wide-eyed novice into a seasoned warrior.

Every expedition I had ever been on taught me invaluable lessons. I learned to trust my instincts, adapt to change, and find strength in adversity. The trials I had endured had sculpted me into the formidable warrior I was today.

As I stood there contemplating my journey, a sense of gratitude washed over me. The challenges I had faced had not only shaped my skills but also revealed the depths of my resilience and determination. I was no longer the wide-eyed novice who had set out on this path; I had grown and evolved, honing my abilities with each encounter.

But this voyage held the promise of something even greater,

something yet undiscovered. My heart swelled with anticipation, knowing that new lands, unseen wonders, and untapped mysteries awaited my arrival. The prospect of stepping foot into the unknown ignited a fire within me—a fire fueled by insatiable curiosity and an unwavering thirst for adventure.

Whispers of distant lands, mysterious artifacts, and unexplored territories fueled my imagination, igniting a fire within me that refused to be quelled. The thought of unearthing hidden treasures, delving into forgotten histories, and conquering new frontiers stirred my spirit, propelling me forward with a surge of determination.

With every beat of my heart, I felt the call of the unknown growing stronger. The thrill of the chase, the adrenaline rush of uncovering ancient secrets, and the satisfaction of overcoming insurmountable challenges awaited me. I craved the intoxicating blend of danger and the discovery that only an adventure of this magnitude could provide.

As the first light of dawn painted the sky with vibrant hues, I found my eyes drawn to the ship that stood at the dock. Its sturdy frame and billowing sails seemed to beckon me, promising untold adventures and endless possibilities beyond the horizon.

As I gazed upon its weathered hull, I couldn't help but imagine the countless tales that had been woven within its timbers. The ship seemed to possess a palpable energy, a whispered invitation to embark on a journey that would forever change the course of my life.

"Hey, you going to stand there daydreaming or load some of this cargo so we can shove off?", said one of the crew members. "

"Apologies, mate," I replied, snapping out of my reverie at the crew member's call. My mind shifted from dreams of adventure to the present task at hand. With a renewed sense of purpose, I set about loading the cargo onto the ship, channeling my energy into the physical labor.

Each crate and bundle became a weight to be lifted and secured, a piece of the puzzle that would enable our departure. The rhythmic movements of my muscles synced with the bustle of the dock, as other crew members joined in the coordinated effort. Together, we worked as a well-oiled machine, driven by a shared purpose and the knowledge that time was of the essence.

The sounds of creaking wood and strained ropes filled the air, intermingling with the shouts and banter of the crew. Despite the physical exertion, a sense of camaraderie permeated the atmosphere, binding us together in a common endeavor.

The atmosphere aboard the Silver Serpent was alive with bustling activity as the crew prepared the ship for its imminent departure. I found myself amidst the whirlwind of tasks, enveloped in a symphony of shouted commands and echoed directives.

"Stow the cargo!" one voice bellowed, its urgency cutting through the air.

"Clear the decks for departure!" called out another, the urgency palpable in their tone.

The energy of anticipation was tangible, electrifying the atmosphere as crew members dashed about, each fulfilling their assigned roles with a sense of purpose. The deck hummed with focused determination and the rhythm of hurried footsteps. The sound of creaking ropes and clattering equipment filled the air, accompanied by the occasional loud thud of crates being positioned.

Caught up in the flurry of activity, the stern voice of a crew member jolted from my thoughts me.

"What on earth are you doing just standing there?" they reprimanded, their words cutting through the clamor. My cheeks flushed with a mix of surprise and embarrassment, bringing me back to the present moment.

"Apologies," I replied, my voice tinged with a hint of self-consciousness. "Making my way to the upper deck now," I added, my words punctuated by determination. Regaining my focus, I maneuvered through the organized chaos, sidestepping barrels and navigating around fellow crew members with practiced precision.

Ascending to the upper deck, a panoramic view of the ship's grandeur greeted me. The billowing sails, taut with the promise of adventure, stretched towards the heavens, ready to harness the wind's power and propel us forward. The sight filled me with awe and a growing sense of excitement at what lay ahead.

As the urgent call of "All hands on deck" resounded through the air, I made my way alongside my fellow crew members, ascending to the upper deck of the ship. Excitement coursed through my veins, anticipation building within me, for I knew that Captain Stormrider was about to address the crew.

As I reached the designated gathering area, my eyes fell upon the figure of our esteemed captain. He stood tall and resolute, his presence commanding respect and instilling confidence. The sun's rays illuminated his weathered face, revealing the marks of countless adventures etched upon his visage.

With a firm yet reassuring tone, Captain Stormrider spoke, his voice carrying across the deck and capturing the undivided attention of every sailor present. Each word he uttered resonated with authority and experience, captivating us all.

"Men, it is time to embark on another voyage, venturing into uncharted waters." Captain Stormrider's voice resonated through the air, drawing my attention and the gaze of the entire crew. His words held a unique blend of excitement and caution, reflecting the thrilling yet unpredictable nature of our upcoming journey.

"Uncertainty and unforeseen challenges will mark our path," Captain Stormrider continued, his voice filled with the wisdom of countless voyages. "But fear not, for we are a crew forged by experience and camaraderie. Together, we shall navigate through the stormy seas and emerge stronger on the other side."

"Valaric," the captain's voice carried a touch of expectation, drawing my focus upon him. "Though you may be new to our ranks, I trust you bring with you the spirit of adventure and a willingness to face the unknown. Your presence here signifies the potential for great things, both for yourself and for the Silver Serpent."

I felt a surge of pride mixed with a tinge of nervousness as the weight of his words settled upon me. Captain Stormrider's acknowledgement of my presence and his recognition of the opportunities that lay before me instilled a renewed sense of purpose.

"Embrace the challenges that lie ahead, for they are the crucible in which our character and resilience are forged," the captain's voice carried a hint of reassurance. "As we embark on this voyage together, I trust that each one of you will bring your unique skills and unwavering dedication to the crew."

"Those who are unfamiliar with life at sea, I advise you to stay out of the way if you are unsure of your duties," the captain's words pierced the air, his tone carrying a stern warning. The weight of his responsibility and the authority he held over the crew were clear in his commanding presence.

As his gaze swept across the assembled sailors, I could feel the weight of his expectations settling upon us all. The atmosphere grew tense, a silent reminder that our journey would demand discipline, skill, and unwavering competence.

"I bear the responsibility of this crew and this vessel," Captain Stormrider continued, his voice unwavering. "Each of you plays a vital role in our collective success. I expect nothing less than complete dedication and a commitment to excellence in all that you do."

His words echoed in my mind, serving as a stark reminder of the importance of our individual contributions to the larger whole. The captain's expectations were clear, and I felt a surge of determination rise within me. I would strive to meet and exceed those expectations, proving myself as a valued member of the crew.

"Discipline and order are the cornerstones of our operation," the captain emphasized, his voice carrying a sense of authority. "Follow orders without hesitation, maintain vigilance, and work together as a cohesive unit. It is through our collective efforts that we will navigate the challenges that lie ahead."

Captain Stormrider's voice resonated with authority and conviction, his words reaching every corner of the deck. The weight of his message hung in the air, underscoring the significance of teamwork and the shared responsibilities that came with life on board the ship.

"Should any of you harbor questions or uncertainties," the captain declared, his voice unwavering, "do not hesitate to seek guidance from your fellow crew members. We are a cohesive unit, relying on each other's strengths to navigate the challenges that lie ahead."

The captain's tone grew solemn as he addressed the potential perils that awaited us on our journey. His words struck a chord within me, reminding me of the ever-present threats that lurked in the vast expanse of the open sea.

"In the face of enemy attacks," Captain Stormrider's voice resounded with determination, "I demand unwavering readiness from every one of you. There will be no room for complacency or indifference on this ship. We sail under the banner of discipline and vigilance."

His words carried a weight that echoed through my being, stirring a heightened sense of awareness within me. The captain's emphasis on discipline served as a stark reminder that our actions, or lack thereof, could have dire consequences for ourselves and the ship.

"Who among you dares to venture into uncharted realms?" Captain Stormrider's voice resonated with a mix of curiosity and excitement. I listened, eager to seize the opportunity that lay before us.

The initial response from the crew was subdued, their voices murmuring a quiet affirmation. But the captain, not content with the tepid reply, raised his voice, determined to evoke a more spirited response.

"It seems none of you caught my drift," Captain Stormrider's words rang out, his tone laced with playful challenge. "I asked, who among you has the courage to delve into new and unknown territories, in pursuit of untold riches?"

This time, the crew erupted in a resounding roar, their unified response reverberating through the air, "Aye Aye, Captain!"

Their enthusiastic affirmation filled me with a surge of adrenaline, a shared determination to embrace the challenges that awaited us in uncharted waters. The prospect of discovering new horizons and unearthing hidden treasures ignited a fire within me, propelling me forward with a renewed sense of purpose.

"Now that's what I like to hear," Captain Stormrider's voice boomed with a delighted tone, his eyes gleaming with satisfaction. His words filled the air, infusing the crew with a renewed sense of purpose and determination.

With a broad smile stretching across his face, the captain continued, "Now, my hearty sailors, it's time to spring into action! Hoist those planks, man your stations, and let's prepare to set sail!" His commanding presence reverberated through the ship, igniting a flurry of activity as the crew responded to his call.

With a surge of adrenaline coursing through my veins, I joined the crew in heaving the heavy planks, feeling the strain in my muscles as we prepared the Silver Serpent for its journey into the unknown. Excitement and anticipation mingled within me, fueled by the prospect of uncharted lands and untold adventures that lay ahead.

As we worked in unison, the ship took shape, every rope pulled taut, every sail unfurled. The Silver Serpent stood tall, her masts reaching towards the sky, eager to harness the power of the wind that would carry us to our destination.

Amidst the flurry of activity, Captain Stormrider's authoritative voice resonated across the deck. "Cast off and set sail!" he commanded, his words imbued with a sense of purpose and determination that resonated within each member of the crew.

Without hesitation, we released the mooring lines, feeling the ship sway as she embraced her newfound freedom. The sea beckoned, its vast expanse stretching out before us, an invitation to explore its depths and unravel its mysteries.

As we raised the sails, the wind caught hold, billowing them outwards with a resounding snap. The ship groaned and creaked, coming alive beneath our feet, as if responding to the call of adventure. The rhythmic sound of the waves lapping against the hull provided a soothing backdrop to our endeavors, further igniting our spirits for the voyage ahead.

"Hoist the Colors!" Captain Stormrider's commanding voice reverberated across the deck, igniting a surge of energy within me. Without hesitation, I sprang into action, joining my fellow crew members in unfurling the vibrant flags and pennants that represented our ship and its crew. As the colorful fabric caught the wind, it soared high above us, a symbol of our allegiance and identity.

As the Silver Serpent left the docks, the crew sang a sea shanty as done on many of their previous adventures.

(Chorus) Hoist the sails and catch the wind. Onward we go, a voyage to begin. With hearts as one, united and strong, sailing to distant shores, where we belong.

(Verse 1) Aboard our vessel, sturdy and grand, sailing forth with a fearless band. To the rhythm of the rolling waves, we sing our shanty, bold and brave.

(Chorus) Hoist the sails and catch the wind. Onward we go, a voyage to begin. With hearts as one, united and strong, sailing to distant shores, where we belong.

(Verse 2) Through stormy seas and tempest's might, we battle the elements day and night. With every heave and every haul, we sing our shanty, one and all.

(Chorus) Hoist the sails and catch the wind. Onward we go, a voyage to begin. With hearts as one, united and strong, sailing to distant shores, where we belong.

(Verse 3) Our destination, a mystery untold, seeking treasures and stories of old. With spirits high and courage aglow, we sing our shanty as we onward row.

(Chorus) Hoist the sails and catch the wind. Onward we go, a voyage to begin. With hearts as one, united and strong, sailing to distant shores, where we belong.

(Outro) So raise your voice, ye sailors bold. Let the sea shanty forever be told. As we embark on this daring quest, together we sail, and we're blessed.

As a newcomer on the deck of the majestic Silver Serpent, I stood transfixed, my eyes wide with wonder, as the sailors' voices melded into a mesmerizing chorus. The captivating sea shanty they sang echoed through the air, carrying tales of daring exploits and far-off lands. Its infectious melody and spirited lyrics ignited a fire within me, stirring a deep longing for adventure and discovery.

With each verse, the energy surged within my veins, fueling my growing excitement. I couldn't help but join in, by humming with the familiar chorus. The words of the shanty felt like an anthem, a celebration of the brave seafarers who came before us, their tales woven into the very fabric of our maritime heritage.

(Chorus) Hoist the sails and catch the wind. Onward we go, a voyage to begin. With hearts as one, united and strong, sailing to distant shores, where we belong.

With each resounding lyric, my determination surged, fueling a fire within me. I had traversed uncharted lands in the past, but this crew, their unbreakable camaraderie and unwavering spirit, made me feel like I had found my true home on the sea. I knew in my heart that this voyage would be unlike any other, a profound opportunity to push my limits, test my mettle, and delve into the secrets that lay shrouded in the mysterious depths of the unknown.

As the chorus echoed once more, my voice rose with newfound confidence.

(Chorus) Hoist the sails and catch the wind. Onward we go, a voyage to begin. With hearts as one, united and strong, sailing to distant shores, where we belong.

The contagious enthusiasm of the crew enveloped me, spreading like wildfire through the ship. The vibrant energy that filled the air ignited a profound sense of unity among us. We were no longer just individuals working alongside each other; we had become a family, bound by a shared purpose and an unbreakable bond.

As the shanty's final chords faded into the winds, a triumphant cheer erupted from the lips of the sailors, carried by the very breeze that would guide us on our daring expedition. My heart swelled with anticipation, the fire of adventure burning within me. Standing tall among my newfound comrades, I embraced the exhilarating prospect of embarking on this remarkable journey aboard the legendary Silver Serpent.

The cheers reverberated through the air, mingling with the crashing waves and the creaking of the ship. In that moment, I felt a deep connection to my fellow sailors, bound by a shared sense of purpose and a yearning for the unknown. The voyage ahead held the promise of uncharted territories, breathtaking discoveries, and unforgettable moments of camaraderie.

## *Chapter 5 The Night*

Lost in the depths of my reminiscences, I was jolted back to reality by a sharp sound slicing through the air, its source shrouded in darkness. A surge of adrenaline coursed through my veins as I unsheathed my sword, the cool touch of the blade comforting my grip. The encounter with the mysterious creature that had ensnared my leg earlier had left me on edge, unwilling to take any chances.

With heightened senses, I stood still, my ears attuned to any further signs of movement or danger. The surrounding darkness hindered my vision, but I remained vigilant, relying on my hearing to guide me. Aside from the serene whispers of the gentle waves caressing the shoreline and the crackling of the nearby fire, there was no other audible disturbance.

The seconds stretched into minutes as I listened and surveyed my surroundings, my gaze scanning the lit beach. Shadows danced in the flickering light, but there was no sign of any immediate threat. The silence weighed upon me, amplifying my apprehension and self-awareness.

I paused, thinking about the chance that my increased unease might be because of my own vivid imagination. "Maybe," I whispered to myself, "my nerves have gotten the best of me, making me nervous about small things."

But deep down, I knew my instincts were wrong. The memory of the creature's grip on my leg lingered, a reminder of the unseen dangers that could lurk in this mysterious realm. I couldn't afford to dismiss any potential threats, no matter how insignificant they might seem.

During an eerie silence, my instincts heightened, alerting me to a faint disturbance in the air. Gripping my mighty sword and raising my trusty shield, I braced myself for the imminent approach of an unknown adversary. The weight of the weapons in my hands provided a reassuring sense of readiness.

With a surge of adrenaline, my senses sharpened, and my eyes darted, scanning the shrouded shadows that enveloped my surroundings. Though engulfed in an abyss of darkness, I relied on my acute hearing, straining to discern any clues from the subtle sounds that penetrated the silence.

There it was, I could hear it—a gentle rustling, the faintest hint of footsteps drawing near. My heart beat faster as I got ready, bracing myself to face whatever was coming. The creature, whatever it was, appeared to have an obvious intention, and its approach was full of mystery.

As the creature closed in, my heart pounded in my chest, and a surge of adrenaline coursed through my veins. I refused to back down in the face of this mysterious intruder. With a primal roar that echoed through the night, I made it known that I would not yield, that I would meet any challenge head-on.

Every muscle in my body tensed as I prepared to defend myself, my grip on my weapon tightening. I locked my gaze upon the shifting shadows, my senses sharpened to their utmost capacity. I would not allow this encounter to catch me off guard.

In a swift, fluid motion, I swung my mighty sword towards the perceived threat, but to my dismay, my strike met nothing but empty air. The elusive creature had evaded my attack with uncanny agility, leaving me disoriented.

Frustration welled up within me, mingling with a surge of determination. I adjusted my stance, gripping my weapon, preparing for the next encounter. The creature had proven itself to be cunning, always one step ahead. I couldn't shake the feeling that I was being toyed with a pawn in its twisted game.

"This adversary is more than just elusive; it possesses an intelligence that surpasses mere instinct," I muttered to myself, my voice filled with a mixture of admiration and frustration. I was up against a formidable opponent, one who was not to be underestimated.

My vigilant gaze darted from side to side, my eyes scanning the darkness to locate the elusive creature or creatures that lurked in the shadows. And then, as if emerging from the depths of a haunting nightmare, a diminutive figure materialized before me, its form discernible in the dim light.

I acted quickly, swinging my sword at the figure, aiming for a decisive hit. But once more, my strike failed, and the figure escaped with uncanny agility. I felt a surge of frustration mixing with the adrenaline that fueled my determination.

To my amazement, I saw something that was beyond belief and even more incredible than I could have imagined. Right in front of me stood a tiny being, only six inches tall, exuding a captivating charm. Its presence was enchanting, and it's mesmerizing features drew my gaze towards it.

The creature possessed a delicate and ethereal beauty. Its large, expressive blue eyes sparkled with an unmistakable sense of wonder, as if they held the secrets of the universe. Pointed ears, resembling those of a mythical creature, peeked out from beneath a cascade of silky fur. The fur draped its plump body in a tapestry of pastel hues, reminiscent of a delicate bouquet of blooming spring flowers.

As I observed closer, I noticed that each strand of its velvety coat shimmered with a subtle iridescence, as if it were infused with fragments of stardust. The creature seemed to radiate a celestial magic, an otherworldly quality that set it apart from anything I had encountered before.

Adorning the creature's back were a pair of ethereal wings, delicate and translucent. They seemed to defy the very laws of physics, as if they were crafted from dreams and wishes. Like gossamer whispers, they fluttered with a mesmerizing grace, each movement an elegant dance that painted the air with a trail of ethereal patterns.

The wings were a canvas of enchantment, their intricate designs shifting and shimmering whenever touched by the gentle caress of light. They appeared to carry the essence of distant galaxies and celestial wonders, as if the creature itself was a bridge between the realms of reality and fantasy.

As I stood in awe of the ethereal being before me, a serene melody filled the air, its soft hum captivating my senses. The gentle vibrations wrapped around me, creating a comforting embrace that eased the tension in my muscles and calmed the racing of my heart. It was as if the creature's very presence radiated a harmonious energy, soothing and enchanting all who had encountered it.

"Well, you pose little of a threat, little one," I remarked, unable to suppress a smile as I observed the endearing creature before me.

Its small size and innocent demeanor evoked a sense of warmth and affection within me. Intrigued by its presence, I couldn't help but express my desire to interact further.

"Can I pet you? You're quite cute," I asked, my voice carrying a gentle tone, eager to extend a friendly gesture towards this enchanting being.

With an air of trust, the tiny creature approached, its curiosity piqued by my welcoming presence. It sniffed my hand, its delicate nose twitching with each inhale. As it recognized my scent, a sense of familiarity seemed to spark within its expressive eyes. The creature's affectionate gesture took the form of gentle rubs against my hand, its soft fur brushing against my skin. I couldn't help but smile, my heart warmed by its gentle touch.

"You truly are a soft and fuzzy little being," I exclaimed, my voice filled with delight as I marveled at the creature's delightful charm.

I extended my hand, creating a secure perch for the diminutive creature. With cautious steps, it climbed onto my palm, displaying a remarkable trust in my presence. Bringing my hand up to my waist, I ran my fingers through its velvety fur, savoring the softness and warmth that greeted my touch. The creature nestled in my hand, emitting a contented purr, as if it had found solace in my companionship.

Curiosity danced in my eyes as I attempted to establish a connection with the enchanting creature.

"So, what shall I call you?" I asked, aware that expecting a verbal response was unlikely.

The creature responded with a steadfast gaze from its mesmerizing blue eyes, understanding my words. Its melodious humming continued, a response filled with unspoken communication and shared understanding.

A moment of inspiration coursed through me, and I declared, "Well, from this moment forth, I shall name you Whisperwind."

The name resonated with the ethereal essence and gentle melodies that emanated from the creature. It felt fitting, a tribute to its otherworldly nature and the unspoken bond we shared. As I met Whisperwind's gaze, I sensed a profound understanding, a silent agreement that acknowledged our connection.

With an elegant movement, Whisperwind climbed up my body, finding a cozy perch on my shoulder. It was as if the creature had found its rightful place, nestled in the warmth of my presence, and taking advantage of the higher vantage point. As I looked at Whisperwind settled on my shoulder, a smile spread across my face, a testament to the deepening bond between us.

Seizing the moment, I acknowledged the importance of tending to the fire, knowing that its continuous glow would ward off the encroaching darkness. With Whisperwind perched on my shoulder, I felt a renewed sense of security and tranquility. I sheathed my sword, knowing that for now, the immediate threat had been quelled, and I secured my shield on my back. The shift in atmosphere was palpable as the tension gave way to a sense of calm. I settled back into my position before the mesmerizing dance of the fire, basking in its comforting warmth and in the presence of my newfound companion.

Settling into a comfortable posture, I felt a gentle weight pressing against my chest. Looking down, I was met with the heartwarming sight of Whisperwind nestled in a curled-up position. A surge of warmth washed over me, as if Whisperwind had found solace in our companionship and recognized the sanctuary I offered. It was a tender moment, reinforcing the bond between us and filling me with a deep sense of contentment.

As I stroked Whisperwind's back, a gentle warmth enveloped us. The presence of this enchanting creature brought solace and companionship, alleviating the need for solitary conversations. A soft chuckle escaped my lips as I spoke to Whisperwind, acknowledging the change in my circumstances.

"Well, my little friend, it seems I no longer have to rely on speaking to myself for company. Your presence is a welcome companion on this journey."

The small creature nuzzled against my hand, as if in agreement, reinforcing the understanding that our connection went beyond mere words.

A pang of hunger resonated within me, a reminder of the physical needs that accompany any arduous journey.

"Come morning, we shall need to forage for sustenance," I declared, my tone resolute.

The growling in my stomach echoed the sentiment, a reminder of the nourishment that awaited our discovery. However, for the present moment, I acknowledge the importance of replenishing my energy and preparing for the challenges that awaited us.

"As the night wears on, it would be wise to rest our weary bodies," I mused, feeling the weight of exhaustion in my voice.

The gentle crackling of the fire provided a soothing lullaby, and the encompassing darkness urged us to seek respite. Aware of the restorative power of sleep, I resolved to make the most of the remaining night, ensuring that we would awaken refreshed and revitalized, ready to face the trials that awaited us at dawn.

With a final affectionate stroke of Whisperwind's fur, I settled into a comfortable position, embracing the quiet stillness of the night. The rustling of leaves and the distant hoot of an owl formed a soothing melody that lulled me into a peaceful state. As the symphony of nature serenaded our dreams, I found solace in the gentle presence of Whisperwind, their warmth and companionship a comforting reminder we were not alone on this remarkable journey. As slumber embraced our weary forms, my mind danced with visions of the adventures that awaited us, ready to unfold in the vast tapestry of the unknown. With a contented sigh, I surrendered to the embrace of sleep, eager for the mysteries and wonders that awaited us in the realm of dreams.

## *Chapter 6 The Crystal*

As the first rays of dawn painted the horizon with hues of gold and pink, I was abruptly awakened by the energetic presence of Whisperwind leaping onto my chest.

Startled from my slumber, I blinked away the remnants of sleep and groggily asked, "What is it, my little friend?"

With a flick of his tail, Whisperwind swiftly hopped off my chest and darted down the beach, casting an expectant glance back at me.

Confusion and curiosity mingled on my face as I mumbled, "What could be so urgent before daylight breaks?"

The behavior of Whisperwind beckoned me to my feet. Stretching my tired muscles, I cautiously trailed the whimsical creature down the sandy expanse, my footsteps tracing the rhythm of the crashing waves. Each step carried me closer to uncovering the mystery that awaited, as whispers of anticipation mingled with the salty sea breeze.

Whisperwind led me to a small pool nestled within the embrace of the sand.

Perplexed, I questioned, "What is it, my friend? What do you want me to see?"

The response came as intense gazes exchanged between us. Whisperwind's eyes fixated on the watery pool, its significance veiled beneath the surface. Sensing that there was more to this ordinary pool than met the eye, I knelt, peering into its depths, ready to uncover the hidden secrets that lay within.

With a mix of curiosity and trepidation, I extended my hand into the pool, my fingertips delicately exploring the unknown depths. The water caressed my skin, cool and soothing, as I reached deeper, searching for what lay hidden beneath the surface. And then, my touch encountered something intriguing—a curved, hard, and smooth object, firmly anchored to the rocky base. Excitement welled up within me as I realized I had stumbled upon a hidden treasure, awaiting its rediscovery after being concealed by the water's gentle embrace.

Persistence paid off as I deftly dislodged the object from its watery sanctuary. As it emerged, glistening droplets cascading from its shell, my eyes widened in recognition—it was a mussel. A sudden realization dawned upon me, and I cast an incredulous glance at Whisperwind. "Were you trying to guide me towards this bounty?" I wondered aloud, marveling at the mysterious understanding between us. The connection between the pool and the potential feast crystallized in my mind, as I realized Whisperwind had led me to this hidden source of sustenance.

Inspired, I delved deeper into the pool, my hands exploring its hidden recesses. My fingertips brushed against more mussels, their presence a revelation. With each successful retrieval, my excitement grew.

"Whisperwind, my astute companion," I exclaimed with gratitude, "you have led us to a nourishing breakfast, and perhaps a stockpile, to sustain us for some time."

The bountiful discovery filled me with a sense of gratitude for the mysterious connection we shared, and a renewed appreciation for the resourcefulness of nature's offerings.

With Whisperwind at my side, we made our way back to the crackling fire, the freshly gathered mussels patiently waiting nearby. The sight of the pile of shellfish filled me with a sense of satisfaction and anticipation. "Now we just need some stones to cook them on," I remarked with a determined tone. With purpose in my stride, I set off towards the direction of the cliffs, confident in my ability to find suitable stones for our culinary endeavor. The promise of a delicious meal sparked a newfound energy within me, driving me forward in search of the tools for our feast.

Amongst the sandy terrain, my gaze fell upon a solitary stone, partially buried in the soft ground. Its modest size, measuring only about two inches in width, belied its potential usefulness. Driven by the desire to gain it, I extended my hand, expecting a straightforward task. However, much to my surprise, the stone proved to be more obstinate than expected, firmly entrenched in its sandy embrace. Determined not to be deterred, I applied more force, my fingers gripping the stone tightly as I exerted a steady pull, determined to liberate it from the earth's grasp.

Realizing that extracting the stone required more than a simple tug, I sighed and said, "Seems like we'll have to put in some extra effort. Let's dig around it and see if we can loosen it up."

With renewed determination, I plunged my hands into the sand, digging around the stone with unwavering resolve. Each scoop revealed a clearer view of the stone, bringing us closer to our aim. The more sand I cleared, the more I marveled at the unexpected challenge.

"Who would have thought that a single stone would put up such resistance?" I remarked with a mix of surprise and admiration for its tenacity.

Persistence paid off as I wiggled the stone back and forth, my hands gripping it firmly. With each movement, the stone gradually loosened its grip on the surrounding sand, finally giving way to my resolute determination.

As I rejoiced in my triumph of removing the stone, a glimmer of light diverted my attention to the spot where the stone had been. An intriguing sight awaited me in the sand, captivating my curiosity. Setting the stone aside, I leaned in closer, driven by an insatiable desire to unravel the secrets hidden beneath the surface.

With each scoop of sand, the object emerged, unveiling its captivating form. A smooth and elongated shape, about six inches long, it exuded an enchanting greenish hue that caught the light and shimmered like a rare gem. Its resemblance to an emerald was undeniable, but its purpose and origin remained veiled in enigma.

As I held the object in my hands, a sense of reverence washed over me. Its smooth surface felt cool and comforting against my skin, as if it held ancient wisdom and untold stories within its very essence. The mysterious greenish glow seemed to hold a magnetic pull, drawing me into a world of possibility and adventure.

Pondering the significance of this concealed treasure, I voiced my thoughts aloud; the words hanging in the air like whispers of curiosity. "Why was it hidden beneath the stone? What mysteries lie within its depths?" My mind brimmed with questions, each one fueling my desire to unravel the enigma before me.

Carefully, I held the object up to the light, examining its smooth surface that seemed to emit a gentle energy. The greenish hue danced under my scrutiny, its captivating glow hinting at an extraordinary nature that lay dormant within. It felt almost alive in my hands, as if it held secrets that only time and patience could unveil.

"If this gem holds no specific purpose, perhaps its value lies in its worth," I mused, my mind contemplating the potential value of the greenish gem.

The possibility of trading it for gold or other valuable resources intrigued me, igniting visions of grander possibilities.

I returned to the comforting warmth of the crackling fire, carrying the stone in my hands. The idea of cooking our gathered mussels on this intriguing stone sparked excitement within me. With a purposeful stride, I made my way back; the anticipation growing with each step.

Arriving at the fire, I set the stone down and gathered driftwood and stones, improvising a small shelf. Carefully arranging the materials, I ensured the stone would receive adequate heat for our culinary endeavor. The crackling flames danced in agreement, casting their glow upon the makeshift construction.

As I placed the stone on the improvised shelf, I could feel the heat radiating through my hands, assuring me of its readiness. The stone transformed into a sizzling surface, eager to fulfill its purpose. With a sense of satisfaction, I knew that this humble stone would soon play a significant role in satisfying our hunger and providing nourishment for our journey.

Eager to savor the succulent flavors that awaited us, I retrieved the mussels we had gathered earlier and carefully arranged them on the heated stone. The tantalizing scent of the sea mingled with the aroma of the crackling fire, creating an intoxicating blend that awakened my senses.

My mouth watered in anticipation as the mussels opened, their enticing aroma filling the air. I instinctively reached behind my back, drawing my trusty dagger, a faithful companion that had served me well on countless occasions. With a flick of my wrist, I skillfully separated the succulent meat from its protective shell, relishing in the satisfying sound of the blade slicing through the tender flesh.

Each bite was a burst of briny goodness, a taste of the sea mingled with the smoky notes from the crackling fire. The flavors danced upon my palate, tantalizing and invigorating. With each mussel I consumed, I felt a renewed energy coursing through my veins, revitalizing me for the journey that lay ahead.

"This is absolutely delightful," I exclaimed with a satisfied smile, my voice filled with contentment.

The flavors of the freshly cooked mussels danced upon my tongue, bringing a burst of savory goodness that perfectly complemented the enchanting atmosphere of our beachside feast.

I extended the second mussel toward Whisperwind, my eyes filled with curiosity and a touch of amusement. The little creature approached cautiously, sniffing at the offering before swiftly retreating, shaking its head in refusal. I furrowed my brow in mild surprise, not expecting such a reaction. "What's the matter, my friend? Seafood not to your liking?" I asked, a hint of amusement lacing my words.

Thinking that perhaps Whisperwind simply had a discerning palate, I offered another mussel. However, to my astonishment, the little creature once again backed away, this time with a more determined gesture of refusal. As I observed Whisperwind darting off towards the dense forest, disappearing from sight, a mix of curiosity and concern welled up within me.

Though I couldn't see Whisperwind amidst the dense foliage, the distinct sound of his wings buzzing and fluttering reached my ears. The rhythmic hum guided my gaze, enabling me to approximate Whisperwind's general direction, even in the absence of visual contact. Intrigued by the creature's curious behavior, I patiently stood there, waiting in anticipation, pondering what Whisperwind could be up to.

After a minute or two, Whisperwind reappeared, delicately holding a green leafy item between his teeth. My eyes widened with curiosity and understanding as I witnessed the tiny creature voraciously munching on the leaf.

"Ah, I see," I exclaimed, a smile spreading across my face. "You're more of an herbivore, aren't you? No wonder you didn't eat what I offered."

Now that the mystery was solved why Whisperwind wouldn't eat what was offered, I peered off into the vast unknown that lay before me, captivated by the mystique of the landscape unfolding before my eyes. Was this uncharted terrain, a realm waiting to be explored by intrepid adventurers? Or perhaps it was a hidden gem, a secret sanctuary concealed from the watchful gaze of the world? As I pondered these questions, a spark of excitement ignited within me, urging me to seek the truth and unravel the secrets that this enigmatic realm held.

My mind retraced the unsettling encounter with the creature that had ensnared my leg, a reminder of the potential dangers lurking beneath the surface of this mysterious realm. I couldn't help but wonder if this place housed other extraordinary creatures, ones yet unseen, waiting to be discovered or perhaps even confronted. Although uncertainty lingered in the air, my adventurous spirit burned brightly, refusing to be dampened by fear.

Whisperwind, perched nearby, provided a comforting presence, its gentle humming acting as a subtle affirmation of our shared contemplations. It felt as if the creature understood the depths of my thoughts, as if we were kindred spirits on this journey of discovery. The bond between us deepened with each passing moment, a partnership forged through curiosity and a shared yearning for the mysteries that lay ahead.

With the remnants of our meal cleared away, my hunger appeased, but my curiosity ignited, I felt compelled to investigate the worn trunk further. I retraced my steps to the spot where I had left it the night before, eager to unlock its secrets. Anticipation coursed through my veins as I reached down and grasped the trunk's sturdy handle, the weight of possibilities lingering in my mind. What mysteries lay hidden within its weathered confines? I could hardly wait to discover the tales it held, eager to delve into the past it might reveal.

## *Chapter 7 The Trunk*

I studied the robust trunk before me, my fingertips exploring the intricate design of the lock. Its intricate mechanisms appeared to be a formidable barrier, guarding the secrets hidden within. The hinges, weathered yet steadfast, bore witness to the trunk's endurance throughout the ages. And the secure seal along the lid told a tale of its time submerged in water, hinting at a watery voyage that added to its mystique.

A spark of creativity ignited in my mind as I thought about the mysterious trunk. Looking for ideas, I turned to my faithful companion, Whisperwind, hoping to find some insight. However, the small creature, while showing empathy in its gaze and soothing hum, didn't have an immediate solution to provide.

Undeterred by the initial setback, I retrieved my trusty dagger from my belt, my fingers gripping its handle with determination. With a hint of optimism, I set out to pick the lock, each precise movement guided by a mix of skill and hope. However, the lock remained intact, defying my attempts.

Whisperwind fluttered around the trunk, its wings creating a gentle breeze that seemed to whisper secrets. I caught a glimmer of movement near the lock, a minuscule glint of light reflected in a tiny crevice. Could this be the key to unlocking the trunk's secrets?

With newfound determination, I attempted to put my trusty dagger in the tiny crevice. I wiggled the dagger in a vertical motion, feeling for any resistance or sign of movement. Whisperwind just watched with keen interest, its eyes gleaming with anticipation. The air was thick with anticipation as I manipulated the tool, applying just the right amount of pressure.

Then a faint click echoed through the air. My heart skipped a beat as the lock surrendered to my efforts. The trunk's lid shifted, offering a tantalizing glimpse of what lay inside.

Whisperwind and I shared a triumphant glance, our eyes sparkling with anticipation. With bated breath, I lifted the lid of the trunk, revealing its long-guarded secrets. The sight that unfolded before us left us awestruck, unable to believe our incredible fortune.

My eyes widened with astonishment as I examined the contents of the trunk. It held a myriad of items that would have been useful during our previous night's ordeal. A sense of longing filled me as I imagined how much easier our situation would have been if we had access to these provisions earlier.

First, my gaze fell upon a sturdy bag, designed for carrying provisions. It was crafted from durable fabric, reinforced with leather straps and buckles, allowing it to withstand the rigors of travel. I couldn't help but think about how this bag would have relieved our burdens, providing a more efficient means of carrying our belongings.

Next, I discovered a rolled-up sleeping mat tucked inside the trunk. The mat was made from a thick, padded material, providing insulation and comfort when laid on the ground. My mind wandered back to the discomfort of the previous night, wishing we had this soft and cushioned surface to rest upon, offering respite from the hard and unforgiving terrain.

As I rummaged further, my fingers brushed against the cool surface of a set of light chain mail. It was woven, providing protection without impeding movement. This discovery ignited a spark of relief within me, realizing that we now possessed a layer of defense against potential threats that may lie ahead.

Last, my attention turned to a package of pemmican, a preserved meat delicacy that had been salted and dried to ensure its longevity. My stomach growled at the thought of nourishing myself with this concentrated source of sustenance. I couldn't help but express my regret, lamenting how our hunger could have been eased had we only been able to access this pemmican earlier.

While I voiced my thoughts, Whisperwind, always a faithful friend, gazed at me with its profound, knowing eyes. Although it couldn't speak with words, the creature's mere presence provided comfort and companionship as we faced our shared obstacles.

I fastened the light chain mail around my body, feeling the comforting weight of the protective armor settle upon me. It provided a sense of security, a layer of defense against the perils that awaited us. With a determined focus, I then gathered the pemmican and the flint and steel, ensuring our essential supplies were stowed in the sturdy bag. Every item had its place, organized to optimize our efficiency and accessibility during our journey.

Meanwhile, Whisperwind, ever the curious and intuitive companion, had climbed up a nearby rock and leaped into the open trunk. I watched with a mixture of amusement and curiosity as the creature explored its contents. The sound of its humming grew louder, showing that something had captured its attention within the trunk's depths.

I approached the trunk, my gaze fixed on Whisperwind's actions. The creature's focused demeanor was intriguing, and I couldn't help but wonder what had piqued its interest.

"What's wrong, boy?" I asked, kneeling beside the trunk with intrigue in my voice.

Surprisingly, Whisperwind didn't look at me.. Instead, its attention remained fixated on the bottom of the chest as it began to paw and scratch at it. The behavior was peculiar, different from its previous interactions with the contents.

Getting closer, I examined the inside of the trunk, focusing on the spot that had caught Whisperwind's attention. I ran my fingers along the bottom, searching for anything unusual. My heart raced with excitement as I wondered if the trunk concealed more hidden mysteries.

Continuing my investigation, I realized that the front corner of the trunk bottom was not square, but rounded off, just enough for me to stick my dagger in and lift the bottom. Testing my theory, I stuck the tip of my dagger in the hole and pried the false bottom of the trunk open.

My excitement heightened as I discovered a vial containing a mysterious liquid, a finely crafted silver dagger adorned with intricate engravings, aged parchment, and a small pouch of gold. I couldn't help but be filled with wonder and eagerness as I made these remarkable finds.

I removed the vial nestled within the hidden compartment. The contents of the vial were a shimmering, translucent liquid of vibrant blue hue. The vial itself was crafted from delicate glass, etched with ornate patterns that danced in the light. As I held it in my hands, I felt a subtle warmth emanating from the vial, as if it held a secret power within its mystical contents.

Placing the vial into my bag, I removed the silver dagger from the hidden compartment in the trunk. Its gleaming blade, forged from the purest silver, sparkled in the light, reflecting an ethereal glow. The hilt of the dagger, carved and adorned with intricate engravings, showcased the skilled craftsmanship that went into its creation.

The etchings on the dagger had a narrative of their own, featuring ancient symbols, mythical beings, or perhaps scenes from heroic tales. Each element was meticulously and accurately engraved into the dagger's handle, imbuing it with a sense of vitality. The designs intertwined and flowed gracefully, coming together to create a mesmerizing work of artistry.

The handle felt just right in my hand, created to offer both beauty and usefulness. Its design made sure the person holding it had a firm grasp, and the silver metalwork featured delicate curves and decorative touches, making it even more attractive and adding to its overall appearance.

The blade, incredibly sharp, had been expertly honed to perfection. Made from pure silver, renowned for its purity and its ability to ward off malevolent forces, it became a powerful tool against supernatural enemies. Its sharpness was unmatched, slicing through the air with precision and grace.

The dagger's remarkable craftsmanship showed it wasn't merely ornamental; it served a clear and important role as a weapon. Its combination of attractiveness and functionality made it a prized possession for skilled warriors and collectors of fine arms alike.

I stored the dagger in my bag and removed the weathered parchment. Its delicate fibers held a wealth of history and knowledge, worn and aged by the passage of time. The surface bore the telltale signs of age, with faded ink and tattered edges, as if it had journeyed through countless hands and witnessed the turning of many eras.

The parchment was a vessel of stories, an ancient medium through which ideas, wisdom, and secrets were conveyed. Its yellowed hue and delicate texture hinted at the long journey it had undertaken, perhaps preserved in the depths of hidden libraries or carried by intrepid explorers across distant lands.

Upon closer inspection, the faded ink revealed traces of symbols, once vibrant and bold. Though time had taken its toll, snippets of text remained, like fragments of a forgotten tale waiting to be deciphered. The writing could be written in flowing calligraphy, elegant, or in a more practical script, reflecting the purpose for which they created the parchment.

After storing the weathered parchment in my bag, I couldn't help but feel a twinge of excitement. Maybe the ancient script held countless untold stories, waiting to be deciphered by someone with knowledge and expertise. The parchment was a puzzle yet to be solved, and I yearned to find someone who could shed light on its contents.

I looked at Whisperwind, feeling a sense of companionship and shared purpose fill the air. The little creature's understanding eyes seemed to convey a silent agreement, as if saying, "Let us seek the wisdom of others who may guide us on this journey." I nodded, grateful for the unspoken affirmation from my loyal friend.

With a determined gesture, I secured the small satchel of gold in my bag. It was a tangible reminder of the possibilities that lay ahead. The gleaming coins held promises of help, trade, and even survival in unfamiliar lands. They would serve as a valuable resource on our quest, a means to get necessities and seek knowledge.

With the artifacts tucked away, I knew the time had come to embark on the next leg of our adventure. My mind pondered the options before us—the unexplored stretch of the beach, the mysterious cliffs beckoning from a distance, and the alluring depths of the forest.

Whisperwind, in its intuitive wisdom, showed our path by directing my attention toward the dense forest. It was an invitation to unravel the mysteries hidden within its depths, a call to discover the unknown and venture into uncharted territories. Not understanding where we were, the invitation to head anywhere was like a new adventure that I enjoyed.

## *Chapter 8 Eldoria Forest*

With Whisperwind in the lead, I headed west into the unknown forest. Within just a few feet, the dense foliage enveloped us, casting dappled shadows upon the forest floor and creating an otherworldly atmosphere. Our footsteps were hushed by a thick carpet of fallen leaves, and the air was infused with the earthy fragrance of moss and decaying wood. My eyes scanned the surroundings, my gaze darting from tree to tree, searching for any signs of life or landmarks that could guide our path.

Whisperwind led the way through the dense forest, maneuvering through the labyrinth of trees, branches, and vines. Its small size allowed it to navigate with ease, while I moved more slowly, pushing aside obstructing foliage and stepping over fallen trunks.

My voice carried through the forest as I expressed my reliance on Whisperwind's guidance.

"I trust you know the way, my friend," I remarked.

Whisperwind responded with a gentle hum, a reassurance that it was indeed leading us in the right direction.

As the path became difficult to discern, my frustration grew. The dense undergrowth seemed determined to obscure our progress. But each time I lagged, struggling to find my footing, Whisperwind sensed my presence and backtracked, circling around to ensure my safety.

After what felt like an arduous hour of trekking through the dense forest, Whisperwind and I found ourselves in an area where the foliage thinned out. Sensing the need for a moment's respite, we settled down on a large rock, our tired bodies craving a brief reprieve.

I unfastened my waterskin and took a refreshing sip, replenishing my parched throat. Out of a gesture of companionship, I poured a small amount of water into a crevice on the rock, offering it to Whisperwind. The avian companion lapped up the water, a testament to the shared exhaustion we both felt. I chuckled. "Thirsty, huh? I can relate. That journey was more demanding than I expected," I remarked, wiping the sweat from my brow.

As I reached into my bag, retrieving a piece of pemmican, I extended it toward Whisperwind, attempting to share a moment of sustenance together. However, the little creature turned up its nose in a display of disinterest. I shrugged, understanding that our tastes and dietary preferences differed.

Sitting there amidst the tranquil forest, I pondered our purpose and the destination to which Whisperwind was guiding us. The sun still hung high in the sky, allowing ample time to find a suitable campsite before nightfall enveloped the land in darkness. I voiced my thoughts, aware of the importance of our preparations.

"We'll need to establish a campsite before nightfall, my friend. The darkness can be unforgiving, making navigation and survival more challenging," I mused, my words punctuated by the affirmative hums and chirps from Whisperwind.

As I prepared to rise from my resting position and resume our journey, an unexpected cacophony of unfamiliar sounds erupted from Whisperwind. The air was filled with a series of low, guttural growls, unlike any utterances I had ever heard. Perplexed, I turned my gaze towards my faithful companion, seeking an explanation.

"What is the matter?"

Just as the unusual sounds emanating from Whisperwind captured my attention, my eyes caught sight of a slender figure dashing towards us. Uncertain whether this sudden arrival was a friend or foe, I unsheathed my sword and raised my shield, adopting a defensive stance. The figure's voice carried towards us, shouting words that were indiscernible to my ears. However, as the figure closed the distance, the words of a female became clearer.

"Get ready for a fight or run!"

Having endured the arduous journey to our present position, I was resolute in my decision not to retreat, knowing that turning back would only lead us into further trouble. The mysterious figure, however, dashed past me and Whisperwind without so much as a glance, leaving us perplexed as to the reason for her frantic haste. As we turned our gaze towards the departing figure, our vision was met with nothing but her receding back, obscuring any clues as to her purpose or destination.

As Whisperwind and I turned around, our eyes widened at the sight of two towering figures, standing at an impressive height of eight feet, in hot pursuit of the fleeing individual. Undeterred by the odds, my experience in confronting formidable adversaries instilled in me the resolve to hold my position. With sword in hand and unwavering determination, I braced myself to engage in combat with the two imposing creatures.

As the towering adversaries closed in, their menacing clubs raised high, intent on striking me, I displayed my agility and reflexes by sliding down and delivering a precise strike to sever the leg of one creature. The injured creature stumbled and crashed to the ground, incapacitated. However, my respite was short-lived, as the remaining creature swung its club with tremendous force toward me. Reacting with lightning speed, I parried the attack, slamming my sword against the club and delivering a powerful counterattack with my shield, crashing into the towering figure's body.

The colossal creature and I engaged in a fierce exchange of blows, our weapons clashing with resounding force. Despite my valiant efforts, the creature's sheer size and resilience made it difficult for me to inflict significant damage. Sensing an opportunity, Whisperwind maneuvered to the other side of the creature, remaining just out of its reach. With a burst of radiant light emanating from Whisperwind, the creature's attention was captivated, providing me with a precious opening. Seizing the moment, I sliced across the creature's arm, leaving a deep gash. Enraged by the wound, the creature's focus shifted away from the bright light, diverting its fury towards me.

As the second massive figure struggled to rise, displeased by the injury to its leg, a sudden cry of agony escaped its lips. It arched its back, as if struck from behind by an unseen force. I couldn't comprehend the cause of this sudden turn of events, but I felt a surge of relief knowing that the second creature was diverted and not advancing towards me.

My focus remained unwavering as I stayed vigilant against the creature I had been engaged in combat with. The severe injury to its arm provided me with a clear opening, and I seized the opportunity with calculated precision. Just as I was about to deliver a decisive strike, a sudden blur caught my attention—an arrow materialized out of nowhere, impaling the creature's chest. The sight stunned both me and my foe, causing a momentary pause in the chaos. Taking advantage of this unforeseen diversion, I pressed forward, delivering the final blow that sent the creature crashing to the ground, its face meeting the earth with a resounding thud.

Turning my attention to the second creature, I braced myself for another grueling confrontation. However, to my astonishment, the massive figure lay motionless on the ground, six arrows protruding from its back like cruel reminders of its swift defeat. Someone had intervened, eliminating the immediate threat before I could even make my move.

With adrenaline coursing through my veins, I sought cover behind the sturdy rock we had rested upon earlier. My heart pounded in my chest, a mixture of exhilaration and caution intertwining within me. I was uncertain if the mysterious archer, who had dispatched the formidable adversaries with a shower of arrows, posed an additional threat or was an unexpected ally. During the tense atmosphere, Whisperwind remained steadfast at my side, a loyal companion whose presence brought a sense of reassurance.

Concerned for Whisperwind's well-being, I turned to him and asked.

"Are you alright?"

In response, Whisperwind emitted his familiar sounds of acknowledgment, assuring me he was indeed alright. The intensity of the recent battle hung in the air, and I couldn't help but express my gratitude to Whisperwind for the crucial distraction that had allowed me to gain the upper hand.

Just then, a woman's voice could be heard coming from the trees.

"That was an intense encounter," she said.

"I would say so," I answered.

"I can't thank you enough for creating that diversion. It played a crucial role in our victory," replied the mysterious lady, still hiding in the trees.

I still couldn't see where she was from where we were standing, but

I could hear her plain as day.

"Well, I don't think believe it was that much of a distraction as the forest has been a lot more challenging and I didn't want to go back the way I came."

"The forest can get kind of thick in some places, so I know what you mean," she answered. "If it is alright with you, I would like to come to thank you for helping me out back there. I don't have any intentions to harm you,", she followed up with.

I responded, my voice tinged with a hint of skepticism, "How do we know you won't shoot us with those arrows, like you did the two beasts?"

With a touch of amusement in her voice, the woman replied, "If I wanted to shoot you, I would have done so earlier when you were in the midst of battle. As you can see, I am a pretty excellent shot." Her words carried a sense of self-assuredness, hinting at her proficiency with the bow and arrows.

I deliberated for a moment, weighing the risks against the possibility of forging an alliance with this mysterious woman. Curiosity and a flicker of trust won over my caution.

"Very well," I consented, lowering my sword. "Come closer, but make no sudden moves. We'll speak face-to-face and decide if we can trust each other."

Emerging from behind the protective cover of the rock, Whisperwind and I observed a faint figure emerging from the dense foliage. The slender figure was clad in a garment that blended with the surrounding trees, concealing her presence. As the figure drew closer, her features became more discernible, revealing a determined expression on her face.

Breaking the silence, the mysterious figure uttered two words that caught me off guard, "Forest Trolls."

Startled, I replied, "What?"

My mind struggled to process this unexpected revelation. The realization that the formidable adversaries we had just faced were indeed Forest Trolls sent a chill down my spine.

Curiosity and a desire for more information compelled me to inquire further.

"You're saying those two massive figures were Forest Trolls?"

The figure nodded, affirming my query.

She continued, recounting her own encounter with the Forest Trolls. "I was enjoying my day out for a relaxing stroll, when they ambushed me. They closed in too for me to use my arrows, so I had to create some distance to survive. That's when fate led me to cross paths with you."

I studied the imposing figures of the Forest Trolls. Laying on the ground before me, their muscular frames commanded attention. Thick, coarse fur adorned their bodies, displaying a range of earthy tones — shades of green, brown, and gray intermingled to grant them the ability to blend into their woodland habitat. As my gaze roamed across their forms, I noticed the rough texture of their skin, punctuated by patches of bark, granting them an uncanny camouflage amidst the trees.

Taking a moment to look back at the mysterious female, my voice was filled with astonishment as I uttered, "By the spirits, I have only heard tales of Forest Trolls in the ancient legends, never have I laid eyes upon one until now."

"There are a few of them in this forest, but they usually aren't this far north," she stated.

"Should we search them for any valuables? Perhaps they possess something of worth."

With a nonchalant gesture, the woman replied, "Feel free to rummage through their belongings, but I must warn you, Forest Trolls rarely carry anything of value."

With a shared understanding, I and Whisperwind approached the trolls, our hands exploring the pockets and crevices of the fallen creatures. After a thorough search, I shook my head in disappointment.

"Nothing of significance here, only their crude clubs.".

The woman nodded. "It is often the case," she affirmed, her tone suggesting that such meager findings were to be expected.

As the woman stood before us, she removed her hood, revealing her face to Whisperwind and I.

"My name is Arabella," she said.

My gaze became fixated on her flowing locks of golden-brown hair that cascaded down her back. Her eyes shimmered like precious emeralds, holding a hint of mystery that captivated me. Her facial features exuded a delicate blend of grace and charm, accentuated by a smattering of freckles that danced across her nose, lending her a youthful allure. As I observed her, I couldn't help but notice how her outfit embraced her petite body, accentuating her ample curves. My mouth hung open, perhaps more than it should have, as her beauty entranced me.

I couldn't help but be enchanted by her radiant beauty, lost in a trance-like state. However, Whisperwind's sudden sound broke through the enchantment, pulling me back to the present moment.

"Um, my name is Valaric, and this is Whisperwind," I choked out, as if I had forgotten my name.

Whisperwind emitted a short humming sound in acknowledgment.

Arabella's eyes twinkled with amusement as she observed the adorable and colorful creature.

"You are quite cute, all fuzzy and vibrant," she remarked, earning a gentle response from Whisperwind.

"So, where are you two heading?" asked Arabella.

"I do not know where we were heading. I was too busy following Whisperwind through the forest and did not know where he was going," I stated with a confused look.

"I found myself stranded on the beach just two days ago with no recollection of how I arrived there or any knowledge of where I am. So now we were just finding a place to seek refuge beyond the shoreline."

"What do you mean you don't know where you are or how you arrived here?" she questioned with her brows furrowed.

"I do not know where I am standing at this moment."

"So, I am going to go out on a limb here and assume that you are not from here either," she mused.

"I am uncertain I even know where here is, for me to say if I am from here or not. So where are we?"

"You are in Eldoria Forest," Arabella stated with a glimmer of amusement in her face.

The name reverberated through my mind, causing me to draw a blank. Eldoria Forest, a place I had never heard of before.

"Eldoria Forest is not ringing any bells. So, I still don't know where I am."

"Would I be correct in stating that since you are not from here and the fact that you have never heard of Eldoria Forest, that you have no place to stay?" asked Arabella.

"That would be correct. We were just planning on setting up camp in the woods for the night and then continue our journey in search of a suitable place to stay."

"How about you two come back to my village and let's see if we can find you a place to stay for the night? Think of it as thank you for saving a damsel in distress from the horrible Forest Trolls," she inquired.

I hesitated, my mind grappling with the irony of Arabella referring to herself as a damsel in distress while displaying her remarkable archery skills against the trolls.

I took a second to look at Whisperwind. "Well, what do you think?"

Whisperwind just responded with his familiar sounds, as if he was giving an approval.

I looked back up at Arabella and said, "I suppose that would be alright."

"Great then. Follow me. I know my way around the woods," she stated.

Arabella, donning her hood once again, led the way back to her village. Whisperwind and I trailed behind, our senses engaged, absorbing the captivating scenery of the surrounding forest and the scenery right in front of us. The sunlight filtered through the canopy above, casting a soft, ethereal glow on the moss-covered ground. The air was filled with the sweet scent of wildflowers and the earthy aroma of the forest.

*Chapter 9 The Deeper Connection*

As we made our way towards the village, my curiosity about Eldoria Forest grew, prompting me to inquire about its intriguing features.

"Tell me more about Eldoria Forest," I asked Arabella, eager to uncover its secrets.

Arabella glanced back at me, a glimmer of excitement in her emerald eyes.

"Eldoria Forest is a place of wonder and mystique," she began, her voice carrying a hint of reverence. "It is said to be enchanted, a realm where ancient magic intertwines with the natural world. The forest is teeming with life, from majestic creatures that roam its depths to ethereal spirits that dwell within the trees."

"The forest is a vast expanse filled with enchanting flora, trees that whisper ancient secrets, elemental springs that possess mystical properties, paths that shift and change, Fae glades where magical beings dwell, cascading waterfalls, hidden caves waiting to be discovered, and a plethora of diverse wildlife," she explained.

My interest was piqued by the notion of shifting paths.

"What do you mean by shifting paths?"

Arabella took a moment to choose her words before responding.

"In Eldoria Forest, the paths and trails possess a mysterious quality. They change and shift, leading travelers to unexpected destinations. What was once a familiar path may whisk you on an different route," she clarified.

This revelation left me pondering their current path and its reliability.

"But how can we be certain that the path we're on will lead us to your village if the paths are prone to shifting?"

"We, the inhabitants of this forest, share a deep connection with its essence. Through our bond with Eldoria Forest, we possess an innate understanding of its ever-changing trails and can navigate them with certainty. The path we tread will guide us to my village," she explained.

I listened to Arabella's words, realizing that gaining a deep connection with the forest was crucial to navigating its shifting paths. I couldn't help but feel a sense of curiosity and determination to understand the forest on a deeper level.

"How does one go about developing such a profound connection with the forest to avoid getting lost amidst these shifting paths?"

Arabella paused their walk, turning to face Valaric.

"Establishing a genuine connection with the forest requires time and a genuine effort to understand its essence," she explained.

Eager to learn, I probed a little deeper.

"And how can we accomplish this task?"

I wanted to get a better understanding of how someone could establish a genuine connection with the Eldoria Forest, so that I would have the ability to move throughout the forest as well.

Arabella took a moment to collect her thoughts, then spoke with conviction.

"Take a moment to look around you," she instructed, as she waved her hand out while turning her body.

"Take a moment to look around and tell me what you see?"

I took a survey of my immediate surroundings, focusing on the trees, grass, vines, and flowers that met his gaze.

"I see the elements of nature that are right in front of me."

"That's part of the problem," she sighed, with a hint of frustration that was clear in her voice. "You're only seeing what's superficial, what's on the surface. You haven't seen the forest."

"I am having difficulty understanding what you mean. Do you see something other than the trees, grass, vines, and flowers?"

After I made that comment, I could see that she was now frustrated with me. Her face was in a blank stare, as if trying to figure out how someone could not understand what she was trying to explain.

"Alright, let's take this from a different perspective. What do you hear?"

I pondered for a moment, recalling the sounds that surrounded me. Trying to listen as I looked around the area.

"I hear the gentle swaying of the trees, the melodic songs of the birds, and the subtle rustling of wildlife," I replied with questions on my face.

A soft sigh escaped Arabella's lips as she shook her head.

"You're not listening," she responded, her voice carrying a tinge of disappointment. "There is so much more happening in the depths of the forest, waiting to be discovered."

As Arabella spoke, I couldn't help but feel a sense of disappointment washing over me. Even Whisperwind, my loyal companion, seemed to express silent disapproval, shaking his head. It was a humbling moment, a realization that I had scratched the surface of understanding the profound depths of the forest I now traversed.

"Close your eyes," Arabella instructed, her voice a soothing melody. "Don't say a word, and just listen to my voice."

I nodded, a sense of anticipation coursing through me as I attuned my senses to the guidance that awaited. I focused on my surroundings, opening myself to the subtle whispers of the forest and the unseen forces that guided its paths.

"Breathe in, allowing the scents of the forest to fill your lungs, "Arabella continued, her words carrying a sense of tranquility. "Notice the aged wood, with its comforting aroma of resin and sap, embodying the strength, stability, and timelessness of the forest."

"Let the air carry to you the fresh scent of leaves, ferns, and mosses, hinting at the promise of new beginnings," Arabella added, her voice dancing with the whispers of nature. "And now, inhale, capturing the sweet fragrance of wildflowers-jasmine, honeysuckle, and lavender — each contributing their ethereal beauty to the forest."

"Keep your eyes closed," Arabella reminded me, her voice filled with anticipation. "Now, with your senses awakened, can you smell these things?" she inquired.

I took a moment to immerse myself in the fragrant tapestry of the forest, my olfactory perception heightened.

"Yes, yes, I can smell these things," I replied, a newfound

appreciation and connection to the forest blossoming within me.

With my eyes closed, I surrendered to the symphony of scents that enveloped me, immersing myself in the forest's essence. In this state of sensory awareness, I discovered the fragrances held a captivating power, allowing me to experience the forest in a unique and vivid way.

As I inhaled, the earthy aroma of damp soil mingled with the sweet scent of wildflowers, awakening my senses, and transporting me to the heart of nature's embrace. I could almost see the vibrant colors of the flowers, the lush greenery of the trees, and the dappled sunlight dancing through the leaves, throughout the olfactory canvas that painted itself within my mind.

"Keep your eyes closed," Arabella urged me, her voice guiding me into a deeper connection with the forest. "Take a moment to listen, to immerse yourself in the symphony of nature that surrounds us."

I kept my eyes closed, allowing my ears to guide me through the enchanting symphony of sounds. The gentle rustling of leaves filled my consciousness, intertwining with the swaying of the majestic trees. It was a melody that evoked a sense of calmness and serenity, as if nature itself were whispering secrets of tranquility into my being.

Amidst the rustling leaves, another presence made itself known— the whispering wind. Its ethereal touch brushed against the leaves and branches, creating a delicate symphony of murmurs. It spoke of the perpetual movement and energy that flowed through the forest, reminding me of the intricate interconnectedness of all living things. With each whisper, I felt a deeper sense of unity with the natural world around me.

And then, the melodic babbling of a nearby brook reached my ears, its rhythmic gurgling and cascading water weaving an enchanting ambiance. In my mind's eye, I could see the clear water flowing over smooth stones and fallen branches, its coolness promising refreshment and renewal. The image of bending down to drink from the brook filled me with a sense of deep connection to the life force that permeated the forest.

Arabella's words resonated within me, painting vivid images of the forest's wonders. I envisioned myself cupping my hands and taking a sip of the cool, pure water, feeling its revitalizing energy flow through me. It was a moment of profound communion with nature, where the boundaries between myself and the forest blurred, and I became a part of its harmonious rhythm.

"Now, open your eyes and tell me what you see," she whispered.

I opened my eyes, allowing my gaze to wander and take in the scene before me.

"I see the trees swaying, their branches dancing to the gentle whispers of the wind. The leaves and flowers adorn the landscape with their vibrant colors, enhancing the majestic beauty of the forest. In the distance, I can see the brook, its crystal-clear waters cascading over the smooth rocks, creating a mesmerizing sight."

"Now that you have a better understanding of how to deepen your connection with the forest," Arabella remarked, her voice filled with a sense of satisfaction. "It's important to continue practicing and meditating to strengthen this bond. By doing so, you will cultivate a deeper connection and attunement with nature."

"Thank you. I have always just gone into a forest, never have I stopped to take in the forest."

"Besides meditation," Arabella spoke in her melodic voice, "I suggest visiting the elemental springs. These sacred springs hold a unique energy that can enhance your connection to the natural world. Each spring embodies the essence of a unique element, offering a profound experience and deepening your understanding of the forest's mysteries."

As we continued our journey towards the village, a profound shift occurred within me. I no longer felt like an outsider in the wilderness, but an integral part of the intricate tapestry of the forest. Every step I took was purposeful, my senses attuned to the subtleties of the natural world that enveloped me.

The trees, with their towering presence, captivated my gaze. I marveled at their majestic forms, swaying in harmony with the gentle breeze. The interplay of light and shadow painted a mesmerizing portrait as sunbeams filtered through the canopy, casting a dappled glow upon the forest floor. The vibrant colors of the flowers and foliage added bursts of beauty, creating a vivid kaleidoscope that stirred my soul.

With each winding path we navigated, I felt a growing connection to the terrain. The forest seemed to guide me, as if it recognized and responded to my newfound understanding. I moved with a fluidity that belied my earlier uncertainty, negotiating the forest's twists and turns. It was as if I had become one with the forest, a symbiotic relationship that fueled my every step.

Whisperwind, my ever-loyal companion, moved alongside me with newfound grace. We shared an unspoken understanding, forged through our shared experiences in this wondrous forest. Together, we wove into the natural surroundings, our presence an echo of the forest's own spirit.

As we approached the outskirts of the village, a profound sense of gratitude welled within me. The journey through Eldoria Forest had not only granted me a deeper connection with nature, but had also unveiled a newfound reverence for its wisdom and resilience. I carried this newfound understanding within me, a gift that would forever shape my perception of the world.

## *Chapter 10 Aurelia*

Arabella's voice carried a curious tone as she turned her attention towards me. The forest's serenity seemed to amplify the gentleness in her voice.

"Tell me, Valaric, where do you come from? I'm intrigued to know of the lands and experiences that have shaped you."

As my gaze softened, my thoughts drifted back to the serene beauty of my homeland.

"I come from a small island known as Aurelia."

"What is it like there?" Arabella asked.

A smile graced my lips as I immersed myself in the memories of my beloved home. With enthusiasm, I painted a vivid picture of Aurelia, my words filled with warmth and nostalgia.

"Aurelia is a place of breathtaking natural wonders. Vast stretches of emerald-green forests as far as the eye can see, with towering trees that seem to touch the heavens. The island is adorned with cascading waterfalls that cascade down moss-covered cliffs, their waters glistening and alive with the soothing sounds of nature."

"Oh, that sounds enchanting," Arabella exclaimed, her voice filled with genuine admiration.

My voice carried a sense of pride as I continued to describe the coastal charms of Aurelia.

"And along our shores, we are blessed with sandy beaches that meet the crystal-clear waters of the ocean," I explained with enthusiasm.

"The sun casts its warm embrace upon the coastline, and gentle sea breezes carry the essence of tranquility. It is a place where the beauty of nature meets the serenity of the sea. The shimmering waves invite you to dip your toes in the refreshing water, while the soft sand welcomes you to relax and unwind. Walking along the beach, you can witness the ebb and flow of the tides, a rhythmic dance that reminds you of the eternal cycles of nature. The coastal landscape of Aurelia is a sight to behold, a haven where one can find solace and be captivated by the harmony of land and sea."

"It sounds breathtaking," Arabella remarked, her voice filled with admiration. "I might have to visit your island one day, Valaric," she added, a hint of wanderlust in her tone.

My face lit up with enthusiasm at the thought of sharing my beloved home with someone new. The prospect of Arabella visiting Aurelia brought a surge of excitement and a sense of pride. I nodded in agreement, unable to contain my anticipation.

"I believe you would love it there and it would thrill me to show you the wonders of Aurelia," I replied.

"Aurelia offers a world of opportunities for those who appreciate its natural beauty and seek a tranquil lifestyle. It's a place where one can find solace, embrace the sea's embrace, and reconnect with the wonders of nature."

"I hope you don't mind me asking," Arabella began, her voice gentle and inquisitive, "but if Aurelia is such a paradise, why did you leave?"

"Aurelia is a haven for those seeking a peaceful life, filled with opportunities to fish, work at the ports, or even open a shop in town. But for someone like me, who yearns for adventure and the thrill of discovering new things, it felt somewhat limiting."

Arabella nodded; her gaze filled with empathy.

"Sometimes, the allure of adventure beckons us to uncharted territories," Arabella pondered. "Maybe Eldoria Forest embodies the very essence of what you yearn for—a realm teeming with enigma, unspoiled splendor, and the opportunity to carve your own destiny."

"I like your thinking Arabella."

Just as I was going to continue that train of thought, Whisperwind emitted a familiar sound.

"What was that sound?" Arabella asked.

"Not sure I can describe the sound, but that was the same sound

Whisperwind made upon the Forest Trolls. So, something is headed this way."

"Quick, let's get up in the trees!" Arabella instructed.

I lifted Whisperwind and found refuge in a nearby tree, ensuring his safety on a sturdy branch. Arabella scaled another tree close by, positioning herself for a strategic vantage point. With unwavering focus, I unsheathed my sword, its glinting blade ready to meet any threat head-on. Arabella, a masterful archer, grasped her bow, poised to rain down a barrage of arrows upon our approaching adversaries.

We sat up in the trees, in complete silence, senses sharpened, attuned to the slightest sound. After a few moments, I could hear a distant rumbling, showing the approach of something large and formidable. The anticipation grew as I could hear the heavy footsteps across the forest floor, drawing dearer to our position.

After moments of anticipation, my eyes fixated upon the origin of the approaching rumble. Emerging from beneath the dappled canopy, a majestic creature commanded my attention—a magnificent wolf. Its coat, a captivating blend of silver and midnight black, shimmered under the gentle touch of sunlight, creating a stark contrast against the shadows of the forest. The intensity of its gaze, its eyes a piercing shade of amber, revealed a profound intelligence and a powerful presence.

My heart skipped a beat as I marveled at the majestic presence of the wolf before us. I did not lose the significance of this encounter on me, and with an excited gesture, I caught Arabella's attention, urging her to join me in witnessing the awe-inspiring sight. I couldn't contain my eagerness to share this remarkable experience with her, knowing that it was an extraordinary moment in the depths of the forest.

As Arabella redirected her focus to the other side of the tree, her eyes widened in astonishment at the sight that unfolded before her. In the grip of overwhelming emotions, she leaped out of the tree, leaving me puzzled and alarmed by her sudden action.

"What are you doing?" I asked, assuming the element of surprise was now over.

"I am greeting my friend," she said with a slight grin on her face.

"What? That huge thing is a friend?"

At that moment I watched as the massive beast bounded over to Arabella, its massive form exuding a surprising gentleness. To my astonishment, Arabella extended her hand and the wolf nuzzled against it, as if seeking affection.

Arabella looked up at me as I was still sitting in the tree.

"Valaric, meet Shadowfang."

"Shadowfang! That massive thing, name is Shadowfang?"

"Yes, her name is Shadowfang, and she is my friend," Arabella remarked. "By the way, you can get down out of the tree now."

"You sure it's safe to climb down the tree? I mean, I don't want that rather enormous wolf eating my little friend here."

"Just get out of the tree," she exclaimed, her voice tinged with a mix of excitement.

I grabbed Whisperwind and made my way down to the base of the tree. Strolling over to where Arabella and the wolf were standing. I was in complete amazement over how big this wolf was. I had seen wolves before, but Shadowfang would have towered over those.

"How does one become friends with an animal that big?"

"I was venturing deep into the heart of the forest, seeking the mysteries that lay hidden within," Arabella recounted, her voice carrying a tinge of nostalgia. "And amidst the dense foliage, my eyes fell upon a fragile wolf pup, its small frame trembling with vulnerability. It was a poignant sight, a lone creature separated from its pack, in need of care and compassion."

I watched as Arabella's eyes grew soft with compassion.

"I couldn't leave the poor creature there, defenseless. So, without hesitation, I brought her back with me to my home, where I could provide the care and nurturing she needed."

"Alright, that makes better sense now how you became friends with a magnificent wolf. At that point Shadowfang wasn't so shadowy or fangy at that point in time."

"Not so much at that point," Arabella confirmed. "The nursing her back to health became my mission. I tended to her wounds, provided her with nourishment, and showered her with love and affection. As the days turned into weeks, and weeks into months, an unbreakable bond formed between us."

"Wow, that sounds like a beautiful story," I exclaimed.

I watched as Arabella's eyes sparkled with pride and gratitude.

"She grew stronger and stronger, but our connection remained unwavering. I protected her when she was just a vulnerable pup, and now, as she has matured into this magnificent creature," she gestured towards the great wolf standing beside her. "She protects me with unwavering loyalty and fierce devotion."

"I can see how that all worked out now, but where was Shadowfang during the Forest Trolls incident?"

"In that instance, I was attempting to be a little stealthier," Arabella explained, her voice carrying a hint of determination. "So, I asked Shadowfang to remain behind while I ventured forward. I mean, come on, you heard her walking up earlier, not stealthy."

"I can follow your train of thought with that one. Her footsteps are quite heavy."

"It appears I ventured deeper into the forest than I had planned, and it was during that exploration that I encountered the Forest Trolls," Arabella recounted, her voice carrying a tinge of unease. "They positioned themselves between Shadowfang and I, forcing me to flee in the direction I did, with them in relentless pursuit."

"Ah, that helps clear a few things up."

"Let's get moving again as we aren't that much further from the village," Arabella said.

We began walking again in the direction we were headed, prior to running into Shadowfang. However, after only walking for a few minutes, we found ourselves face-to-face with a group of guards. The guards were dressed in the same distinctive attire as Arabella, but with firm grips on their spears, that were pointed at us.

"Halt," commanded the leading guard, his voice laced with authority. "State your identities and explain why you are bringing an outsider here. You know well that the King has forbidden outsiders in our realm."

My thoughts raced with questions. Who were these guards? What kind of village was this? What kind of village has a king? What are we going to do? Do we fight?

I stood and watched as Arabella reached up and removed her hood, revealing her face to the guards. The guard's stern expressions softened, and they all dropped to their knees, their spears lowering in a show of reverence.

"Princess," they exclaimed in unison, their voices filled with a mix of awe and respect.

My eyes widened as I struggled to process the unexpected revelation.

"Princess," I blurted out without thinking.

Arabella turned towards me, a mixture of amusement and understanding in her eyes.

"Yes, Valaric," she replied with a gentle smile. "I am the Princess of this realm, and these guards are here to protect me and our people. We have a unique connection to the forest, and our village operates under a unique set of rules."

I took a moment to absorb this revelation, allowing it to sink in and reshape my understanding of the situation. My perception shifted as I glanced at the guards, their unwavering posture before Arabella spoke at volumes. I realized she held a position of great significance and bore the weight of leadership, carrying the responsibility of guiding and protecting her people.

## *Chapter 11 Kingdom of Vindoria*

As Arabella continued talking with the guards, I looked at Whisperwind with confusion and disbelief.

"Did you know she was a princess?" I asked Whisperwind.

Whisperwind's face showed no emotion as he pivoted to look at me, his eyes giving nothing away. Arabella briefly glanced back, a soft smile appearing on her lips, before returning her focus to the guards. My question had been louder than I meant it to be, causing her to briefly turn her gaze.

Arabella turned in my direction.

"I bet you are wondering how come I didn't tell you I was a princess," she exclaimed.

"Well, the thought had crossed my mind! Seems like that is information that a person should know, so they know how to properly address someone."

"There are many reasons, Valaric," she responded with a mischievous smile. "For one, it's not always wise to reveal one's royal stature when wandering alone in the woods. It attracts unnecessary attention and trouble."

A chuckle escaped her lips as she continued, "And let's be honest, you would have probably acted all weird and different around me, just like you are now."

"I don't know what you are talking about Ara, ugh, I mean Princess."

"Yes, that is exactly what I am talking about right there," she said with a laugh.

I became even more puzzled; the amazement giving way to a somewhat embarrassed understanding. I couldn't help but feel sheepish as I recognized my own exaggerated response. Even Whisperwind, sitting close by, seemed to let out a quiet, musical laugh, as if teasing me for my momentary loss of control.

In that moment, the head guard spoke with a firm tone, his concern clear in his voice, "Princess, we cannot permit the outsider to roam around the Kingdom."

"Very well, then restrain him with shackles and lead us to my father," Arabella responded.

"Shackles?" I exclaimed.

"You can either enter with shackles under guard or face the sharp ends of the pointy sticks these guards are holding," she gestured.

"Alright, shackles it is, but may I inquire where you intend to escort us? We are still only in the forest."

"You really have learned nothing, have you?" she remarked.

As the guards secured the shackles around my wrists, we advanced. And with each step we took, a breathtaking transformation unfolded before us. It was as if a veil of enchantment lifted, revealing a realm of magic that materialized out of thin air. Before our eyes stood a magnificent kingdom, resplendent in its ethereal beauty and captivating splendor.

Bewildered by the abrupt transformation, I turned my gaze back, only to see the familiar forest we had just departed from. The stark contrast between the two scenes was nothing short of astonishing. My curiosity surged within me, and I couldn't help but burst forth with a mixture of excitement and bewilderment. Questions swirled in my mind, begging for answers in this extraordinary realm before me.

"Wait! What just happened? How did we get here? What is transpiring?" I exclaimed, my voice brimming with eagerness. "There was nothing in front of us, so where did all this splendor originate from?"

Arabella fixed her gaze upon me, a gentle laughter escaping her lips as she responded, "Valaric, it seems there is still much knowledge for you to gain."

Her voice held a touch of amusement and affectionate teasing. "Didn't you grasp the lesson earlier? That seeing isn't always necessary to acknowledge something's existence," she stated, reminding me of our previous conversation.

Brimming with enthusiasm, I yearned to gain clarity and understanding of the situation.

"Well, yes, but our earlier discussion revolved around birds, wind rustling through the leaves, and a babbling brook—not an entire kingdom emerging amidst these woods," I said, with amazement in my voice.

"Valaric, I will explain everything to you in due time. But at this moment, it is crucial that we make our way to my father, the King," she exclaimed with a sense of urgency, emphasizing the importance of their current task.

While making our way through the kingdom, I found myself unable to resist taking in the wonders that surrounded me. My eyes wandered in awe as I spotted what appeared to be dwellings intricately constructed within the trunks of towering trees.

Unable to contain my curiosity, I asked, "Um, are those homes built inside the tree trunks?"

Arabella responded with a hint of pride in her voice, "Why, yes, they are."

As I kept looking around, I couldn't help but be entranced by the glowing mushrooms, impressive buildings, and colorful plants lining our path. The kingdom's beauty and enchantment sparked many questions in my mind, making me even more curious and eager to uncover the hidden mysteries within this magical world.

"Arabella, I have so many more questions."

Arabella, ever patient, reassured me with a serene tone, "In due time, Valaric. There will be moments to address your questions."

Upon their arrival at the castle, the guards escorted us inside, leading them to where the King sat upon his majestic throne.

Arabella, with a touch of shyness, greeted her father, saying, "Hello, Father. How has your day been?"

The King's expression, serene, clouded with concern as he responded, "My day was going well until this minor incident, daughter." There was a hint of disappointment in his voice as he continued, "What is the meaning of this? Why do you dare to defy me and bring an outsider into our kingdom, jeopardizing the safety of everyone within?"

With determination in her voice, Arabella stepped forward and explained, "Father, this outsider saved my life from two menacing Forest Trolls."

The King, now intrigued but still stern, inquired, "How did you find yourself in such a perilous encounter with Forest Trolls, and where was Shadowfang, your loyal protector?"

Arabella took a deep breath and recounted the tale to her father, hoping to convey the urgency of the situation and the noble character of Valaric.

She recounted the incident in full, vividly describing the courage and unselfishness I had shown. Her words carried a deep sincerity as she narrated the events step by step, wishing that her father would grasp the real significance of my deeds. Arabella longed for her father to understand and accept my presence in the kingdom with no restrictions or guards.

"How many times have I told you not to venture out alone?" the King questioned with a sense of authority and worry at the same time.

Arabella, feeling a mixture of remorse and determination, began, "I know, Father, but."

Before she could finish her explanation, the King interrupted, his tone firm. "No 'buts'," he asserted, making his point clear. "You are the royal heiress to the throne, and we cannot afford any harm to come your way," the King declared, his concern for her well-being clear in his words.

"Yes, Father," Arabella replied, acknowledging her father's concerns, and accepting the weight of her responsibility as the future ruler.

"As for you, Valaric," the King addressed me, his voice laced with a mix of gratitude and respect, "it appears we owe you a considerable debt of gratitude for risking yourself to save my daughter, the princess."

The King's words had a deep impact on me, expressing a heartfelt thankfulness for the brave deed I had done. His sincere appreciation moved me, making me realize even more the importance of what I had done and how it had affected the kingdom.

In a commanding tone, he ordered the guards, "Remove the shackles from him." The clinking sound of metal unlocking filled the air as it freed me from restraints.

"Now," the King continued, his gaze fixed upon me, "what brings you to the Kingdom of Vindoria? What is your purpose here?"

Still filled with a sense of wonderment, I replied to the King with honesty, "Your Highness, I must admit that I am uncertain of my exact whereabouts. I found myself in a place unknown to me." Taking a breath, I recounted my extraordinary journey, sharing my story with the King, hoping to shed light on my presence in the kingdom.

"These are indeed unique circumstances," the King acknowledged, his tone filled with a mixture of curiosity and caution. "Throughout the history of our kingdom, we have rarely encountered an outsider within our walls," he exclaimed, emphasizing the novelty of my presence.

After careful consideration, the King decided. "You may stay in our kingdom," he declared. "However, for your own safety and to prevent you from doing anything illegal, a guard will be assigned to watch over you," the King stated, emphasizing the need for caution.

"Tomorrow, we shall arrange for you to meet with our esteemed cartographers," the King informed me, his voice filled with reassurance. "Their expertise will provide you with a better understanding of your current location and circumstances," he continued, emphasizing the importance of gaining clarity.

"If we can provide you with knowledge of where you have been, it may prove invaluable in guiding you towards where you go," the King remarked, highlighting the potential value of the forthcoming meeting with the cartographer.

"Take this and wear it around your neck," the King instructed, extending a metal medallion attached to a chain.

I accepted the medallion, my fingers tracing its surface, and my eyes widened in awe as I beheld the designed insignia.

In the heart of the medallion, a majestic crown commanded attention, its splendor enhanced by radiant gemstones that shimmered with regal allure. Encircling the crown, an exquisite border showcased the harmonious fusion of ornate vines and leaves intertwined to form a tapestry of natural beauty.

Beyond the border, symbols of strength and power made their presence known. A noble lion, fierce and dignified, stood as the embodiment of courage and protection, while an elegant eagle soared beside it, representing vision and wisdom.

Adorning the bottom of the medallion, a banner unfurled, bearing the king's motto in elegant script. The Latin words "Fortitudo et Sapientia" adorned the banner, serving as a reminder of the King's commitment to both strength and wisdom in his rule.

"In the event of any troubles, present this medallion, and all within the kingdom will recognize it as a symbol of my authority," the King instructed, his voice carrying an air of reassurance.

I nodded, acknowledging the importance of the task at hand, and fastened the medallion around his neck.

"Guards, please accompany Valaric and his loyal companion to their assigned quarters," the King commanded, his voice resonating with authority.

Turning his attention to Arabella, he assured her, "We will have ample time to continue our conversation later."

Arabella, understanding the need for privacy and the pressing matters at hand, replied, "Indeed father, we shall discuss further when the time is right."

Valaric and Whisperwind were escorted to their assigned quarters, where a vigilant guard took position just outside the door. I settled onto the bed, and Whisperwind joined me.

Looking at Whisperwind, I couldn't help but express my bewilderment, asking, "Do you have any idea what exactly happened?"

Whisperwind let out a series of gentle hums, conveying a sense of surprise and amazement.

"A Princess," I repeated, my voice filled with disbelief. "We were simply wandering through the forest, not knowing where our path would lead, and now we find ourselves within the walls of a grand castle. By the way, Whisperwind, do you remember where we were originally headed?"

In response, Whisperwind gazed at me with a knowing look, acknowledging my words without providing a direct answer.

"Good talk buddy," I exclaimed.

"After all that has transpired, I believe I direly need a drink."

Determined to unwind and escape the weight of recent events, I stepped out of my quarters and approached the guard stationed nearby.

"Excuse me, could you please direct me to the local alehouse?"

The guard, sensing my need for a moment of relaxation, offered me clear directions. Grateful for his help, I set off towards the alehouse, the guard by my side, expecting the refreshing respite that awaited me.

72

## *Chapter 12 The Ale*

As the guard and I arrived at the alehouse, we could hear a lively atmosphere. Patrons were laughing, talking, clanking mugs against tables, and sounded like they were having a good time. Once I opened the door, the place became silent as the patrons quietened down, their curious gazes fixated on my unfamiliar presence. I thought about closing the door and heading the other way.

"Don't worry, they're intrigued. Outsiders are a rarity in our kingdom," the guard assured me. "While these people may not have encountered an outsider within our borders before, they're accustomed to seeing them elsewhere. Rest assured; they mean you no harm."

As I processed the guard's words, a realization struck me. I knew my mere presence in this unfamiliar place had sparked the curiosity of the surrounding locals.

"Do you think it's safe for us to sit down and enjoy a drink?"

The guard nodded, a warm smile on his face. "This kingdom is known for its peace and hospitality. If we remain together, there should be no cause for concern. Let's find a table and savor a drink in the company of newfound friends."

As we settled into our seats, the guard signaled the barkeep for a round of ales to be brought to our table. I took a moment to take in the alehouse's ambiance. Its rustic charm was clear, with solid wooden beams intersecting above, and walls adorned with aged tapestries and weathered paintings portraying scenes from a bygone era. The soft, golden light enveloped the space, casting a warm and inviting glow upon the worn yet comfortable furniture, enticing patrons to find respite and camaraderie amidst the revelry.

Long, polished wooden tables were scattered throughout the ale house, inviting camaraderie, and fostering a sense of communal gathering. The worn, comfortable benches and chairs whispered stories of countless patrons who had found solace, celebration, and camaraderie within these very walls.

Behind the bar, shelves lined with an impressive assortment of wooden casks and gleaming bottles showcased a vast selection of ales, ranging from pale and golden to rich and dark, each promising a unique blend of flavors and a momentary escape from the outside world. Skilled bartenders moved with practiced grace, pulling taps, and pouring frothy libations into sturdy tankards.

The atmosphere was alive with merriment as locals and visitors alike engaged in lively conversations, their laughter intermingling with the occasional strum of a lute or the haunting melody of a fiddle. The clinking of tankards and the hearty toasts of friends filled the air, creating a harmonious symphony of conviviality.

With a satisfying clink, the barkeep placed two tankards on the table, signifying a moment of camaraderie. The guard and I mirrored each other's actions, lifting our tankards in unison. Our eyes met, a silent exchange of understanding passing between us, before we proclaimed "cheers" and brought the vessels to our lips, savoring the refreshing taste of the ale.

As I took that expected first sip, the ale caressed my palate, its smoothness akin to velvet gliding. It was a sensation that embraced my senses, enveloping my mouth in a comforting embrace. The liquid's gentle warmth, like a fond farewell from a dear friend, lingered, inviting me to savor the experience.

The taste was a symphony of flavors, crafted by skilled brewers who understood the art of ale-making. Notes of toasted malt danced across my taste buds, offering a gentle sweetness that balanced with a subtle hint of caramel. The richness of the malt was complemented by a delicate touch of earthy hops, imparting a mild bitterness that added depth and complexity to the brew.

"This ale is exceptional. Some of the best I ever had in all my travels," I stated as I took another sip.

"This ale house lives up to its reputation as the best in the entire kingdom," added the appreciative guard.

"By the way, what is your name?"

"I am Sir Gregory," came the guard's reply, accompanied by a nod.

"Well, it's a pleasure to meet you, Sir Gregory."

"Likewise," acknowledged Sir Gregory, with a nod and a friendly smile.

As we enjoyed our ale, the barkeep came back to the table. "Will you be having anything to eat?"

"What's the special tonight?" asked Sir Gregory.

"Goulash and bread," replied the barkeep.

"Yes, bring us two bowls, please," said Sir Gregory.

"And another round of ales," I added.

As we awaited our goulash and ales, my gaze fell upon the medallion hanging around my neck, bearing the words "Fortitudo et Sapientia."

"What does Fortitudo et Sapientia mean?" I asked.

"Strength and Wisdom," responded Sir Gregory with confidence.

I took a few moments to reflect on the experiences I had had here.

"Well, it seems fitting, based on what I have seen."

"Tell me a little about yourself, Sir Gregory. What is your story?"

Sir Gregory straightened his posture, a sense of pride emanating from him as he replied, "I am a member of the immediate guard for the kingdom, entrusted with the responsibility of being the first line of defense should any threats arise."

"How does one become a member of the immediate guard for the kingdom?"

"Through years of service and fortitude," Sir Gregory stated, with a half chuckle. "Sometimes I believe it is a right place and right time situation sometimes."

As we were talking, the barkeep dropped off the goulash and ale for us to enjoy. We dug in, but kept our conversation going.

"Are you from this area, or do you come from another location?"

A nostalgic gleam appeared in Sir Gregory's eyes as he answered, "Indeed, I hail from a long line of Vindorians."

"Vindorians? What are Vindorians," I asked.

"Vindorians are the revered guardians of the forest," Sir Gregory explained, his voice filled with a sense of reverence. "Our role is to safeguard the woods from external threats and preserve its beauty, which grants us an intimate understanding of its secrets and mysteries."

"That's remarkable," I exclaimed. "I suppose you can traverse the moving pathways in the forest, like the Princess?"

"Yes. Being able to understand the secrets takes time to accomplish through meditation though," Sir Gregory stated.

"Interesting. Do you possess any other unique skills?"

A proud smile crossed Sir Gregory's face as he continued, "Indeed, we possess other talents as well. Many of us have a knack for crafting intricate carvings and decorative pieces using fallen branches and reclaimed wood. It allows us to honor the forest's gifts in a creative and meaningful way."

"That's impressive. Does the kingdom have a wise council?"

Sir Gregory's gaze turned thoughtful as he spoke. "The elders, they are the keepers of wisdom. They hold the profound knowledge of ancient tales, legends, and the rich history of our kingdom, passed down through countless generations. They are the pillars of wisdom and guidance, ensuring our heritage and traditions endure."

Leaning back in my seat, I couldn't help but be captivated by the sense of unity and togetherness within the Vindorian community. With a subtle gesture, I signaled the barkeep for another round of ale, eager to prolong this delightful experience. The atmosphere of the alehouse was brimming with camaraderie, as conversations flowed, and tales were shared with enthusiasm. It was a space where strangers became friends, where stories intertwined and memories were forged.

"In my homeland, we have a diverse mix of people from all walks of life, each possessing their unique skills and talents," I mentioned.

"Where abouts are you from," Sir Gregory asked.

"I am from Aurelia. There is no kingdom, but there is a bustling port people travel in and out of all the time. So, we have ship builders, local shops, adventurers like myself, and many other trades."

"Interesting. So, it sounds as if you do not worry about outsiders too much," said Sir Gregory.

Before I could answer, the barkeep dropped off another round of ales for us to enjoy.

"Not so much," I replied. "Tell me, Sir Gregory, do you have a designated place to practice your skills?"

A playful smile danced upon Sir Gregory's lips as he replied, "Indeed, we have a training ground designed for honing our prowess. If you're up for a challenge, we can visit it tomorrow and engage in some practice together."

"Oh, I assure you, Sir Gregory, I am more experienced than you might think. I'm eager to put my skills to the test."

"I suppose we will have to put your skills to the test tomorrow."

"Sounds like a plan. Well, I suppose it's time to call it a night."

Sir Gregory commented, "Leaving so soon? Are you admitting defeat already, my friend? You're quite a lightweight!"

"No, not at all. I just need to refocus on my original plan of exploring and understanding this kingdom. But hey, if you're up for more drinks, we can continue another time."

Sir Gregory grinned, unable to resist a friendly jab. "Ah, I see. So, the rumors about your tolerance were true then, lightweight!" The playful banter between them sparked a friendly rivalry.

However, both Sir Gregory and I realized that prolonging our evening of indulgence in the ale house would not be the wisest choice. With a sense of reluctance, we bid farewell to the lively atmosphere and jovial company, preparing ourselves for the journey back to the castle. As we embarked on the familiar path, we couldn't help but notice a subtle shift in the surroundings. The once brisk stroll now seemed longer and more arduous, as if time itself had slowed down to test our resolve.

## *Chapter 13 The Tour*

The next morning, I was awakened from my slumber as Arabella barged into my room with an infectious energy. She wielded a shield and sword, her excitement radiating through the air. "Good morning!" she exclaimed, gleefully striking the shield against the wall. Startled by the unexpected noise, I rubbed my eyes, trying to shake off the remnants of sleep.

"What in the world is going on?" I asked.

"I thought I would come and get you going this morning, so I can explain more about our kingdom, as promised," Arabella explained, as she hopped onto my bed with an enthusiastic grin.

"You're not like the princesses from fairy tales, are you," I asked with a chuckle.

Arabella rolled her eyes. "No, I'm afraid not. But trust me, there's a lot more to our story than meets the eye. Now, come on! I have other things to attend to today, but I said I would explain everything to you, and I intend to keep my word."

I let out a sigh, realizing there was no escaping her determination.

"Alright, alright, I'm moving," I huffed, as I threw off the covers to prepare for the day ahead.

As I trailed behind Arabella, anticipation coursed through my veins, filling me with a sense of curiosity and excitement. The prospect of venturing into the Kingdom of Vindoria ignited a fire within me, stirring my imagination with visions of untold mysteries and thrilling adventures that lay ahead.

As we embarked on our journey through the kingdom, an

additional guard joined our side, replacing Sir Gregory, who was most likely catching up on much-needed rest. The presence of the additional guard brought a sense of security and reassurance as we traversed the winding paths and explored the captivating corners of the kingdom.

As we walked, Arabella turned to me and asked, "So, how much did Sir Gregory fill you in last night?"

"Not too much, just that everyone here is called a Vindorian and they protect the forest or something like that," I replied.

"Yes, that's true, but there's so much more to our kingdom than just that. Today, I want to take you to Elemental Springs. It's a place of great beauty and power."

"Elemental Springs? What are they?" I asked, with a look of confusion.

"They are natural springs in our kingdom that are infused with the essence of the elements," Arabella explained. "Each spring represents a unique element: earth, water, fire, and air. They hold significant spiritual and magical energy."

"Sounds fascinating. Just lead the way, and I'll follow behind you."

With Arabella as my guide, I followed her through the enchanting paths of the kingdom, eager to discover the wonders that awaited us at the elemental springs. Little did I know this journey would unveil even more extraordinary aspects of the Kingdom of Vindoria.

As Arabella and I walked through the kingdom, the vibrant colors of nature enveloped us. Lush greenery, delicate wildflowers, and the sweet scent of blooming blossoms filled the air. The sounds of birds chirping and leaves rustling created a symphony of tranquility. Each step revealed a new breathtaking vista, with sunbeams filtering through the canopy above, casting a warm and ethereal glow on our surroundings.

Arabella glanced back at me with a warm smile and asked, "Isn't this place beautiful? The elemental springs hold a special place in the hearts of our people. They are not only sources of natural beauty, but also places of great significance."

I nodded, captivated by the serene surroundings.

"I can see why. It feels like a realm untouched by time. What else can you tell me about these elemental springs?"

"Legend has it that the elemental springs are sacred gifts given upon us by the ancient spirits of the land. Each spring represents one of the four elements that shape our world," she said with enthusiasm.

"Here we are," Arabella exclaimed, as we approached the first spring. "This is the Earth Spring. It symbolizes stability, grounding, and the life force that flows through the land. Many come here to seek solace, meditate, and reconnect with the earth's energy."

As I approached the spring, a gentle, earthy energy enveloped me, drawing me closer. The crystal-clear water bubbled forth from the ground, shimmering in the sunlight, as if it held a secret of its own. Kneeling by the spring, I cupped my hands, letting the cool water flow through my fingers, eager to taste its purity.

"It's remarkable," I followed up with.

Arabella guided me from one spring to another, each unveiling a distinct essence and purpose. As we arrived at the Water Spring, a serene pool greeted our eyes, mirroring the vast expanse of the sky above. Arabella's voice resonated with reverence as she shared the secrets held within this sacred place.

She spoke of the Water Spring's purifying nature, its ability to cleanse not only the body but also the spirit. The tranquil waters were said to possess healing properties, soothing ailments, and rejuvenating weary souls. I could almost sense the gentle touch of the water, its coolness soothing and invigorating all at once.

Next was the Fire Spring, where a small flame danced atop the water's surface. Arabella cautioned me to approach with care.

"Fire represents passion, transformation, and the spark of creativity within us. It can be a powerful ally when channeled."

"I can understand that perspective."

We arrived at the Air Spring, where a gentle breeze rustled the nearby trees. Arabella inhaled, savoring the fresh air.

"Air signifies intellect, communication, and the power of the mind. It encourages clarity, inspiration, and the ability to adapt," she stated as she exhaled.

As we left the springs behind and continued our walk, I asked, "Are there more hidden wonders in this kingdom, Arabella? It seems like there is so much to explore and learn."

"Indeed, Valaric. Our kingdom holds many secrets, ancient ruins, mystical forests, sacred grove, and creatures of myth. We scratched the surface. But for now, let's savor the magic of the elemental springs and cherish the bond we're forming on this adventure."

As we continued our exploration of the kingdom, the path led us to a secluded part of the forest where the remnants of ancient ruins stood. The air felt charged with history and mystery, beckoning us closer.

Arabella paused and gazed at the weathered stone structures, adorned with intricate carvings. "Valaric, these are the ancient ruins of our ancestors," she said, her voice filled with reverence. "They are remnants of a civilization that thrived long before our time."

"What secrets do these ruins hold? What stories lie within these ancient walls?" I questioned.

"These ruins hold the echoes of a forgotten era. They were once a thriving city, a center of knowledge and art. The people who lived here were known for their wisdom and connection to the mystical forces of the land."

I stepped closer to a beautifully carved pillar, tracing the intricate patterns with my fingers.

"It's incredible to think about the lives that were here, the knowledge that was accumulated. What caused the downfall of this civilization?"

"Legends speak of a great calamity that befell our ancestors. A catastrophic event, perhaps a natural disaster or a conflict with external forces, led to the decline and eventual abandonment of this once-thriving city."

"And what remains of their knowledge and wisdom? Are there any records or artifacts that have been preserved?"

Arabella nodded. "Some of their wisdom has been passed down through oral traditions, carefully guarded by our elders. However, many of their writings and artifacts have been lost to time. There are whispers of hidden chambers and forgotten libraries within these ruins, waiting to be discovered by those who possess a keen eye and a thirst for knowledge."

"I would love to explore these ruins further, to uncover the secrets that lie within. Is it possible to gain access to these hidden chambers?"

"It is said that those who prove themselves worthy, with a genuine passion for preserving history and a deep respect for the ancient ways, may be granted permission to enter the hidden chambers. I believe you have the spirit of an adventurer, Valaric. Perhaps one day, you will unravel the mysteries of these ruins."

As we left the ancient ruins behind, we ventured deeper into the heart of the kingdom, making our way towards the mystical forests that lay ahead. The air grew thick with enchantment, and the sounds of nature seemed to harmonize with our footsteps.

"Valaric, prepare yourself to witness the true magic of Vindoria. These mystical forests hold secrets and wonders beyond imagination."

"What makes these forests so special? What kind of magic lives within?"

"These forests are not like any other. They are alive with ancient energy, infused with the essence of nature itself. It is said that the trees whisper ancient wisdom, and the creatures that dwell here possess powers beyond comprehension."

"Powers? Are there beings with magical abilities in these forests?" I questioned, with my eyes wide open.

Arabella nodded; her gaze fixed on the path ahead.

"Indeed. Within these woods, you may encounter mystical creatures, beings attuned to the natural forces of the kingdom. Some can manipulate elements, while others can heal, communicate with animals, or even shape-shift."

"That sounds incredible! I've heard stories of such creatures, but I never thought I'd have the chance to witness their existence firsthand."

Arabella's voice carried a note of caution. "Remember, Valaric, these creatures are guardians of the forest. They are wary of outsiders and protect their realm. It is crucial to approach them with respect and reverence, for they hold a delicate balance within this enchanted land."

"I understand. I will tread lightly and honor the ancient magic that thrives here."

As we ventured deeper into the forests, the atmosphere shifted. Sunlight filtered through the dense foliage, casting ethereal patterns on the forest floor. The air hummed with an unseen energy, and whispers seemed to dance in the breeze.

Arabella gestured to the towering trees that surrounded them.

"These majestic beings hold ancient wisdom and serve as the guardians of this sacred realm. Each tree has a story to tell, a tale of resilience, growth, and interconnectedness."

"To think that these trees have witnessed countless generations, their roots intertwining with the very fabric of this kingdom. It's quite humbling."

Arabella smiled, her voice soft. "Indeed, Valaric. These forests hold a delicate balance of power and tranquility, a testament to the harmony between nature and the mystical forces that live within. Let us continue our journey and may the wonders of these woods fill your heart with awe and reverence."

"Valaric, we are approaching the sacred grove, the source of the Vindorian wizards' power. It is here that they connect with the mystical forces that flow through Vindoria."

"So, this is where the wizards draw their magical abilities from? How do they tap into this power?"

"Within this grove, the very essence of nature converges with ancient energies. The trees here serve as conduits, channeling the raw magic that permeates the land. The wizards commune with the spirits of the forest, forging a deep connection and awakening their latent powers."

"That's incredible! To have such a direct connection with the natural magic of the kingdom. It must be a profound experience."

Arabella's smile grew, her voice tinged with excitement. "Indeed, it is a sacred and transformative journey. The wizards undergo rigorous training, learning to attune their spirits to the harmonies of nature and harness the elements that flow through the grove. They become vessels of power, entrusted with the responsibility to wield magic for the greater good."

"They are the guardians of the mystical energies, the protectors of the delicate balance between the natural world and the realm of magic. I can only imagine the wisdom they have gained."

Arabella nodded; her gaze fixed on the vibrant foliage ahead. "Their journey is not just about gaining power, but also about understanding the interconnectedness of all living things. They learn to respect the delicate harmony that exists between magic and nature, using their abilities to heal, protect, and nurture the kingdom."

"Thank you, Princess, for sharing these insights with me. "It truly deepens my understanding of the Kingdom of Vindoria and its magical heritage."

"You're welcome, Valaric. I'm glad I could offer you some glimpses into our rich traditions. Now, as for your training with Sir Gregory, I won't keep you any longer. I have a few other things to attend to within the kingdom."

"Already. I was rather enjoying myself learning about the kingdom and spending time with you. It was like walking through a fairy tale."

"Yes, I must get back to some other things in the kingdom. We will have more time later. Maybe we can go out on an adventure."

I nodded appreciatively. "That would be a grand idea. I suppose I will make my way over to the practice grounds to meet up with Sir Gregory then. Until our paths cross again, Princess."

With our parting words, Arabella and I embarked on our separate paths. I followed the guard, allowing him to lead me through the enchanting and winding paths of Vindoria. Our destination was the practice grounds, where I expected the opportunity to test my skills against Sir Gregory, honing my abilities in the art of combat.

## *Chapter 14 The Practice Grounds*

After a lengthy trek, the guard and I reached our destination - the practice grounds. Sir Gregory, already in attendance, wore a mischievous smile as he greeted us. His playful remark echoed through the air, setting a lighthearted tone for the upcoming encounter.

"Ah, there you are! I was starting to think you were nursing your wounds from last night in your room."

"No, not quite. The Princess was kind enough to give me a tour of the kingdom. It's a fascinating place with a rich and unique history," I replied with a faint chuckle.

"Well, that's fine, but enough stalling. Get yourself in here and let's have some fun, Mr. Big Talker," he teased, beckoning me to join him on the training grounds.

"Alright, Sir Gregory, I'm ready for the challenge. Let's see what I'm made of," I declared, stepping forward with determination.

With unwavering resolve, I stepped into the sparring ring, gripping a wooden sword and shield. My eyes reflected a fierce determination as I prepared myself for the forthcoming challenge.

Sir Gregory, equally equipped, smirked and taunted, "Let's see what you're made of."

We circled each other in the sparring ring, a tense anticipation filling the air. I tightened my grip on the hilt of my sword, my focus on Sir Gregory. With determination, I swung my blade towards him, intending to land a decisive blow. However, Sir Gregory's expertise shone through as he deflected my attack, countering with a swift strike to my side. The impact took me by surprise, a jolt of pain reverberating through my body.

"You'll need to be quicker than that," Sir Gregory jeered.

With unwavering resolve, I thrust my sword forward, aiming to catch Sir Gregory off guard. However, his mastery of defense proved formidable once again, as he deflected my attack with precise movements. Using his shield, he applied just the right amount of force to knock me off balance, testing my stability and resilience.

As Sir Gregory moved in for another attack, I expected the strike, sidestepped, and retaliated with a series of rapid sword swings. My strikes were calculated and precise, forcing Sir Gregory to deflect and dodge with agility.

The spar intensified as both of us engaged in a fierce exchange of blows. My skills began to shine as I displayed improved speed and agility, matching Sir Gregory's prowess with each strike.

The clashing of wooden swords echoed through the practice grounds as we tested each other's limits. My determination and growing proficiency pushed Sir Gregory to his own limits, forcing him to employ advanced defensive maneuvers to keep up.

The spar continued, our swords colliding with intensity and skill. My technique evolved with each passing moment, showcasing my innate talent for combat. The onlookers watched in awe as the clash between the aspiring knight and seasoned guard unfolded before them.

"Not too bad there, Valaric," said Sir Gregory, a hint of approval in his voice. The exchange of blows with wooden swords had left both men winded, but eager for more. "Where did you learn to wield a sword?" he asked.

"I was fortunate to receive training in the art of swordsmanship from a very young age," I replied. "Growing up, I was immersed in a world where warriors and combat were revered. It became ingrained in me, and I developed a natural affinity for handling a blade."

"It seems your skills have shaped your path, leading you to seek new adventures," he mused. "I can see that you take great pride in honing your abilities."

"Indeed, Sir Gregory. The mastery of combat has always been a driving force for me. It not only grants me the means to protect myself and others, but also opens doors to new horizons and thrilling experiences."

"You speak with conviction, and your prowess in swordsmanship is clear," he remarked. "But I wonder, how do your skills fare with other weapons? Are you as versatile as you are skilled with a sword?"

"I'm always eager to explore new realms of combat. If you're up for it, Sir Gregory, let's put the swords aside and engage in a friendly bout with spears. I am not as skilled in spears as I am in swords, but isn't that what we are doing here? To help develop our skills."

"Spears, you say. An excellent choice," he responded, his voice filled with eagerness. "Very well, Valaric. Let's see how your adaptability translates to another weapon. Prepare yourself."

With a mutual understanding, the wooden swords were set aside, and we retrieved long spears from the nearby arsenal. The transition felt natural to me as I grasped the sturdy shaft of the spear, feeling the balance and weight of the weapon.

In the practice ring, we circled each other, spears held at the ready, our focus locked in determined anticipation. With the change of weapon, my mind adapted, recalibrating my techniques and strategies for the spear.

As the spar begun, the clash of wooden spears echoed through the air. I explored the limits of my agility and adaptability, launching calculated thrusts and parrying Sir Gregory's counters. The extended reach of the spear added an additional dimension of strategy to our dance of combat.

Intensity mounted as our movements grew more fluid and instinctive. My proficiency with the sword transitioned to the spear, showcasing my versatility and quick thinking. I employed feints, agile footwork, and well-timed strikes to keep Sir Gregory on his toes.

Equally skilled with the spear, Sir Gregory countered with his own repertoire of techniques, matching my agility and skill blow for blow. The training ground transformed into a flurry of spinning spears and calculated lunges, fueled by our mutual respect and determination.

The spar persisted, with each of us pushing the other to our limits, exploring the intricacies of spear combat. Moments of near misses and blocked strikes exemplified our mastery of the weapon. As the bout drew to a close, Sir Gregory and I stood, chests heaving, sweat trickling down our brows. The spar had tested our mettle and deepened our bond.

"Well fought, Valaric," Sir Gregory acknowledged. "Your adaptability and quick thinking with the spear are commendable. It's clear that your dedication to the art of combat extends beyond the confines of a single weapon."

"Thank you, Sir Gregory. It was a thrilling experience, and your expertise pushed me to new heights. I'm humbled to have sparred with such a skilled warrior."

As the sun began its descent, casting a warm golden hue over the kingdom, we made our way back to the familiar paths of the castle. The exhaustion from the day's exertions weighed on our weary bodies, but our spirits remained uplifted.

"We will have to do this again," Sir Gregory remarked. The day's training had invigorated him, fueling his desire for more exhilarating sparring sessions.

I nodded in agreement.

"Absolutely, Sir Gregory. Our dedication to honing our skills demands that we continue pushing ourselves. We mustn't let complacency dull our blades or our spirits."

We strolled side by side along the road, our footsteps creating a harmonious rhythm. The trials we had faced together throughout the day had forged a deep camaraderie, strengthening our bond as fellow warriors. Our shared pursuit of mastery and the unspoken understanding between us fostered a sense of unity.

As the castle came into view, its majestic silhouette standing tall as a testament to the enduring spirit of the kingdom, a surge of anticipation coursed through me. I couldn't help but feel an exhilarating sense of readiness for the future that lay ahead. The road stretched before us, brimming with countless challenges and adventures, beckoning us onward.

"Rest well, Sir Gregory. Today was but the beginning of a remarkable journey we shall undertake together."

Sir Gregory clasped my shoulder, a firm grip that conveyed unspoken trust and camaraderie. "And rest well yourself, Valaric," he replied. "The path we walk is not an easy one, but together, we shall rise to every challenge that comes our way."

I found the idea of embarking on adventures with Sir Gregory quite appealing, as it allowed me to gauge his abilities and strengths. Understanding the capabilities of those around you is crucial, as it determines whether you need to protect them or if they can hold their own. From what I witnessed, Sir Gregory was skilled and self-reliant. It gave me confidence, knowing that I could rely on him as a companion during our future escapades.

With a last nod of mutual understanding, we bid each other goodnight, our weary bodies craving the embrace of rest. As we retreated to our separate chambers, our minds buzzed with the vivid memories of the day, already weaving visions of the future encounters that lay ahead. The excitement of what awaited us filled the air, fueling our dreams and igniting the anticipation for the journeys yet to come.

## *Chapter 15 The Earthbound Gorgons*

The first rays of sunlight pierced through the canopy of trees, casting dappled shadows on the forest floor. Sir Gregory headed to Valaric's quarters. A new day had dawned, bringing with it a call to duty and an urgent mission.

"Valaric, grab your gear," Sir Gregory announced. "We are going to investigate an issue at one of the elemental springs in the heart of the forest."

"Do we have any information about the issue?"

"Not exactly. The esteemed elders have summoned us to assess the situation, determine the cause, and take action. Our task is to gather as much information as we can and report back to them with our findings."

As I walked alongside Sir Gregory, our strides filled with purpose and determination, a familiar figure appeared before us in the bustling streets. It was Shadowfang, a majestic wolf whose presence signified the imminent arrival of Arabella, the Princess of Vindoria.

"You didn't think I would let you two have all the fun, now did you?" Arabella's voice carried a mischievous tone as she joined them.

"Princess, you know very well that your father would have my head if I allowed you to come along on this perilous journey," Sir Gregory protested.

A confident smile played on Arabella's lips as she dismissed Sir Gregory's apprehension.

"Well, it's a good thing you're not letting me come. I am choosing to join you," she stated.

As I observed the exchange between Sir Gregory and Arabella, I found myself rendered silent, understanding that my opinion held little weight in this matter. I stood back, a mere observer, as they engaged in a discussion that encompassed the clash between duty and the yearning for adventure.

As our group ventured deeper into the forest, my gaze turned back towards the distant kingdom. Confusion furrowed my brow, and I couldn't resist the urge to turn to Arabella, seeking clarification and an explanation for the course we were embarking upon.

"How come I can now see the kingdom, but I couldn't before when we arrived?" I inquired.

"That's because of the medallion you wear," she explained. "It serves as a symbol of your connection to the kingdom and grants you access. It lets others know the king authorizes you himself."

"Thank you for enlightening me. I was wondering what would happen if I were to leave the kingdom. Would I be able to find my way back?"

Arabella's voice held a reassuring tone as she responded, "As you grow closer to the heart of the forest, it will guide you back to the kingdom, even without the medallion. The connection between the forest and the kingdom runs deep, intertwining their energies."

As we pressed forward along the path, Whisperwind assumed the role of our guide, forging ahead with unwavering confidence. Sir Gregory took up position behind him, his watchful gaze scanning our surroundings. Arabella walked alongside me, her presence offering a sense of reassurance and camaraderie. And bringing up the rear, Shadowfang maintained a vigilant watch, ensuring our safety from any potential threats lurking behind us.

"That's quite the little companion you have there, Valaric. He seems to have an uncanny sense of our destination," stated Sir Gregory.

"I'm not sure if he knows our exact path or if he circles ahead of me. It's as if he's checking the path in the direction we're headed and then doubles back to ensure we haven't deviated," I followed up with.

"Can you understand his sounds or communicate with him?" Sir Gregory inquired.

"Not communicate, but I'm recognizing certain sounds and their meanings," I explained.

"Quite fascinating," Sir Gregory acknowledged.

Arabella, unable to contain her admiration, interjected with a cheerful comment, "He's cute, with his lovely pastel colors."

"Yes, his appearance adds to his charm," I said with a soft chuckle.

With some lighthearted exchange, we continued our trek through the forest, guided by Whisperwind's instinctual navigation and my growing understanding of my companion's unique mannerisms.

At that moment, Whisperwind emitted a distinct sound, capturing everyone's attention.

"That sound shows something ahead of us," I let everyone know.

Aware of the gravity of our circumstances, we huddled together, our collective focus sharpened. Each of us attuned our senses, listening for any rustle in the underbrush, scanning the surroundings for any signs of danger. The air seemed charged with anticipation as we prepared ourselves for whatever lay ahead, drawing strength from our unity and shared purpose.

Sir Gregory took charge, instructing Shadowfang, "Keep a vigilant eye on our rear side." Turning to Arabella and I, he added, "Princess and Valaric, remain right here and stay alert."

Meanwhile, Sir Gregory advanced towards the source of danger, using his stealth and expertise. The tension in the air was palpable as Arabella and I held our weapons at the ready, with our eyes fixed on Sir Gregory's gradual approach to uncover the nature of the imminent threat.

Sir Gregory returned to the Princess and I, his face etched with concern, to share the details of his discovery.

"I've observed two Earthbound Gorgons near the earth elemental Spring," he reported.

Eager to understand the threat they faced, I inquired about these mysterious creatures.

Arabella stepped forward her voice filled with knowledge. "Earthbound Gorgons are formidable beasts with hardened, stone-like skin," she explained. "Their natural defense renders them resistant to conventional attacks."

"So, we're up against gigantic creatures that can withstand most forms of assault?" I questioned. "How are we supposed to confront such a formidable challenge?"

Sir Gregory, ever the experienced warrior, interjected, "while their resistance poses a significant challenge, we must think strategically. We need to exploit their weaknesses and find alternative means to disrupt their defenses."

Arabella nodded in agreement, "indeed, we cannot rely on brute force. We must seek unconventional methods, exploiting their vulnerabilities and unsettling their stability."

"How are we supposed to do that?" I asked.

Arabella, ever resourceful, responded, "I have a plan."

We huddled together to discuss our strategy for subduing the powerful creatures.

With the plan in place, Arabella took charge.

"Alright, everyone, get into position," she commanded.

Each of us assumed our positions with calculated precision, our hearts pounding in anticipation of the imminent confrontation. We stood tall and resolute, ready to face the Earthbound Gorgons with unwavering determination. The air crackled with a palpable tension, as if the very atmosphere held its breath in anticipation of the clash that was about to unfold.

Drawing upon her deep connection with the elements, Arabella channeled the forces of nature to aid our cause. The ground beneath us erupted with a surge of power as mighty roots and vines burst forth, entangling the massive forms of the Gorgons. Their movements were disrupted, their balance thrown off by the entwined vegetation that acted as a natural barrier against their onslaught.

During the chaos, Shadowfang displayed her remarkable agility, pouncing upon one of the Gorgons with fierce determination. Her swift and calculated attacks stunned the creature, leaving it vulnerable and struggling to regain its footing. Simultaneously, Whisperwind emanated blinding rays of light, blinding the second Gorgon, and weakening its ability to defend itself.

Seizing the moment, I surged forward with my sword at the ready. With focused precision, I targeted the exposed weak points on the fallen Gorgon's stony hide, delivering precise and powerful strikes. Each blow reverberated with the force of my determination, causing the creature to waver under the onslaught.

Not to be outdone, Sir Gregory exhibited his mastery of combat, using his spear to launch himself into the air. Executing a daring aerial maneuver, he descended upon the second Gorgon with relentless force, his strike landing with a thunderous impact that sent shockwaves through the ground.

Capitalizing on the opportunity created by Sir Gregory's assault, Shadowfang launched into a frenzied onslaught, her fangs and claws tearing into the downed Gorgon. Meanwhile, Arabella provided additional support, her arrows finding their mark on the creature's formidable exterior, weakening it further.

Together, our coordinated efforts and unwavering determination turned the tide against the Earthbound Gorgons, their once overpowering presence now met with fierce resistance and relentless assault.

After an arduous and intense struggle, the air cleared, revealing a scene of collective exhaustion and accomplishment. Beads of sweat trickled down our weary faces, mingling with the grime and dirt that marked our bodies. The battle had been fierce, demanding every ounce of strength and resilience we possessed. But in the end, our unwavering determination and coordinated efforts had prevailed, and the Earthbound Gorgons lay defeated before us.

"Valaric, you did well for your first battle against Gorgons," praised Sir Gregory.

I nodded. "Thank you, but it was Arabella's well-constructed plan that made it possible."

"Now that the Gorgons are defeated, what's our next move?" I asked as I scanned the area for potential dangers.

Arabella's gaze fell upon the large rock that had been placed upon the earth element.

"First, we must restore the balance," she declared.

As we approached the colossal rock, its imposing presence loomed before us, evoking a sense of daunting challenge. Determination etched across our faces we shared a silent agreement to overcome this formidable obstacle together. Sir Gregory positioned his spear, ready to use it as a lever, while Arabella and I braced ourselves for the imminent exertion of our combined strength.

With focused intent, we applied our collective force, pushing against the unyielding weight of the rock. Inch by inch, we felt the resistance give way, as the massive obstacle budged. It was a genuine test of our physical prowess, demanding every ounce of our determination and perseverance.

With a final push and a collective sigh of relief, the rock rolled away from the earth elemental, its weight no longer obstructing its freedom. The element, awakened from its temporary stasis, stood tall and resolute, its connection to the earth restored.

Exhausted but satisfied, Sir Gregory wiped the sweat from his brow.

"That was no simple task with such a sizable rock."

Arabella nodded in agreement.

"Indeed, but we've restored the balance, and that's what matters," she stated.

Still attempting to catch our breath and start our celebrations, for dealing with the Gorgon's and clearing the Earth Element, our celebrations were cut short.

In a cruel twist of fate, the Gorgon's massive arm swung toward Sir Gregory with devastating speed. The horror unfolded before my eyes in agonizing slow motion, as I watched the blow connect with its intended target. Sir Gregory's body was sent hurtling through the air, crashing down with bone-crushing force upon the unforgiving ground.

The impact reverberated through the air, each tremor echoing the terror that surged within me. Fear surged through my veins like wildfire, igniting a blaze of adrenaline and urgency. Every fiber of my being screamed for action, for a chance to protect and save my fallen comrade.

With trembling hands and a heart pounding in my chest, I rushed forward, my instincts kicking into overdrive. The world around me blurred as I unsheathed my sword, the metallic glint reflecting the fear that danced in my eyes. Determination etched deep lines on my face, a testament to the indomitable spirit that burned within.

In that harrowing moment, I fought against the rising tide of panic, channeling my fear into resolve. The weight of the situation bore upon my shoulders, but I pushed forward, my trembling hands wielding the sword with desperate precision. Every strike was fueled by the fear of losing Sir Gregory, every movement a testament to the depth of our bond.

As the blade pierced through the Gorgon's stony exterior, I felt a fleeting surge of triumph amidst the prevailing fear. The creature staggered, dazed by the force of my blow, affording me a brief respite from the terror that consumed me. Yet, the battle was far from won, the fear lingering like a specter at the back of my mind.

But my focus could not waver, for the dire situation demanded my unwavering attention. The fallen Gorgon was but a temporary victory in the face of the impending danger that still loomed over us. Fear gnawed at the edges of my consciousness, urging me to act swiftly, to tend to Sir Gregory's fallen form and protect him from further harm.

"Sir Gregory, stay with us," I pleaded.

As fear surged through my veins, I suppressed its paralyzing grip and focused on the task at hand. Drawing upon the basic first aid knowledge I possessed, I assessed the severity of Sir Gregory's wounds. Blood stained the ground beneath him, a grim reminder of the danger that had befallen us.

With trembling hands, I applied firm pressure to the wound, trying to stanch the flow of blood. Time was of the essence, and every passing moment heightened the urgency to get Sir Gregory back to the safety of the kingdom where he could receive proper medical attention.

Arabella's voice resonated with urgency as she called upon Shadowfang for help. "Shadowfang, run like the wind and bring back the guards to help us carry him back to the kingdom," she commanded.

Shadowfang sprinted towards the castle, her agile form disappearing into the distance.

Whisperwind, sensing the gravity of the situation, emitted a new, enchanting hum, his wings fluttering with purpose. A soft glow enveloped the injured Sir Gregory, its soothing aura casting a temporary respite on the bleeding, providing some relief to the team. I watched with a mixture of hope and concern, knowing that Whisperwind's power had its limits and that they needed additional help.

Arabella's gaze was unwavering as she assessed the situation. She knew they couldn't afford to waste precious time. "Valaric, we must do what we can to stabilize him," she said, her voice steady yet filled with concern. "We need to support his injuries and make sure he remains conscious until help arrives."

## *Chapter 16 A Life in the Balance*

Each second felt like an eternity, the weight of the situation pressing upon us like a suffocating fog. The surrounding forest seemed to hold its breath, as if aware of the gravity of Sir Gregory's condition. With every labored breath he took, his life force slipped further away, and our hope hung by a fragile thread.

Whisperwind, sensing the urgency, emitted his healing auras with unwavering determination. But their effects were fleeting, only providing a temporary respite from the relentless bleeding. Drawing closer, Arabella clasped Sir Gregory's hand, her eyes filled with an unwavering resolve.

"Sir Gregory, stay with us," she implored, her voice laced with both concern and a glimmer of reassurance. "We need you here. Don't let go."

Sir Gregory's once vibrant eyes now held a distant, weakened gaze, his essence fading before our very eyes. Every labored breath was a testament to the immense struggle that consumed him, as if each inhalation required a Herculean effort. The tenuous grip he had on consciousness felt as fragile as a fraying thread, threatening to sever at any moment. My heart weighed down with worry, I stood steadfast by Sir Gregory's side, offering an unwavering presence as a pillar of support.

Whisperwind, with ethereal wings fluttering with renewed determination, emitted healing auras that enveloped the fallen knight. The creature's essence pulsed with otherworldly energy, offering a lifeline amidst the encroaching darkness. Though the healing power was potent, it could only provide temporary relief, unable to mend the profound damage that had befallen Sir Gregory.

As the seconds stretched into agonizing minutes, the surrounding forest seemed to reverberate with the weight of the situation. The towering trees stood as silent witnesses; their branches outstretched like compassionate sentinels.

Arabella, her voice trembling with emotion, leaned closer to Sir Gregory's ear, her words filled with heartfelt urgency. "You have fought bravely, Sir Gregory. Your journey is not over. Stay with us," she urged, her words a plea infused with the deepest respect and gratitude. "We need your wisdom, your guidance. Hold on."

Time stretched before us, each minute feeling like an eternity. My gaze remained locked on Sir Gregory, a mixture of fear and determination in my eyes. The weight of the moment pressed upon me, igniting a fierce resolve within my being. We couldn't afford to lose Sir Gregory, not now, not after just getting to know him.

The forest fell into an expectant hush as Arabella and I remained vigilant, our focus fixed on the approaching sound. The rhythmic footfalls grew louder, racing towards us with an urgency that stirred a mix of apprehension and anticipation. My grip tightened around the hilt of my sword, instincts urging me to be prepared for any outcome. Arabella, her bow poised with an arrow notched, mirrored my readiness, her gaze fixed on the forest's edge.

Then, emerging from the foliage, Shadowfang bounded into view, her presence a welcome sight amidst the tension. Arabella and I lowered our weapons, relief washing over us like a gentle breeze. It was Arabella's loyal companion, bearing news or aid, rather than an unknown adversary.

Shadowfang approached with a grace that belied her swiftness, her eyes reflecting a blend of concern and determination. She had come to our side, her loyalty unwavering even in the face of adversity. My sword found its sheath once more, while Arabella's bow was lowered with a relieved sigh. We knew that Shadowfang's arrival brought reassurance and the potential for a helping hand.

With renewed hope, Arabella and I watched as Shadowfang turned and retraced her steps, heading back towards the castle. Our hearts swelled with gratitude, knowing that her departure meant that help was on its way. We stood by Sir Gregory's side, his condition still precarious, but now bolstered by the imminent arrival of help.

The distant sounds of approaching footsteps grew louder, a symphony of determined strides echoing through the forest. Arabella and I strained our ears, listening as the rescue party drew closer. Our anticipation peaked as the footsteps multiplied, showing multiple individuals. Relief washed over us in waves, knowing that soon we would have the aid and resources needed to transport Sir Gregory back to the castle.

Arabella leaned closer. "Hold on, Sir Gregory," she implored, her words a plea infused with unwavering determination. "Help is on its way. We won't let you down. Don't give up now."

My gaze remained fixed on the forest's edge, my resolve firm. The echoes of approaching footsteps grew louder, filling the surrounding space with a sense of imminent rescue. The combined efforts of Shadowfang's return and the impending arrival of reinforcements brought a glimmer of hope, weaving a thread of determination that bound us together in our mission to save Sir Gregory.

Help had arrived, the guards summoned by Shadowfang's swift return. They approached with a sense of urgency and purpose; their eyes filled with concern as they assessed the critical condition of our esteemed knight.

The guards gathered around Sir Gregory, their experienced hands maneuvering with practiced precision. They secured him onto a makeshift stretcher, ensuring that he was stable and ready for the journey back to the castle. Arabella and I exchanged a glance, our unspoken communication reflecting both a shared determination and a glimmer of hope. We would accompany Sir Gregory every step of the way, our unwavering support a testament to our friendship.

As the guards lifted the stretcher, I walked ahead of them, my steps measured yet filled with an unyielding determination. Arabella remained close to Sir Gregory, her hand resting on his, her presence offering solace and reassurance. Together, we embarked on the arduous journey back to the castle, our hearts heavy with the weight of uncertainty, but fortified by the unbreakable bonds of loyalty and friendship.

Whisperwind led the way, his wings fluttering with a sense of urgency, while Shadowfang remained ever watchful at the rear, ensuring our path remained clear. The group pressed forward, our steps quick and determined, our focus unwavering. We knew that every passing moment was critical, and the castle, with its skilled healers, held the best chance for Sir Gregory's survival.

The journey back felt both eternal and fleeting, time warped by the weight of our mission. The forest paths, once filled with the excitement of adventure, now seemed to stretch endlessly as our sole purpose became returning Sir Gregory to safety. Every rustle of leaves, every crack of a branch, seemed to carry a whispered plea for his recovery.

With each passing moment, the castle loomed larger on the horizon, its silhouette a beacon of hope in the fading light. We quickened our pace, a surge of determination coursing through our veins. We knew the healers awaited our arrival, ready to do everything in their power to save Sir Gregory's life.

As we approached the castle gates, our steps filled with a mixture of anticipation and trepidation. The fate of our dear comrade hung in the balance; the outcome was still uncertain. But we held onto the glimmer of hope, knowing that within those ancient walls lay the chance to turn the tides and breathe life back into our fallen knight.

## Chapter 17 The Cartographer

Back within the sanctuary of the castle walls, the healers worked to tend to Sir Gregory's injuries, their experienced hands navigating the delicate task of restoring his strength. I stood by Arabella's side, offering support and comfort amidst the sterile surroundings.

Aware of my limited role in the healing process, I understood the need to focus my efforts elsewhere. The weight of responsibility urged me to fulfill the task assigned by Arabella's father. With a reassuring glance towards Sir Gregory's bedside, I communicated my intentions to Arabella, assuring her of my commitment to the task at hand.

"Arabella, there is little more I can do here for Sir Gregory," I whispered. "As your father suggested, I shall make my way to the cartographers and gather information. We must remain vigilant and prepared, even in these uncertain times."

"Thank you for everything Valaric," she replied with a sad look on her face.

With resolute determination, I made my way through the corridors of the castle, my steps purposeful and my mind focused. The room where the cartographers worked was my destination, the place where I hoped to find answers and unveil the secrets of the unknown land that surrounded me.

A guard assigned to accompany me, followed behind. Together, we sought the guidance and expertise of the cartographers, hoping that their extensive knowledge and detailed maps would offer insight into my current whereabouts.

As I entered the room, a flurry of activity greeted me. Maps adorned the walls, their intricate lines and markings telling tales of uncharted territories and hidden paths. The cartographers, engrossed in their work, looked up, their eyes filled with curiosity at an unknown visitor.

I approached one cartographer, a seasoned individual with ink-stained fingers and a weathered expression. With a respectful nod, I spoke, my voice laced with anticipation, "I seek your guidance, wise cartographer. I find myself in unfamiliar lands, and I yearn to understand the lay of this unknown territory. Any knowledge or maps you can provide would be appreciated."

The cartographer's face contorted into a scowl as he addressed me with an air of impatience. "And who might you be? What brings you here, disrupting our work? We have no time to entertain intruders like you," he spat with disdain. "Leave now, before you become more of a nuisance."

I stood in the room, taken aback by the cartographer's hostile response. The rudeness in the cartographer's tone was unexpected, and it halted my words. Despite the unwelcoming reception, I maintained my composure, understanding that patience and diplomacy were necessary in this situation.

"I apologize if I have disturbed you," I replied, my voice steady despite the cartographer's dismissive attitude. "I understand you are busy, but I come seeking your guidance and knowledge. I find myself in unfamiliar lands and need maps or any information you can provide to help us navigate and understand this unknown territory."

"I heard you the first time; there's no need to repeat yourself," scoffed the cartographer, his tone laced with annoyance. "Once again, who are you and why have you invaded our domain? We have no interest in entertaining court jesters like you," he huffed, dismissing me with a wave of his hand.

"My name is Valaric, hailing from the kingdom of Aurelia. I have been tasked by the king himself to gather information about our current location," I replied, my voice carrying a hint of irritation. I eyed the cartographer with a touch of frustration, hoping he would finally take my inquiry.

The cartographer's voice dripped with sarcasm as he retorted, "Ah, so the almighty king has sent you, and now you expect us to drop everything and cater to your needs, do you?" A smirk played on his lips. "Well, my dear Valaric, you can wait in that corner over there, and if, by some miracle, we find the time, we may grace you with our help." He ended his statement with a dismissive snort, uninterested in my purpose.

I bit back the sharp words that threatened to escape my lips as I confronted the dismissive cartographer. My frustration simmered beneath the surface, but I chose my words carefully. "Look," I began, my voice laced with restrained annoyance, "you keep repeating that you have no time. But I wonder, what is your time worth to you?"

With a deliberate air of defiance, I reached into my pouch and pulled out a shining gold coin. I held it aloft, catching the light and emphasizing its value. "Here," I said, my tone challenging, "one gold coin. How much time are you willing to spare now?"

The cartographer's eyes widened at the sight of the precious metal, and a flicker of interest danced across his face. He hesitated for a moment before finally gesturing for me to approach.

"Well, well now, young Valaric," he responded, his tone veiled in false affability, "there's no need to be so testy. We will be more than happy to assist a person of your fine stature." "Now, what is it you would like to know, Valaric?" asked the cartographer, a hint of newfound respect in his voice. My persistence had shifted the dynamics of our interaction, compelling the cartographer to be more accommodating.

"Can you show me a map of our current location, along with the surrounding lands?"

The cartographer, no longer dismissive but somewhat eager to please, reached into a pile of documents and retrieved a map. With practiced hands, he unfurled it onto the sketching table, smoothing out the creases and revealing a detailed depiction of the area.

Pointing to a marked spot on the map, the cartographer proclaimed, "Here we are." I viewed the map, searching the surrounding islands, but did not see Aurelia on it.

"Do you know where Aurelia is in relation to my current location?" I inquired, my voice tinged with a mix of hope and concern. I yearned for any clue that would bridge the gap between my homeland and the unfamiliar lands I found myself in.

The cartographer's response was less than encouraging. "Never heard of any place called Aurelia before," he replied, his tone dismissive and disinterested. My heart sank, my hopes for a clear connection dashed in an instant.

Confusion clouded my mind as I grappled with the disheartening realization. How could my homeland be so unknown in this vast realm? Determined to seek answers, I pressed further. "Well, at least tell me where we are," I urged, hoping to gain some footing in my quest for understanding.

The cartographer, more forthcoming with geographic information, revealed my current location. "We are in the Kingdom of Vindoria, nestled within the heart of the Eldoria Forest," he stated. My mind raced, taking in the significance of our whereabouts, but I yearned for more specifics.

Frustrated yet driven, I probed further, seeking clarity about the land we found ourselves in. "But on what land, island, or mass does the Eldoria Forest reside?" I pressed, hoping for a breakthrough in my quest for knowledge.

The cartographer's response fell short. "That's it, that is all that we know," he admitted, a hint of frustration seeping into his voice. "The Kingdom of Vindoria spans over 500 verdant spans and is at the center of the Eldoria Forest. Beyond that, our knowledge is limited."

"Can you provide me with detailed maps of the Kingdom of Vindoria and the Eldoria Forest, ones that I can take with me?" I requested, my eyes fixed on the cartographer with a mix of urgency and determination. I knew that possessing accurate maps would be essential for navigating the unfamiliar terrain and uncovering the secrets that awaited me.

The cartographer, ever quick with a retort, responded with a touch of snark. "I could, but of course, you know these things just don't draw themselves," he said, his tone laced with a hint of annoyance. I sighed, recognizing the need to appease the cartographer's ego to get what I sought.

Putting aside our banter, I reached into my pouch and retrieved a second gold coin, holding it up for the cartographer to see. "Fine, enough of your haggling," I conceded, my voice tinged with a touch of exasperation. "But for this additional coin, you will provide me with not just ordinary maps, but ones that mark locations known to hold valuable resources or secrets."

The cartographer's eyes gleamed at the sight of the shimmering gold coin. Greed and curiosity intertwined as he contemplated the offer. Finally, he nodded in agreement, unable to resist the allure of potential riches. "Very well, young Valaric," he agreed, a sly smile playing at the corner of his lips. "For the second coin, I shall provide you with maps that include markers for hidden treasures, sacred sites, and other lucrative locations known to those who seek adventure and wealth."

Reaching into the stack of crafted maps, the cartographer retrieved the requested maps with practiced ease. Carefully unfurling the parchment, he straightened out the creases, revealing the intricate details of the Kingdom of Vindoria and the expansive Eldoria Forest. With a steady hand and keen eye, he marked several key locations that might pique my interest.

As the cartographer finished his task, he presented the maps to me, and I accepted them. Expressing my gratitude, I flipped the two gleaming gold coins onto the table, their distinct clinking sound reverberating through the room. With a nod of acknowledgment, I bid farewell to the cartographer and made my way out of the chamber, maps in hand, ready to embark on my new journey armed with knowledge and direction.

## *Chapter 18 The Elders*

After bidding farewell to the cartographers, I made my way to check on Sir Gregory, my heart heavy with concern. As I approached the healing quarters, I couldn't help but feel a mix of anxiety and hope. Stepping inside, I found Arabella by Sir Gregory's side, her eyes fixed on his pale form.

"How is he doing? Any changes or updates?" I asked.

Arabella sighed, her expression reflecting the weight of the situation. "No changes," she replied. "He is still teetering on the edge, fighting to hold on."

"What have the healers said? Why is there no change?"

Arabella reached out, placing a comforting hand on my arm. "I understand your frustration, but we remember that healing from injuries of this nature takes time," she explained, her voice filled with a gentle reassurance. "The healers have done all they can, and Sir Gregory's fate now rests in the hands of time and his own resilience."

"You're right, Arabella. We must remain steadfast and allow Sir Gregory the time he needs to recover."

"As I can be of no immediate help here, I shall venture to the kingdom elders and seek their wisdom regarding the enigmatic items in my possession."

Arabella nodded in agreement, a faint smile crossing her lips. "That is not a bad idea, Valaric. It will keep you occupied and prevent you from worrying about Sir Gregory's well-being while we await any developments."

My gaze softened as I looked at Sir Gregory, my concern for him still clear. "Indeed, it is best to grant him the peace he needs for now."

Arabella placed a comforting hand on my arm, her eyes filled with gratitude. "Should there be any changes in Sir Gregory's condition, we will send a swift messenger to the Elders' Hall to summon you back."

"Thank you, Arabella. Your support means the world to me."

Filled with anticipation and a glimmer of hope, I left the healing quarters and headed for the Elders' Hall. The crystal, vial, dagger, and parchments in my bag added to my curiosity and desire for answers. These objects remained enigmatic, but their potential significance hinted at a profound discovery awaiting.

Approaching the grand Elders Hall, its imposing doors served as portals to ancient wisdom. Inside, the revered elders, guardians of knowledge, and custodians of deep secrets resided. They held the key to shedding light on the true nature of the artifacts.

Entering the chamber, I found myself in the company of these esteemed elders, emanating wisdom and experience. The room was filled with an aura of reverence and anticipation, as if it held the secrets to a hidden realm of knowledge.

Standing before them, I spoke with respect and curiosity, "Greetings, esteemed elders. I am Valaric, a traveler from Aurelia. Today, I seek your guidance and knowledge regarding certain artifacts that have come into my possession."

Placing the crystal on the table before the elders, I took a deep breath and unraveled the tale of my discoveries. "The first item is a crystal I stumbled upon along the shores, just outside the mystical Eldoria Forest." The crystal shimmered with an ethereal glow, as if reflecting the ancient secrets hidden within its translucent depths.

I held the vial containing the mesmerizing blue liquid, its contents swirling with an air of enchantment. "The second item is a vial, which holds a mysterious and potent blue elixir. Its origin and purpose remain a mystery to me, compelling me to seek your wisdom."

With a sense of reverence, I revealed the crafted dagger, its hilt adorned with symbols of power. "The third item is this remarkable blade, discovered within a hidden compartment of a trunk washed ashore. Its craftsmanship and hidden purpose have intrigued me."

I placed the ancient parchments on the table, their delicate pages hinting at centuries of wisdom waiting to be unraveled. "The fourth item is these ancient parchments, preserved within the same trunk.

They bear inscriptions and symbols that elude my understanding, yet I sense their significance."

As I watched the esteemed elders examine each artifact, my heart swelled with anticipation. Their collective wisdom and experience brought forth a profound understanding of the significance of these discoveries. I could sense the weight of their knowledge and the gravity of the moment as they engaged in hushed discussions, sharing insights and referencing their vast repository of information.

One elder, his hands adorned with age-old symbols, retrieved an ancient book from a nearby shelf. Its weathered pages held the secrets of generations past, and I couldn't help but feel a sense of awe as they flipped through its pages. They searched for any mention or connection to the mysterious items I had presented before them, and I knew that within those ancient texts lay the potential for uncovering long-buried truths.

As I stood by, observing the esteemed elders, I couldn't help but be captivated by the atmosphere in the chamber. Each page turned held the potential to unlock hidden truths, and I could sense the weight of anticipation that filled the room. The elders' experienced hands scanned the ancient text, tracing their fingers over faded illustrations and deciphering cryptic symbols.

In the chamber's silence, their collective knowledge merged with the timeless wisdom contained within the ancient book. They sought to unravel the mysteries and unveil the significance of the crystal, the vial, the dagger, and the parchments. It was as if the elders were weaving together the threads of ancient lore, connecting the artifacts to long-forgotten stories and legends.

Their shared insights and discoveries seemed to shed new light on the origins and purpose of these items. I could feel the energy in the room shift, as the elders' faces displayed a mix of curiosity, reverence, and anticipation. The weight of their accumulated knowledge hung in the air, mingling with the aura of the artifacts themselves. I knew we were on the brink of uncovering a deeper understanding of the mysteries that had brought me here.

With a calm and measured voice, one elder addressed me, curiosity gleaming in their eyes. "Could you please recount for us, once more, the exact circumstances in which you discovered these intriguing artifacts?"

Taking a deep breath, I gathered my thoughts before speaking. With a mix of fascination and caution, I recounted the events, including every pertinent detail.

"The crystal," I began, "was unearthed from the sand just outside the borders of the Eldoria Forest. Its radiant allure caught my eye as if they meant it to be found."

As I shifted my gaze towards the vial, dagger, and parchments, I continued, "The vial, the dagger, and the parchments were hidden within a secret compartment of a weathered trunk that had washed up on the beach. It was an unexpected discovery, shrouded in mystery."

The elder leaned forward, engrossed in the content, and inquired further, "And how did you come to encounter these items? What led you to this encounter?"

Taking a moment to compose myself, I recounted the events that led up to my discovery of the artifacts. With a mix of excitement and trepidation, I shared the tale with the esteemed elders, including every significant detail. Their eyes were fixed on me, their expressions attentive and filled with the weight of their knowledge and experience.

"An intriguing tale of events," stated the elder, his voice laced with curiosity. "Please, lift your pant leg on the leg that the mysterious creature grabbed you," he instructed. The elders leaned in; their gazes focused on the marks left by the creature's grasp.

As I bared the exposed area, the elders' eyes were fixed on the imprints left by the creature's touch. The complex pattern of interwoven lines and symbols etched upon my skin seemed to bewilder and fascinate them. It was as if they were gazing upon a language from another realm, one unknown to mortals like us. The marks pulsed with a mysterious energy, hinting at a deeper meaning beyond mere physical contact.

The knowing glances exchanged between the elders hinted at their understanding of such mystical phenomena. They were well-versed in ancient texts and lore that spoke of mystical creatures and their markings. The imprints on my skin appeared to be indicators of a profound connection, a bond forged between me, a mortal, and a being of extraordinary origin.

With utmost care, the elders traced their fingers over the imprints, their touch gentle yet purposeful. To my amazement, the marks responded, emitting a faint glow that mirrored the elders' astonishment. It was as if the lines were alive, shifting and rearranging themselves in response to their touch, revealing hidden patterns and arcane symbols that held deep significance.

I stood there, absorbing the unfolding revelation, my heart pounding with both excitement and trepidation. The elders were unraveling the enigma of markings, and I could feel that their knowledge and insight were guiding them toward a deeper understanding of the mysterious bond between myself and the creature that had left its mark upon me.

With each passing moment, the elders delved deeper into the meaning behind the marks adorning my leg. My encounter with the creature was no mere coincidence, but a destined event of profound significance. The marks were not just physical reminders; they held the key to hidden knowledge and potential.

In hushed whispers, the elders discussed the significance of the marks, their minds filled with ancient prophecies and forgotten wisdom. They recognized I was now connected to a realm beyond their understanding, linked to a greater purpose that would reveal itself in due time. The marks symbolized my unique destiny, a path that would intertwine with the mysterious creature and the unfolding events in the realm.

As I stood there, absorbing their words and the weight of their insights, a mix of awe and trepidation filled my heart. The elders' revelations opened a door to a new world of possibilities, unveiling a destiny that had been written in the stars. The journey that lay ahead was bound to be filled with challenges, but I knew that with the guidance of the elders and the strength of the mysterious marks upon my leg, I was ready to embrace my role in the unfolding tale of destiny and discovery.

Finally, the elder stepped forward, his voice carrying the weight of insight and revelation. "These artifacts are not ordinary trinkets. They hold the whispers of ancient tales and the echoes of forgotten realms."

"The crystal," the elder continued, "is a fragment of a long-lost relic imbued with potent energies. It is said to possess the ability to reveal hidden truths and unveil pathways obscured by illusion." As he spoke, the crystal seemed to shimmer with an inner radiance, as if acknowledging its own purpose.

"The vial contains a concoction crafted by the alchemists of old. It is rumored to possess transformative properties, capable of altering the very essence of its imbiber, be it physical or metaphysical."

"The dagger," the elder's voice took on a solemn tone, "bears the mark of an ancient order of guardians. It is a weapon steeped in history, capable of severing the ties of enchantments and protecting against forces that seek to manipulate the fabric of reality." The dagger gleamed with a resolute purpose; its edge honed for battles unseen.

"The parchments are fragments of forgotten knowledge, fragments of maps, prophecies, and incantations. They hold the potential to unlock hidden realms, unveil long-lost treasures, and decipher the secrets of the past." The parchments whispered of forgotten wisdom, waiting to be revealed once more.

"Regrettably, we cannot provide you with further information regarding the meaning of the marks on your leg," expressed the elder with a tone of solemnity. "These marks go beyond a mere injury caused by a creature's grip. They bear a profound significance, a convergence of powers that elude our current understanding."

With a respectful nod, I thanked the esteemed elders for their invaluable time and the profound insights they had shared. As I placed the artifacts back into my bag, a sense of anticipation welled up within me.

"I will return in the future, hoping to learn more from your continued research and any further revelations regarding both myself and these artifacts."

Leaving the hallowed halls of the Elders, I carried with me a newfound sense of purpose. The knowledge gave upon me by the esteemed elders would serve as a guiding light, driving me to seek answers and unravel the secrets that lay dormant within the artifacts.

With every step, my mind raced with possibilities, envisioning a future where the marks, the crystal, vial, dagger, and parchments would find their rightful place in the grand tapestry of my destiny. I knew that my return to the Elders Hall would not only mark a reunion with wise sages but also serve as a catalyst for deeper understanding and the uncovering of hidden truths. The journey ahead promised adventure and revelation, and I was eager to embrace it with an unwavering determination to fulfill my role in the unfolding tale of destiny and discovery.

## Chapter 19 The Mission

As the heavy doors of the Elders Hall closed behind me, I found myself enveloped in a momentary solitude, my mind still abuzz with the wisdom shared by the esteemed elders. However, before I could immerse myself in contemplation, a sense of urgency disrupted the tranquility. Without warning, a messenger approached me with an air of haste.

"Valaric, I have a message from the princess. You are to come to the healing chamber," the messenger relayed.

My heart skipped a beat at the mention of the healing chamber. My mind raced to Sir Gregory, fearing the worst. The urgency in the messenger's voice ignited a sense of apprehension within me, driving me to seek answers.

"Is it about Sir Gregory?"

"I don't know the details. I was sent down here to request your immediate presence," he replied.

"How long have you been standing out here?" I asked.

The messenger hesitated before responding, "Fifteen minutes."

"Why did you not come into the hall and inform me sooner? What if the matter is urgent?"

"We may not enter the Elders Hall unless we have a specific task or message for the elders," the messenger clarified.

"Thank you for delivering the message. I shall make my way to the healing quarters with utmost haste," I declared.

Without further delay, I set off towards the healing quarters, my strides purposeful. The urgency in the air fueled my determination, driving me to reach the healing chamber as swiftly as my legs could carry me.

As I raced through the corridors, my mind buzzed with worry and anticipation. The fate of Sir Gregory hung in the balance, and I couldn't bear the thought of any more delays. The path before me blurred as I focused on reaching the healing chamber, my heart pounding with a mix of apprehension and hope.

Time seemed to stretch as I weaved through the castle's labyrinthine hallways, my thoughts consumed by the possibilities awaiting me. With each step, my resolve grew stronger, my determination unyielding. The weight of responsibility rested upon my shoulders, urging me forward, fueling my pace.

I arrived at the entrance of the healing quarters, my breath heavy and my heart pounding in my chest. Steadying myself, I pushed open the door and stepped inside, ready to face whatever news awaited me. The healing chamber buzzed with activity, and my eyes sought the princess, hoping to find answers and reassurance in her presence.

"Arabella, you sent for me?" I inquired.

"Yes, we need your help," she responded.

"What is it? How can I help?"

"The healers require your aid. We need you to embark on a journey to the cliffs located just north of here," she explained.

"What will I find there?"

"There is a specific plant that grows on those cliffs, possessing remarkable healing properties. The healers believe it may hold the key to Sir Gregory's recovery," Arabella revealed.

"I will do whatever it takes to retrieve the plant and help Sir Gregory. But how will I be able to identify the plant amidst the vastness of the cliffs?"

"One of the healers will accompany you on this journey. Their expertise will guide you in identifying the specific plant," she assured him.

Recognizing the challenges that lay ahead, Arabella continued, "I must warn you; the journey will not be easy. It will take at least two days of arduous travel to reach the cliffs. The path may test your endurance and resolve."

"I am prepared for the journey. I will depart at first light."

With a sense of purpose, I reached for my map, eager to mark the approximate location of the cliffs. "Do you have any information about the exact whereabouts of this plant within the cliffs?"

Arabella's expression softened with a touch of uncertainty. "We have an approximate location, but the exact spot remains unknown. Nature is elusive."

"I will trust in our collective knowledge and intuition to guide us to the plant," I stated, folding the map with care. "I will return with the healing plant and do everything in my power to aid Sir Gregory's recovery."

"I will send Shadowfang with you on this journey as well to aid with the task," Arabella stated.

"Having Shadowfang by our side will provide an extra layer of protection. Her familiarity with the area will be an invaluable asset. Is there anything else I should know about the journey?"

"No, just move and remain vigilant. Time is of the essence," she emphasized.

As our conversation neared its end, Arabella shared one last piece of information.

"Before you settle in for the night, my father, the King, has requested your presence."

"The King wishes to see me?"

"Yes, it is a matter of importance. I suggest you make your way to him without delay," she advised.

"I will head to the King's presence with utmost urgency. Thank you for informing me."

However, before I could take a step towards the door, Arabella's hand grasped mine, and our eyes locked in a moment of connection.

"I thank you for your help, Valaric. I know this journey and the tasks ahead are a lot to ask," she expressed.

My gaze softened as I reciprocated her appreciation.

"Think nothing of it, Arabella. The well-being of Sir Gregory and the kingdom is of utmost importance to me. I will do my best to fulfill this duty."

Guided by one of the castle guards, I embarked on my journey to the King's current location. We traversed the magnificent corridors of the castle, our footsteps echoing against the polished stone floors. As we arrived at a grand meeting room, adorned with intricate tapestries and symbols of regal authority, the guard announced my presence to the King.

Seated at the head of a long table, the King acknowledged the guard's announcement with a slight nod. He motioned for the guard to allow me entry into the room. With a sense of anticipation, I stepped forward and crossed the threshold into the chamber. The room greeted me with an air of solemnity and significance.

Taking a moment to survey my surroundings, my gaze swept across the well-lit space. Candle chandeliers bathed the room in a warm, flickering glow, casting dancing shadows upon the walls adorned with age-old tapestries. My attention was drawn to the centerpiece of the room—a sturdy table crafted from the finest wood, its polished surface reflecting the gentle illumination from above. Its presence hinted at the countless meetings and decisions that had shaped the kingdom's history.

As my eyes wandered, I also noticed the regal portraits adorning the walls. Ornate frames showcased the visages of esteemed figures, their gazes following my every move. These were the faces of previous kings, their expressions a testament to their leadership and legacy. I couldn't help but feel a sense of reverence for those who had come before me, recognizing the weight of their responsibility and the profound impact they had left on the kingdom.

"Valaric, come in and take a seat," commanded the King.

I approached the table and bowed my head in acknowledgment. "Thank you, your Highness."

"I have been informed that you will embark on a journey tomorrow to retrieve a particular plant," the King stated.

"Your Highness, I have only just agreed to undertake this task," I stated as I pondered how the news about the mission had already reached the king.

A small smile played at the corners of the King's lips as he leaned back in his chair. "Word travels within these walls, Valaric," he explained. "When acts of bravery and compassion occur within our kingdom, they do not go unnoticed."

"I assure you, your Highness, it was a duty I accepted. When Sir Gregory was in need, I did what any person would do to aid a comrade."

"Indeed, you are not a native of our kingdom, and as we have expressed, trust towards outsiders is not easily granted," he remarked. "However, I must acknowledge that your actions have not given me reason to suspect any ill intentions towards our realm."

"Your Highness, I assure you I bear no ill will towards anyone. As an adventurer, my purpose is to seek new experiences and challenges, not to bring harm or discord."

"I see," the King said, his tone softened. "While trust is not easily gained, actions can speak louder than words."

A flicker of relief passed through my eyes, grateful that my intentions were being acknowledged, albeit with caution. The King continued, his voice carrying a hint of concern.

"The journey that lies before you will be arduous and fraught with danger. Considering this, I will assign a few more guards to accompany you and ensure your safety as you retrieve the plant."

"Thank you, your Highness. Their presence will provide reassurance and aid in our mission."

"Before you embark, make a stop at the castle kitchen," the King instructed. "Stock up on provisions and supplies that will sustain you and your companions throughout the journey. It is vital to be well-prepared."

"I will follow your guidance, your Highness. Your wisdom and support are deeply appreciated."

As I prepared to take my leave, a mixture of anticipation and determination swirled within me. The challenges that awaited were formidable, but with the added guards and provisions from the castle kitchen, I knew I had the resources to face them head-on.

With a final bow of gratitude, I exited the meeting room, my mind already consumed by thoughts of the upcoming journey. I understood the weight of the King's expectations and the need to prove myself worthy of the trust placed upon me. In the days to come, I would face trials and uncertainties, but I was determined to uphold my values and complete the mission entrusted to me.

## *Chapter 20 The Journey Begins*

The next morning, the courtyard outside the castle became the gathering point for our expedition. I, along with Whisperwind and Shadowfang, arrived early, eager to embark on the journey. Soon, the others emerged from the castle to join our group. As I realized I was unfamiliar with their names, I decided it was time for introductions.

"Ah, allow me to guess," I exclaimed with a playful grin. "We have the healer, the skilled archer, and the mighty swordsman, am I right?"

Everyone released a slight chuckle at my attempt to break the ice.

"I am Valaric, a swordsman hailing from Aurelia," I said. "And this," I gestured towards the mystical creature perched on my shoulder, Whisperwind. He possesses a uniqueness that sets him apart. And I'm sure you all are already acquainted with Shadowfang, the ever-loyal companion of our esteemed Princess."

"I am Aria, a healer with a few additional skills," she announced.

Her long, chestnut-colored hair cascaded down her back in loose waves, shimmering under the sunlight. As she spoke, I couldn't help but feel a sense of reassurance emanating from her, knowing that her healing abilities would be invaluable on our journey.

As Aria introduced herself, I couldn't help but be captivated by her presence. Her emerald green eyes seemed to hold a hint of magic that reflected the depths of her healing abilities.

Her face, graced with high cheekbones and a soft, graceful jawline, conveyed a gentle and kind nature. The warmth and empathy in her aura were clear, and Valaric felt an instant sense of comfort in her company.

Aria's attire further emphasized her elegance and sophistication. The flowing robes made from exquisite Vindorian fabrics draped over her slender figure, while intricate patterns and delicate embroidery added an extra layer of beauty to her appearance.

"Hello everyone, my name is Ethan, and I am an archer." Ethan stated.

Ethan stood at an impressive height of six feet, with an athletic build that spoke of his agility and strength. Ethan's commanding presence was enhanced by his confident demeanor.

His visage was characterized by a strong, angular jawline, accentuated by a well-groomed beard that framed his face and matched the chestnut brown hue of his hair. His hair fell in waves, reaching just below his ears. But it was his piercing eyes that drew attention, a deep shade of blue that held a mixture of determination and mischievousness, hinting at the adventures he had seen.

"Hello everyone, my name is Lucas, and I am a swordsman," said Lucas.

Lucas stood at an impressive height of six feet and a few additional inches, possessed a powerful and well defined muscular build, emphasized by his broad shoulders. His face was chiseled and rugged, displaying a strong jawline that exuded determination and resilience. Lucas's facial hair was meticulously groomed, with a well-shaped beard and hints of stubble that added a touch of rugged charm. His steel-gray eyes, framed by thick eyebrows, seemed to hold a penetrating gaze, reflecting his unwavering focus and intensity during combat.

His dark hair, trimmed, cascaded just above his shoulders, adding an air of mystique to his formidable presence. Adorned in black leather armor that hugged his physique, Lucas showcased both style and practicality, allowing for fluid and agile movements in the heat of swordplay.

Scattered across his muscular arms were visible scars, etched reminders of the battles he had faced and the risks he had confronted as a seasoned and skilled swordsman. These marks served as a testament to his unwavering commitment to his craft and his willingness to put himself in harm's way for the greater good.

"Now that we have acquainted ourselves with one another. I trust that everyone comprehends the nature of our mission and the destination we must reach," I inquired.

In response, a unanimous nod rippled through the assembled team, signifying their understanding.

"Are there any lingering queries or uncertainties before we embark on this journey?" I asked.

Again, a collective shake of heads, articulating they had no questions that plagued their minds regarding the imminent task at hand.

"Very well. Let us set forth and fulfill this important quest together," I followed up with.

Our journey began, our footsteps navigating through the dense forest. Whisperwind, the agile creature, took the lead, his keen senses guiding us through the surroundings. I followed behind, scanning the environment for any signs or obstacles along our path. Ethan, with his bow at the ready, maintained a vigilant position, prepared to protect, and provide cover when needed.

Aria walked beside me, radiating grace and purpose. Her healing skills were honed, and she remained alert to any potential dangers. Lucas, the seasoned swordsman, moved with silent strength, his presence commanding respect and assurance. Meanwhile, Shadowfang, Arabella's loyal companion, remained at our backs, her senses sharp and attentive.

As we ventured deeper into the forest, nature's symphony embraced us. The whispering wind rustled through the branches, creating a soothing melody. The gentle calls of birds and the occasional rustle of small creatures contributed to the harmonious rhythm of our journey. Babbling brooks provided a refreshing soundtrack, their crystal-clear waters flowing with serene tranquility.

"Valaric, could you tell us some things about Aurelia?" asked Ethan.

"What would you like to know?"

Ethan pondered for a moment before asking, "Well, what is it like there? Are there vast forests?"

I nodded and replied, "Indeed, Aurelia boasts its fair share of forests. However, I must admit that my connection to those forests is not as profound as the bond I've formed with Eldoria Forest."

"What do you mean by your connection to those forests is not as profound with the forests of Aurelia?" asked Aria.

"During my travels through the forests of Aurelia, I have felt the gentle caress of the wind, heard the rustling of leaves, and listened to the symphony of woodland creatures. But I realize now that I never immersed myself in the forest's essence, as I have had the opportunity to do in Eldoria Forest. Unlike Eldoria Forest, Aurelia's forests lack the enchantment of elemental springs and the presence of mythical creatures. To my knowledge, creatures like trolls or gorgons do not inhabit those woods, or at least, I have never encountered them in all my journeys through the forests while growing up."

"So, in Aurelia, the forests are mostly inhabited by regular animals," Ethan asked.

I nodded, affirming Ethan's assumption. "That's correct. The forests of Aurelia are home to a variety of wildlife, such as deer, foxes, rabbits, and countless bird species. They possess their own beauty, but they lack the mystic allure and magical inhabitants found in Eldoria Forest."

"I don't know if I could imagine a place with just animals in the forest," stated Ethan.

"I can understand that sentiment, Ethan. The forests of Aurelia may not be as fantastical as Eldoria Forest, but they possess their own charm and beauty," I stated.

"Are all the people in Aurelia part of the same culture or tribe?" inquired Lucas.

"No, we have tribes that share similar cultures, but Aurelia is also home to many individuals from different backgrounds who have settled there over the years. Aurelia has a bustling port that serves as a gateway for people to come and go as they please. It allows for trade, resupplying of provisions for ships, and even facilitates travel to other lands."

"What is a port?" asked Ethan.

"A port is a designated area along the coast where ships can dock. It serves various purposes, such as providing a safe harbor for ships, enabling them to resupply their provisions, engage in fishing activities, or even embark on voyages to other lands. It's like a hub where land and sea connect, facilitating trade and travel."

"Ah, I see. It must be fascinating to have such a lively place where people from different lands come together," Ethan exclaimed.

I nodded, appreciating Ethan's grasp of the concept. "Indeed, it brings a diverse mix of cultures, ideas, and experiences to Aurelia. It creates a dynamic environment."

"So, have the three of you encountered many outsiders during your own journeys?" I asked?

"Not too many, I'm afraid," Ethan admitted. "The forest itself seems to deter most people, with its shifting paths and enchantments. Many wanderers end up getting lost or stumbling upon the likes of trolls and other creatures that dwell within its depths."

"It seems Eldoria Forest prefers to keep its secrets hidden," I mused. "The allure of its mysteries is both captivating and perilous."

"Well Aria, how about you? Have you had a lot of outsider experience?" I asked.

"I have seldom come across anyone from outside the kingdom," she admitted. "My responsibilities as a healer keep me within the safety of the castle walls. This journey will be one of the farthest treks I have undertaken into the forest, and I embrace it as a new adventure."

I nodded, appreciating Aria's eagerness to explore beyond her usual confines. "The forest has much to reveal to us, and I'm certain it will be a transformative experience for all of us."

"Lucas, have you encountered many outsiders?" I asked.

"I have encountered a few more outsiders during my travels," he disclosed. "However, they were always deep within the forest or out on the remote cliffs and mountains. None have ventured close to the kingdom itself."

"The wilderness holds many secrets, and it seems the forest and mountains guard them," I remarked.

"How did you end up in the kingdom?" inquired Lucas.

"It was all quite accidental" I admitted. "Whisperwind and I set off on a stroll through the forest, without a clear destination in mind. I followed Whisperwind, trusting his instincts as we ventured deeper into the unknown. To this day, I still do not know where he was leading me."

"So, it was all down to sheer luck?" Ethan remarked.

"Yes, indeed. It was a stroke of fortunate happenstance that brought us to the Kingdom's doorstep," I replied.

"Aria, could you share with us what a typical day looks like for you?" I inquired. However, before she could respond, our conversation was abruptly interrupted by the peculiar noises emanating from Whisperwind up ahead.

"Everyone, stay where you are," I instructed. The group halted, their attention now focused on the mysterious sounds permeating the air.

"What in the world is that noise?" asked Ethan.

"That, my friends, is Whisperwind's way of alerting us to something nearby that doesn't have friendly intentions," I said. "It's a useful signal, as the noise goes unnoticed by the source of the threat or, if they hear it, they often mistake it for just another ambient sound in the forest."

"Ethan, would you be willing to venture ahead to investigate what Whisperwind detected?" I asked. "Whisperwind will guide you with his buzzing sounds, ensuring you don't walk into any danger. With your exceptional eyesight and familiarity with the forest's inhabitants, you're better equipped to spot any potential threats or clues," I acknowledged.

"Yes" Ethan replied.

"The rest of us can wait here while Ethan gathers information. Once he returns with some insights, we can strategize" I directed.

After about ten minutes, we saw Ethan heading back our way.

"What did you see, Ethan?" I asked.

"There are three Forest Stalkers up ahead," Ethan stated.

"What are Forest Stalkers?" I asked.

"Forest Stalkers possess sleek ebony fur that blends with the shadows, allowing them to move undetected. Their feline-like grace is contrasted by razor-sharp claws and teeth, hinting at their lethal capabilities," Ethan followed up with.

"Now that we are aware of what we are up against, does anyone have a plan to confront these creatures?" I asked.

Lucas stepped forward, his voice steady and his gaze focused. "I propose that Ethan, Shadowfang, and I move ahead to confront the threat head-on," he declared. "Meanwhile, Valaric, your role will be to stay here and protect Aria."

"I can defend myself, you know," Aria insisted.

Lucas met her gaze, his expression filled with sincerity. "I have no doubt in your abilities, Aria," he assured her. "However, your expertise in identifying the plant we seek, and your healing skills, make you invaluable to our mission. You are the only one who can provide immediate aid should any of us be injured."

"Lucas is right, Aria," I concurred. "Your knowledge and healing abilities are vital to our success. We need you by our side, ready to offer your guidance and support."

Aria's expression softened, and I could see her understanding the significance of her role and the impact she could have on our mission. Her willingness to accept the responsibility was clear in the determined nod she gave.

With the plan in place, Ethan, Shadowfang, and Lucas advanced towards the location where the creatures had been spotted. Their steps were calculated, and their senses heightened, prepared for any surprises that lay ahead.

After a few minutes of silence, Aria and I could hear sounds of the intense battle. Our focus was drawn to the commotion unfolding ahead, our thoughts filled with concern for our comrades engaged in the fight.

"I hope they are prevailing," I murmured.

Aria nodded in agreement, her eyes reflecting both worry and a desire to be of help.

"I share your sentiments," she replied. "It's frustrating not knowing the exact circumstances or how we can lend our support."

"It seems we have an unwelcome visitor on our hands," I stated as I tightened my grip around my weapon.

As every muscle in my body tensed, my senses heightened, preparing for the impending danger. Time seemed to slow as the creature revealed itself, emerging from the shadows. My focus sharpened, homing in on the imminent clash that awaited me.

But just as the creature unveiled its true nature, a sudden and unexpected intervention occurred. Bolts of lightning, crackling with raw power, struck with precision and lethal force. The creature was engulfed in a blinding cascade of electrical energy, its existence extinguished.

I stood frozen for a moment, my eyes widening in disbelief. The swift and devastating display of elemental power had obliterated the threat before I even reacted. Glancing around, I tried to make sense of the unexpected turn of events. The source of the lightning attack was still unclear, leaving me in awe and wonder.

Just then, I heard a voice behind me, "Told you I could take care of myself," Aria stated.

"What the? How in the," I exclaimed, unable to find the right words to express my surprise.

With a hint of amusement in her voice, Aria replied, "I tried to tell all of you."

I couldn't help but chuckle at her remark, my initial shock giving way to a sense of admiration for her hidden abilities.

"That may have been something you might have mentioned at our initial meeting," I exclaimed. "You know, the fact you could cook a beast from the inside!"

"Well, surprises keep things interesting, don't they?" she quipped, with a playful glint in her eyes.

"Indeed, they do," I replied. "But now, let's go see how the others are doing."

The battles were just wrapping up as Aria and I were getting to where the others were located.

As the battle unfolded, the forest became a whirlwind of movement and conflict. Lucas's strikes were swift and deadly, exploiting the creature's weakened state to deliver a fatal blow. With a last swing of his sword, he dispatched the wounded Forest Stalker, ensuring it posed no further danger.

With one enemy vanquished, Lucas turned his attention to Shadowfang's plight, rushing to aid his faithful companion in her fierce struggle. Together, their combined strength and skill overwhelmed the Forest Stalker, and Shadowfang emerged triumphant, panting, but sustained some injuries.

Ethan, with his relentless barrage of arrows, found an opening in the creature's defenses. His arrow found its mark, delivering a fatal blow to the third Forest Stalker. It fell to the forest floor, its threat silenced forever. As the adrenaline subsided, the forest returned to a peaceful calm, and the companions stood united, victorious in the face of a formidable foe.

"Make sure they are all extinguished before walking away," I instructed, emphasizing the importance of thoroughness. "We cannot afford to make assumptions like we did before, which led to Sir

Gregory's injury."

"Why did you bring Aria here before we came back to get the two of you," questioned Lucas.

A wry smile played on my lips as he shared the events that had unfolded in their absence. "Trust me, she doesn't need any help," I replied. "Aria revealed a remarkable ability, one that I did not know she possessed. She single-handedly took care of the adversaries."

"That's incredible," Lucas exclaimed. "We have quite the formidable team, it seems."

"Indeed, we do," I affirmed. "Now, let's finish our task and ensure there are no lingering threats. We cannot let any more surprises hinder our progress."

With the Forest Stalkers defeated, Aria and Whisperwind shifted their attention to tending to the wounded. Shadowfang, having taken the brunt of the battle, received immediate care from Aria's healing abilities. Lucas expressed his gratitude for Shadowfang's valiant effort, knowing that her presence had made all the difference in contending with the formidable creature.

We breathed a collective sigh of relief as they assessed the aftermath of the confrontation. Thanks to our coordinated efforts and skilled combat, we emerged victorious with no major injuries to impede our progress. The threat had been decisively eliminated, and a sense of accomplishment washed over us.

I acknowledged the team's success, my voice filled with pride and satisfaction. "Well done, everyone. We have faced this challenge head-on and triumphed. Let us take a moment to regroup and replenish our strength before we continue our journey."

## Chapter 21 The Air Elemental

"Does anyone know where we are approximately?" asked Aria.

"I don't have an exact answer, but let's consult the map to see if we can gather our approximate location," I suggested.

We had been on the move for a short time, perhaps an hour, or at most, an hour and a half. I scanned the intricate lines and markings on the map, tracing our path and comparing it to our surroundings. After a few moments of careful examination, I pointed to a spot on the map.

"It seems we are here," I said.

"If possible," Aria began, her voice filled with anticipation, "let's make our way towards this elemental spring area over here. It's conveniently in route, and it would be an ideal location for a meditation session."

"That sounds like a plan," I affirmed, folding the map, and stowing it back in my pack. "It's an opportunity for us to replenish our energies and seek the guidance of the elements. Let's make our way to the elemental spring and embrace the tranquility it offers."

"Well, how many more encounters like the previous one do you think we'll have on this journey?" I asked.

Lucas and Ethan exchanged a brief but meaningful glance, their shared experiences speaking volumes. "More times than any of us would probably want to in these woods," Lucas replied, his tone carrying a hint of weariness. "The creatures we face out here play a crucial role in keeping our kingdom safe. They act as natural guardians, preventing both the creatures themselves and any outsiders from reaching our domain."

"It's a necessary defense mechanism," Ethan added. "While it may seem like a necessary evil, it serves to safeguard the Vindorians and maintain the sanctity of our kingdom. Outsiders find it challenging to breach our borders because of these very creatures."

"I suppose it's a necessary sacrifice for the greater good," I mused. "In Aurelia, one could spend days or even weeks in the woods encountering nothing like what we've faced."

"We shouldn't linger here any longer if we want to make progress," I remarked. "Is everyone ready to resume our journey and continue our quest?" I inquired, seeking their confirmation.

In response, a chorus of nods swept through the team, their determination clear in their resolute expressions. I rose from my position, readying myself to move forward toward the towering cliffs that marked our path. With Whisperwind leading the way, we set off, our feet guided by a shared purpose and a renewed sense of determination.

"Aria, what other hidden capabilities do you possess?" I asked.

"I possess the ability to conjure various types of elemental spells," she revealed. "However, it's important to note that some spells are more potent than others."

"Is that why you wanted to visit the elemental springs?" I asked, connecting the dots.

Aria nodded, a serene smile gracing her lips. "Indeed. The elemental springs serve as a source of power and inspiration. When I meditate there, I can tap into their energy and enhance the strength of my spells. I try to make it a daily practice whenever circumstances allow."

"You know, Valaric, the elemental springs are not only beneficial for me but also a great place for you to connect with the forest," Aria suggested. Her voice carried a gentle encouragement.

"The Princess mentioned the same thing, and I can see the wisdom in it. Unfortunately, I haven't had the chance to pause and immerse myself in that experience yet."

"Meditating at the elemental springs not only deepens our connection with the natural surroundings but also enhances our understanding of the forest," Ethan explained. "While I may not have the opportunity to do it daily like Aria, I seize the chance whenever it presents itself."

"Does it help with traversing the forest and gaining knowledge of the area?"

Ethan nodded. "Absolutely," he affirmed. "By embracing the stillness and attuning ourselves to the forest's rhythms, we gain insights into its secrets. It grants us a deeper understanding of its paths, hidden enclaves, and the creatures that dwell within."

"I find all of this quite intriguing, especially since we don't have these kinds of natural wonders back in Aurelia. Although the forests themselves remain unchanged, except for the shifting seasons, the paths created by animals and people remain the same unless a new trail is forged."

The thought of animals and their role in their journey sparked a question in my mind. "Speaking of animals, why are we traversing on foot rather than riding animals that might transport us much faster?"

Lucas met my gaze and offered a knowing smile. "The forest poses its own challenges that even animals would struggle with. Their speed would be compromised amidst the dense foliage and bringing them up the cliffs would render them vulnerable to danger."

"Ah, I see," I acknowledged.

After another half an hour of walking, we arrived at our destination —the elemental springs. I gazed upon the springs, noting their resemblance to the ones I had encountered before. The distinct characteristics of each elemental spring—air, fire, earth, and wind— were clear to me, providing a sense of familiarity and understanding.

"I'm glad we made it," Ethan expressed, his voice tinged with a hint of fatigue. "It felt like we were walking for hours."

"Alright, so how do we do this?" I asked. "Since you all know what you are doing, I can watch over everyone to ensure we are safe while you meditate."

"There's no need for that. We have Shadowfang and Whisperwind who can alert us if any danger approaches. You can immerse yourself in the meditation experience," Lucas stated.

Aria chimed in, her voice gentle and reassuring. "Here, just sit down next to one of the elementals to get started. We will guide you through the process, and once you're settled, we'll begin our own meditations."

"Does it matter which one I sit next to?"

"For you, it may not matter as much. Each elemental offers a unique experience, and sitting next to any of them will provide you with unique insights. Choose the one that resonates with you, and the rest of us will select the others," Aria answered.

I contemplated for a moment, considering my options, before choosing to sit near the air elemental. The gentle breeze whispered through the surrounding trees, beckoning me to embrace its essence. As the others positioned themselves near the remaining elementals, I observed their serene postures and closed eyes, realizing that I too, should adopt a similar approach.

With a newfound sense of purpose, I closed my eyes, allowing my thoughts to drift to the encompassing forest. I directed my attention to the rustling leaves, the soft murmurs of the wind, and the ever-present presence of the air element. Gradually, I let go of external distractions, focusing on my connection with the element of air.

In my mind's eye, I visualized myself blending with the air, feeling its invisible currents flow through me. I imagined myself as a part of the forest, intertwining my essence with the gentle whispers of nature. With each breath, I absorbed the purity and vitality that the air element offered.

As I sat in my meditative state, I surrendered myself to the ethereal embrace of the air elemental. The rhythm of my breath matched the gentle cadence of the wind, allowing me to feel weightless and free, as if I were soaring through the sky. My consciousness expanded, and I transcended the boundaries of the physical realm.

In this state of blissful tranquility, my senses heightened, and I became attuned to the subtle whispers of the air. It whispered secrets and revealed hidden knowledge, offering glimpses of the interconnectedness of all things. With each inhale, I absorbed the wisdom carried by the wind, and with each exhale, I released my doubts and limitations.

As I embraced the essence of the air element, I felt a profound connection to the world around me. It was as if I had ascended above the towering trees, granting me an encompassing view of my surroundings. From this elevated perspective, I could see the intricate tapestry of nature, the interplay of light and shadow, and the delicate dance of life.

The visions that unfolded before my mind's eye were awe-inspiring. I witnessed how the wind could be harnessed to aid our journey, to carry messages from one place to another, and to create pathways through impenetrable obstacles. I saw how the air currents could guide us, revealing hidden trails and unveiling the secrets of the forest.

With each passing moment, I felt an intuitive understanding of how to use the power of the wind to our advantage. I saw the potential to manipulate the breeze to our will, to redirect its course, and to create pockets of stillness or gusts of force when needed. These insights offered me a newfound resourcefulness, enabling us to navigate the challenges that lay ahead.

In this harmonious communion with the air elemental, I noticed my potential. I realized that by harnessing the power of the wind, I could become an instrument of change and transformation. The visions instilled in me a profound sense of purpose, as I recognized the role I had to play in shaping the destiny of our quest.

As I emerged from my meditative state, a surge of energy coursed through my veins, revitalizing my entire being. I opened my eyes, and to my surprise, I found the rest of the group fixated on me, their expressions a mix of curiosity and wonder.

Puzzled by their intense gaze, I couldn't help but ask, "What's the matter? Why is everyone staring at me like that?"

Aria, Ethan, and Lucas exchanged glances before Aria spoke up, her voice filled with awe, "It's because you have been meditating for hours, Valaric. You went deeper than anyone we have ever seen before. Most people only meditate for about fifteen minutes."

Perplexed, I took a moment to observe my surroundings. To my astonishment, I realized that the sun was almost on the horizon, casting a warm golden glow across the landscape.

"How did the day pass by so quickly?" I exclaimed.

Lucas couldn't help but chuckle. "Well, it did indeed pass by quickly, but that's because you were in a profound state of meditation for much longer than you realize."

"But I only felt like I meditated for about 10 minutes, at most. How is that possible?"

Aria stepped forward, her eyes shimmering with excitement. "Valaric, when you delved into your meditation, you entered a realm of profound connection and exploration. Time operates differently in that realm, and what may have felt like minutes to you was, in fact, hours in the waking world."

My mind struggled to comprehend the magnitude of what Aria was telling me. I had traversed the boundaries of ordinary consciousness and ventured deep into the realm of spiritual awakening.

Curiosity brimming within her, Aria couldn't resist asking, "Tell us, Valaric, what did you see during your journey? What revelations did the elemental springs give upon you?"

Taking a deep breath, I gathered my thoughts before I began recounting the visions and insights that had unfolded before me. I described the ethereal landscapes I had traversed, the whispers of ancient wisdom I had heard, and the profound connection I had forged with the elemental forces.

I spoke of the vibrant colors that danced before my eyes, the melodies that resonated within my soul, and the profound unity I felt with the natural world. I shared how the elemental springs had revealed secrets of the forest, intricate ways to harness the power of wind, and how I had gained a heightened sense of purpose and clarity.

As I wove my tale, the rest of the group listened intently, captivated by the vividness of my descriptions and the depth of my experience. Each word I spoke painted a vivid picture in their minds, transporting them to the realms I had visited.

As I finished sharing my journey, a profound sense of awe and reverence filled the air. The group realized that my meditation had not only granted me personal insights, but had also deepened our collective understanding of the elemental forces that surrounded us. The experience had brought us closer together, united by a newfound appreciation for the interconnectedness of the natural world and the power that lay within it.

"We should set up camp nearby for the night," I suggested. "It's getting dark, and it wouldn't be wise to stumble upon nocturnal creatures. We need to ensure our safety."

As I looked around, I saw the rest of the group nodding in agreement, each of us understanding the importance of resting and regaining our strength. Together, we organized ourselves, finding a suitable campsite nestled in a secluded area, shielded by the protective embrace of the forest.

As I sat by the flickering campfire, its warm glow illuminating our faces, I couldn't help but feel the weight of responsibility pressing down on me.

"Tomorrow, we must make better time. We need to move faster than we did today. I don't want to let everyone down by falling behind on our journey."

Ethan placed a reassuring hand on Valaric's shoulder. "Valaric, journeys are rarely smooth and swift. We remember that progress is not always measured by the distance covered, but by the lessons we learn and the challenges we overcome."

Aria chimed in, her voice soothing yet firm. "And let us not forget the value of rest and reflection. Our meditation at the elemental springs has already gifted us with renewed clarity and deeper connections. Trust that it will guide us in the days to come."

As I took a deep breath, I let their words sink in. I realized that the weight I felt wasn't a measure of my leadership's worth, but a reflection of my commitment to the mission we all shared. Nodding at their understanding, I made a silent promise to myself to let go of unnecessary self-imposed pressure.

At that moment, I chose to embrace the present and cherish the camaraderie and wisdom we shared around the campfire. Tomorrow would indeed bring new challenges, but I knew we were in it together. The bond we had forged would be our source of strength and support, carrying us through whatever trials lay ahead.

## *Chapter 22 The Hidden Grotto*

As the night settled around the camp, I found myself lost in the mesmerizing dance of the crackling flames. The warm glow cast gentle shadows upon the surrounding trees, creating a tranquil atmosphere amidst the wilderness.

In the flickering light, memories of the day I set foot on the Silver Serpent--the vessel that launched me into this extraordinary journey--came rushing back. I reminisced about the mix of emotions that swelled within me as I bid farewell to the familiar comforts of my homeland. Anticipation and uncertainty mingled in my heart as I embarked on this uncharted path.

The crackling fire seemed like a portal to the past, stirring a whirlwind of emotions within me. Faces of my loved ones saying their farewells flashed before my mind's eye—the pride in their eyes, the undercurrent of worry, and the hope they held for my endeavors. The camaraderie I had shared with my companions on the ship—the laughter, the shared stories, and the unspoken bond we had formed — echoed in my thoughts, reminding me of the connections that had been woven along this journey.

My mind wandered back to that unforgettable moment when I stood on the deck of the Silver Serpent, facing the vast expanse of the cerulean sea. The ship's sails billowed with the wind, gracefully propelling us forward on our journey. The open waters seemed endless, inviting me to embrace the untamed adventure that awaited us.

As we sailed further away from the harbor, the initial chaos of departure had settled into a serene calm. The crew members, having completed their tasks, now stole glances at the expansive blue canvas that surrounded us. Their eyes reflected the ocean's tranquility, and a sense of awe and reverence filled the air.

Observing the crew going about their duties, each member immersed in their tasks to ensure the ship's smooth operation, I marveled at the unity and dedication that bound us together. The sounds of ropes being secured, the occasional creak of the ship, and the distant call of seagulls created a symphony that harmonized with the rhythm of the waves. It was a beautiful melody of camaraderie and purpose that underscored our shared voyage into the unknown.

As I joined my fellow shipmates in marveling at the mesmerizing sight of the open waters, I couldn't help but feel an overwhelming connection to the vastness of the sea. It symbolized limitless opportunities, uncharted territories, and a world yet to be explored.

The gentle sway of the ship beneath my feet offered a soothing reassurance, as if nature itself cradled us on our voyage. Time seemed to stand still as I allowed myself to be fully present in the moment, relishing the salty breeze caressing my face and the rhythmic lullaby of the ocean serenading my soul.

Turning my gaze from the expansive water, I approached a man diligently working on tying knots in a sturdy rope. Intrigued by the sailor's experience, I struck up a conversation. I was eager to learn from someone intimately familiar with these waters and the art of sailing, hoping to gain insights that would enrich our voyage even further.

"So, how long have you sailed alongside Captain Stormrider?"

The man paused momentarily, glancing up from his task. "I've had the honor of traversing the high seas with Captain Stormrider for a good five years now," he replied. "And let me tell you, those years have been filled with wondrous sights and extraordinary adventures."

"I can only imagine the wonders you've witnessed during your time at sea."

"Aye, you wouldn't believe the things I've seen," the sailor responded. "Captain Stormrider has led us to uncharted lands and exotic destinations. I've witnessed marvels beyond my wildest dreams, encountered cultures and creatures I never knew existed."

"You speak of remarkable journeys. Who among the crew would

you recommend for the most extraordinary tales?"

"Ah, if it's grand adventures you seek, then you must talk to Finnegan over there," he suggested. "He's sailed the high seas for over a decade, and his tales could keep you spellbound for hours. He's witnessed wonders and dangers that would make your heart race."

I nodded appreciatively, grateful for the sailor's guidance. With newfound anticipation, I set my sights on Finnegan, eager to hear the legendary seafarer's accounts and dive deeper into the captivating world of their maritime journeys.

"Hello again Finnegan."

The seasoned sailor glanced up from his work, giving Valaric a friendly nod.

"Hey Valaric, good to see you again. What can I do for you?"

I straightened my posture, eager to dive into the realm of Finnegan's storied experiences.

"I've heard whispers of your grand adventures with Captain Stormrider," I remarked with anticipation. "Sailing the open seas for so long, I can only imagine the extraordinary tales you have to share."

Finnegan's eyes sparkled with the memories of countless voyages.

"Aye, Captain Stormrider has led us on many daring expeditions, always seeking uncharted lands and unexplored horizons," he responded. "He possesses a unique ability to spot opportunities and push the limits, allowing us to witness wonders that most can only dream of."

"I yearn to hear those captivating stories of your adventures, Finnegan. While we sail these waters, I hope you'll find time to share some of those remarkable tales. There's nothing quite like immersing oneself in the tales of past adventures."

"Once, on a fateful night beneath a sky dotted with countless stars, we set sail for the distant Isle of Avalora," Finnegan began. "Legend had it that the isle held ancient treasures and untold wonders, obscured by treacherous waters and mists."

I leaned in closer, hanging on to every word as Finnegan skillfully painted the scene.

"We charted a course through tempestuous seas, our ship buffeted by fierce gales and towering waves," Finnegan continued. "Yet, undeterred by the challenges, Captain Stormrider steered us with unwavering determination, his eyes ablaze with the thrill of the unknown."

"As we neared Avalora, a dense fog descended, enveloping the ship in an eerie embrace," Finnegan narrated. "Navigating blindly, we relied on our instincts and the captain's uncanny intuition. And that's when we saw it—a faint glimmer of light, like a beacon in the darkness."

My imagination soared as he envisioned the mystical isle shrouded in mist, its secrets waiting to be unveiled.

"We approached the source of the ethereal glow," Finnegan continued. "And what we discovered left us in awe—a hidden cove, its shores adorned with luminescent sea flora, casting an otherworldly radiance upon the waters."

He paused for effect, allowing the weight of the revelation to settle. "It was a place untouched by time, where enchantment danced with reality," Finnegan whispered. "We immersed ourselves in the cove's ethereal beauty, witnessing rare marine creatures, their vivid hues shimmering in the underwater realm."

"But our time in Avalora was too precious to pass by," Finnegan's voice resonated with determination. "The allure of the island's mysteries pulled us deeper into its embrace, urging us to explore its uncharted realms."

"On the following morning, Captain Stormrider and we the valiant crew set foot on the sandy shores of that mystical island. The air was thick with the scents of the sea and exotic blossoms, creating a heady mix that beckoned us to explore."

"As we ventured deeper into the heart of Avalora, a feast for the senses awaited. The verdant forest engulfed us, its towering trees creating a lush canopy above. Colorful birds flitted amidst the branches, their melodious songs echoing through the air," Finnegan continued.

I sat and listened to the tale that Finnegan was telling. I could imagine myself with them on this amazing journey. Finnegan had the gift of telling stories like no one I had ever heard before. You could get a feel for what was going on, especially when sitting on the very ship that the adventure happened on.

"The sunlight danced through the foliage, painting the forest floor with a tapestry of light and shadow. We pressed on, eager to uncover the island's hidden treasures," Finnegan narrated.

"Imagine our astonishment when we stumbled upon cascading waterfalls, their pristine waters flowing into inviting pools of turquoise. The coolness of the water washed away the weariness from our journey, refreshing both body and soul," Finnegan described.

"But the true marvel awaited us in the heart of Avalora," Finnegan continued, his tone dropping to a hushed whisper. "Concealed behind a veil of cascading water, a hidden grotto emerged. As we stepped into that ethereal chamber, a sight beyond imagination greeted our eyes."

"A mesmerizing display of bioluminescent creatures painted the walls with their radiant glow. Delicate mushrooms cast a soft, phosphorescent light, transforming the grotto into a realm that defied reality itself," Finnegan exclaimed, his hands gesturing as if to recreate the magical scene.

"The air crackled with an otherworldly ambiance as we stood in awe, basking in the brilliance of the bioluminescent beings. It was a sight that would forever be etched in our memories, a testament to the untamed beauty and enchantment of Avalora"

"But, dear friends, the tranquility was short-lived. From the shadows emerged a monstrosity straight out of nightmares. Fangs dripped with venom, and its twisted form sent shivers down our spines," Finnegan continued. "With a screech that chilled us to the bone, the creature lunged at us, hungry for blood."

"Swift as lightning, Captain Stormrider sprang into action, his voice like thunder as he commanded us to defend ourselves. Swords clashed, spells crackled, and the battle for our very lives began. The grotto, once a sanctuary of beauty, now echoed with the sounds of war."

"Amidst the chaos, we fought with all our might, never faltering in our resolve. Our blades met the creature's scaled hide, and our spells ignited with fury. Yet, the creature fought back with a relentless ferocity, testing our mettle."

"But let me tell you, my friends, we were not the crew of the Silver Serpent for naught," Finnegan exclaimed. "With every swing of our weapons, every surge of magic, we pushed back the foul beast. Captain Stormrider's leadership guided us through the fray, his unwavering resolve inspiring us to keep fighting, even in the face of danger."

"As the battle reached its climactic peak," Finnegan continued, "our hearts pounded in our chests, adrenaline coursing through our veins. Captain Stormrider's voice rang out above the chaos, rallying us to deliver one final blow. 'This is our moment, me hearties!' he cried, his words fueling our determination."

"With a renewed vigor, our swords clashed against the creatures, with a ferocity born of desperation," Finnegan emphasized. "Spells crackled and exploded, their arcane energies weaving a tapestry of power and destruction."

"The creature fought back with a savage fury," Finnegan exclaimed. "Its claws slashed through the air, and its fangs snapped. But we stood strong, forming an unbreakable wall of defense. We shielded one another, protecting our comrades from the creature's relentless onslaught."

"Captain Stormrider, the epitome of bravery, led the charge with unwavering resolve."

Finnegan's voice rose with admiration as he spoke.

"With his sword held high, he struck a decisive blow, severing the beast's venomous tail. A triumphant roar erupted from our throats as we witnessed our enemy weakened, its defenses crumbling."

"Sensing victory within our grasp," Finnegan continued, "we unleashed a relentless barrage of attacks. Flames engulfed the creature, scorching its scales, while ice encased its limbs, rendering it immobile. Lightning crackled and danced around its writhing form, electrifying the air with raw power."

"And then, in a dazzling display of might and magic, the creature let out one final, earth-shaking roar. Its monstrous body convulsed, and with a blinding flash, it disintegrated into a swirling vortex of dark energy, dissipating into the air."

"Silence settled over the battlefield, allowing the weight of their victory to sink in. As the echoes of battle subsided," he continued, "we stood amidst the aftermath, panting but triumphant. And there, amidst the disturbed rubble, we beheld a sight that took our breath away."

"Glinting amidst the chaos," Finnegan spoke with reverence, "were the treasures we had unearthed. Gold coins spilled from cracked chests; their sheen undiminished by time. Jewels of vibrant hues adorned the ruins, casting a mesmerizing kaleidoscope of colors. It was a sight that spoke of untold wealth and hidden secrets."

Finnegan's voice carried a note of amazement as he recounted the moment.

"We exchanged knowing glances, our eyes reflecting the shared realization that we had stumbled upon a fortune beyond our wildest dreams. With cautious steps, we gathered the glittering riches, each gem and coin a tangible reward for our valorous deeds."

"Captain Stormrider, ever wise and insightful," Finnegan said, "reminded us that these treasures held a deeper meaning. They symbolized our triumph over adversity, the challenges we had overcome, and the bonds we had forged in the crucible of battle."

"And so, my friends," Finnegan concluded, "we carried our newfound wealth back to the Silver Serpent. Each of us felt a sense of accomplishment and gratitude. The gold and jewels adorned our ship, their radiance serving as a constant reminder of our strength and courage."

"That was some adventure," I exclaimed.

"Aye," Finnegan replied with a knowing smile, "and that was just one of the grand adventures we have taken under Captain Stormrider's command. The tales we could tell, my friend!"

"I can't wait to be on an adventure like that and see what this world offers. The wonders, the challenges, the mysteries waiting to be unraveled."

Finnegan nodded, "Ah, you have yet to taste the thrill of the open seas, the exhilaration of battling mighty foes, and the joy of discovering hidden treasures. But fear not, my friend, for the world is vast, and there are countless adventures that await us."

We shared a moment of quiet anticipation, our minds wandering to the untold wonders that lay ahead. The possibilities were endless, and our spirits soared with the promise of future escapades under Captain Stormrider's command.

"Brace yourself, Valaric," Finnegan said with a mischievous grin, "for the adventures we seek are but a breath away. The call of the unknown beckons, and together, we shall embark on journeys that will leave our hearts pounding and our souls forever changed."

"I am ready, Finnegan. Ready to face the challenges, ready to embrace the unknown, and ready to carve our names into the legends of this vast and wondrous world."

## Chapter 23 The Mystery

Lost in memories of my time aboard the Silver Serpent, Aria pulled me back to the present. Startled, I blinked and turned to face her, realizing that I had been drifting into my thoughts.

"Hey Aria, what are you doing up?"

"I couldn't sleep, and it's dawn, anyway. So, I thought I'd get an early start to the day," Aria replied.

Aria's curious gaze met mine as she observed my distant expression. "You seemed deep in thought when I walked up. What were you thinking about?"

"I was just lost in thoughts of the Silver Serpent."

Aria's brow furrowed, confusion flickering across her face. "Silver Serpent? Was that some kind of creature you battled?" she asked, seeking clarification.

"No, my dear Aria, the Silver Serpent was not a creature. It was a ship—a vessel that carried me on countless grand adventures before I found myself here."

"Ah, I see. It must have been quite an extraordinary experience. Perhaps you could share some of those tales with me one day," she suggested.

"Certainly, Aria. I would be more than happy to regale you with stories of our daring exploits, the wonders we encountered, and the bonds forged aboard the Silver Serpent."

"I suppose its time to rouse the others, so we can set our course towards the cliffs," I suggested.

Aria nodded in agreement, her eyes scanning the horizon. "Indeed, we have a long journey ahead, and the path ahead remains shrouded in uncertainty," she remarked.

"I'll go wake the others, so we can gather our belongings and prepare to embark on the trail."

Aria settled herself in a comfortable spot, her gaze fixed on the emerging colors of the sunrise. "I've already made all the preparations, so I think I'll stay here and savor the beauty of the rising sun. Take your time and gather the others," she stated.

As Aria settled into her spot, she allowed herself to be present in the moment, embracing the serene ambiance of the unfolding sunrise. The first rays of light peeked over the distant horizon, casting a soft golden hue across the land. The sky transformed into a canvas of vibrant colors, with shades of pink, orange, and purple blending into a breathtaking display.

A gentle breeze rustled through the surrounding foliage, carrying with it the scent of dew-kissed flowers and the invigorating freshness of a new day. Aria closed her eyes, inhaling, allowing the tranquil energy to seep into her very being.

As she opened her eyes, her gaze was drawn to the dance of light and shadow that played across the landscape. The sun's rays bathed the rolling hills and distant mountains, casting long, captivating shadows that stretched towards the horizon. The world seemed to awaken with each passing moment, as birds chirped their melodic symphony and small creatures emerged from their nocturnal hideouts.

Aria marveled at the delicate beauty of nature's artwork. The morning dew shimmered like a sea of diamonds on the blades of grass, reflecting the golden sunlight. The leaves of nearby trees rustled, creating a soothing melody that accompanied the vibrant chorus of nature awakening to a new day.

Lost in the captivating scenery, Aria's gaze shifted upwards to the sky. She watched in awe as wispy clouds painted trails across the vast expanse, their colors evolving with the changing hues of the sunrise. The celestial canopy seemed to embrace the emerging light, as if celebrating the birth of a brand-new day.

I made my way to wake up the rest of the group, greeting them with spirited determination. "Morning, everyone! Time to rise and shine," I announced.

Ethan, still groggy from sleep, grumbled in response, "There's just something wrong with waking up this early in the morning to start the day."

Lucas, known for his boisterous nature, couldn't resist a playful jab at Ethan. "Just like an archer to sleep most of the day away," he teased.

I nodded in agreement with Lucas. "Indeed, we have a long journey ahead, and we've already lost some time with our detour to the Elemental Springs yesterday," I reminded them.

Ethan let out a sigh, accepting the reality of the situation. "Yes, I know, but that doesn't mean I have to like it," he muttered.

In a matter of minutes, Ethan and Lucas were ready to embark on the day's adventures. They glanced at each other, acknowledging their readiness, and then turned to me.

"Let's go meet up with Aria so we can hit the trail," I suggested.

Ethan, Lucas, Shadowfang, Whisperwind, and I followed the path to the location where I had left Aria to enjoy the sunrise. As we reached the spot, confusion clouded our faces.

"Um, this is where I left her when I came to get everyone. Where did she go?"

Ethan chimed in, his voice tinged with skepticism. "You sure this is where she was? Maybe we got the location wrong."

"Well, I am pretty sure. We were sitting right here, talking and watching the sunrise."

Growing perplexed, I interjected, "She knew I was going to get you and head back this way so we could start our trek. It makes little sense for her to disappear."

The group exchanged concerned glances, our minds racing with explanations.

"Well, where did she go?" Lucas asked, his voice filled with worry.

With each passing moment, the weight of uncertainty pressed upon us like a heavy burden. We continued to scan the surroundings, hoping for even the faintest sign of Aria's presence. The rustling of the wind in the trees seemed to carry a haunting sense of unease, amplifying our anxiety.

My heart sank as I realized Aria was nowhere to be found. She had vanished without a trace, leaving us puzzled and concerned. Determination coursed through our veins as we rallied together, refusing to succumb to despair.

We spread out, searching every nook and cranny, calling out her name in desperate hope she would respond. The forest echoed with our voices, but there was no answer, no sign she was nearby.

As we ventured further, the shadows of the forest seemed to grow darker, intensifying our sense of urgency. Something unexpected had transpired, and the mystery of Aria's disappearance loomed before us. The fear of the unknown propelled us forward, driving us to unravel the enigma that had befallen our companion.

"Shadowfang, can you pick up her scent?" I asked.

Shadowfang, the keen-nosed companion of the group, sprang into action. She lowered her head to the ground, sniffing around the area in search of any trace of Aria. After a few moments, her tail wagged, and she followed a faint trail.

Ethan, Lucas, Whisperwind, and I followed behind Shadowfang, our eyes darting around the surroundings, searching for any trace of our missing companion. Each step filled us with a mixture of anticipation and concern as we delved deeper into the unknown.

With Shadowfang leading the way, her keen senses guiding us, we headed westward, following the trail of Aria's scent. Urgency propelled us forward, our hearts burdened by the uncertainty of her fate. We scoured the landscape, scanning every inch, hoping for any clue that could lead us to her, but the answers remained elusive.

Undeterred, we continued our search, calling out Aria's name with hope in our voices. The echoes of our pleas reverberated across the expanse, but there was no response, only the haunting silence that surrounded us. The lack of any immediate sign or sound left us spellbound, our minds racing with worry and countless questions.

With each stride, the landscape revealed its untamed beauty and the enigma it held. The sun's rays painted long shadows on the rugged terrain, adding weight to our quest. Amidst the uncertainty, we clung to hope, steadfast in our resolve to find our missing companion.

Shadowfang traced Aria's scent, guiding us towards a concealed cave nestled deep within the forest. As we approached, caution took over, our footsteps becoming more measured, aware of the mysteries that might await us inside.

My voice broke the silence, filled with a mixture of curiosity and concern. "Do you think it's possible she went into the cave?"

Lucas, displaying his usual skepticism, voiced his doubts. "Why would she walk into a cave when she knew we were about to head out in the other direction?"

"That's a question we'll have to ask her when we find her," I replied. Turning my attention to Shadowfang, I asked, "Do you still have her scent?"

Shadowfang, ever faithful, pressed forward into the cave, but before she could take another step, Lucas's urgent voice pierced the air. "Stop!" he yelled; his words filled with caution. The group halted, their hearts pounding in their chests.

"What's the holdup?" I asked.

Lucas took a deep breath, his eyes scanning the cave's entrance. "These hidden caves can be treacherous," he warned. "They're shrouded in mystery, darkness, and often conceal traps or shifting paths. We must prepare ourselves before we venture further."

Lucas's words resonated with the group, serving as a poignant reminder of the potential dangers lurking within the cave's depths. Without hesitation, we assessed our supplies, ensuring we had all the gear and provisions. Each of us double-checked our equipment, determined to be prepared for whatever challenges awaited us inside.

With our preparations complete, we stood shoulder to shoulder, united in our determination. The uncertainty ahead only strengthened our bond, fueling our resolve to face whatever trials lay in wait. As we took our initial steps into the unknown cave, a mixture of anticipation and trepidation filled our hearts. We knew this path would test our mettle and camaraderie, but we embraced it with unwavering courage, ready to overcome whatever obstacles came our way.

## *Chapter 24 Ancient Wisdom*

"Princess, Sir Gregory is still in the same condition," the healer reported.

"Thank you. I have important things to do at Elder's Hall," I replied. "Please inform me if anything changes with his health."

"Yes, Princess. If Sir Gregory's condition improves or worsens, we will send a messenger to find you," the healer assured.

"Thank you," I expressed my gratitude.

"You're welcome, Princess," the healer responded.

Sir Gregory's life still hung in the balance because of his serious injuries. The healers had tried everything they could think of, but they were waiting for a vital plant that a team was out getting.

I didn't want to leave Sir Gregory, but there was nothing more I could do to help. Part of me hoped he would wake up and see me there, supporting his recovery. Sadly, I had tasks to complete in the Kingdom. One of them was gathering information about the ruins for Valaric.

Not wanting to waste any more time, I went to Elder's Hall. When I reached the door, I went inside and talked to one elder.

"Good morning, Princess. How are you today?" inquired the elder.

"Good morning, Elder. Can you assist me with some information?" I inquired.

"What kind of information are you seeking?" the elder inquired.

"I'd like to access a manuscript about the ruins," I mentioned.

"The ruins? That's an unusual request coming from you, Princess," remarked the elder.

"I understand. I'm trying to gather some information for Valaric. Just looking for general knowledge," I explained.

"I see. Come with me," the elder invited.

We strolled past a few shelves packed with books before we turned into one aisle. When we were about halfway down, the elder halted, glanced around, and then took out a manuscript.

"Here you are, Princess. This is the manuscript you're looking for about the ruins," the elder said.

"Thank you. Is there a spot where I can sit and read it?" I inquired.

"Just continue down this aisle, and there are chairs with tables where you can sit down to examine the document. And, of course the manuscript must stay in this room," the elder explained.

"I understand," I replied.

The elder turned and walked back down the same aisle we came from. I turned and headed in the opposite direction to find the tables. As I reached the end of the aisle, I spotted the table the elder had mentioned.

I started reading the manuscript, hoping to find some information for Valaric. The manuscript was quite old but contained some details about the ruins that might be useful to him. There wasn't any specific guidance on exploring the ruins, but it provided minor details, like the layout. It was a starting point, at least.

Just as I was about to turn the next page, I recognized my father's voice. No one else spoke to the elders in such a commanding manner and tone. I suppose being King had its advantages.

Hearing his voice, I moved closer to eavesdrop on their conversation. I retraced my steps up the aisle I had walked down earlier, wanting to be close enough to listen in without joining the discussion.

The elders, who had a powerful presence and looked wise, had a lot of knowledge and a deep respect for the king. When my father greeted them, he spoke with a powerful voice that showed he was in charge, recognizing how valuable their gathered wisdom was.

"Respected elders," he started, speaking to them with the highest respect and honor, "I stand here before you in search of knowledge and insight regarding the outsider known as Valaric. While he has been among us, what have we come to know? What secrets have we uncovered about him?"

His curiosity about Valaric and the enigmas surrounding him seemed to drive my father to seek their counsel, wishing that they could reveal more about this stranger who had entered our world.

The elders, their faces bearing wrinkles from years of wisdom, exchanged knowing looks, acknowledging his quest for knowledge. After a moment of thought, one elder spoke, his voice heavy with the wisdom of many years. "Valaric's presence has sparked interest and discussion among us," he began. "We've observed his actions and listened to his words, trying to understand his true character and intentions."

"And what have you found? What information can you share about this stranger?" he inquired. The King's tone held a mix of excitement and curiosity, as he desired to uncover the secrets and knowledge the elders had gathered during Valaric's time among them.

The elders, their voices blending together like a harmonious choir, shared their collective wisdom with him. "Valaric possesses a noble heart and an unwavering determination," one elder stated, his tone showing both admiration and caution. "But he bears a mysterious mark from the ancient ones, a mark he gained on our shores. Its true meaning still eludes us," the elder explained.

"The ancient items he carries in his bag seem innocent enough," another elder commented. "They are relics from a long-gone time, fragments of an ancient past. However, it's the combination of these items—the crystal, the potion, the dagger, and the parchments—along with the mark on his leg, that hints at potential abilities we can't yet fathom," he added.

Another elder nodded in agreement, his expression deep in thought. "These artifacts, older than both of us and our predecessors, carry an unmistakable sense of power," he observed. "However, the full scope and nature of this power remain hidden, buried beneath the sands of time."

The other elders leaned closer, their faces filled with curiosity and fascination. The allure of these ancient relics and Valaric's enigmatic mark captured their shared imagination. They could sense that this outsider held more secrets than met the eye, and that his journey was linked to their own history.

"Valaric's presence among us seems to hold the potential to unlock long-forgotten secrets," pondered one elder. "It's as if destiny's currents have brought him to our shores, carrying with him the weight of forgotten knowledge and dormant abilities."

The elders looked at each other, their minds filled with thoughts and ideas. They knew their journey was now connected to Valaric's, and that the fates of their people were linked in ways they didn't understand yet.

"We should be careful and take our time," one elder suggested. "These items and the mark on his leg are significant. They have the power to influence our future, so we need to be cautious as we explore this unknown path."

The elder leaned in, his long years of wisdom making him a compelling figure. "Until we uncover the hidden meaning behind this mark, we may never grasp how much Valaric can do and what his true abilities are," he said.

"The Sacred Grove will be our place of refuge, where we'll perform the ancient ceremonies of our forebears," the elder declared. "By connecting with the divine, we'll ask the Gods to share more secrets and understanding about Valaric's mysterious mark."

The other elder, his expression wise and cautious, nodded in agreement. "Until we have unraveled the depths of this enigma, it is prudent to maintain a vigilant watch over Valaric," they advised. "Let us remain vigilant, observing his actions and intentions, for in the delicate balance of discovery lies the key to understanding his true purpose."

"In this moment, I've assigned one of my most trusted advisors to keep a close watch on Valaric," the King said. "They're with the team on their current mission to get the plant that might help Sir Gregory recover."

"What?" I muttered to myself. My father had put a spy in the group with Valaric to get the plant needed for Sir Gregory. I wondered who it could be—Aria, Lucas, or Ethan? It made me question how you could trust someone who was there just to spy on you.

Recognizing the need for more information, the King added, "I expect them to report any important observations or discoveries to me." His words stressed how crucial their findings were, understanding their potential impact on the kingdom and its people. He knew that the insights they gained from Valaric's presence could change our understanding of the world outside our borders, and he was determined to be informed about every detail.

"When you find more information and discoveries, please inform me," the King asked. "I will ask for your advice, as the road we're on is connected to Valaric's journey."

Afterward, my father left Elders Hall in a hurry. I needed to learn more about this informant, so I started heading for the exit. However, I was stopped by the elder who had helped me earlier.

"Um, Princess. Are you forgetting something?" the elder asked.

"I don't think so," I replied.

The elder then looked at the manuscript I was holding.

"I was just returning the manuscript to its proper place, esteemed elder," I explained.

With the book back where it belonged, I left Elders Hall and followed my father. Seeing that he was heading toward his chambers, I seized the opportunity to access one of the secret passages hoping to uncover more information.

The King entered his chambers and called for the head guard to join him. When the head guard arrived, the King gave his orders. "Once the group comes back from their urgent mission," he said, "send a guard to let me know right away. I need to be informed about their return and any updates."

Understanding the seriousness of the situation, the head guard nodded with determination. "Of course, your Majesty," he replied. "I'll pass your message to all my guards. We'll ensure swift communication once the mission is done."

Satisfied with the head guard's response, the King dismissed him. "Valaric might just be a distraction for a bigger threat. Maybe he's scouting the area until his companions arrive to cause trouble," he muttered to himself.

My father seems to have a problem with Valaric, but it might just be because Valaric is an outsider. It might not be personal at all. Still, I'm curious to find out who's spying on Valaric and giving information to my father. That's a mystery.

I'll know where my father is when the group comes back. That's the only way to discover who's working with Valaric. But it might also give me insights into Valaric's intentions, in case he's trying to harm us.

With no more information to gather here, I returned to Elders Hall. On the way, I thought about Valaric's situation. So far, he has done nothing wrong and has been helping us. But I couldn't help but wonder, could it all be a trick? Is he trying to gain our trust just to harm us later on?

As I neared the entrance of Elders Hall, a guard emerged from the shadows, and his demeanor showed he had urgent news that demanded my immediate attention.

My heart sank as I realized that all the thoughts occupying my mind moments ago had now taken a back seat. With a mixture of worry and concern, I turned to the guard, ready to hear the news he had to share.

The guard wasted no time in emphasizing the seriousness of the situation. "Princess Arabella," he started, "I'm sorry for disturbing your thoughts, but there's important information regarding Sir Gregory."

My mind filled with anxiety. Sir Gregory's condition had been very precarious, and any update was of utmost importance. I steeled myself, prepared to face whatever recent developments had arisen.

The guard continued, his words carrying a significant weight. "I've been instructed to bring you back to the healing area. There have been recent changes in Sir Gregory's condition, and it's essential that you return."

My heart felt heavy, torn between my desire for solitude and the responsibilities that came with being a princess. After taking a deep breath, I regained my composure and nodded in acknowledgment. "Thank you for informing me," I replied. "Lead the way back to the healing area. I'll address this matter right away."

*Chapter 25 The Gem Golem*

As we ventured deeper into the cave, darkness enveloped our surroundings, making it difficult to see. In anticipation of this, we had prepared makeshift torches using flint and steel before entering, casting a flickering glow that danced against the cave walls. With our weapons ready, we braced ourselves for the unknown that lay ahead.

"This cave was not marked on the map the cartographers provided," I said.

Lucas, seasoned in the mysteries of the Eldoria Forest, responded, "That's part of the allure of this forest. It conceals hidden caves, secret passages known only to a few."

I nodded, acknowledging the ever-shifting nature of this enchanted forest. Retrieving the map, I marked the location of the discovered cave, ensuring it would be added to our knowledge for future reference. The mystery of Aria's presence in this cave continued to perplex me, but I was determined to unravel the enigma that surrounded her sudden disappearance.

Ethan, who voiced his thoughts. "I can't comprehend why or how Aria ended up in this cave. There were no signs of struggle or any sign that she was taken forcefully."

"You're right. Aria knew we were regrouping and about to set off on our journey. It's unsettling to think about what could have led her here, leaving no trace. Well, we'll figure all of that out later. For now, let's just keep pressing forward to find her. It appears Shadowfang still has a decent scent and is pressing forward on her trail."

As we ventured deeper into the cave, the path became labyrinthine, with many twists and turns leading in different directions.

Ethan's sudden remark broke the eerie silence. "Do you smell that? It's as if something was burned."

We paused, inhaling the acrid scent that permeated the air. Our eyes scanned the surroundings, and then our attention was drawn to a charred object nestled against the cave wall.

Lucas approached the object and inspected it. "Looks like that may be the remains of a Lumiguan," he said.

"A Lumiguan? What is a Lumiguan?" I inquired.

"A Lumiguan is a small lizard-like creature that dwells in caves. It possesses a remarkable ability to emit a soft, luminescent glow. However, when it feels threatened, it can unleash a fierce attack," Lucas stated as he pointed at the burnt remains. "Something encountered this Lumiguan and set it ablaze."

"Well, maybe we are still currently on the correct path. Who do we know can do something of this nature?"

As we continued our descent down the winding path, our eyes scanned the surroundings, and our attention was drawn to a few more burned animals scattered along the way. Each charred creature served as a macabre confirmation that we remained on the right track within the intricate labyrinth of tunnels.

Our journey persisted and a faint glow emerged in the distance, casting an ethereal light upon the cave walls. Our movements became more cautious, our steps measured and silent, as we approached the source of the illumination. As we drew nearer, the glow intensified, revealing a breathtaking sight. The cavern was adorned with luminescent stones, their inherent radiance casting a mesmerizing luminescence that permeated the space. The stones illuminated the cave, providing us with much-needed visibility in the otherwise dark and treacherous environment.

"I wonder if these stones only glow in this cavern or if their luminescence extends to other places."

Lucas, drawing from his knowledge passed down through the generations, replied, "I do not know for certain. The stories and rumors I've heard from the elders mention a place called the Glimmering Caverns. It is said to be like this, adorned with walls of sparkling gems like amethysts, emeralds, sapphires, and other precious stones. However, finding the Glimmering Caverns has proved elusive for centuries."

"What tales surround the Glimmering Caverns?"

Lucas continued, "According to the elders, the Glimmering Caverns were once an adventurer's dream, but they were treacherous to navigate and filled with fierce creatures."

"With such valuable gemstones, one would assume that this place would have been marked on every map."

"The reason the entrance is not on any maps may be that the entrance consistently shifts, and the trails in Eldoria Forest always seem to shift," Lucas explained.

"I can follow that logic," I responded. "If the entrance to the cave shifts, then it would be quite difficult to accurately mark its location on a map. That explains why no one has found it for centuries."

Seizing an opportunity, I reached down and picked up one of the luminescent stones, carefully placing it in my bag. The stone's ethereal glow illuminated my surroundings, offering a source of light that could prove invaluable in our quest through the dark and treacherous cave.

"We can examine this later to determine if its luminescence is exclusive to this cavern or if it maintains its radiance beyond these walls."

As we ventured deeper into the caves, the luminescent walls grew brighter, casting an ethereal glow on our surroundings.

"It's quiet in here," Ethan remarked. "Considering the trail of burned creatures we've encountered; I would have expected more signs of life, or at least some unsettling noises."

"We've been walking for what feels like hours through these winding passages. I can't shake this feeling of being lost in a labyrinth," said Lucas.

"We'll find our way out of this maze once we locate Aria. But before that, we must uncover the truth behind her disappearance and determine where she has gone," I said.

We pressed on, our resolve unyielding, as we searched for any signs that would lead us to Aria's whereabouts and guide us out of the labyrinth of caves. With every step forward, our hearts remained steadfast, driven by the shared determination to find our missing companion and unravel the mysteries concealed within the depths of this subterranean realm.

As we continued pressing forward in the cavern, a palpable sense of unease filled the air. Whisperwind, our trusty companion, emitted low, guttural growls, a familiar warning sign that danger lurked nearby. Our instincts, sharpened by past encounters, kicked in, and everyone came to a sudden halt, their senses attuned to the surroundings.

"Can anyone glimpse what lies ahead?"

Ethan, straining his eyes in the dimly lit surroundings, responded, "I can't see anything beyond these luminescent walls on either side of us."

Recognizing the urgency of the situation, I took it upon myself to venture ahead, determined to uncover the mystery that lay in our path. With measured steps, I moved, prepared to confront whatever awaited us in the shadows of the cavern.

My senses heightened as I inched closer to the source of the looming threat. Gradually, the faint grumbles grew louder, resonating through the cavern walls. The deep, reverberating sound hinted at a colossal presence, yet my eyes had not yet laid sight upon it. Guided by curiosity and a dash of trepidation, I continued my stealthy approach, each step a deliberate effort to unravel the enigma before me.

As I neared a large rock formation, I seized the opportunity to peer around its protective embrace. And there, my gaze fell upon a sight that left me awestruck. The creature that stood before me was immense, an embodiment of resplendent gemstones that shimmered and glimmered with ethereal light. Its sheer size spoke of tremendous strength and posed a formidable challenge for our group.

However, amidst the grandeur of the gemstone creature, my attention was drawn to a corner of the chamber where Aria lay motionless. Concern gripped my heart as I pondered her condition, uncertain if she still clung to life. With the urgency of my discovery weighing upon me, I knew that my primary responsibility was to return to the group and relay the information I had gathered.

Stepping back, I retraced my steps, mindful not to disturb the tranquility of the chamber any further. The weight of my observations burdened my thoughts, compelling me to hasten back to my comrades and share the perilous truth that awaited them.

"I found Aria, but she's lying motionless in a corner," I explained upon my return. "Unfortunately, there's a massive creature in the same area."

Lucas recognized the description. "Sounds like a Golem, most of them are made of stone."

"Does anyone have a plan to deal with this creature?"

"Golems could be overcome with blunt force," said Lucas.

"We can't just leave her behind, even if she's no longer with us."

"Well, I guess we can 'Boudreaux it'," I said, causing confusion among his companions.

"What do you mean by 'Boudreaux it," Ethan asked.

"You know, when people do something reckless with enthusiasm and gusto. Boudreaux it."

"Alright, let's Boudreaux it!" Ethan responded.

"That's the spirit," he encouraged, his voice filled with determination.

I turned to Lucas, urging him to join in. "Come on, Lucas, you can do it."

Lucas took a deep breath, mustering his resolve. "Let's Boudreaux it," he said, perhaps lacking the same level of enthusiasm, but ready to face the challenge, nonetheless.

We prepared ourselves, weapons at the ready, and charged towards the fearsome beast.

I reached the Golem first, deflecting its powerful sword strikes. Ethan unleashed a volley of arrows, each finding its mark and causing the creature to stagger. Lucas positioned himself on the other side of the beast, slashing and striking with precision.

However, despite our bravery and skill, the formidable Golem remained impervious to my and Lucas' swords, as well as Ethan's arrows. Our relentless assault only seemed to enrage the creature further, driving it into a frenzy. The Golem retaliated with a swift and powerful swing of its right arm, slamming me against the cavern wall, leaving me stunned.

Turning its attention to Lucas, the Golem seized him with both hands, tossing him like a lifeless doll against the wall. The impact rendered Lucas unconscious, lying motionless on the ground. With two of our companions incapacitated, the Golem, now free from our attacks, set its sights on Ethan.

Determined to continue the fight, Ethan unleashed a final barrage of arrows, pouring all his strength into each shot. But to his dismay, the Golem's gem-like exterior proved impenetrable. Undeterred, Ethan maintained his assault, hoping to buy me and Lucas some time to recover.

Shaking off the impact, I regained my footing and lunged at the Golem from behind. My sword struck the creature's back, but the Golem whirled around, delivering a devastating blow that sent me crashing into another wall.

As Lucas remained unconscious and I struggled to recover, Ethan stood alone against the advancing Golem. The massive creature, its presence dominating the cavern, moved closer with each calculated step, its gem-like exterior gleaming with an ominous glow.

Despite the gravity of the situation, Ethan summoned every ounce of strength and resolve within him. Undeterred by the overwhelming odds, he launched himself at the Golem with unwavering determination. Each strike he delivered was a testament to his exceptional skill and the desperation that fueled his actions.

However, just as the battle seemed to reach a tipping point, Shadowfang, Arabella's faithful companion, leaped forward, teeth bared, aiming to sink his fangs into the Golem's impenetrable exterior. Alas, even the wolf's valiant effort proved fruitless, as the Golem remained impervious to his attack.

In a swift and merciless countermove, the Golem seized Ethan, its colossal strength overpowering him. With a brutal force, it slammed his head against the unyielding wall, causing his consciousness to fade away as darkness enveloped his senses.

Realizing the futility of my sword and shield against the mighty Golem, my mind raced, seeking a glimmer of hope amidst the chaos. My eyes darted around the surroundings, searching for any sign of salvation from this formidable adversary.

The Golem, sensing my movement, turned its colossal form towards me, closing in with measured steps. I knew I stood no chance against the overwhelming strength of the Golem. But I refused to succumb to despair. Determined to find a way, I continued to scour my immediate surroundings, grasping for a solution to turn the tides of this perilous encounter.

In my frantic search, my gaze fell upon my bag. With a spark of realization, my eyes locked onto a small vial nestled amidst my belongings. Its radiant blue hue shimmered like the luminescent stones that adorned the cave walls.

In a moment of desperation, I uncorked the vial, my mind resolved and my determination unyielding. With a fleeting thought that echoed our earlier reckless resolve, "We're going to Boudreaux it," I raised the vial to my lips and swallowed the luminous blue liquid in one swift motion.

Instantly, a remarkable transformation swept through my body. The ancient markings etched upon my leg, remnants of my encounter with the creature on the shoreline, blazed to life with a radiant glow. The once faint symbols now glimmered with clarity, as if imbued with an otherworldly power.

An electrifying surge coursed through my veins, awakening dormant strength and resolve. The mystical properties of the potion had tapped into an ancient energy, resonating deep within my very being. Empowered by this newfound might, I stood ready to confront the towering Golem that loomed before me.

As my gaze shifted, my attention was drawn to the dagger markings and gems that adorned my surroundings. In a moment of intuition, I realized that the very essence flowing through my veins had ignited a connection to these ancient artifacts. Without hesitation, I seized the nearby ancient dagger, my fingers wrapping around its hilt.

As if guided by an unseen force, I braced myself for the impending strike of the Golem's mighty arm. With lightning speed and unwavering precision, I thrust the ancient dagger upward, its keen edge meeting the Golem's descending limb.

To my astonishment, the blade sliced through the Golem's arm with astonishing ease, as though cutting through warm butter. The air filled with a resounding clash of metal against gemstone, echoing through the cavernous chamber. A spray of fractured gem shards scattered into the air as the Golem recoiled in pain and surprise.

With each strike, I could feel the power coursing through me, fueling my every move. Seizing the opportunity as the Golem staggered back, I rose to my feet, my determination unyielding. Closing the distance between us, I lunged forward with unbridled intensity.

In a display of remarkable agility and precision, I swung the ancient dagger with unmatched finesse, cleaving through the Golem's remaining arm. The clash of metal against gemstone resounded through the chamber, mingling with the Golem's anguished roar. As the arm disintegrated into a shower of fractured shards, the Golem writhed in pain, its majestic form now marred by the ravages of battle.

Summoning my last reserves of energy, I gathered all my might for one last strike. With a surge of unwavering determination, I drove the ancient dagger deep into the Golem's heart, piercing through the gem-like exterior. The chamber trembled as the Golem's essence quivered, teetering on the edge of annihilation.

In a resounding crescendo, the Golem shattered into thousands of glittering gem shards, cascading through the air like a luminous storm. The chamber was engulfed in a dazzling spectacle of refracted light, illuminating my triumphant figure amidst the fragments of my vanquished foe.

Breathing heavily, I stood amidst the aftermath of the battle, my body pulsating with the echoes of my formidable feat. The threat of the Golem had been vanquished, its presence reduced to a scattered tapestry of radiant gemstones.

## Chapter 26 The Hidden Message

With the Golem's shattered remains scattered across the chamber, I wasted no time in rushing to Aria's side. Relief washed over me as I discovered she was still breathing, her unconscious state a testament to the ferocity of our encounter. "She's just knocked out, like the rest of us when facing that monstrous Golem," I remarked, a mix of concern and reassurance in my voice.

Assured of Aria's stability, I turned my attention to my fallen comrades, Lucas and Ethan. With steady hands and a sense of urgency, I tended to their wounds, applying bandages to aid in their healing. The two sustained some deep cuts from the encounter, but nothing too life-threatening. The camaraderie shared among us was palpable, even in our silent vulnerability.

Shadowfang and Whisperwind, ever the resilient companions, remained unscathed by the battle's aftermath. I met the loyal eyes of Shadowfang, and I couldn't help but offer a wry smile, acknowledging the wolf's steadfastness even in the face of such perilous encounters.

"That was quite a tough battle we faced."

As I surveyed the chamber, my mind replayed the harrowing moments we had just endured. The Golem's formidable strength and unyielding defense had tested our limits, pushing us to the brink of our capabilities. It was a battle we had emerged from, scarred but victorious. The sense of camaraderie and triumph filled my heart, knowing that we had overcome a tremendous challenge together, and it strengthened our resolve to face whatever lay ahead in this enigmatic realm.

As I caught my breath, my thoughts turned to the future, to a time when we could leave such formidable foes behind. "May we never have to face another creature like that," I spoke aloud, the weight of my words resonating through the chamber. In the quiet aftermath, I couldn't help but feel a renewed sense of unity and gratitude for my companions. We had overcome tremendous odds, standing together in the face of danger. Their unwavering support and camaraderie had made all the difference in our victory. With this shared strength, I knew we could face any challenge that lay ahead in this realm.

Aria came around first. "What happened?", she asked. "All I remember is getting drawn into this cave by some force, and then I ran into this rather enormous creature made of gems," Aria stated.

"Yes, Lucas identified it as a Golem, unknown if he still stands by that answer, after now seeing and getting beat up by the thing," I replied.

"What happened to the creature?" asked Aria.

"The creature has been eliminated."

"How? I threw all the magic I had at the thing and nothing phased it," remarked Aria.

"I must have found a weak point on the creature and got a lucky strike", I replied, not wanting them to know that I had taken the potion.

Deep down, I felt a sense of uncertainty. The effects of the potion I had ingested still lingered within me, its true nature and consequences yet to be understood. As I weighed the ramifications, I kept this information to myself for now, not wishing to add any unnecessary worry or speculation to our already burdensome journey. Our focus needed to remain on finding a way out of this labyrinth and reuniting with the rest of the team. There would be time for reflection and understanding once we were back in the embrace of daylight.

As Aria and I engaged in conversation, our focus was interrupted by the returning awareness of Lucas. Regaining his senses, his voice cut through the air, filled with confusion and concern.

"What happened?" Lucas inquired.

I took a moment to gather my thoughts, considering how best to summarize our encounter with the formidable Golem. "We faced a formidable creature, my friend. It dealt us a severe beating, throwing us against the walls with substantial force."

Lucas's eyes widened, recalling the brute strength of the Golem. "But where did it go?" he pressed, searching for answers in the aftermath.

"It shattered into thousands of gem shards," I explained, gesturing to the scattered remnants of our vanquished foe.

As we gathered our composure, I shared my decision to keep the nature of the potion to myself for now, not wanting to add any unnecessary worry to our already burdensome journey. The battle had left us with scars, both visible and hidden, yet our unity and resilience remained unshaken.

Lucas's confusion only deepened. "But... how? I witnessed the Golem hurling you against the wall."

Sensing the need for a simple explanation, I repeated the same vague account I had shared with Aria, omitting the details of my potion-induced surge of strength.

"Well, sometimes fortune smiles upon us amid battle," I replied with a shrug. "I found an opening and struck a decisive blow. It was a stroke of luck, I suppose."

As the conversation unfolded, Ethan regained consciousness. "Why does my head feel like I've immersed it in a wine barrel overnight?"

Anticipating Ethan's inquiries, I spared him the trouble of seeking answers by providing a condensed version of our recent exploits. I addressed his potential questions with practiced ease, leaving no room for further probing.

As we sat together, a sense of shared astonishment enveloped us, our minds swirling with the magnitude of what we had just experienced. The air crackled with a mixture of disbelief and wonder as we contemplated the extraordinary events that had unfolded within the depths of the cavern. The weight of our encounter lingered, and the experience had left an indelible mark on each of us.

"As much as I enjoy discussing formidable creatures, let's stay focused on our mission to retrieve the plant," I interjected, steering the conversation back to our primary objective. "We're disoriented, and our exact location and time elude us," I added, emphasizing the urgency of our situation.

Scanning the group, I gauged their readiness to press forward. "Is everyone capable of continuing our journey, at least to make our way out of this cave?"

Each member affirmed their readiness with a resounding yes, though I knew they harbored a silent hope that we wouldn't encounter any more daunting creatures on our path to exit the cavern.

"Before we depart, let's take a few moments to gather some of these gemstones," Ethan suggested. "After the beating we've endured, it's only fair to reap a small reward for our efforts before we resume our journey," he reasoned. The idea appealed to us all, and we began collecting a few of the radiant gemstones as souvenirs, a reminder of the formidable Golem we had faced and the triumph that followed.

Agreeing with Ethan's suggestion, we dispersed, each of us handpicking the larger gemstones scattered across the cavern floor. Our hands worked, filling our pockets and pouches with the shimmering remnants of the defeated Golem. The gems, though valuable, also served as tangible reminders of our hard-fought victory.

As we gathered our belongings and prepared to navigate our way through the labyrinthine tunnels, my eyes caught sight of mysterious writing etched onto the wall. Intrigued, I caught the attention of my companions. "Does anyone know what this writing means?" I inquired, pointing to the inscription.

Confusion clouded the faces of Ethan, Lucas, and Aria as they stared at the blank wall.

"What writing? I see nothing," Ethan remarked, voicing the sentiments of the others.

My brow furrowed in puzzlement. "Are you telling me that none of you can see this right here?" I questioned, pointing at the wall.

The response from my friends was unanimous—they saw nothing but mere marks on the stone surface. Lucas couldn't resist a playful jab.

"Did you hit your head harder than we thought, Valaric? There's nothing there," he quipped. Doubt crept into my mind. Perhaps the battle had taken a greater toll on me than I realized.

However, I knew I wasn't mistaken. My eyes were drawn to the clear, legible words before me. The inscription read, "Victor of Glimmering Caverns possesses mystical abilities within the caverns." Uncertain of its significance and why I alone could perceive it, I kept the discovery to myself for the time being. The message held a secret meant only for me, and I felt compelled to uncover its true meaning before sharing it with the group.

The team embarked on the journey through the enchanting luminescent caverns, with Whisperwind leading the way, followed by myself, Aria, Ethan, Lucas, and Shadowfang guarding our rear. As we ventured deeper into the twisting passages, small creatures scurried about, catching our attention. Aria, showcasing her command over fire, dispatched the critters, leaving nothing but smoldering remnants in their wake.

Although our progress wasn't rapid, we continued to press onward, determined to reach the cave's exit and salvage what remained of the day. Each member of the group understood the implications of this detour—their mission to get the crucial plant for Sir Gregory was being delayed once again. We persevered, aware of the importance of our goal.

With every step, our anticipation grew as we neared the end of the labyrinthine caverns. The sight of daylight filtering through the last stretch of the tunnel filled us with a renewed sense of joy and relief. The prospect of resuming our original path and getting back on track fueled our excitement.

"Finally, it seems we've reached the end of this maze," I exclaimed. Eager to step out of the caverns and resume our journey, we made our way towards the exit.

As we emerged from the depths of the caverns, a collective realization washed over us. The surroundings were unfamiliar, devoid of any recognizable landmarks or features. Ethan was the first to voice his confusion.

"This isn't where we entered the caverns."

Lucas, having experienced the shifting nature of the caverns, responded with a knowing tone, "The caverns are known for their constant shifting, which is why they've remained uncharted and hidden for centuries."

The group exchanged bewildered glances, trying to make sense of our current predicament. Aria's voice carried a hint of perplexity as she asked, "If we're not where we were before, then where exactly are we?"

Retrieving my map of the Eldoria Forest, I hoped to gain some clarity in our current location. As the group observed our surroundings, I examined the map, searching for familiar landmarks.

It was Lucas who, with a spark of recognition, revealed our position.

"We're at the beginning of Serpents Pass," Lucas declared.

Puzzled, I inquired, "How do you know?"

"I've been here before, on one of my previous expeditions," Lucas explained.

I studied the map, attempting to reconcile our unexpected arrival with our intended destination. "We find ourselves where we would have been if we had left from our original location this morning," I observed, trying to make sense of the situation.

Aria, still perplexed by the unlikely coincidence, questioned, "How is that possible?"

"I suppose, as Lucas suggested, the caverns have a tendency to shift, and by sheer chance, we've ended up in the right place," I speculated. The events left a lingering sense of wonder in the air. Could it be mere luck, or did the cryptic inscription on the cavern wall hold some hidden significance?

"Considering the time, it's too late to begin the ascent up the mountain pass. We might as well set up camp here for the night," I suggested, considering the fading daylight.

Lucas nodded in agreement, adding, "We should be able to reach the plant location and make it back down within a day once we start tomorrow."

With the decision made, the team prepared to settle in for the night. Exhausted from our eventful day in the Glimmering Caverns, we welcomed the opportunity to rest and recharge. We knew that tomorrow's journey would present its own set of challenges, as the location of the plant we sought was difficult to reach.

*Chapter 27 Serpents Pass*

The following morning arrived with a renewed sense of purpose and determination. We rose early, eager to begin our ascent up the formidable Serpent's Pass and complete our mission before nightfall. I was aware of the challenges that lay ahead and sought Lucas's insights on the treacherous trail.

"Tell us more about Serpent's Pass, Lucas," I inquired.

Lucas took a deep breath, preparing to shed light on the daunting path that awaited us. "Well, let me paint you a picture," he began. "Serpent's Pass is not for the faint of heart. It's a narrow and winding trail that weaves its way through the rugged peaks of the surrounding mountains. Its name comes from the serpentine twists and turns that resemble the sinuous motion of a snake."

"The pass is flanked by steep cliffs and precipitous drops on either side, posing a constant threat to anyone who ventures upon it. There will be moments where we must navigate treacherous sections with little margin for error. Nature has thrown in its own challenges, such as fallen rocks, fallen trees, and other obstacles that we'll need to overcome." His words resonated with the gravity of the task that lay ahead, reminding us of the perilous journey that awaited us on Serpent's Pass.

"Sounds like a fun and interesting little stroll we have ahead of us," I remarked.

The team shared a brief chuckle, knowing that humor could be their ally in facing the arduous trials that awaited them on Serpent's Pass.

"In terms of creatures, there are a few we should be wary of?"

"I've come across a few formidable creatures in my previous expeditions through these mountains," Lucas responded. "First, there are the Serpentkins, venomous snakes that inhabit these parts. Their bites can be quite dangerous if not treated promptly because of the venom they inject in their victims. We'll need to keep an eye out for them and exercise caution."

Lucas continued; his voice filled with caution. "Then there are the Winged Harpies. These fearsome avian creatures possess razor-sharp talons and emit piercing cries. They swoop down from the skies, attacking with precision. We must be prepared for attacks from above."

"Last, but certainly not least, the Rock Golems," Lucas said. "The Rock Golems are like the Gem Golem but are made of rock. They didn't seem as tough as the Gem Golem, but still very formidable."

I listened, noting the potential threats that lay in wait. "So, attacks from above, below, and even in front of us with those Rock Golems similar to the one we encountered in the Glimmering Cavern."

"Well, I guess there's no better time than the present to embark on our adventure. Is everyone ready to go?" I asked.

Aria, displaying her unwavering resolve, expressed her readiness to embark on the challenging journey. "I'm ready whenever you are," she stated. Ethan echoed her sentiment, assuring the group that he was prepared for whatever lay ahead. Lucas, though reserved, voiced his agreement, signaling his readiness to face the perils of Serpent's Pass.

"Perhaps we should adjust our formation this morning, allowing Lucas to take the lead. His experience with Serpent's Pass will be invaluable to us," I suggested.

Lucas welcomed the idea, acknowledging the advantage his knowledge could bring to their expedition.

With the new formation in place, Lucas stepped forward, assuming the role of the trailblazer. Ethan followed behind, ready to support Lucas and navigate the challenges that awaited them. Aria, Shadowfang and I formed the middle. Our collective focus sharpened as we advanced through the twisting path. I kept Whisperwind stowed in my bag, recognizing the difficulty the terrain presented for the small creature.

As we emerged from the embrace of the forest, an intriguing sight greeted our eyes—the entrance to the Glimmering Caverns stood before us, unchanged from where we had left it the day prior. The significance of this discovery was not lost on me. The Eldoria Forest was notorious for its unpredictable nature, with pathways shifting like sand in the wind. Yet, there it was, the entrance, a beacon of familiarity amidst the ever-changing landscape.

Without hesitation, I retrieved my trusty map and marked the location of the cavern's entrance. This marked spot would serve as a vital anchor, ensuring we wouldn't lose track of the Glimmering Caverns and their mysteries in the future. Its location on the map symbolized the beginning of our exploration and the potential for extraordinary discoveries within the cavern's depths.

"I can't help but wonder if our presence somehow disrupted the usual movement of the caverns," I pondered aloud.

"It's hard to say for certain, but it's worth noting if the entrance remains fixed when we return," said Ethan.

I nodded in agreement, acknowledging the practicality of monitoring the cavern's stability. "You're right," I affirmed, "keeping track of any changes will be essential for our future endeavors."

With their observations noted, we shifted our focus back to the task at hand. "Well, time's wasting. Let's press forward, retrieve what we came for, and make our descent."

With determination in our hearts, we embarked on our arduous ascent through Serpent's Pass, our sights set on retrieving the precious plant that held the potential to aid Sir Gregory. Aware of the challenge that lay before us, we summoned our collective strength and resilience, ready to conquer the mountain and return before darkness enveloped the land.

The initial part of our journey proved manageable, with a moderate incline that tested our endurance but did not deter our resolve. However, we understood that the genuine test awaited us as we ventured deeper into the pass, where the path would become more treacherous.

"How frequently do you find yourself in these parts, Lucas?" I asked.

Lucas replied with a hint of familiarity in his voice, "I've traversed this pass a few times, as it's often considered the most viable route to navigate through the mountain and reach the other side of Eldoria Forest."

"What lies beyond the mountain range? Is it just an extension of the forest?"

Lucas responded with a light chuckle, "Indeed, it's the continuation of the forest on the other side. However, accessing that area poses its own set of challenges, which is why it remains less explored compared to this side."

"So, despite some having ventured there, there's a high likelihood of unexplored wilderness?"

"That is indeed a possibility," Lucas confirmed.

"Once we accomplish our current task, it might be worth venturing to the other side to uncover the mysteries that lie beyond."

Aria's eyes sparkled with intrigue as she responded, "That sounds like an enticing prospect. It would offer a welcome change from our daily routines, and I've noticed significant growth in my skills just throughout this journey alone."

Ethan nodded in agreement; his mind captivated by the potential for further discoveries. "Indeed, there may be even more hidden treasures awaiting us, similar to the gems we got after our triumphant encounter with the Golem in the cavern."

As we walked, our imaginations soared, envisioning the unexplored landscapes and the secrets that lay beyond the mountain range. I found solace in the notion that our journey did not have to end with the completion of our current task—there was a vast world waiting to be discovered, brimming with new challenges, treasures, and experiences.

Just as we were about to delve further into our conversation about future adventures, a distinct noise resonated from Whisperwind. My expression shifted, recognizing the significance of the sound. "Ah, that can only mean one thing," I remarked, my voice filled with a mix of caution and anticipation.

"I have seen nothing yet," Lucas reported. The group readied their weapons, preparing for whatever awaited them on their path.

Adjusting the formation, I positioned myself in front of Lucas. Considering the best strategy to protect Aria and Ethan, who could attack from a distance, I decided that Lucas and I would handle anything that got too close.

As we advanced, we spotted six Serpentkins basking in the sun, blocking our path.

"No way to sneak past them; they've got us cornered," Lucas pointed out.

"Well, they haven't noticed us yet, so let's plan."

We discussed our approach, devising a strategy to deal with the Serpentkins.

"Alright, on my signal, let's launch our attack," I commanded.

We prepared themselves, ready to face the menacing Serpentkins head-on.

I counted down, my voice steady. "Three, two, one," I announced, starting our coordinated assault.

In perfect synchrony, Ethan released a well-aimed arrow, while Aria conjured a powerful lightning attack aimed at the nearest Serpentkin. The unexpected strike caught the creatures off guard, causing them to writhe in pain and confusion.

Before those two Serpentkins could figure out what happened, they were hit again by another arrow and lightning strike. This tactic eliminated the first two Serpentkins. Before the rest of the Serpentkins could figure out what happened, Ethan and Aria struck the next closest two Serpentkins.

Although the initial strike didn't eliminate the Serpentkins, it dealt damage, weakening their defenses. This provided an opening for Lucas and I, too engage in close combat. With our swords at the ready and shields raised, we closed in on the first two Serpentkins, aiming to sever their heads from their bodies.

Meanwhile, Aria and Ethan prepared for another round of attacks, ready to unleash their skills once more. However, as Ethan released his arrow, one of the Serpentkins advanced, causing the projectile to veer off course and miss its intended target. Now, four resilient Serpentkins were closing in on the group, their venomous fangs gleaming in the dim light.

As the closest Serpentkin lunged at me, I raised my shield to parry its ferocious strike. The force of the impact sent a jolt through my arm, revealing the true strength of these formidable adversaries. "These creatures pack quite a punch," I grunted, determined to press on despite the challenge they posed.

"Watch out for their venomous bites! We don't want anyone getting poisoned," Lucas stated.

I took heed of Lucas's warning, understanding the threat posed by the Serpentkins' deadly fangs. As Lucas and I fought to fend off the relentless creatures, Aria and Ethan used their ranged attacks to chip away at the adversaries from a distance. Ethan's precise shot landed in the eye of one Serpentkin, while Aria's lightning sent another into a writhing frenzy. The combined efforts of the team proved effective against these reptilian foes.

Amidst the chaos of battle, Lucas and I found ourselves locked in a fierce struggle with the Serpentkins. However, in the heat of the fight, one of the Serpentkins grabbed hold of my leg, pulling me with force. Panic and urgency filled my voice as I cried out for help, signaling that the creature was dragging me away. Reacting, Ethan launched a flurry of arrows towards the Serpentkin, attempting to free me from its grip. However, he had to hold back his assault as Lucas rushed to my aid, ensuring he didn't harm me.

In a frantic struggle, I swung my weapon at the Serpentkin, attempting to free myself, but the awkward position hindered my leverage and effectiveness. Just as the situation seemed dire, Lucas sprang into action, seizing the opportunity and delivering a decisive blow. With a fierce attack, he severed the end of the Serpentkin's tail that had gripped my leg.

"Thank the heavens," I exhaled with relief, my voice. "Now, someone help me get this thing off," I called out, my determination undiminished.

Lucas and I were freed from the clutches of the Serpentkin, and Aria and Ethan turned their focus towards the remaining assailants. Their combined onslaught proved too much for the Serpentkin to handle, as a barrage of attacks extinguished its existence.

Now, with only two Serpentkins remaining, the odds tilted in our favor. Lucas and I, fortified by our shields and armed with our swords, stood firm, holding the Serpentkins at bay. Ethan and Aria, unleashing a flurry of arrows and lightning bolts, provided relentless support from a distance. As the battle raged on, our coordination and unwavering determination proved to be a formidable force.

With our combined efforts, we triumphed over the remaining Serpentkins, albeit not without a few scrapes and bruises. I, in particular, withstood the injuries, my resilience clear despite the pain I endured. Despite the challenges we faced, our resilience and unity had prevailed once again.

"Indeed, the challenges of Serpent's Pass serve as a natural deterrent, preventing easy exploration of the other side of the mountain range," I acknowledged, wincing as Aria and Whisperwind began tending to my wounds, their healing abilities bringing me relief.

Lucas nodded in agreement, understanding the gravity of the situation. "It's not just the physical obstacles, but also the unknown dangers that await on the other side. It's a treacherous path that demands resilience and caution."

As we took a moment to recover and regain our breath, I couldn't help but feel a pang of wounded pride. Being carried off like a rag doll had bruised my ego more than my body. Fortunately, our injuries were superficial, mere bumps and bruises that would heal with time and rest.

Now that everyone had been tended to and preparations were made, we forged ahead on our trek through Serpent's Pass. I couldn't help but express my dislike of snakes. "I hope we encounter no more of those. Snakes have never been my favorite creatures," I admitted.

Ethan chimed in, reflecting on our recent encounter. "They were larger than I had imagined when Lucas described them to us," he remarked.

"Well, it wouldn't have been as exciting if I had given away all the details beforehand," Lucas responded with a mischievous grin.

"I never imagined they would be capable of pulling a grown man around by the leg. That was quite a surprise."

We shared a hearty laugh, finding humor in the unexpected turn of events. The camaraderie among us grew stronger with each challenge we faced together.

"Does anyone know how much further the cliffs are from here?" Aria inquired, looking ahead.

Lucas pointed in a specific direction and replied, "The cliffs are over in that direction, but this is where the trek becomes more challenging. The paths become treacherous, filled with obstacles."

"That's what makes this plant so special. Its rarity and the difficulty of obtaining it add to its value," Aria remarked.

"I wonder why no one has ever attempted to bring a part of the plant back and cultivate it in the kingdom."

Aria offered her understanding on the matter. "I have attempted it in the past, but it seems there is something about this location and altitude that allows the plant to flourish. It requires the specific conditions found here."

I furrowed my brow, intrigued by the plant's adaptability. "It's fascinating how an environment that appears more challenging can actually provide the ideal conditions for growth," I mused.

As our team forged ahead, we found ourselves in a perilous stretch of the journey, where a single misstep could spell disaster for any individual. The rocky terrain grew treacherous, testing our agility and balance. We had to rely on one another, offering helping hands and guidance to navigate around daunting obstacles.

Every member of our team, except for Shadowfang, faced the challenges with a mix of determination and caution. Our footsteps were calculated, our movements deliberate as we maneuvered over the rugged terrain. The air was filled with focused energy as we aided one another, lending support and encouragement.

Meanwhile, Shadowfang, true to her lupine nature, leaped and bounded over the obstacles, displaying an astonishing grace and agility. Her wolf-like instincts guided her every movement, allowing her to navigate the terrain with apparent ease. The rest of us watched in awe and amusement, sharing a lighthearted laugh at Shadowfang's impressive display of natural prowess. Even in the face of danger, her presence brought a sense of comfort and camaraderie to the team as we continued to conquer the challenges together.

"The good news is, we have a little farther to go," Lucas announced. "The bad news is that the path ahead doesn't get any easier," he added.

I couldn't help but inject some sarcasm into the conversation. "Well, that's just fantastic," I remarked. "I was really hoping for a break in the relentless challenges we've faced on this journey." I paused for a moment before voicing my observation. "Does anyone else feel like this entire trip has been a nonstop struggle?"

I continued, sharing my perspective. "Back in my homeland, spending weeks in the woods would involve encountering nothing more than the usual woodland creatures. Even when we ventured out on adventures, we rarely encountered as many creatures as we have in just these three days," I reflected.

Ethan chimed in, offering his own insights. "While I don't venture too far from the Kingdom, I've witnessed my fair share of battles, even within its borders."

"As you venture deeper into uncharted territories, the likelihood of encountering creatures and challenges increases exponentially," Lucas explained.

"Based on what we've experienced, it's clear that an individual traveling alone would have little chance of successfully crossing Serpent's Pass to reach the other side of Eldoria Forest," I concluded.

Lucas nodded in agreement. "That pretty much sums it up."

We persevered, pushing through the treacherous path as we navigated over and under various obstacles. Every step was a test of our determination and physical agility. However, our shared goal and the urgency of our mission propelled us forward. As we conquered the last obstacle, our eyes were greeted with a breathtaking sight--the clearing of the cliff, where the sought-after plant awaited us, holding the key to saving Sir Gregory's life.

The sight that unfolded before us was awe-inspiring. The cliff's edge was adorned with a magnificent display of vibrant flora, a stunning array of colors that seemed to dance in the gentle breeze. It was a sight witnessed by anyone, a hidden gem reserved for those who dared to venture through the arduous path of Serpent's Pass.

"Wow," Aria whispered in awe.

"Indeed, this place is a true marvel. Few have the privilege of experiencing such natural wonders firsthand," I remarked, my voice filled with appreciation for the unique opportunity we had been granted.

"I can understand why Aria joined us on this quest. With so many plant species gathered in one place, it would be a daunting task for anyone to identify the right one," Ethan admitted.

"You're right, Ethan. We're fortunate to have Aria's knowledge and guidance in this endeavor," I acknowledged, grateful for her presence. "Why don't we take a moment to rest and replenish our energy? We can enjoy a well-deserved meal before retrieving the plant and making our way back down," I proposed.

"We mustn't linger for too long, though. The safety of this place is compromised by the creatures in Serpent's Pass," Lucas reminded us.

"You're right, Lucas. We'll take a brief respite, ensuring we're recharged, but we won't overstay our welcome."

After replenishing our energy with a quick meal, we took a moment to savor the majestic view that unfolded before us. Each member marveled at the enchanting beauty of the flora-filled clearing; a scene that seemed almost otherworldly.

While Aria admired the surrounding foliage, her keen eyes spotted the plant they had sent us to retrieve. With a determined expression, she plucked enough, ensuring we would have an ample supply for our mission and beyond.

"Take some of this plant with you," Aria suggested. "Let's each carry a portion, just in case. We'll ensure its safe arrival, regardless of any unforeseen circumstances. And having a surplus can be valuable for future needs as well," she explained as she distributed the plant among the team members.

Following Aria's guidance, we each placed our portion of the plant in our bags, securing it for the journey ahead. With our mission accomplished and the precious cargo safeguarded, we took one final lingering look at the picturesque site, cherishing the memory of the breathtaking scenery.

Bracing ourselves, we prepared to embark on the descent down Serpent's Pass once again. Determined and united, we set our gaze forward, ready to face the challenges that awaited us on our journey back. The trials we had conquered had only strengthened our bond, and as we navigated the treacherous path together, I knew we could overcome anything that lay ahead.

## *Chapter 28 The Tumble*

As we made our way down Serpent's Pass, following Lucas's lead, we retraced the treacherous path we had climbed. Ethan, Aria, Shadowfang, and I followed behind, navigating the rugged terrain.

"I have to admit, I thought coming down would be easier," Ethan confessed. "But this path seems just as demanding as when we ascended."

"It's surprising how the same obstacles that tested us on the way up continue to challenge us on the way down," Aria remarked. "I guess the mountain doesn't discriminate."

"Regardless of the difficulty, we have to keep pushing forward. We've come this far, and we can't let the descent discourage us," I added.

Shadowfang, our loyal companion, maneuvered through the rocky terrain, providing a sense of calm and reassurance to the group. Her presence served as a reminder that we were not alone on our journey.

"The view overlooking the cliffs, surrounded by such vibrant flora, was a sight to remember," Ethan said. "But let's be honest, it doesn't make this descent any more enjoyable."

As we descended further down Serpent's Pass, we engaged in lighthearted conversation and jokes to ease the strain of navigating the challenging terrain. The sound of laughter and friendly banter filled the air, providing a welcomed distraction from the physical discomfort we experienced along the way.

Through our conversations, we found solace in each other's company, forging stronger bonds as we shared stories, reminisced about past adventures, and exchanged humorous remarks. The camaraderie among us created a sense of unity and made the arduous journey a little more bearable.

Despite the physical demands and the delays we encountered, we maintained a positive outlook. We found comfort knowing that we had got the plant we needed, even if it meant being behind schedule. The satisfaction of accomplishing our goal fueled our determination to push through the remaining challenges.

Each of us carried a sense of pride and fulfillment. Our minds were filled with admiration for our collective achievement, knowing that we had overcome many obstacles and persevered in the face of adversity. This shared sense of accomplishment brought a renewed sense of purpose and motivation as we continued our descent.

Though our bodies endured pain and fatigue, our spirits remained uplifted by the bonds we had formed and the sense of progress we had made. With every step, we inched closer to the end of Serpent's Pass, guided by our unwavering determination and the support we found in one another.

"Once we're back, I'm going straight for a hot bath to wash off all this muck. It feels like we've been out here for ages, but it's only been a couple of days," Aria said.

"Absolutely," I replied, nodding in agreement. "This journey has been one of the most challenging experiences I've had in a long time. It's taken a toll on all of us."

As we continued along the pass, our fatigue clear in every step, a sudden scream from Ethan pierced the air. "Ah!" he yelled, the sound of panic and surprise echoing through the surroundings. The entire group froze in their tracks, our attention shifting to Ethan and the unexpected event that had just unfolded.

Scanning the ground beneath Ethan's feet, we searched for answers. It didn't take long for us to realize that the earth had given way beneath him, causing him to slide down into a crevice in the pass. Time seemed to stand still as a mix of concern, fear, and determination filled the air.

Lucas leaped into action, assessing the situation. "Ethan! Can you hear us?" he called out. "Stay calm and let us know if you're injured."

Aria, Shadowfang, and I, our hearts pounding, gathered around the edge of the crevice, trying to glimpse Ethan. The tension was palpable as we awaited his response, hoping he was unharmed and able to communicate.

Concerned for Ethan's well-being, I took charge of the situation. "We can't waste any more time. We need to get down there and find out if he's injured and how badly," I asserted.

The team retrieved the ropes from our packs and secured them to sturdy boulders, using them as anchors for our descent.

"Lucas and Shadowfang, stay up here and be ready to assist us," I instructed. "Aria, Whisperwind, and I will go down the ropes to assess the situation and provide aid if needed."

With Whisperwind nestled inside my bag, Aria and I descended the rope. The drop was not a Vertical descent, but more like a steep slide, making it impossible to climb back up without help.

As we made our way down, the darkness engulfed us, casting an eerie atmosphere. I called out Ethan's name, my voice echoing through the cavernous space, but there was no immediate response.

The silence was deafening, heightening my apprehension and sense of urgency. My heart pounded in my chest as we reached the lower area, our feet landing on the uneven ground. With cautious steps, we ventured deeper into the darkness, searching for any sign of Ethan.

My senses heightened, my eyes scanning the surroundings, straining to catch even the faintest sound. Aria held her breath, her focus sharpened as she listened. Whisperwind, too, perked up, his senses attuned to any potential danger lurking in the shadows.

After what felt like an eternity, a weak voice reached our ears.

"Valaric...I'm down here," Ethan called out.

"Shh, I think I heard something," I whispered.

Aria strained her ears, her senses heightened. And then we heard it.

"Valaric," came the voice from the depths of the crevice.

"I can hear him," Aria confirmed.

Determination surged through us both as we prepared to locate Ethan.

"It sounded like it came from that direction over there," I stated.

In a moment of realization, I remembered the luminescent stone I had placed in my bag, a precious memento from our previous adventure in the Glimmering Caverns. I rummaged through my bag, and to my relief, the stone was still glowing. "Well, it's not much light, but it's better than nothing," I said, holding up the stone to cast a dim glow around us. "Let's head in that direction and see if we can find him."

As we ventured toward the source of Ethan's voice, our eyes adjusted to the limited illumination provided by the glowing stone. Shadows danced around us, heightening our sense of unease.

With each step, the tension mounted, as if the very darkness around us held its breath. My grip tightened on my sword, ready for any potential threat that may emerge from the shadows. Aria followed, her instincts sharp and senses on high alert.

As we ventured deeper into the unknown, the faint sound of movement broke the silence—something stirring in the darkness. Aria and I exchanged wary glances, our hearts pounding in our chests. We were not alone.

As Aria and I navigated through the darkness, we pressed forward, our gazes fixed on the ground and surroundings. The feeble glow of the luminescent stone cast a dim light, allowing us to see two to three feet in front of us. Every step was taken with caution, our senses on high alert, knowing we were not alone in this treacherous place.

Our efforts were rewarded when Ethan's voice called out, a glimmer of hope cutting through the oppressive darkness.

"Hey, over here," he exclaimed.

My heart lifted as I caught sight of Ethan's form, illuminated by our meager light. "He's over here," I informed Aria.

As we reached Ethan's side, our attention turned to his well-being.

Are you hurt?" I asked.

Ethan winced; his voice strained. "Just my ankle. I tried to get up, but it's too painful to put weight on it."

Aria sprang into action, retrieving bandages from her pack. "Let's get you wrapped up and give your ankle a chance to heal."

I took a defensive stance, keeping a vigilant watch over our surroundings, my grip tightening on my weapon.

Whisperwind, ever attuned to our needs, emanated a soothing aura as he focused his healing abilities on Ethan's injured ankle. Gentle waves of warmth washed over him, easing his pain and promoting the healing process. We remained alert, knowing that our presence in the crevice had not gone unnoticed, ready to defend ourselves against any potential threat.

As Aria wrapped the bandages around Ethan's ankle, securing them in place, a sense of relief and gratitude washed over our team. Though we were still deep within the crevice, we had reunited with our fallen comrade, and now our focus turned to ensuring his mobility and our safe return to the surface.

"I sure wish we had more light in here, so we could see what else is around us," I murmured.

Ethan, ever resourceful, spoke up. "Here, there's a torch in my bag that we didn't use earlier."

Grateful for the solution, I retrieved the torch from Ethan's bag. With steady hands, I struck the flint against the steel, creating a shower of sparks that ignited the torch. Flames flickered to life, casting a warm glow that illuminated our surroundings, revealing the crevices and corners of our enclosed space. The torch's light brought a newfound sense of security, and we proceeded, feeling more at ease with the added visibility.

The increased light provided a sense of relief and security, allowing us to better assess our surroundings and detect any potential threats that might lurk nearby. My sharp eyes scanned the area, taking in the details, ready to react if needed.

As the torch bathed the crevice in its gentle radiance, I couldn't help but think of the luminescent stone I had used earlier. I realized its value in providing a soft, continuous glow that aided our navigation in the darkness.

"If we ever find the Glimmering Cavern again," I mused, "we need to collect a few more of these stones. They truly do help with our visibility."

Pausing for a moment, I pondered, a playful smile tugging at my lips. "Although," I continued, "maybe we can find ones that are a little bigger than this small thing. It wouldn't hurt to have even more light at our disposal." The idea of carrying larger luminescent stones sparked a lighthearted conversation among the team, easing the tension in our precarious situation.

As Aria and Whisperwind tended to Ethan's injured ankle, I surveyed our immediate surroundings. The torch's comforting glow provided some visibility, but its limited reach prevented me from discerning our location.

Gazing into the depths of the pass, my eyes strained to capture any details that might reveal our current position. It seemed we were within a hollowed-out section, a small pocket carved by nature's hand. The rough and jagged walls were clear evidence of the pass's treacherous nature, while the obscured ceiling loomed above.

My mind raced with questions about the implications of our surroundings. Was this hollowed-out section a natural occurrence, shaped by geological forces? Or perhaps it held the remnants of some long-forgotten event, a reminder of the pass's tumultuous history. Curiosity and caution blended within me as I pondered the mysteries of this confined space.

As Aria attended to Ethan's well-being, my attention was drawn to a mysterious object tucked away in the corner of our surroundings. It bore a resemblance to the luminescent rocks we had encountered before, but it was different—it was embedded in the wall, almost like a shelf, emitting an intriguing orange glow. My curiosity was piqued, but I also remained cautious, unsure of what this sight might entail.

"Almost finished here," Aria's voice brought me back to the present, and I felt relieved to hear that Ethan's ankle was bandaged and Whisperwind's healing powers had been effective. He seemed to recover well. I turned my focus back to Ethan, wanting to ensure his well-being before proceeding.

"How are you feeling, Ethan? Can you get up? We should make our way out of here once you're ready," I inquired.

Ethan nodded; a glimmer of recovery clear in his eyes. "I'm feeling better already. Just give me a few more minutes, and then I'll be good to go." His determination bolstered my own, and I couldn't help but feel optimistic about our chances of making it out of this crevice and back to the surface.

Satisfied with Ethan's response, my curiosity got the better of me, and I felt compelled to investigate the mysterious object I had glimpsed earlier. I positioned the luminescent stone near the group, casting a soft glow in the immediate vicinity, allowing us to see better.

"Before we leave, I want to take a quick look in that corner over there," I explained.

As I approached the corner of the area, my heart raced with a mix of excitement and caution. The mysterious object came into focus, revealing an astonishing sight—a large, magnificent egg nestled in a crafted nest. Its size was impressive, dwarfing any chicken or bird egg I had ever seen. The egg's surface shimmered with a vibrant reddish hue, resembling the flickering flames of a roaring fire. Intricate patterns adorned its shell, resembling swirling embers and molten lava.

The discovery of such an extraordinary egg left me awestruck, but my instincts kicked in. I turned my gaze, scanning the surroundings, understanding that where there's an egg, there's a creature responsible for its creation. The presence of the egg meant that its formidable parent may not be too far away. I couldn't shake the feeling that we were not alone, and we needed to remain cautious as we explored further.

Feeling a sense of urgency, I relayed the discovery and description of the egg to the rest of the group. Ethan's eyes widened as he processed the information.

"That sounds like a Fire Drake egg," Ethan remarked. "They are legendary creatures that haven't been seen for ages. This egg must have been here for a considerable amount of time."

Considering the egg's significance and potential scientific value, I proposed the idea of taking it with us for further investigation by the Elders.

"Perhaps the Elders can shed light on its origins and provide insight into the reappearance of Fire Drakes," I suggested.

Ethan nodded in agreement, recognizing the importance of preserving this rare specimen. "It's a good idea," Ethan affirmed. "We can present it to the Elders and let them decide how to handle this remarkable discovery."

My fingers explored the surface of the egg, searching for any signs of damage or openings. To my surprise, the egg remained intact, its smooth exterior not showing a recent hatching. The egg was as hard as a rock to the touch. What intrigued me even more was the warmth emanating from the shell, as if some hidden fire burned within. The enigma of the Fire Drake egg left us with a sense of wonder and excitement, but we remained cautious, knowing that the creature responsible for it might still be nearby.

I secured the remarkable egg in my bag, feeling the weight of responsibility and wonder with each step as I rejoined the rest of the group. We would soon depart from this strange hollow within the pass, but I remained vigilant, ever aware of my surroundings.

As I returned, my gaze remained watchful, open to any other discoveries that might captivate my attention. In the far corner, a peculiar crevice caught my eye, its mysterious allure beckoning me. The torch's flickering light struggled to penetrate the depths, leaving me with more questions than answers.

My heart pulsed with curiosity and caution, torn between the potential for an alternate route and the possibility of unforeseen dangers. The thrill of exploration tugged at my adventurous spirit, urging me to venture further into the unknown. Yet, I reminded myself of our paramount objectives—ensuring Ethan's well-being and delivering the plant to the kingdom.

"There's an opening to a pathway in that corner over there," I exclaimed, gesturing towards the mysterious crevice. "We should mark this location on our map for future exploration."

Pulling out my worn map, I noted the spot where Ethan had fallen, ensuring we wouldn't forget the entrance to this enigmatic path. The prospect of unraveling its secrets ignited a sense of intrigue within the group, but we knew our current priority was to regroup and continue our journey.

Turning to address the team, my gaze swept across their determined faces. "Are we ready to move forward?" I asked, seeking confirmation.

Ethan, attempted to stand, testing the strength of his injured ankle. With a determined expression, Ethan nodded. "I can manage. It's a little sore, but I can still walk."

"Excellent," I replied. "Let's make our way back to the ropes and climb out of this area."

Securing Whisperwind in my bag, we headed towards the ropes, prepared to ascend. However, our plans were interrupted as Lucas and Shadowfang came sliding down the path, surprising me.

"What are you two doing down here?" I asked.

Lucas explained the situation, his voice laced with urgency. "We can't go up that way. Winged Harpies were headed in our direction, and we didn't stand a chance without Aria and Ethan. So, we made the split-second decision to slide down the hole to avoid being detected."

Lucas took a moment to compose himself before responding.

"Winged Harpies are formidable avian creatures," he began. "They possess razor-sharp talons and emit piercing cries that send shivers down your spine. Their agility in the air is unmatched, enabling them to swoop down from above and strike their prey with deadly precision."

I listened, a sense of apprehension settling over me. The Winged Harpies sounded like formidable adversaries, and facing them without our weaponry was a dangerous prospect. I cast a grateful glance at Lucas, acknowledging his sharp senses for alerting us to the approaching danger.

"Well, it's a good thing you both made it down here safely," I remarked. "We must be cautious and contemplate our next move."

"There are two options," I began, considering our circumstances. "We can wait here for a while, hoping the Harpies will leave, or we can explore the passage in the corner over there."

"What does everyone want to do?"

Lucas chimed in, "Given that the way we came in is not an option for the next few hours, we can either wait it out or embark on a brief adventure. If we don't find a way out, we can always return here to check if the coast is clear."

"How are you feeling, Ethan?"

"Thanks to Aria and Whisperwind's excellent care, I'm feeling pretty good. I'm open to exploring if that's what the group decides," Ethan stated.

Aria, her eyes filled with curiosity, shared her opinion. "Let's make the most of this time and see what else this place offers. Since we're waiting anyway, why not explore further?"

I looked around the group and found no objections. "If everyone agrees, let's venture forth and see what lies beyond. We'll stay vigilant and assess the situation as we go."

With our decision made, we prepared to delve deeper into the unknown. We understood the risks and potential rewards that awaited us. With our determination unwavering, we embarked on our impromptu exploration, eager to uncover the hidden secrets of Serpent's Pass.

## *Chapter 29 The Chamber*

Lucas took the lead, with Aria and Ethan following behind. Shadowfang and I formed the rear, creating a close-knit group. Aria held the torch, providing a flickering glow that helped us navigate the darkness, even though our visibility was limited.

We advanced step by step, moving toward the open passage that beckoned us into the uncharted territory. Each of us remained vigilant, alert to any potential dangers that might lie ahead.

Crossing the threshold, we entered the unexplored region, and a mix of excitement and apprehension filled the air. The torch's light cast eerie shadows on the walls, giving us mere glimpses of the unfamiliar surroundings. The path stretched out before us, winding deeper into the mysteries that awaited.

Ahead of us, the path unfolded with a series of winding turns, curving in different directions without revealing its destination. Observing our progress, I remarked on the paths meandering nature.

"It seems like this path twists and turns, but it doesn't have a clear direction," I said. "However, considering that we found the egg in the area we were just in, it's reasonable to assume that this pathway will lead us to the outside."

Lucas, intrigued by my mention of the egg, sought further clarification. "Egg?"

I nodded and elaborated on our recent discovery. "Yes, we stumbled upon an egg in the previous area," I explained. "We believe it holds significance, so we've brought it back to the elders for further investigation."

As we ventured deeper, we found ourselves in yet another open area, reminiscent of the previous one. However, the entrance to this space was obstructed by a peculiar white substance, resembling spiderwebs, but thicker and stronger. Lucas drew his sword and sliced through the dense strands, creating an opening for us to pass through.

"What do you see up there?" I asked Lucas.

"Uncertain, but those webs were thick enough to warrant using my sword," Lucas replied.

My face contorted with concern and dread. "I hope it's not what I think it is," I muttered, my mind conjuring images of giant spiders lurking beyond the webs.

"The substance seems thick," I said. "Don't say it! I can't stand spiders; they give me the creeps!" I exclaimed; my voice tinged with a shiver of fear.

Lucas chuckled and reassured me, "Well, I was going to say that it's too thick for me to believe it's just spiders. But now that you mention it..." His sentence trailed off, leaving a touch of amusement hanging in the air.

As we stepped into the room, a flurry of scurrying sounds filled the air, and it became apparent that the creatures were not fleeing but converging upon us.

Lucas's voice trembled with urgency as he warned, "Prepare yourselves. These things are headed this way, and it doesn't sound like just one or two of them."

The creatures came into view, confirming Lucas's fears. "Um, Valaric, you will not like this answer, but they are indeed spiders," exclaimed Lucas, panic lacing his voice. "However, they may be small enough to fit in the palm of your hand, but they are rather large for spiders."

My excitement was obvious in my voice as I responded, "That's what I was afraid you were going to say." We prepared to defend ourselves against the impending arachnid onslaught.

Lucas turned to Aria, urging her, "Aria, see if you can concentrate on fire directly in front of me. We need more light, and maybe we can scorch a few of these creatures as well." Aria wasted no time and conjured a burst of flames illuminating the area. Lucas's voice filled with excitement, "Holy Mother of."

"What? What is it?"

"There are more than just a few spiders in here. Get ready to swing that sword," Lucas said.

Even as Lucas finished his sentence, the first spider reached him. With a swift and decisive blow, Lucas eliminated the immediate threat. However, the challenge now lay before us as the remaining hundred spiders.

"They are easy to stop individually, but there are a lot more than just one or two in front of us," Lucas stated.

"Aria, can you project a wall of fire instead of individual hits?" Lucas asked.

"Say no more," responded Aria.

She moved her hands in a graceful motion, unleashing a stream of fire in front of our group, ensnaring many of the spiders within the bright blaze. The creatures emitted painful cries as it engulfed them in the flames. However, a few agile spiders evaded the fire and continued their relentless advance, resembling fiery balls dashing toward us.

"Spread out," Lucas commanded as he impaled another spider with his sword. With the increased light from the fire, Ethan unleashed a flurry of arrows toward the spiders still at a distance, while I swung my sword at any spider that ventured near me. Shadowfang, with her mighty teeth, tore into the spiders as they drew closer.

"The fire is working. It keeps some of them at bay, catching them in the wall of fire and allowing only a few to advance," Lucas observed.

"Maybe we should concentrate another round of fire behind the first wall, trapping them in the middle and forcing them to choose a direction," I stated.

Aria attempted another round of fire, as Lucas had proposed. Unfortunately, the results fell short of our expectations. The second wall of fire pushed the spiders toward us, causing them to converge in our direction, desperate to escape the scorching flames.

"Oh, not good," Lucas exclaimed. "More are coming through this direction instead of retreating." Aria, undeterred, attempted another fiery assault, catching quite a few spiders. However, their numbers continued to swell in our direction. We fought, slashing and striking anything that came within reach, arrows whistling through the air. The task was arduous, and the odds seemed daunting.

Just as the situation appeared grim, I proposed a new plan. "We need to come up with another strategy," I declared. "There are far too many of these creatures advancing toward us. Why don't we fall back into the hallway? We can concentrate our fire in a single location, forcing them to run through even more flames."

"You mean retreat and create a wall of fire between the walls, us, and this area," Aria clarified.

I nodded and outlined the formation. "Yes, Lucas and I will be up front, with you and Ethan right behind us. If the spiders breach all of that, they will be severely weakened by the time they reach us."

"That sounds like a solid plan. Let's put it into action," Lucas agreed.

We maneuvered back into the corridor, positioning themselves for their defensive strategy. Aria conjured a wall of fire covering the last five feet in front of us, halting the spiders' relentless pursuit.

"It's working! They are so fixated on reaching us they are running straight into the flames," Aria exclaimed.

"Let's keep this until we have dealt with a significant number of them," I suggested.

We continued employing this technique for a few moments, neutralizing our adversaries. No spiders could penetrate our fiery barrier, and the sounds of their demise echoed through the chamber.

"Alright, let's go see what our situation is now that the fire has gone down, and no more spiders seem to come through," I said.

With Lucas and I out in front, we sauntered forward back into the area we were in a few minutes ago. Our plan worked, and the spiders' numbers dwindled down to almost nothing. The team continued to finish the rest of the spiders that continued to head in our direction, either by sword, arrow, or fire.

"That was intense," stated Ethan, still catching his breath.

"Yeah, that was not the most enjoyable part of this journey," I agreed. "But let's not dwell on that. Look over there. There's an opening in that direction. Let's head that way," I suggested, determined to find an exit from this labyrinth.

We made their way across the spider-filled area, our senses on high alert. As we entered the new passageway, we couldn't believe our eyes. We found ourselves in a chamber that seemed to hold a treasure trove of lost relics and forgotten artifacts from ancient times.

"Would you look at this?" exclaimed Lucas.

"Oh, we see it, but what are these things?" Aria inquired; her curiosity piqued.

We took in our surroundings, marveling at the crafted statues, the ornate jewelry gleaming in the dim light, the display of weapons adorned with engravings, and the parchment papers rolled up.

"I'm not sure," Lucas admitted, his voice filled with wonder. "But these items have been resting here undisturbed for a considerable length of time."

We stood in amazement, feeling as if we had stumbled upon a hidden chamber that human eyes hadn't seen in ages.

We explored the area, examining each artifact with reverence and curiosity. It was a captivating sight, a glimpse into the past, and we couldn't help but feel a sense of reverence for the history contained within those ancient walls. We couldn't resist imagining the stories behind each artifact, the lives of the people who once possessed them, and the significance they held in their respective eras.

"Let's gather a few of these items and take them back to the Elders. They might identify their significance," suggested Lucas.

"I'm all for it," Ethan chimed in, eager to uncover the secrets held within the artifacts.

"Are you finding anything interesting over there?" asked Lucas.

"I believe these are manuscripts, and those fragments seem to be parts of ancient maps," I explained.

"They just look like old parchment paper with some ancient symbols on them. How can you determine what they are," Lucas asked.

"This manuscript mentions Thalondor, describing the glorious civilization that once thrived there," I revealed.

"Thalondor is nothing but ruins now. We don't speak of it or venture anywhere near that area," Aria said.

"I did not know. Perhaps these manuscripts hold secrets and knowledge that your people are unaware of," I proposed. "We should bring a couple of them back for the elders to examine."

"He might be onto something. These manuscripts could contain information that has been lost to us," Ethan added.

"So, you can also decipher these ancient symbols," Lucas asked.

I nodded. "Yes, from the one in your hand, I can gather that there are more hidden chambers like this one, concealed within Serpent's Pass," I divulged.

"That's quite interesting because people have been traversing this pass for ages, and there are no stories of hidden chambers," Lucas remarked.

"Well, we are standing in one, aren't we? It seems these chambers have remained a secret until now," I pointed out, leaving the team pondering the mysteries that lay before us.

"With this discovery, I'm more convinced than ever that the way out lies in the direction we were heading. There's no other explanation for how all this stuff ended up here without some kind of entrance," I declared. "Let's gather what we can carry and keep moving. Hopefully, we haven't lost too much time since we still need to make our way back," I added.

We took a moment to pack some items we had found in the chamber, ensuring their safe transport. Once everyone had secured their belongings, we agreed it was time to continue our journey.

As we surveyed our surroundings, we noticed another corridor leading in the opposite direction of our previous path. We regrouped and ventured down the corridor, our steps echoing through the dimly lit passageway. The path unfolded much like before, with twists and turns, until we reached a dead end. Frustration threatened to creep in, but Lucas's sharp eyes caught a glimmer of light.

"Look over there, light," Lucas exclaimed.

"There must be a hidden passage or a movable wall," I suggested.

We scanned the area, searching for any sign of a mechanism or lever that could unlock the path.

"Spread out and feel along the wall. There has to be something that opens this passage. How else could they have brought those statues in here?" I instructed.

We fanned out, their hands gliding across the cold stone walls. Then, Ethan's fingers brushed against something peculiar—a mechanism of sorts.

"Everyone, come over here," Ethan called out.

We gathered around; their eyes fixated on the discovery. Uncertainty hung in the air.

"Well, what does everyone think?" Ethan asked.

"It could be the way out, but it could also be a trap," Lucas cautioned.

"We should spread out, just in case," I suggested. "If you're uncomfortable, Ethan, I can push it for you."

"No, I'll do it. But everyone, move away, just in case," Ethan requested.

With cautious anticipation, the team spread out, creating a safe distance. Ethan applied pressure to the mechanism, and a distinct click resonated through the corridor. Moments later, a sliver of light streamed in through the now-opened passage.

Excitement surged within them, the possibility of finding their way out igniting their spirits.

"Let's push against the wall to see if we can open it further," Lucas suggested.

He and I approached the wall, leaning into it with all our might. Slowly, the wall yielded, revealing the outside world. We surveyed their surroundings, ensuring no lurking creatures threatened their escape. Satisfied, we stepped out into the open.

"We should close this entrance and make it appear untouched, so no one else stumbles upon it," Lucas proposed.

"Good thinking," I said.

We worked together, sealing the door, and rearranging the surroundings to erase any trace of our presence.

"Does anyone know where we are now that we're out?" Ethan inquired.

We glanced around, searching for familiar landmarks.

"I know where we are," Lucas declared. "We're close to the entrance to Serpents Pass, where we started this morning. If we head in this direction, we'll be back where we began," he explained.

"That's good news. It means we're still on track," I remarked. "Let's keep moving so we can set up camp in the same area as last night," I suggested.

We descended the hill, eager to leave Serpents Pass behind and return to familiar grounds. We maintained an impressive pace, propelled by the anticipation of a well-deserved rest after the exhausting trek. Finally reaching the bottom, our eyes were drawn to the entrance of the Glimmering Caverns, still standing in the exact spot where we had discovered it the night before.

"That's intriguing. For centuries, no one could find the entrance, and yet we stumble upon it two days in a row, in the same location," Lucas remarked.

"Perhaps defeating the Golem disrupted its ability to move the entrance," I speculated.

"I don't know. It's just strange," Lucas concluded.

"Well, if the entrance is still there tomorrow morning, we should take a quick detour to the chamber with the luminescent stones. We could grab a couple of larger ones to carry with us, especially for areas like the one we just traversed," I suggested. "It shouldn't take us long, considering how valuable they are."

Lucas nodded in agreement.

Having arrived at the same location we had camped in the previous night; the team wasted no time setting up camp once again. Weary from the day's arduous journey, we relished the opportunity to rest and rejuvenate our weary bodies. The familiar surroundings brought a sense of comfort, and we settled in, ready to recharge for the adventures that awaited us on the following day.

## *Chapter 30 The Kiss*

We gathered around the crackling fire; their faces illuminated by the dancing flames. Aria and I sat on one side, while Ethan and Lucas occupied the other, engaged in lively conversation about our recent expedition. Whisperwind, our faithful companion, nestled closer to the fire, reveling in its comforting warmth, while Shadowfang darted around, embracing the freedom of the night.

"I never, in my wildest dreams, imagined we would stumble upon something like that chamber today," remarked Ethan.

"Indeed, it took us by surprise. Our sole purpose was to retrieve the plant needed to save Sir Gregory," I replied. A mischievous grin spread across my face. "I suppose you could call the ground giving way beneath you a stroke of luck," I chuckled.

Laughter erupted from the group.

"Who would have thought that my clumsy slide would be a fortunate turn of events?" added Ethan.

"And to think, for a moment there, we thought we might have to spend the night atop Serpent's Pass," Lucas stated with a hint of relief.

"I'm intrigued to hear what the elders will make of the artifacts we found," Ethan mused.

"I imagine it will be hailed as a significant find, one that could unveil long-lost knowledge from the past. However, it also carries the potential to challenge everything we know, turning our understanding upside down," I explained.

"How so?" asked Lucas.

"Over time, as stories are passed down through generations, they change, evolving until the facts of centuries ago become distorted or even lost in the narratives of today," I revealed. "Yet, you will be returning to your kingdom with authentic documents from the past, written by those who lived in those times. Although they could still be accounts shaped by oral traditions, they hold the potential to shed light on the unknown, offering glimpses into aspects we are unaware of today," I concluded.

"Well, aren't we feeling wise and philosophical?" Ethan said as he chuckled.

"Ya, I suppose you're right. What do I know? The one who still hasn't figured out where he came from," I chuckled.

"You never told us how you defeated Golem while the rest of us were knocked out," Lucas probed.

I paused for a moment, reflecting on the swift and intense encounter. "There's nothing much to tell. It was more of a lucky strike when I attempted to block the Golem's blow to minimize my pain," I explained.

"Well, that was one fortunate shot because I know both of us were pounding on that thing for a while, and we couldn't find any vulnerable spot to even make it flinch," Lucas remarked.

"Look, everything happened so quickly. I couldn't give you a detailed account even if I tried. I'm just glad we all made it out alive," I confessed.

"Indeed, that's what matters," Ethan said.

Leaning back, I reflected on the encounter with the Golem and the intriguing ability I had discovered—the ability to see inscriptions on the cavern walls that remained hidden from the others. My thoughts also turned to my newfound capacity to read the ancient symbols on the manuscripts and map fragments. This reminded me of the parchment papers I had retrieved from the trunk that washed up on the beach.

"What do you have there?" asked Aria.

"Just some parchments I found in a trunk that washed up on the beach. I haven't had the chance to survey them and decipher their contents yet," I replied.

"What are they?" Ethan inquired.

"The elders mentioned they are fragments of forgotten knowledge—

pieces of maps, prophecies, and incantations. They believe these parchments hold the potential to unlock hidden realms, unveil long-lost treasures, and reveal the secrets of the past."

"Well, isn't that interesting? Can you make sense of it?" Ethan interjected.

I sighed, aware of the limitations posed by the dim light. "I can make out a few symbols, but it's challenging without proper illumination. The symbols seem to speak of distant lands, lands beyond the forest, filled with darkness, or something to that effect," I shared. "I need to take the time to study these parchments in daylight so I can see them more clearly," I remarked.

"It's possible that lands exist beyond the forest. We may never know, given the vastness of the forest itself. It would take more than a few days to reach its edge," Lucas stated.

I nodded, contemplating the vastness of the unknown beyond the familiar boundaries of their forest home. The prospect of hidden realms and lost treasures stirred a mix of excitement and trepidation within me. I couldn't wait to delve deeper into the mysteries these parchments held, knowing that they might hold the key to unraveling the secrets of the past and unveiling new wonders that lay beyond the horizon.

Our tranquil moment shattered when a familiar sound emanated from Whisperwind, putting us on high alert. In an instant, we sprang to our feet, weapons at the ready, our focus fixed on Whisperwind, who was sensing something. We mirrored the Shadowfang's intense stance, prepared to confront any threat that might approach. However, as seconds turned into minutes, nothing appeared before us. Despite the lack of a visible danger, Whisperwind persisted with the warning sound, leaving us puzzled. We watched as Whisperwind backed away, still fixated in a specific direction.

"What is it, Whisperwind? What do you see?" I asked. Confused and uncertain, the group exchanged glances, trying to make sense of the situation. Then, a distinct crack reverberated through the air, not from the direction we expected, but from beneath my feet--where Whisperwind had been pointing. All eyes darted downward, drawn to my bag. Reacting, I reached inside and, as if guided by an invisible force, grasped an egg nestled within. Another crack resonated from the egg, filling the air with anticipation.

I realized the source of the mysterious sounds. I held the egg, and to the amazement of the others, a small creature emerged. The sight left us in awe, witnessing the birth of a new life—a world full of wonder and boundless possibilities unfolding before our eyes.

All eyes were fixated on the mesmerizing sight unfolding before us as the creature emerged from its egg. The air crackled with anticipation as Ethan broke the silence, his voice filled with certainty. "It's a fire drake."

My skepticism prompted me to inquire, "But how can you be so sure? It's been ages since anyone has laid eyes on one."

"The resemblance is uncanny, just like the ancient paintings I've studied in the distant past."

The fire drake's majestic form revealed itself, adorned with delicate horns atop its head and scales that shimmered in hues of red, orange, and gold. As it broke free from its confinement, the air stirred by its tiny wings, a profound sense of wonder enveloped everyone. Bearing witness to a creature believed to be extinct was a breathtaking spectacle.

Moved by the sight before me, I reached up with my other hand, stroking the fire drake's head, imparting a reassuring touch.

Aria, overwhelmed by the spectacle, exclaimed, "Wow, that was amazing." She couldn't help but notice the connection forming between the fire drake and me, prompting her to remark, "It seems to like you."

"How can you tell?" I asked.

"Because it hasn't bitten your finger off for touching it," Aria chuckled.

"Well, I suppose that could be true."

"What are you going to call it?" Aria asked.

I pondered for a moment, grappling with the challenge of assigning a name to a creature of unknown gender.

"I must admit, I'm uncertain. How does one even determine the gender of such a remarkable being?"

My inquiry was met with silence, as the truth dawned upon us all-- we were venturing into uncharted territory, where knowledge of fire drakes was scarce.

"Considering we've been referring to it as a fire drake, I assume it possesses the ability to breathe fire, as the legends suggest?"

"Indeed, according to the tales of old, fire drakes unleashed mighty flames upon their enemies in the heat of battle," Ethan interjected.

Inspired by the legends and the nature of our newfound companion, I proposed a few names: "In that case, we could name it Ignatius, Pyrothor, or Flamebringer."

Lucas, offering his own suggestion, chimed in, "How about Scorch?" The name hung in the air, carrying a sense of intensity and power.

I repeated the name, "Scorch? An intriguing choice." Pausing for a moment, I addressed the fire drake, seeking its silent approval. "What do you think of the name Scorch?"

Although the fire drake couldn't respond in words, its demeanor showed no objection. I smiled, finding reassurance in the lack of fiery repercussions. "Well, taking a cue from Aria's analogy, since Scorch hasn't attempted to singe my fingers, I believe Scorch it is."

"This is amazing," Aria stated, "as the egg sat in that chamber that Ethan fell into for who knows how long, but then hatches the day we bring it out of that chamber."

"Maybe with my bag sitting right here next to the fire, caused the egg to warm up enough to get it moving. I have no other ideas behind that, as I know nothing about these things."

Scorch, our newfound companion, laid in my lap as we contemplated the mysterious circumstances of its hatching.

The group savored the warmth of the crackling fire, our bodies tired from the day's adventures. As the night deepened, our voices wove tales of triumphs and discoveries, laughter punctuating the air. Yet, with passing time, weariness claimed our spirits, and the urge for rest emerged.

Feeling the weight of fatigue tugging at my eyelids, I decided it was time to retire for the night. I gathered my belongings, my mind still processing the day's events. Aria, sensing my departure, voiced her own desire for rest, her voice carrying a touch of gratitude.

"You know," Aria began, her voice gentle yet filled with genuine appreciation, "I never thanked you for saving my life in the treacherous Glimmering Cavern. Amidst all the chaos and uncertainty, you risked everything for me."

My heart fluttered with surprise and warmth as I brushed off her gratitude with a humble response. "It was nothing," I insisted. "I am certain you would have done the same for me."

In that moment, our proximity intensified, and our souls seemed to draw closer. Aria, recognizing the significance of the moment, stepped closer to me, her intentions clear. Her lips found their way to mine, expressing gratitude and affection in a single, tender kiss. The world seemed to fade, leaving only the sweet connection we shared, a moment filled with warmth and a newfound sense of closeness.

The unexpected gesture surprised me, and I felt my senses electrified as her lips touched mine. Aria's lips were soft and inviting, leaving an indelible impression upon my own. In that moment, the world seemed to pause, and I savored the sweetness of the moment.

As the kiss concluded, Aria turned and retreated towards her designated sleeping area. I stood there, my mind swirling with a whirlwind of emotions, perplexed by what had just transpired. I was frozen, my mouth agape, unsure of how to navigate this uncharted territory that had unfolded before me. The kiss had ignited a rush of feelings within me, and I wrestled with questions and emotions I had never faced before. It was a moment that left me both thrilled and apprehensive, eager to explore this newfound connection, yet uncertain of the path that lay ahead.

I couldn't believe what had just happened, as Aria's unexpected kiss left me in a state of electrified surprise. Her lips were soft and inviting, and the sensation lingered on my own as I stood there, trying to process the moment. It felt like time stood still, allowing me to savor the sweetness of that brief encounter.

My heart was racing, and I grappled with a mix of excitement and uncertainty. The kiss had ignited something within me, something I had never experienced before. Questions and emotions flooded my mind, and I felt as if I was treading on uncharted territory.

Thrilled by the connection we had shared, I also felt apprehensive about what it might mean for our friendship and the journey ahead. It was a moment that changed everything, and I couldn't help but wonder about the path that now lay before us.

*Chapter 31 The Luminescent Stones*

As the sun rose on the following morning, our team knew it was time to prepare for the journey back to the kingdom. With our bags laden with the treasures we had discovered on our arduous path, we were aware of the considerable distance that still lay ahead of us. We were determined not to waste any time, knowing the potential value of returning to the Glimmering Caverns to collect more stones while the entrance remained accessible. The possibility of uncovering more secrets and hidden wonders drove us to press onward without delay.

"How did everyone sleep? Restful slumber, I hope," Lucas asked.

Aria, always cheerful, was the first to respond. "I slept like a dream, Lucas. It was a peaceful night indeed."

"I slept ok," I said.

"For being out here, I say I slept pretty decent," answered Ethan.

"Thats's good and how did you sleep, Lucas?" I asked.

"Not too bad at all. I believe yesterday took all my energy, so I slept hard," Lucas said.

"Good deal. Well, if everyone is about ready to go, I would say let's get moving as we have a couple of days' journey back. We need to get this plant back to the kingdom, so we have some chance of saving Sir Gregory."

We rallied together, ready to resume our journey, and to our relief, the entrance to the mystical Glimmering Caverns remained steadfast in its position.

With a renewed sense of purpose, I took the lead, my voice resolute.

"Let's venture into the cavern and retrieve more of those radiant, luminescent stones. They proved invaluable, especially in the area where Ethan encountered his mishap."

Conscious of the need to make haste, I emphasized the importance of efficiency. "If we act, we won't lose much time. We may never get the opportunity to get the rocks again if no one has seen the tunnel entrance for years."

With a determined stride, we ventured once more into the depths of Glimmering Caverns, our objective clear: to secure more of the coveted luminescent stones. I led the way, my steps purposeful, and my companions close behind. Whisperwind fluttered inside my bag, while Scorch, nestled alongside, emanated a comforting warmth. Our unity and determination gave us strength as we delved deeper into the cavern's mysteries.

Aria, Ethan, Lucas, and Shadowfang formed a vigilant rear guard, their senses heightened, and weapons ready. This time, the cavern appeared sparser in its population of creatures, yet a few still lurked in the shadows. Swift and coordinated, we neutralized any threats we encountered, dispatching them with precision and efficiency.

As we advanced through the labyrinthine passages, our footsteps echoing through the cavern's ancient corridors, the luminescent stones revealed themselves like scattered stars, casting a gentle glow that illuminated our path. Our determination grew with each radiant gem we gathered, knowing the potential these stones held to aid us in our quest.

"Here are some sizable ones that should fit in a bag, yet emit enough brightness to illuminate dark areas," I announced, displaying the selected luminescent stones.

Ethan nodded in agreement, recognizing their practicality. Each member of the team collected two larger stones, their hands cradling the palm-sized treasures. These stones surpassed the original one I had retrieved, a testament to our successful endeavor. The sight of our growing collection filled us with hope and assurance as we continued to explore the depths of the Glimmering Caverns.

"See? That didn't take us long at all," I remarked. We had secured the luminescent stones, ensuring our journey would be well-guided in the face of darkness or uncertainty.

"Alright, everyone, it's time to make our way out. We don't want to prolong our return to the kingdom any further. We're already a day behind schedule to get these plants back in hopes of saving Sir Gregory," I declared, a sense of urgency in my words.

As we retraced our steps along the familiar path, heading back from the depths of the Glimmering Caverns, my thoughts wandered to the words I had encountered during our previous expedition. My voice was audible. I uttered the cryptic inscription to myself, "Victor of Glimmering Caverns possesses mystical abilities within the caverns." The significance of those words lingered in my mind, leaving me curious and intrigued about the secrets the caverns might still hold.

The inscription continued to linger in my mind, intriguing me with its hidden meaning. Despite my continued pondering, the true nature of those mystical abilities remained shrouded in mystery, eluding my grasp. Countless questions danced in my thoughts, their answers just beyond my reach. What could those abilities entail? How might they manifest within the depths of the caverns?

Another intriguing occurrence captured my attention--the blue potion I had consumed during my desperate act to defeat the formidable Gem Golem. It was that very potion that had granted me an unexpected advantage, enabling my victory in our intense battle. However, since that pivotal moment, I had noticed subtle shifts in my reality. An undercurrent of peculiar occurrences seemed to follow in my wake, evoking both wonder and bewilderment.

Most striking of all was my newfound ability to decipher ancient symbols etched upon parchment, a skill that had eluded me prior to imbibing the mysterious blue elixir. The potion had brought forth changes within me, opening doors to unexplored facets of myself. It was as though the caverns' secrets were revealing themselves to me, guiding me towards a destiny intertwined with ancient prophecies and forgotten knowledge.

As I reflected upon the mysterious connections between the inscription, my newfound abilities, and the transformative power of the potion, I couldn't help but feel both awe and trepidation. Each revelation deepened my curiosity, driving me to uncover the hidden truths concealed within the caverns. The words had captivated my mind, leading me on a quest for understanding.

Lost in the labyrinth of my contemplations, I found myself disconnected from the world around me. Lucas's attempts to engage me in conversation went unnoticed, as it engrossed me in the mysteries that tugged at my thoughts. It was only when he persisted with his questions that it jolted me back to reality, rejoining the present moment.

"Valaric, what do you think?" Lucas asked, his voice reflecting both curiosity and a hint of exasperation.

Startled, I refocused my attention on my companion. "About what?" I inquired; my mind still entangled in the enigmas that had captured my thoughts.

Lucas sighed; his patience was apparent. "Weren't you listening? We were all discussing our plans to enjoy a refreshing ale at the renowned Ale House once we return to the kingdom."

My eyes widened with recognition, snapping me out of my reverie. A warm smile played on my lips as memories flooded back.

"Ah, yes! The Ale House, where I first met Sir Gregory," I recalled, a touch of nostalgia coloring my words. "I have fond memories of that place."

"Indeed, it was there that our paths intertwined, where friendships blossomed amidst laughter and merriment," Lucas reminisced.

A flicker of excitement danced in my eyes as I embraced the prospect of indulging in the delights of the Ale House.

"When we return, we shall make it a priority to quench our thirst with the finest ale and revel in the camaraderie of shared stories," I declared. The thought of returning to that familiar haven of joy and companionship uplifted my spirits, reminding me that beyond the caverns, there awaited moments of simple pleasure and cherished connections with my friends.

"Interesting," Ethan began, his voice filled with a sense of intrigue. "I have a couple of places I've been meaning to explore, but they require a team to accomplish. If anyone's interested, we could embark on another adventure together."

Excitement flickered in the eyes of the group as they expressed their enthusiasm for another joint expedition.

Aria, however, interjected with a reminder of her own priorities. "Before we set off on any new escapades, I must visit the elemental springs."

Ethan reassured her, "Oh, don't worry. I didn't mean we would embark on another journey as soon as we returned. We all deserve a few days of relaxation before diving into new endeavors."

Laughter erupted among the group, their shared understanding of the need for respite resonating.

As the laughter echoed around me, my mind was transported to the memory of my previous meditation session near the springs. The gentle flow of water, the whispers of the wind, and the vibrant energy of the place had enveloped me, transcending the boundaries of time. I felt a sense of peace, a connection to something greater than myself, and I wondered if there was more to the elemental springs than met the eye. It was a realm of mystery and wonder that beckoned me, inviting me to explore its depths in search of hidden truths.

As I pondered the possibility of repeating the experience, questions flooded my mind. Would time slip away from me once more? What unseen realms might I encounter during an extended meditation session? Curiosity swelled within me, urging me to seek answers.

Lost in my introspection, the prospect of returning to the elemental springs presented a unique opportunity for exploration and self-discovery. In the depths of my being, a longing for understanding and connection beckoned, urging me to delve into the mysteries concealed within the springs' ethereal embrace.

Aria's voice pierced through my contemplations, bringing me back to the present.

"I see light up ahead!" she exclaimed, breaking the spell of my wandering thoughts. My attention snapped back, and I realized we were nearing the exit of the cavern. The team felt a wave of relief wash over us, knowing we were on our way back home.

However, as we stepped out of the cavern and surveyed our surroundings, confusion and disbelief clouded our expressions. This was not the expected exit. Instead, we stood on the outskirts of the kingdom.

"Um, what is going on?" asked Aria.

Silence fell upon the group as we exchanged puzzled glances, searching for answers that eluded us.

Lucas, breaking the silence, ventured an explanation, his tone tinged with perplexity. "I thought the opening had become stationary near Serpent's Pass after all this time. How could it have transported us here?"

My mind whirled with thoughts and possibilities. Could this be one of the mystical abilities referenced in the words I had read on the cavern wall? The notion seemed absurd, almost comical. I entertained the idea of entering the caverns with a specific destination in mind and upon exiting, finding myself where I had intended. It sounded like something out of a fanciful tale rather than reality.

"We can unravel this mystery later," I declared. "For now, let's prioritize delivering the plant to the healers. We find ourselves back a day early instead of a day late."

We nodded in agreement, their focus shifting to the immediate task at hand. With a newfound sense of purpose, we set off towards the kingdom, carrying the precious plant that held the hope of saving Sir Gregory's life.

I took a step back, allowing Aria to assume the responsibility of receiving the fragments of the plant from each team member. With utmost care, we entrusted her with the precious cargo, knowing she would ensure its safe delivery to the healers. As Aria gathered the plant pieces, a sense of accomplishment swelled within the group. We had completed our mission early, a feat that filled us with anticipation and pride.

Despite our celebratory mood, an uneasiness lingered in the air. Little did we know that our jubilation would soon be overshadowed by unforeseen events.

## *Chapter 32 The News*

"Hello, Princess. How are you today?" inquired the head guard.

"I'm doing fine. And you?" I replied.

"I'm good. Have you heard the news?" he asked.

"What news?" I inquired.

"The team that went to retrieve the plant for Sir Gregory has returned. They appeared mysteriously just outside the Kingdom," explained the head guard.

"That's quite interesting," I remarked.

"Yes, indeed. I'm on my way to inform your father about it," said the head guard.

"Well, have a good day. Goodbye," I said.

"Goodbye," responded the head guard.

Now that I was aware the team had returned, I needed to reach my secret hiding spot to eavesdrop on some information. Especially because I knew the head guard was on his way there at that moment. Perhaps I could discover the identity of the informant and learn what they knew.

I hurried through the castle corridors to reach my hiding place. Fortunately, I arrived just in time, as the head guard was entering my father's chambers.

"What is it?" the King asked.

Unfazed by the outburst, the head guard maintained his composure and spoke with utmost respect, "Your Highness, I bring tidings of the group's return, including the outsider, Valaric."

"Impossible!" the King exclaimed. "There is no way they could have traversed Serpent's Pass and returned."

"Have you, yourself, seen them?" asked the King.

"Yes, your Highness, they have indeed accomplished their mission. Each member of the group carried a piece of the plant, which they entrusted to Aria for the healers."

"Well, it seems the outcome is of little consequence now," he muttered under his breath.

"Your Highness, my guards reported the group emerged from one of the hidden caverns," he revealed.

"A hidden cavern?" he exclaimed.

"Yes, your Highness," he affirmed. "It appears they have stumbled upon an elusive cavern concealed within our realm."

"Have you dispatched guards to investigate the entrance?" the King asked, his voice brimming with anticipation.

"Your Highness, I sent guards to explore the cavern," he confessed. "However, they returned, claiming they could not locate the entrance from which the group emerged."

"This cannot be," he grumbled, a mix of disbelief and annoyance in his voice. "You must send them back. Leave no stone unturned until we find the entrance."

"As you command, your highness," he acknowledged, his voice reflecting his unwavering determination. "I will conduct a thorough search and reveal the hidden entrance to the cavern, as you command, your highness," he said with unwavering determination.

"Do not return until you have discovered the entrance," he commanded, his voice brooking no argument.

"I shall not rest until unveil the cavern's hidden secrets," the head guard vowed, just prior to exiting the room.

As I watched the head guard leave, I thought to myself, that is very interesting. Some type of hidden cavern that allowed them to arrive a day earlier than expected. I didn't expect them back until after five days.

I wondered what this cavern was all about. It seems my father wanted to know as well, since he has the guards searching all over the place for the entrance. Why not ask the team about it? Maybe we could gather more information that way.

I think I will just do that; I thought to myself. However, just as I was about to step out of the secret passage, someone else knocked on my father's chambers. Who could this be, I wondered. Well, I guess I will stick around and find out.

"Your Highness," the informant began, "please accept my apologies for the delay in delivering my report. I have arrived as swiftly as possible to provide you with the information you seek."

"Well, what did you observe on your little outing?" the King questioned, his tone laced with impatience.

The informant stood before the King, relaying every detail of the journey, starting from Valaric's extended meditation at the air elemental spring to his astounding victory over the Gem Golem and his newfound ability to decipher ancient transcripts.

"Valaric devoted an extraordinary amount of time to the air elemental spring, immersing himself in its essence," the informant explained. "While it is not uncommon for individuals to spend prolonged periods there, his meditation lasted for more than half a day. It was as if he tapped into the very currents of the air, drawing strength and focus from its energy."

"How could an outsider spend that much time in a meditation session? Most people take less than fifteen minutes as most," questioned the King.

"I do not know," said the informant. "Valaric also somehow defeated the Gem Golem in Glimmering Cavern's all by himself."

"What? Impossible. How could he have defeated the Gem Golem?" asked the King.

"We do not know, your Highness, as we were all knocked out," said the informant. "He claims to have struck a fortunate blow while defending himself, but we cannot dismiss the possibility that there is more to it than mere luck. His agility, cunning, and prowess in combat far exceeded our expectations."

"So, let me guess. The hidden cavern you all emerged from today was Glimmering Caverns," asked the King.

"Yes, your Highness," said the informant.

"My guards cannot find that entrance, even though they saw where you all emerged," said the King.

"We haven't figured out what is going on with Glimmering Cavern," said the informant. "We went in and came out at Serpent's

Pass. The entrance didn't move for two days. We gathered some luminescent rocks and ended up here. We still haven't figured out how."

"Interesting. Well, I have my guards searching for the entrance as we speak. Is there anything else that you have on Valaric?"

"Indeed, your Highness. Valaric's ability to decipher the ancient transcripts further deepens the enigma surrounding him. He reads the inscriptions with ease, as if he has an innate understanding of their meaning."

"We must proceed with caution," he declared. "Continue to monitor Valaric's actions by any means possible, gather more intelligence, and report any significant developments. We cannot afford to underestimate the depths of his mysterious talents."

"Thank you for the information. You may be excused," said the King, waving a dismissive hand.

"Thank you, your Highness," the informant replied before leaving.

As I observed the informant leaving my father's chambers, I couldn't believe what I had just witnessed and heard. I had placed my trust in that individual, and they had revealed everything as if it were of no consequence. I couldn't help but wonder how many times this person had betrayed me. How often had they gone to my father to report on my actions?

I knew I had to confront this person as soon as possible. The silver lining was that I had heard nothing that suggested Valaric was working against us. It seemed like he was doing everything in his power to assist us. However, regardless of how many times he had saved the kingdom, my father would still be informed of it.

Before I knew it, my father was also exiting his chambers as well. I wonder where he is headed to in such a hurry. Looks like the perfect opportunity to follow him to see where he is going, I thought.

I exited the secret place and followed my father through the castle. It appeared as if he was headed towards Elders Hall. I believe I will take a shortcut and beat him there.

I arrived just seconds before my father and headed to the same aisle I was on the last time I was here looking up the ruins. All I saw was my father yank the doors open, revealing the council of elders gathered within. Their gazes turned towards him, their expressions a blend of anticipation and wisdom.

Before the King could utter a word, one elder spoke, his voice carrying the weight of newfound knowledge.

"Your Majesty, we were just about to send a messenger to you so that we may share newfound information with you," they announced.

"Please, enlighten me," he requested, a hint of eagerness in his voice.

"Your Highness, it seems the team has returned with some ancient artifacts from Thalondor," said the elder.

"What? I was not informed of this information. What did they find?" asked the King.

"It seems they found a secret chamber in Serpent's Pass that contains a lot of artifacts about Thalondor. They brought back some trinkets, weapons, and some manuscripts that Valaric can interpret somehow."

The elder's subsequent revelation deepened the intrigue surrounding the Outsider Valaric and his abilities. The mention of Valaric's proficiency in deciphering the ancient manuscript, written in cryptic symbols recounting Thalondor's glorious past, added another layer of mystery to the unfolding narrative.

"I was informed that the outsider Valaric could read ancient text, but I had no clue it was from Thalondor. However, that he could read ancient text was the reason I came to see all of you," said the King.

However, a shadow of disappointment fell upon the conversation as the elder shared the unfortunate truth: "the ancient symbols were inscribed in a language so ancient and obscure that even the esteemed council of elders found themselves unable to unravel its meaning."

The King's patience waned, his frustration clear in his booming voice as he demanded clarification. "So, apart from the fact that you can't decipher the ancient script, what are you trying to convey?" The weight of the unknown loomed upon him, fueling his desire for answers.

With a composed demeanor, the elder articulated their aim, emphasizing the urgency to delve deeper into the secrets of Thalondor. They revealed that, at present, Valaric stood as the sole individual capable of unraveling the mysteries concealed within the ancient texts and artifacts. The council recognized the significance of his role in their pursuit of understanding.

The King's response carried a tinge of skepticism and weariness. "So, let me guess," he retorted, a note of resignation in his voice. "You require Valaric to remain within the kingdom for an extended duration, am I correct?" His question served as a subtle reminder of the potential consequences and risks that accompanied the outsider's presence.

"With your permission, of course, your Majesty," the elder acknowledged, understanding the weight of their request.

The King, caught between the urgency to unlock the mysteries of Thalondor and his concerns regarding the potential repercussions, conceded to their proposition. His tone carried a hint of resignation as he issued a warning to the council.

"It seems you leave me no choice," he declared. "But let it be known that if any harm befalls this kingdom because of his presence, the responsibility rests on your shoulders," the King stated as he stormed out of Elders Hall.

Oh my I thought, as I watched my father storm out of the hall. He was furious, based on everything I could hear. I need to look into all of this, but first, I need to find Valaric.

With that I exited the hall and asked some guards if they knew where Valaric was located. After a few minutes, I figured out that he was at the elemental springs. Wasting no more time, I headed that direction.

When I made it to the elemental springs, Valaric was in a meditative state at the springs. The weird piece, he stayed in that meditative state for another couple hours. When he finally came out of a meditative state, I must have startled him, because he looked surprised to see me.

"Princess, what brings you here?" he asked.

I took a moment to compose myself before responding. "It took me some time to locate you. I had to inquire with the guards about your whereabouts. It took me an hour to get to you. Then I waited for another couple of hours while you meditated."

A look of disbelief crossed his face as he protested, "But I assure you, I have only been here for fifteen to twenty minutes at most." The unexplained distortion of time added another layer of mystery to the already nature of the elemental springs.

"You possess a strong affinity with the elementals, both in presence and perception. Your connection seems to extend beyond the ordinary," I remarked, my words bringing a sense of recognition to his face.

"You were the one who advised me to meditate for a better connection with the surroundings," Valaric acknowledged.

I nodded; my gaze softened. "Yes, I suppose I did. But Valaric, I didn't come here to discuss the elemental springs. There is something I must tell you," I interjected, my tone now somber.

"Please share."

Taking a deep breath, I conveyed the heavy news with empathy, "Sir Gregory passed away two days ago."

## Chapter 33 The Toast

The news of Sir Gregory's passing struck me like a heavy blow. My mind raced, replaying the events of our mission and scrutinizing every decision I had made. I couldn't shake the feeling that there must have been something more I could have done to ensure our success and prevent this tragic loss.

Maybe we should have taken the time to check on the Earthbound Gorgons at the Elemental Springs in Eldoria Forest, I thought. Perhaps there was a lingering threat that we had overlooked, a danger that could have been neutralized if only we had been more thorough.

The weight of regret settled upon my shoulders as I contemplated the what-ifs and the missed opportunities. I understood that dwelling on the past would not change the present, but I couldn't help but feel a pang of responsibility for not considering every angle of our mission. Losing Sir Gregory weighed on my heart, and I couldn't help but wonder if there was a way I could have altered the outcome.

"Valaric, there was nothing you could have done to change the outcome of the current situation," Arabella reassured me. "Sir Gregory was an experienced knight in this kingdom, well-versed in the threats that dwell in the forest. His passing was a tragic loss, but it was beyond our control."

I listened to Arabella's words, appreciating her attempt to console me. However, my mind was still consumed by thoughts of what could have been.

"I understand," I replied. "We took significant risks to fulfill the task, but in the end, it feels like it was all in vain."

Arabella chimed in, "It wasn't all for nothing, Valaric. Through this journey, you have gained the respect and companionship of new allies within the kingdom. That is something valuable."

I nodded, acknowledging Arabella's perspective. We had formed strong bonds and earned the trust of our comrades. Yet, the weight of our perilous encounter in the Glimmering Caverns still hung upon me.

"Yes, I gained new allies," I admitted, "but let's not forget that we nearly lost our lives in those treacherous caverns."

As I spoke, a mixture of gratitude and unease filled my heart. I recognized the significance of our achievements, but I couldn't shake off the lingering sense of danger we had faced. It was a stark reminder of the perils that awaited us in our quest to protect the kingdom.

"Well, enough about this," I said with a hint of determination. "I am going to head over to the Ale House and raise a glass to Sir Gregory's memory. Are you coming?"

Arabella hesitated for a moment, aware of the unconventional nature of her presence in such an establishment. However, she recognized the significance of honoring Sir Gregory and the importance of being there for me at this moment.

"Well, while it is not customary for a princess to enter such a place, I suppose I can make an exception," she replied.

"Excellent! We should gather the others and give Sir Gregory a grand send-off, a celebration befitting his valor."

Turning to the guard who had been following me, Arabella spoke, her eyes fixed on his.

"Go find Aria, Ethan, and Lucas. Inform them we will be at the Ale House, bidding farewell to Sir Gregory. It's time to honor his memory and celebrate his noble spirit."

The guard hesitated, torn between his duty to protect me and carrying out the princess's command. However, Arabella's unwavering gaze and firm tone left him with no choice.

"Yes, Princess," he replied, bowing his head before departing to fulfill his mission.

Arabella turned back to me, her expression one of determination and support.

"Let us make this a memorable send-off, a tribute to the heroism and sacrifice of Sir Gregory. Together, we shall honor his memory and find solace in the camaraderie we have forged on this journey."

At that moment, a small head emerged from my bag, catching Arabella's attention.

"Oh my, what is that?" she asked.

I couldn't help but grin as Scorch, the hatched Fire Drake, made an adorable appearance.

"Well, everyone said it was a Fire Drake," I explained. "When Ethan stumbled upon a hidden chamber, he found the egg just sitting there. We intended to bring it back for the elders to examine, but it hatched."

"Aww, it's cute," she cooed, stroking Scorch's head. "And what do you call this little one?"

Valaric smiled, his eyes gleaming with affection for the tiny Fire Drake. "Scorch," I replied. "It seemed like the perfect name for this fiery companion."

"Indeed, a fitting name for a Fire Drake. I have a feeling this little one will grow up to be quite magnificent," Arabella stated.

"Time will tell," I said. "Scorch hatched just yesterday, but already it seems to have taken a liking to me."

As we continued our conversation, Scorch nuzzled against my hand, emitting a warm and comforting aura. The bond between us was clear, a connection that went beyond words. In the presence of this newfound companion, I found solace and a glimmer of hope amidst the challenges we faced.

"Let's head over to the Ale House and meet the others," I suggested, a faint smile forming on my lips. The weight of recent events lingered, but the prospect of gathering with our companions offered a brief respite.

Arabella nodded, her gaze filled with gratitude and admiration. However, before we embarked on our way, she leaned in and gave me a hug. It was a tender gesture, an expression of appreciation and warmth.

"Thank you," she whispered. "Thank you for risking your life to save someone you knew, someone to whom you owed nothing."

My eyes met hers, my expression reflecting a mixture of humility and determination. "There is no need for thanks, Arabella," I replied, my voice steady. "In times of peril, I would hope that others would extend a helping hand, just as you did for me."

A touch of sadness crossed Arabella's face as she shook her head.

"I wouldn't be so sure," she responded, her voice tinged with a hint of melancholy. "You first came to my rescue, a stranger, and then went above and beyond to assist Sir Gregory. While Vindorians often extend such kindness to their own, it is less common for outsiders to receive such unwavering support. That is why I want to express my deepest gratitude."

I reached out and placed my hand over Arabella's, a silent reassurance of my unwavering loyalty. "Arabella, faced with adversity, unity and compassion, should transcend borders and origins," I said, my voice filled with conviction. "We are all connected, bound by the threads of humanity. It is in our moments of need that we must come together, regardless of our differences."

As we strolled towards the Ale House, my bag carried the soft rustling of Whisperwind's wings and the occasional playful movement of Scorch, the Fire Drake. Arabella, eager to hear about our recent journey, turned her attention to me.

"So, tell me everything about your expedition," she inquired with genuine curiosity. "What did you encounter? What sights did you behold?"

I smiled, captivated by the opportunity to share our adventure with Arabella. I recounted the thrilling moments and the camaraderie that bound our group together. Taking the time to describe the majestic beauty of the Glimmering Caverns, with their shimmering crystals and an ethereal glow. I painted a vivid picture of our ascent to the cliffs, the breathtaking view that greeted us, and the delicate plant nestled amidst the rocks.

As I delved deeper into our tale, my words resonated with excitement and wonder. I spoke of the hidden chamber we had stumbled upon, filled with long-lost artifacts from a forgotten era. The air was thick with mystery and intrigue as I shared the details of our exploration, our teamwork, and the dangers we had faced together.

Arabella listened, her eyes sparkling with curiosity. "It sounds like I missed quite an eventful trek," she exclaimed. "The allure of adventure is strong, and I long to be a part of the next expedition. It seems like an extraordinary experience."

I nodded, understanding Arabella's yearning for the thrill of discovery. "Indeed, it was an incredible journey," I acknowledged.

"And I know future adventures will be captivating. Your presence would add a touch of brilliance to every step we take."

As the Ale House drew nearer, Arabella and I brimmed with eagerness and excitement, our conversation animated. Upon entering the lively establishment, our eyes scanned the room until we spotted Lucas, Ethan, and Aria already seated at a table. I pointed towards our group.

"Over there," I said to Arabella.

Navigating through the bustling crowd, we joined our friends at the table. The atmosphere carried a mix of solemnity and camaraderie as the weight of our recent loss lingered in the air.

I motioned to the barkeep, signaling for a round of ales to be brought to our table. As the drinks arrived, the clinking of mugs resonated in the room, drawing the attention of our companions. We all gathered our mugs and raised them in a heartfelt toast, honoring the memory of Sir Gregory, a valiant knight who had given his life in service to our cause.

"To Sir Gregory, may his fire and fight continue into the afterlife?" I raised my mug high, the flickering candlelight reflecting in my eyes. The words carried a weight of reverence and respect, an acknowledgment of the fallen knight's bravery and unwavering spirit.

"For though I knew him only, in the time we spent together, Sir Gregory proved to be a remarkable knight who extended his hand in friendship," I continued, my voice tinged with a mix of sorrow and gratitude. The table fell into a momentary silence, each person reflecting on their own memories of the valiant knight.

"To Sir Gregory," the words rang out in unison as we all raised our mugs, the clinking of mugs echoing through the room. The golden ale flowed down our throats, a bittersweet reminder of the fleeting nature of life.

As the ale soothed our parched throats, we took turns sharing stories, recounting adventures we had embarked on alongside Sir Gregory. Tales of battles fought, victories won, and narrow escapes danced in the air. Laughter punctuated the somber atmosphere as we reminisced about the humorous mishaps and light-hearted moments that had woven through our trials.

Amidst the stories and laughter, there was a shared understanding that this was not only a time for mourning, but also a time for celebration. It was a celebration of Sir Gregory's life, his unwavering dedication to the kingdom, and the immeasurable contributions he had made. Each one of us at the table honored his memory by recounting the impact he had on our lives and the lessons he had imparted.

As the evening unfolded, we raised our mugs in countless toasts, savoring the shared memories and cherishing the bond we had forged through our journeys together. In those moments, our grief was tempered by the strength we drew from one another, finding solace in the understanding that Sir Gregory's legacy would live on through our own actions and deeds.

The Ale House, once a place of revelry and merriment, transformed into a sanctuary of remembrance, a sacred space where we honored and celebrated the fallen. Amidst our laughter and tears, we paid tribute to Sir Gregory's unwavering spirit, vowing to carry his legacy forward and ensure that his fire and fight would forever burn bright in our hearts.

As the night ended, we exchanged bittersweet smiles and heartfelt embraces, our souls a little lighter and our spirits fortified. Leaving the Ale House, we carried with us the memories of our fallen comrade and the shared bond that would forever unite us. Sir Gregory would be missed, but his legacy would endure, immortalized in the hearts and minds of those who had the privilege of knowing him.

## *Chapter 34 Land*

Seated in the solitude of my room back in the castle of Vindoria, my mind wandered back to the lively atmosphere I had just encountered with my friends at the Ale House. The echoes of laughter and heartfelt toasts still reverberated in my ears. It had been a much-needed respite from the weight of recent events. As I attempted to relax and unwind from the day's events, my thoughts trailed off again to my comrades of the Silver Serpent and how I had arrived in this area.

The crew from the Silver Serpent, my companions on the treacherous journey, remained shrouded in mystery. What had become of them? How had I found myself in my present circumstances?

Images flickered in my mind's eye—snapshots of perilous encounters, moments of camaraderie, and faces etched with determination. The memories were fragmented, like scattered puzzle pieces waiting to be connected.

As I sat in contemplation, my thoughts turned to the tale I had heard from Finnegan, the story of the legendary Grotto. The mere mention of its name ignited a spark within me, igniting my adventurous spirit. The prospect of new discoveries and uncharted territories stirred my soul like never.

I had experienced my fair share of adventures in the past, each one leaving an indelible mark on my journey through life. But this time, it was different. The prospect of sailing alongside Captain Stormrider and his esteemed crew filled me with a potent mix of excitement and anticipation. The allure of the unknown beckoned, and I felt an unyielding desire to embark on this new adventure and uncover the secrets that awaited in the uncharted waters of the Grotto.

I yearned for the thrill of the unknown, the adrenaline that coursed through my veins when faced with the unexpected. I longed to witness sights that no eyes had beheld before, to stand on shores untouched by human footprints and breathe in the intoxicating scent of uncharted territories.

As I reminisced, my mind drifted back to the initial week on the ship, which had passed with no significant events. The crew sailed across the vast expanse of the ocean; their course guided by the gentle caress of the wind. It was during this tranquil period that we focused our efforts on maintaining the ship, ensuring it was prepared for any challenges that lay ahead.

The atmosphere aboard the Silver Serpent was one of camaraderie and shared experiences. The crew members, with their vast knowledge and seafaring wisdom, regaled each other with tales of their past voyages. Their stories painted vivid pictures of lands they had discovered and encountered during their time aboard the ship.

Sitting on the deck, surrounded by the vastness of the ocean, we would gather, our voices intertwining with the rhythmic sounds of the waves. We would recount our encounters with mythical creatures, describe the breathtaking beauty of faraway lands, and share the challenges we had faced on previous expeditions.

At that poignant moment, I spotted Captain Stormrider amidst the bustling activity on the ship. Seizing the chance, I approached the seasoned captain, grateful for the opportunity to express my gratitude and enthusiasm.

"Captain, I wanted to express my sincere appreciation for allowing me to be a part of this grand adventure, for granting me the opportunity to explore uncharted lands." I voiced my gratitude. "I was chatting with Finnegan, and the stories he has about previous adventures are amazing."

A wry smile curved Captain Stormrider's lips as he acknowledged my words. "Ah, so you've been having a chat with Finnegan, have you?" he replied.

I nodded. "Indeed, Captain. His stories have ignited my imagination and filled me with anticipation. From what I've heard, this promises to be an extraordinary opportunity for an adventurer like me."

Captain Stormrider's gaze shifted, lost on the horizon beyond. His weathered face bore the weight of countless voyages and untold tales. When his eyes met mine again, there was a glimmer of shared determination.

"Valaric, lad," the captain began. "Every voyage is an adventure, a test of will and courage. It's not just about exploring new lands, but also discovering the depths of your own character. It's about facing challenges head-on and forging bonds with your shipmates that will withstand the fiercest storms."

"While we have journeyed to uncharted lands, braved the perils of dense jungles, and uncovered precious treasures, the true essence of an adventure lies not only in the events themselves but also in how they are recounted and immortalized," Captain Stormrider explained.

I furrowed my brow, grappling with this perspective. "But Captain, aren't the actual experiences and discoveries what define an adventure? Surely, the tales we weave are inspired by the real exploits."

Captain Stormrider nodded, acknowledging my viewpoint. "Aye, lad, the experiences and discoveries form the foundation of an adventure. But it is the art of storytelling that transforms a mere series of events into legends that stand the test of time."

He gestured toward the crew as they went about their tasks, their camaraderie clear even in the simplest actions. Valaric, an adventure is more than the sum of its parts. It is the spirit of the crew; the bonds forged in the face of adversity, and the triumphs and setbacks that shape the narrative. It is the tales shared around a campfire, the embellishments that stir the imagination, and the captivating way in which those stories are passed down through generations."

I listened to Captain Stormrider, feeling the weight of his words sink in. It wasn't just about the external events; it was about the lasting impact those experiences had on the crew and the stories they would carry forward in time.

"The legends that endure," the captain went on, "are a blend of truth and embellishment. They capture the very essence of our journey, painting vivid pictures in the minds of those who hear them. These tales inspire others to seek their own adventures, sparking a sense of wonder and wanderlust."

A mischievous glint in his eyes, Captain Stormrider asked, "Have you ever heard the one about the mighty whale?" I shook my head, intrigued and eager to hear more.

"Well, there was once a small fishing boat," he began, launching into a story that transported me to a world of excitement and wonder. I was completely captivated by the captain's storytelling as the images unfurled in my mind like a vivid tapestry.

But just as the tale reached its peak, the deckhand's voice rang out, interrupting our moment of shared storytelling.

"Land ho!" they exclaimed, pointing towards the distant shore.

Captain Stormrider's gaze shifted from me to the horizon, his face alive with excitement and determination.

"Ah, it seems our story will have to wait for another time," he said. "But fear not, my young adventurer, for a new chapter in the chronicles of Captain Stormrider and the Silver Serpent is about to unfold."

My heart raced with anticipation, knowing that this was just the beginning of our grand journey. The uncharted land before us held secrets waiting to be discovered, challenges to be overcome, and triumphs to be celebrated.

As the ship sailed through the open sea, the land grew closer with each passing moment. My fellow crew members, brimming with excitement, watched as the unfamiliar terrain beckoned us toward its mysteries. The air was charged with a sense of adventure, and I could feel the Silver Serpent beneath my feet, as if it too shared in our eagerness.

Captain Stormrider stood at the helm; his eyes fixed on the horizon. His voice carried across the deck, commanding both authority and enthusiasm.

"Maintain course and heading," he called out. The crew, well-trained and disciplined, sprang into action, ensuring the ship stayed on its intended path.

The helmsman's grip tightened around the wheel, adjusting the ship's direction as Captain Stormrider's commanding voice resonated through the salty breeze. With purposeful movements, the crew scanned the horizon, eager for the possibilities that lay ahead on this uncharted journey.

Among my comrades, I felt a rush of excitement and curiosity surging through my veins. The allure of exploring new lands, discovering hidden treasures, and encountering untamed wonders ignited a fire within me. I was ready to step onto that foreign soil and embrace the thrilling unknown.

As our ship drew nearer to the unexplored territory, the crew's spirits soared. Each member carried their own dreams and aspirations, united by a shared desire for discovery. We yearned to leave our mark on these untamed lands, to witness landscapes that had never graced our eyes.

The wind carried the scent of possibility, and the waves whispered tales of the adventures that awaited us. Our determination mingled with the saltwater, fueling our resolve. We were the bold few, destined to chart a course into the unknown and etch our names in the annals of exploration. Together, we sailed forward, ready to embrace whatever wonders and challenges this uncharted journey had in store.

As the uncharted land loomed larger with every passing moment, its beauty and mystery beckoned to the crew of the Silver Serpent. Eager to set foot upon this virgin soil and embrace the tales that awaited them, we held our breath in anticipation. Captain Stormrider's unwavering command echoed in our ears, a constant reminder of the responsibility we bore as we ventured into the unknown.

"Release the anchor!" Captain Stormrider's voice boomed, and the crew lowered the heavy anchor, its weight sinking into the depths to secure the massive ship. With the boats prepared and ready, we embarked on the adventure, Valaric among those eager to explore the mysterious land.

As the boats glided into the water, we propelled ourselves towards the territory. Each stroke of the paddle drew us closer, our hearts brimming with excitement and curiosity. Our anticipation swelled, ready to set foot on this unfamiliar soil, eager to uncover its hidden wonders and expand our knowledge. I felt a surge of eagerness coursing through myself, seizing the opportunity to discover and learn in this captivating new environment. With each oar's pull, we embraced the adventure that awaited, prepared to leave our mark on this uncharted land and etch our names in the annals of exploration.

Once we reached the shoreline, we coordinated our efforts to pull the boats up onto the sandy beach. Captain Stormrider, our fearless leader, eagerly took the first step onto the foreign land, feeling the grains of sand beneath his boots.

As he prepared to explore the uncharted territory, a distinct knocking sound on my door interrupted my thoughts, snapping me back to the present moment, and I stood in my room, disoriented.

With a mixture of curiosity and confusion, I made my way towards the door, each step serving as a transition from the vivid world of my imagination to the more mundane reality around me. As I reached the door, uncertainty clouded my mind, wondering who could seek my attention. My hand hesitated for a moment before turning the doorknob, revealing a familiar face on the other side.

"Oh, hello Aria," I greeted. "I wasn't expecting you. What brings you here?"

"May I join you?" Aria's voice floated through the doorway, her presence adding a touch of intrigue to my solitude. I looked up, surprised yet intrigued by her unexpected visit.

I stepped aside, welcoming her into my room. "Of course, please come in," I said, gesturing for her to enter.

Aria entered with a confident stride; her eyes locked with mine. She spoke in a playful tone, her words dripping with allure.

"Considering the wonderful time we had at the Ale House, I thought perhaps we could extend the merriment a little while longer," she suggested, a seductive glint in her eyes.

My lips curved into a charming smile as I met her gaze. "I can't object to such an enticing proposition," I replied, my voice laced with anticipation.

In that moment, a mutual understanding passed between us, as if the air crackled with an electric current. We moved closer, our bodies gravitating towards each other. As our arms encircled one another, we shared a tender embrace, our hearts beating in synchrony.

The room seemed to fade away, leaving only the two of us entwined in each other's arms. Time stood still as we reveled in the moment's intimacy, relishing the connection that had blossomed between us. Our embrace was a testament to the unspoken bond that had formed, a testament to the chemistry that had grown beyond friendship.

## Chapter 35 The Tale of Thalondor

The following morning, I stirred from my slumber, feeling a sense of rejuvenation that had eluded me for quite some time. The softness of the bed embraced me, a stark contrast to the hardness of the beach or the forest floor. As consciousness returned, I recollected Aria, who had paid me an unexpected visit the previous night.

My hand reached out, searching for any lingering trace of her warmth, but the space beside me lay empty of her presence.

"Ah, it seems she slipped away in the night's quiet," I murmured, the words escaping into the stillness of the room.

A subtle smile carved my lips as I recalled the tender moments we had shared. Though brief, our encounter had left an indelible impression on my heart. The memory of our embrace lingered, filling me with a mix of longing and contentment.

I scanned the room, my gaze landing on the slumbering forms of Scorch and Whisperwind nestled in the corner. The responsibilities of the day beckoned, urging me to rise and tend to pressing matters. My voice resonated through the room, breaking the silence.

"Well, my companions, it's time to rouse from our peaceful slumber. We have important tasks ahead of us," I declared, addressing both Scorch and Whisperwind. They responded with simultaneous yawns, uninterested in the impending activities.

Undeterred by their lack of enthusiasm, I chuckled at Scorch and Whisperwind's nonchalant reaction. With a renewed determination, I continued, "Our first order of business is to visit the elders. Perhaps they have uncovered valuable information about the mysterious mark on my leg or any artifacts we retrieved from our recent journey."

As if in agreement, Scorch stretched its tiny wings, emitting a small flame as it yawned once more. Whisperwind, meanwhile, arched his back and stretched, revealing its satisfaction with the leisurely morning.

I lifted Scorch and Whisperwind, placing them inside my bag to ensure their comfort during our journey. As I opened the door, a familiar guard stood in my path, maintaining his dutiful post. I couldn't help but chuckle at the sight.

"Well, it seems one must go to great lengths to prove their harmlessness around here," I remarked. With my companions secured, I ventured out into the castle's corridors, in route to the Elders Hall. However, my path intersected with Arabella, brightening my morning.

"Good morning, Princess," I greeted Arabella. She returned the greeting, curiosity twinkling in her eyes.

"How did you sleep?" Arabella inquired, showing genuine concern. I smiled in response.

"Far better than my nights spent on the forest floor," I confessed, as Scorch and Whisperwind peeked out of my bag, acknowledging their presence.

"Good morning to both of you," Arabella said, extending her hand to caress their heads. The magical creatures purred and chirped in response.

"Where are you headed with such determination this morning?" Arabella asked, her interest piqued.

"I was making my way to the Elders Hall to seek information," I replied, emphasizing the significance of the matter. Arabella's eyes widened with understanding.

"May I join you?" she requested.

"Of course," I responded. "In fact, it's best if you accompany me. The information we seek likely concerns your people as well."

As we meandered through the labyrinthine corridors, Arabella and I engaged in a captivating conversation. Her eyes brimming with curiosity, she broke the silence.

"Do you believe the items you brought back hold great

significance?" she inquired.

I pondered for a moment before responding, my gaze fixed on the path ahead.

"I cannot say for certain," I admitted, "as we could not inspect them. However, it is possible that they unveil hidden truths from the past, knowledge that has eluded everyone."

Arabella nodded, absorbing my words. "Even if they don't reveal groundbreaking discoveries, they can still serve as corroborative evidence, reinforcing what we already know," she remarked.

I smiled, appreciating Arabella's insight. Our shared curiosity and desire for understanding forged a bond as we continued our journey towards the Elders' Hall. With each step, we expected uncovering the secrets that lay within the artifacts, eager to shed light on the history that had been veiled in obscurity.

After traversing the vast corridors, Arabella and I reached the grand entrance of the Elders' Hall. The towering doors swung open, revealing the solemn atmosphere within. The elders, engrossed in their scholarly pursuits, gathered around a table adorned with the artifacts brought back from Serpents Pass.

"Good morning, esteemed elders," I greeted with a respectful nod. "I inquire if any further revelations have emerged from my previous visit or from the items we returned with."

The elders acknowledged our presence, their eyes still fixed upon the objects. One elder, his voice laden with wisdom, addressed Arabella and I.

"Good morning, Princess and Valaric," he replied, his tone measured and calm. "As you can see, we have been examining the artifacts, but our progress in uncovering their true nature has limitations."

The Elder's eyes narrowed in curiosity as he leaned forward. "We have been informed that you possess the rare ability to decipher some of the ancient symbols. Can you confirm if there is any truth to this rumor?" he inquired, his voice filled with anticipation.

My brows furrowed as I considered the Elder's question. Memories of our time in Serpent's Pass resurfaced, reminding me of the symbols I had encountered.

"Indeed, there is some truth to that claim," I admitted. "While in the pass, I deciphered a few of the symbols we encountered. However, because of the limited lighting and time constraints, I couldn't delve into them. Our priority was to retrieve the healing plant and return."

"Would you mind looking at this manuscript that your team returned with to see if you can read the tales written on the manuscript?" asked the elder. I accepted the manuscript with a gentle grasp, my eyes drawn to the ancient text that adorned its delicate pages.

As I delved into the contents of the manuscript, my mind became immersed in a world long forgotten, a tapestry of words and stories that breathed life into the faded ink. With each deciphered line, the tale of Thalondor, once a magnificent jewel of civilization, unfolded before my eyes.

"The manuscript tells of a time when Thalondor stood as a radiant beacon, a kingdom that shimmered with the brilliance of culture, artistry, and intellectual pursuits," I began. "It speaks of a Kingdom that boasted magnificent architecture, intricate and ornate, reaching for the heavens in its grandeur."

My eyes sparkled with enthusiasm as I continued to unravel the manuscript's secrets. "Thalondor thrived on rich traditions and fostered a vibrant community," I explained. "Within its walls, countless schools and academies flourished, drawing scholars, philosophers, and intellectuals from far and wide. It was a place where knowledge and wisdom were revered, where ideas blossomed, and creativity knew no bounds."

The tales inscribed on the manuscript painted a vivid picture of a Kingdom alive with intellectual discourse and artistic expression. My words breathed life into the past, conjuring images of bustling marketplaces adorned with colorful tapestries and vibrant artworks, where the symphony of voices, echoing with debate and contemplation, filled the air.

"The manuscript speaks of brilliant thinkers and visionaries who called Thalondor their home," I continued. "Their minds ignited like the very flames of inspiration, shaping the destiny of the kingdom and leaving an indelible mark on the annals of history."

"What else does it say?" inquired the elder with a mixture of anticipation and curiosity, his eyes fixed on me as I held the precious manuscript in my hands. Now well-acquainted with the tales inscribed within the ancient text, I embarked on an enlightening narration, breathing life into the pages.

"The manuscript delves into the legendary Army of Thalondor," I began, my voice carrying a tone of admiration and respect. "It paints a vivid portrait of a formidable force, armed with high-quality weaponry and donning impenetrable armor. The soldiers of Thalondor were renowned for their unwavering discipline, forged through rigorous training and a commitment to excellence."

My words painted a picture of a military force that stood as a symbol of power and protection, revered both within the boundaries of Thalondor and beyond.

"The reputation of the Army of Thalondor extended far and wide," I continued. "Their valor on the battlefield struck fear into the hearts of neighboring regions and earned the respect of even the most formidable adversaries. They were the guardians of Thalondor's borders, ensuring the safety and security of the Kingdom."

As my narrative unfolded, the manuscript revealed yet another facet of Thalondor's vibrant existence. "Thalondor was not only a seat of military might but also a bustling trade hub," I disclosed. "Nestled amidst the verdant landscapes, Thalondor enjoyed strategic access to the sea and the surrounding regions, fostering prosperous trade routes that connected distant lands. Merchants and traders thrived within the city's walls, their wares and goods enriching the cultural tapestry of Thalondor."

The imagery evoked by my words painted a bustling scene of commerce and exchange, where merchants from far and wide converged to showcase their exotic treasures and engage in lucrative transactions. Thalondor stood as a vibrant crossroads, a melting pot of cultures, where goods, ideas, and stories flowed, breathing life into the city's very essence.

My voice resonated with a deep appreciation of the intricacies of Thalondor's economic prowess.

"The wealth amassed through trade not only contributed to the prosperity of Thalondor but also fueled the flourishing of arts, architecture, and intellectual pursuits," I continued. "The city's coffers overflowed with riches, nurturing an environment where creativity and innovation thrived."

"Does it mention how Thalondor fell to ruins?" inquired the elder in a somber tone, his eyes searching mine for any glimmer of insight. Turning the pages of the manuscript, I scanned the ancient text for clues that would unveil the city's tragic fate.

"As I delve deeper into the manuscript," I began, "there was a series of cataclysmic events and conflicts that befell Thalondor, plunging it into ruin." My fingers traced the faded symbols on the parchment, as if attempting to draw forth the echoes of the past.

"The tales speak of dark forces driven by envy and an insatiable thirst for power," I continued, my voice filled with a sense of foreboding. "These forces, unleashed upon Thalondor, sowed chaos and discord, setting the stage for a great war. The Armies of Thalondor and its valiant citizens fought, their spirits unwavering, but the relentless onslaught of their adversaries eroded their strength."

My words painted a picture of a city consumed by strife and embroiled in a desperate struggle for survival. The manuscript offered glimpses into the courage and resilience of Thalondor's inhabitants, who clung to their homeland even as darkness closed in.

"In an act of desperation, the people of Thalondor resorted to a potent enchantment," I revealed. "This enchantment caused the very land to shift and twist, birthing Eldoria Forest to remove and contain the encroaching dark forces." My words hung heavy in the air as the profound sacrifice made by Thalondor became clear.

As my gaze fell upon the last page of the manuscript, I read the last lines with a mix of hope and determination. "The concluding passage speaks of a prophecy, a glimmer of hope amid the ruins," I shared. "It tells of a day when Thalondor shall rise again, called upon to stem the tides of an impending great battle. The destiny of Thalondor is intertwined with its return to former glory, a beacon of light against the encroaching darkness."

"What a great battle," inquired the elder, his eyes filled with curiosity and concern. I furrowed my brow, flipping through the manuscript once again in search of more answers.

"I don't have all the details," I confessed, a hint of frustration in my voice. "The manuscript alludes to a forthcoming great battle, but it doesn't specify the exact nature or origins of the conflict." I glanced up at the elder, a sense of unease permeating my expression. "What I know is that the enchantment enacted by Thalondor's inhabitants should contain the encroaching darkness for one thousand years."

The elder's face betrayed a mix of anticipation and trepidation. He understood the significance of the timeline mentioned in the manuscript. "How long has Thalondor been in ruins?" I questioned, my voice filled with a mix of curiosity and empathy.

"According to the records and historical accounts we have discovered," the elder began, "Thalondor has languished in ruins for one thousand years." The weight of that revelation hung in the air, a poignant reminder of passing time and the enduring remnants of a once-great civilization.

"We have to notify the King at once," declared the elder, urgency lacing his words. His voice reverberated through the chamber, cutting through the air like a clarion call. With a firm resolve, he commanded, "Call for a messenger!"

The messenger, alerted by the elder's authoritative tone, stepped forward, his eyes filled with concern. "You must inform the King," the elder instructed, his voice tinged with a somber note, "that we bear grave news and that preparations for the worst must be made."

I exchanged a puzzled glance with Arabella. We were unaware of the gravity of the situation, our minds grappling to comprehend the unfolding events. Sensing our confusion, the elder turned his attention to me, his gaze piercing yet filled with a glimmer of hope.

"Lucas mentioned you had discovered parchments, maps of other hidden locations akin to the chamber you found in Serpents Pass," the elder inquired, his voice tinged with curiosity. He sought to glean any information that could shed light on the mysteries surrounding our current predicament.

I nodded, my expression reflecting a mixture of understanding and uncertainty. "From what I could gather by examining those parchments," I responded, my voice measured, "they appeared to be maps depicting hidden locations similar to the chamber we discovered."

Amidst the swirl of excitement and commotion, a small head popped out from my bag. Scorch's vibrant scales shimmered under the flickering light, capturing the attention of the elder.

"What is that creature in your bag," inquired the elder, his eyes filled with intrigue and a hint of trepidation.

My face beamed with pride as I lifted Scorch from my bag, introducing him to the elder. "This is Scorch, a fire drake. We found his egg in the same area where we discovered all these artifacts. To our astonishment, the egg hatched near a raging fire."

The elder's curiosity peaked, and he expressed a desire to examine Scorch up close. I handed the young fire drake to the elder, allowing him to observe the creature's features and demeanor.

"When did he hatch?" inquired the elder, his eyes scanning Scorch's tiny form with keen interest.

"He hatched two days ago, on the night before our return from the mission to retrieve the plant," I responded.

The elder's eyes widened with astonishment as he processed the information. With a sense of urgency, he hurried to retrieve a book from the nearby shelves. Pages were turned, accompanied by the sound of whispered incantations under his breath.

"That creature is far too large to be a fire drake at only two days old," the elder exclaimed, a mix of surprise and awe coloring his voice. "Based on its size and vibrant colors, this can only be one thing—a dragon."

My eyes widened in disbelief, my mind struggling to comprehend the revelation. "A dragon," I repeated, my voice tinged with a blend of astonishment and uncertainty.

The elder nodded with certainty, his gaze fixed upon the book's illustrations and descriptions. "Indeed, my boy. According to the details outlined in this ancient tome, the creature you hold in your hands is none other than a dragon."

The realization hung in the air, filling the chamber with a profound sense of wonder and intrigue. My thoughts raced, contemplating the significance of our discovery—a dragon, a mythical creature steeped in legends and power, had entered our lives in the most unexpected manner.

*Chapter 36 The New Mission*

As the grand doors of the Elder's Hall swung open, revealing the imposing figure of the King, an air of tension and urgency permeated the room. The echoes of his booming voice reverberated through the chamber, demanding an explanation for the commotion that had disrupted the tranquility of his castle.

Gathering his composure, the wise elder stepped forward, bowing before the King. "Welcome, your Majesty," he began, his voice filled with both reverence and concern. "We find ourselves amid grand discoveries and uncertainties, prompting the urgency that fills these halls."

The King's piercing gaze bore into the elder, his eyes demanding answers. "Explain the meaning of this intrusion and the sense of doom that hangs in the air," he commanded.

Taking a deep breath, the elder composed his thoughts, knowing the weight of their revelations would shape the fate of their kingdom. With measured words, he unveiled the recent discoveries, recounting the insights gleaned from the ancient manuscript Valaric had deciphered.

As the elder's voice resonated with wisdom and conviction, he painted a vivid picture of Thalondor's glorious past, its fall into ruins, and the prophecy that spoke of its destined revival. The King listened, his skepticism and curiosity intertwining as he grappled with the magnitude of the revelations.

"How can we be certain that his understanding of the manuscript is accurate?" he inquired, with a hint of skepticism.

The elder, acknowledging the King's astute observation, bowed his head in humility. "Your observation is wise, your Majesty," he conceded. "Indeed, none of us possesses the ability to decipher the ancient symbols with absolute certainty. However, Valaric's knowledge and intellect have proven invaluable in our quest for understanding."

"Father," Arabella spoke up. "I believe in Valaric's sincerity, to the best of his abilities. I have a suggestion, if you would be open to it."

Curiosity piqued; the King turned his attention to his daughter. "I am all ears," he replied, a glimmer of interest shining in his eyes.

Arabella continued, her words flowing with a sense of purpose. "The parchments over there hold valuable information about hidden chambers within Serpent's Pass. It is possible that these chambers may provide further insights into the thousand-year-old enchantment. My suggestion is to send Valaric, accompanied by a skilled team, back to Serpents Pass to seek these hidden chambers. If he finds them, it will lend greater credibility to his claims."

The King pondered Arabella's proposal, contemplating its potential benefits. "I am uncertain of what this will prove," he mused, voicing his reservations. "But very well, we can put this theory to the test. Valaric, if your ability to read the symbols is genuine, locating a few chambers within Serpents Pass should not pose a significant challenge."

"Your Highness, I must emphasize that the parchments are over a thousand years old. The passage of time has altered the landscape, making finding these chambers more challenging than one might expect."

"So, you're suggesting that you cannot read the symbols and that this is all a ruse?" he questioned.

"No, your Highness, that is not what I am implying. I assure you; I can read the symbols to the best of my abilities. However, the transformation of the land over a millennium introduces uncertainties and obstacles that we must confront."

The room fell into a momentary silence as the King absorbed Valaric's explanation, his gaze alternating between the determined faces of his daughter and the young scholar. After a contemplative pause, the King spoke, his voice laced with a mix of caution and resolve.

"Very well, we shall put your claim to the test, Valaric. Return to Serpents Pass with a team and endeavor to find these hidden chambers. The success of your mission will not only validate your abilities, but will provide us with valuable insights into the truth that lies within the ancient symbols."

"Summon Aria, Ethan, and Lucas," commanded the King, as he turned to the messenger. "Valaric, you shall lead the expedition back to Serpents Pass alongside Aria, Ethan, and Lucas, in search of additional chambers within the pass," he declared, his gaze unwavering.

Arabella, filled with determination, stepped forward, her voice eager yet respectful. "Father, I too wish to accompany them on this mission," she pleaded.

The King's stern countenance remained unyielding as he intervened, cutting off Arabella's appeal. "I forbid it," he stated, his tone leaving no room for negotiation. "You are the future of this Kingdom, and I will not jeopardize its fate on a mere scouting expedition," he affirmed, his words echoing with a resolute resolve.

My gaze focused on the elders, my voice filled with a mix of anticipation and curiosity.

"I'm eager to embark on this quest, but I wonder, what are we seeking within Serpents Pass? In the chamber we discovered, there were many intriguing objects, and while our primary aim is to retrieve as much as possible, should we be prioritizing a specific item or artifact?"

The elders exchanged knowing glances; their faces etched with the weight of ancient knowledge. One of them stepped forward, his voice carrying a hint of solemnity.

"Valaric, our aim is twofold. We must gather all that we can from the chamber, for each artifact holds a fragment of the past, whispering tales of power and wisdom. However, above all, we must seek anything that might hold the key to vanquishing the encroaching darkness. We seek a weapon, an insight, or a hidden path that will lead us to victory, preserving our kingdom's prosperity without befalling the same fate that befell Thalondor."

I absorbed the elder's words, the gravity of our task sinking in. My gaze flickered across the chamber, where weapons and ceremonial trinkets stood as silent sentinels of a forgotten era. I couldn't help but wonder if they held secrets capable of turning the tide. With a determined nod, I spoke, my voice tinged with determination.

"In our previous exploration, have any of these artifacts revealed clues or unveiled knowledge that could aid us? Has any weapon or ceremonial trinket shed light upon the path we must tread?"

The elders' expressions grew somber, their eyes reflecting the weight of their journey.

"While some artifacts have given glimpses of ancient wisdom and hinted at untapped potential, their true significance remains veiled. They are pieces of a grand puzzle, awaiting our efforts to decipher their purpose and unlock their hidden truths. It is through our exploration and collective wisdom that we shall uncover the path forward."

Just as the conversation reached its climax, the doors of the Elder's Hall swung open, revealing the figures of Aria, Ethan, and Lucas. Their arrival brought a renewed sense of purpose to the room, as they stood before the King, ready to fulfill their duty.

Lucas, his voice steady and filled with determination, broke the silence. "Your Highness, we have answered your call. How may we be of service?"

The King's gaze shifted from elder to Lucas, his voice firm. "Valaric will lead an expedition back to Serpents Pass and I want you three to accompany him. Explore the depths once more, for we suspect that there are more chambers awaiting discovery, similar to the one you unveiled a few days ago."

Lucas, ever the practical thinker, chimed in, "If we are to delve deeper into the pass and retrieve additional artifacts, we will require extra hands to aid in carrying the precious items back to safety."

The King nodded in agreement, his eyes scanning the room. "Very well. I shall assign a few guards to accompany you on your journey."

With a sense of urgency, the King concluded, "Now, time is of the essence. Head towards the pass before daylight fades. May fortune favor your endeavors and return with haste."

I took charge, my voice commanding yet filled with camaraderie. "Gather the supplies for our expedition. Meet at the same location as last time in fifteen minutes. We shall make our final preparations before venturing into the unknown."

After the allotted time had passed, the team assembled once again at the familiar meeting point, now accompanied by four additional guards. We stood united; our resolve unyielding, ready to embark on a new chapter of our adventure. Our aim was clear: to seek more chambers akin to the one we had discovered, hoping to unearth something that would aid us in our current quest.

As we set forth into the depths of the Eldoria Forest, our footsteps resonating with determination, a peculiar sound reverberated through the air, growing louder and more distinct with each passing moment.

Alerted by the approaching noise, Lucas voiced his frustration. "Just when our journey has begun, we must confront an obstacle already."

With eyes scanning our surroundings, everyone braced themselves for a potential encounter, ready to face whatever lay ahead. The anticipation built, adrenaline coursing through our veins. However, much to our relief, the source of the sound revealed itself to be none other than Shadowfang, our fears unfounded.

"Shadowfang, we mistook you for some formidable creature preparing to engage in battle," Lucas admitted with a mixture of relief and amusement.

Puzzled by Shadowfang's unexpected appearance, I raised an eyebrow. "It is peculiar that Arabella did not mention sending Shadowfang to accompany us on this journey."

"What's with all the standing around? Don't we have an important mission to embark upon?" Arabella's voice broke through the silence, her determination clear in her words.

"What are you doing here?" I asked, a mix of surprise and concern in my voice.

Arabella met my gaze, her resolve unwavering. "I am coming along. I want to witness this firsthand," she declared.

I attempted to interject, citing the King's explicit instructions. However, before I could finish my sentence, Arabella cut me off with a response fueled by unwavering conviction.

"I understand what the King said, but there is too much at stake for me to stand by. We must take action."

Her words hung in the air, resonating with a sense of urgency. The gravity of our mission weighed upon us all. Arabella's determination ignited a spark within the group, reigniting our purpose. I acknowledged the gravity of the situation, succumbing to her resolute spirit.

"Who am I to impede a Princess on a quest of great importance," I mused. "Let us proceed," I added, my voice laced with newfound determination.

## *Chapter 37 Winged Harpies*

As we continued our journey, Lucas's sharp eyes caught sight of something at the edge of his vision. He pointed towards a concealed entrance, obscured by foliage.

"Could that be the entrance to the Glimmering Caverns?" Lucas questioned, a mix of surprise and intrigue in his voice.

I studied the entrance, my mind racing with possibilities. "It bears a striking resemblance," I replied, contemplating whether it was mere coincidence or if the cryptic inscriptions we had discovered held a deeper meaning. However, my thoughts were interrupted by the guard, expressing disbelief.

"That's impossible! We combed this entire area for the entrance," the guard exclaimed.

I raised an eyebrow, my curiosity piqued. "So, you're saying that the entrance was not here when you conducted your search? And why were you searching for it?" I inquired, my tone filled with suspicion.

The guard hesitated for a moment before answering. "It wasn't here, and the King ordered us to find the entrance," he admitted, hinting at a hidden agenda.

My expression hardened as I pressed for more information. "Why would the King task you with such a mission? And how did he even come to know about the entrance?" I questioned.

The guard shifted uncomfortably. "We don't question the King's orders; we carry them out," he responded, evading my inquiries.

Thoughts raced through my mind as I considered the implications of the King's knowledge about the entrance. The revelation hinted at a secret informant or undisclosed motives.

"Interesting," I thought to myself, recognizing that someone must have divulged the entrance's existence to the King.

"Shall we venture inside and see if it leads us to Serpents Pass?" proposed Ethan, his curiosity piqued. Each member paused, considering the possibilities that lay before us.

"Even if we don't find ourselves at Serpents Pass, we can still take a few moments to gather more luminescent rocks for those without them," I acknowledged, recognizing the practicality of the idea. "In the worst case, we spend a few minutes collecting the rocks, but in the best case, we secure both the rocks and a passage to Serpents Pass," I concluded.

"He raises a valid point," Aria chimed in. "No matter the outcome, there's little to lose in attempting it," she added, echoing the sentiment shared by the group.

"Very well, let's venture forth and gather the luminescent rocks," I conceded, a glimmer of anticipation in my eyes.

The group ventured deeper into the winding paths of Glimmering Caverns; our steps guided by the soft glow of the luminescent rocks. As we approached the radiant formations, I instructed everyone to gather only a few, emphasizing the need to conserve our strength for the journey ahead. The anticipation grew as each member handpicked one or two rocks, ensuring we had enough to illuminate the hidden chambers we hoped to discover.

Arabella and the guards were captivated by the ethereal beauty surrounding them. They marveled at the brilliance of the cavern; its walls adorned with a mesmerizing display of luminescence. Time seemed to stand still as we immersed ourselves in the otherworldly glow.

Sensing the need to press onward, I interrupted their reverie. "As captivating as this sight is, we must not lose focus. It's time to continue our journey," I urged, rallying Arabella and the guards. They tore their gaze away from the radiant spectacle and collected their designated rocks.

With our supplies in hand, we retraced our steps toward the cavern's entrance, ready to embark on the next phase of our adventure. However, as we emerged from the cavern, Arabella and the guards were flabergasted to be stand at the entrance of Serpent's Pass. Disbelief mingled with awe as they exchanged astonished glances."

"I knew it would work," Ethan declared, his confidence vindicated by our unexpected arrival.

Arabella couldn't help but inquire, "But how? How did we end up here?"

"That, Princess, remains a mystery," Lucas replied with a wry smile.

Aria chimed in, revealing a similar experience. "We encountered a similar phenomenon when we returned from Serpents Pass before."

"Well, no matter how we got here, we are here now," I remarked, acknowledging the inexplicable turn of events. "Let's focus on the task at hand and gather the items they sent us to retrieve. We can discuss the peculiarities of our journey later, as I doubt we will find a satisfactory explanation."

Deep down, I already held an understanding of why and how we had arrived at Serpent's Pass. However, realizing that it would be challenging to convey such revelations, I opted to keep my thoughts to myself for the time being.

My practical approach was met with agreement.

"You're right, Valaric. Let's keep moving,' concurred Lucas. Turning to me, he inquired, "Have you examined the parchments to determine our next destination?"

I retrieved the ancient parchments and studied the intricate symbols and markings. "Based on my deciphering, the chamber we seek should be further ahead, a short distance from here, on the left side of the pass wall," I informed the group.

The group advanced along the winding path of Serpents Pass in our pursuit of the hidden chamber depicted on the parchment. However, our quest for the chamber was soon overshadowed by a startling realization—we were not the sole inhabitants of the pass. As we pressed forward, a faint but ominous sound caught Lucas's attention.

"Did anyone else hear that?" Lucas questioned, his senses heightened by the eerie atmosphere.

Perplexed, Aria scanned the surroundings, trying to identify the source of the mysterious sound. "Hear what?" she asked, her voice filled with curiosity and concern.

Ethan, however, drew everyone's attention to the skies above. With an urgent tone, he exclaimed, "I think he means those!" His outstretched finger pointed upward, revealing a flock of winged harpies soaring through the air.

The group grasped the gravity of the situation. Lucas, ever vigilant and experienced, took charge. "Prepare yourselves, everyone. We're facing a winged harpy attack," he declared, his voice unwavering despite the impending danger.

"I suppose these are the same harpies Shadowfang and I encountered a few days ago, just before we leaped into the chamber with all of you," Lucas speculated, recalling their previous encounter. "Given that, our best offense and defense will be our bows and magic, unless we catch one of them on the ground."

Lucas's observation resonated with the group as they prepared to face the incoming threat. Arrows were notched, and magical incantations whispered under their breaths. Each member of the team steeled themselves for the impending battle, aware that a single well-placed arrow or a powerful spell could disrupt the relentless advance of the harpies.

Ethan, driven by his impulsive nature, wasted no time in taking action. Drawing his bowstring taut, he let loose an arrow that soared through the air, finding its mark, and striking one harpy. However, the wounded creature persisted, its determination unshaken, while the rest of the flock followed suit, closing in on the group.

"The good news is that we can hit them," Ethan replied to his companions. "But the bad news is that a single arrow won't bring them down, and they are all converging on our location."

"Well, let's see if we can amplify that harpy's pain," Aria declared, her voice filled with determination as she unleashed a crackling lightning bolt toward the injured creature. "Direct hit, and it's going down," she exclaimed, a glimmer of satisfaction in her eyes.

As the harpy fell, the group's momentary triumph was overshadowed by the daunting reality that these things were hard to eliminate. Valaric assessed the situation, acknowledging the odds stacked against them. "Twice as many of them as there are of us, and we're trapped between two walls with nowhere to escape," he observed with a touch of grimness. "Let's focus on launching ranged attacks and take down as many as we can before they're upon us."

Eager to combine their efforts, Ethan proposed a coordinated strategy. "Princess, aim for the second one, and I'll target the first," he instructed, his voice firm. "Aria, unleash your lightning bolts as soon as our arrows find their marks."

With our plan in motion, we unleashed our attacks with precision and synchrony. Arrows soared through the air, finding their targets, while Aria's lightning bolts crackled with raw energy, striking the harpies, and adding to their assailants' agony. Our combined assault proved effective, felling a significant number of the oncoming harpies. However, despite our success, a determined few persisted, continuing their relentless advance toward us.

"Quick, let's repeat the same strategy as before," I stated. "Guards, gather here and be prepared to raise your shields as soon as they launch their arrows," I instructed. The guards positioned themselves, ready to shield the group from the impending attack.

Arabella, Ethan, and Aria eliminated two more harpies with precise strikes, but now the remaining creatures closed in, bringing the fight close. Sensing the imminent threat, we moved closer, seeking refuge under the protective cover of the shields.

"Brace yourselves," I called out as the harpies collided with the shields, their ferocious attacks attempting to breach our defense. The impact was forceful, causing a few guards to stumble and injuring one at the back of the formation.

"We need to get some shots off, even in such close range," Ethan voiced his concern. Determination flickered in his eyes as he spoke. "Just create a small opening for me to aim and shoot," he requested.

We adjusted their positions, creating a small gap within the shield formation, granting Ethan the opportunity to draw his bow. With precise aim, he released an arrow, striking one harpy. However, the damage inflicted was not sufficient, and the harpy's fate remained unclear amidst the chaos.

With the injured guard lying defenseless on the ground, the harpies intensified their assault, targeting their attacks on the vulnerable individual. The rest of the group continued to unleash a barrage of arrows and lightning bolts, trying to fend off the relentless creatures.

"One guard is down and injured," Lucas shouted, his voice filled with concern.

Aria, torn between the urge to heal the injured guard and the necessity to continue launching lightning bolts, sought guidance. "What should I prioritize? Healing the guard or attacking the harpies?" she asked.

"Keep unleashing lightning bolts! If we divert our attention from bringing down the harpies, they'll overwhelm us," Lucas responded with conviction.

Amidst the chaos, my keen eyes detected a harpy lingering on the ground, injured but not yet defeated. "Watch out! There's one on the ground, still posing a threat," I warned the others.

Taking swift action, Lucas switched his focus from ranged attacks to close-quarters combat. With a determined expression, he drew his sword and closed in on the injured harpy. With a powerful strike, he eliminated the grounded threat.

"Stay vigilant and keep aiming for their downfall. I believe there are only five left in the sky," Ethan stated.

Aria, Arabella, and Ethan continued their relentless assault, channeling their arrows and lightning bolts towards the remaining harpies, hoping to eliminate the looming threat.

With each precise strike, the harpies faltered, their once menacing presence waning. "It seems like the remaining harpies are retreating," Ethan reported.

I sensed a momentary respite and urged my companions to check on the fallen guard. Lowering Whisperwind to the ground, I entrusted the loyal creature to administer the initial healing. Aria made her way to the guard's side, her heart heavy with anticipation.

Her examination yielded a grim outcome. Aria's voice trembled as she relayed the tragic news. "I'm afraid the guard didn't make it," she said, her words carrying the weight of loss.

"Indeed, this was not an outcome we wanted," I remarked, my voice tinged with exhaustion and lingering tension.

Lucas, his tone filled with understanding, chimed in, offering insight into our daring decision to enter the chamber." You now understand why Shadowfang and I took the leap. It was a formidable challenge, even for two skilled archers and a lightning caster. There was no other option for us," Lucas explained.

I nodded, realizing the gravity of our actions. "Let us now pay our respects to our fallen comrade and ensure that we bring him back to the kingdom with the dignity he deserves," I suggested, my voice firm.

Together, we organized ourselves, making the preparations to honor our fallen companion. With unwavering determination, two of the remaining three guards stepped forward, ready to bear the weight of their fallen comrade and carry him back to the kingdom. It was a solemn task, a solemn duty, but one we approached with reverence and solemnity.

As the remaining members of the party pressed forward in our search for the first hidden chamber, I scanned the surroundings with keen eyes. Upon reaching a particular location, I turned my gaze to the right, a spark of recognition igniting within me.

"Wait a moment," I spoke up, my voice filled with realization. "Isn't this where we emerged from the first chamber?" I questioned, seeking confirmation from my companions.

Lucas nodded, a wry smile gracing his lips. "Indeed, you have a sharp memory. We arranged the area to appear undisturbed, so as not to arouse suspicion."

My mind raced with possibilities. "Alright, everyone, let's search the vicinity. There must be a mechanism here, like the one we discovered on the other side," I directed, urgency clear in my voice.

The party dispersed, our hands moving with increasing speed and determination, exploring every nook and cranny. Amidst the flurry of our search, it was Aria who, through a stroke of luck or intuition, stumbled upon the concealed mechanism.

"I think I found something," Aria announced, her voice filled with a mix of excitement and relief.

Our group gathered around her, anticipation palpable in the air. With a decisive push from Aria, the hidden passageway revealed itself, though not wide enough for immediate passage.

"We've uncovered the entrance," I declared. "Now, let us combine our strength and pry it open wide enough for us to enter."

With concerted effort and unwavering determination, the team worked together, leveraging our combined strength to widen the opening. Our persistence paid off, granting us access to the secrets concealed within.

As we stood on the threshold of the revealed chamber, a mixture of trepidation and anticipation filled our hearts. We knew that beyond these ancient walls lay the potential for untold knowledge, and with each step we took, our journey into the unknown continued.

## *Chapter 38 The Armies of Thalondor*

As we stepped into the first chamber, we pulled out our luminescent rocks, casting an ethereal glow that illuminated the winding paths before us. Step by step, we made our way through the labyrinthine passages, our anticipation building with each turn.

We arrived at the entrance of the chamber, and what we beheld left us breathless. The sheer grandeur of the ancient space struck us like a reverberating chord, resonating with the weight of a thousand years of untouched history. It was as if time had stood still within these walls, preserving a forgotten era that had long been sealed off from the rest of the world.

Statues of regal figures lined the chamber, their stone gazes fixed in stoic reverence. Weapons gleamed with an ancient luster, a testament to the skill of their long-lost craftsmen. Delicate jewelry adorned pedestals, shimmering with an otherworldly radiance. And amidst it all, stacks of parchment lay, holding secrets and tales waiting to be unveiled.

Our team stood in awe, our eyes dancing across the magnificent tableau before us. This chamber, much like the previous one, held a similar trove of treasures, artifacts that whispered stories of a forgotten era. It was a sight that filled us with both reverence and curiosity, beckoning us to delve deeper into the mysteries that lay shrouded in the shadows of time.

I marveled at the sight before me, my eyes tracing the intricate details and ancient artifacts that adorned the chamber. Arabella, standing beside me, shared in my awe, her curiosity piqued by the unknown wonders that lay within.

"Look at all of this," I exclaimed.

Arabella's gaze shifting from one fascinating object to another couldn't help but feel a sense of wonder. "Does this chamber resemble the one you encountered?" Arabella inquired, her voice filled with genuine curiosity.

I nodded, a smile playing at the corners of my lips. "Indeed, the layout and essence of this chamber have striking similarities to the one we discovered before."

As the rest of the party explored the chamber, our collective excitement filled the air. Driven by my thirst for knowledge, I made my way towards the parchments that lay nearby, eager to unravel the secrets inscribed upon them.

"I'll inspect these parchments," I stated. "Let us know if anyone stumbles upon something more intriguing than what we already discovered at the Elders' Hall," I added.

After spending a considerable amount of time poring over the parchments, I took a moment to assess our findings. We had searched for any trace of new information, but the manuscripts contained mostly familiar accounts of Thalondor's structure and daily operations. Disappointment weighed upon our hearts, for our hopes of uncovering prophecies or insights into the thousand-year-old enchantment remained unfulfilled.

"I'm afraid there isn't much here that we haven't already seen," I admitted. "These manuscripts provide a deeper understanding of Thalondor's inner workings, but they offer no direct mention of prophecies or the duration of the enchantment."

"Perhaps it's time we turn our attention to the second hidden chamber, as the King had requested. Who knows, it might hold more substantial clues. We can always return to this chamber, if need be," said Lucas.

"You're right. Let's make our way back to the entrance and venture forth to the next chamber. Perhaps there, amidst the undiscovered secrets and untold tales, we will find the answers we seek."

We retraced our steps back towards the entrance of the chamber, our anticipation growing as we hoped to discover another hidden chamber. Once we reached the entrance, we exited and closed it behind us, ensuring that the chamber remained concealed, just as we had done with the first one.

"Now, where do we go from here?" Ethan asked.

"I'm examining the parchments as we speak," I replied. "If we continue in the same direction we were heading, we'll reach a wall. At that point, our only options will be to turn left or right."

"I am familiar with that location," said Lucas. "Great, Lucas! Lead the way," I exclaimed, a spark of hope lighting up my eyes. I followed Lucas, who confidently took the lead with a sense of purpose.

The rest of the team, filled with anticipation, fell into step behind Lucas. We navigated the winding paths of the Serpent's Pass until we reached the location described on the map.

"Alright, team, let's get to work," I declared. The group dispersed, their hands exploring every inch of the wall, searching for any sign of a hidden mechanism or passage. Hope and anticipation filled the air as we embarked on our quest to uncover another secret chamber.

Minutes turned into what felt like hours as we combed through the wall, our fingers tracing the ancient stone, seeking any irregularity or subtle hint that would lead us to our next discovery. Doubt crept in, casting shadows on our confidence in my ability to decipher the ancient symbols. Then it occurred, almost in unison, "I found something," Lucas and Arabella exclaimed, their voices intertwining in a chorus of exhilaration.

We stood there, stunned by the dual discovery. Uncertainty and caution hung in the air as we contemplated the implications of our findings. My voice broke the silence, voicing the unease that had settled among us.

"Did both of you find something?" I asked.

Lucas and Arabella nodded in unison, their expressions mirroring the shared surprise.

"I was afraid you were going to say that." We, now faced with the prospect of two mechanisms, exchanged uncertain glances. Our minds raced with possibilities, wondering if one was a trap while the other held the key to unlocking the passage.

"We must consider the possibility that one of these could be a trap while the other opens the passage."

"No offense, Princess, but in this case, we cannot afford for you to pull either of them," I cautioned.

"Lucas, are you willing to take the risk and pull one mechanism without knowing what may occur?" I asked. The weight of responsibility lay heavy in my words.

Lucas nodded. "Yes, I am prepared. Have Aria ready to heal, just in case, though."

As we regrouped in the original passageway of Serpent's Pass, the tension mounted. Lucas positioned himself in front of the mysterious mechanism, his heart pounding with anticipation. Uncertainty filled the air as they all gathered, their eyes fixed on Lucas, unsure of what would transpire.

"I'm getting ready to push it," Lucas declared. "Everyone, be on the lookout." We stood alert, their senses heightened, ready to react to any unforeseen danger.

Lucas took a deep breath, his hand trembling as he prepared to activate the mechanism. "In three, two, one," he counted down. With a resolute push, the mechanism responded with a satisfying click.

"Nothing happened," Lucas stated.

"Are you sure you pushed it correctly?" Ethan asked.

"I'm uncertain. Is there a wrong way to push it?" Lucas replied.

"Alright, that's not getting us anywhere. Lucas let's switch places. I'll push the other mechanism."

With Lucas now standing alongside the others, I positioned myself in front of the second mechanism. Uncertainty hung in the air as we contemplated the possibility of this being the trap we had feared. I could sense the collective apprehension, knowing that they were all watching me, hoping for a different outcome this time.

Taking a deep breath to steady my nerves, I assessed the situation. The first mechanism had yielded no results, leaving me wary yet determined to proceed cautiously.

I glanced at my companions, seeking reassurance. "Is everyone out of the way?" I inquired, my voice laced with a mix of caution and resolve.

"Yes," they confirmed in unison.

I braced myself, preparing for the unknown. With a flicker of determination in my eyes, I pushed the mechanism, unsure of what awaited us. A collective breath was held as we waited for any sign of progress.

Suddenly, a crack appeared on the wall, emerging from the center between the two mechanisms. It started as a hairline fracture, widening and revealing a hidden passageway. The team's tension eased as the realization dawned upon us that no danger had been triggered.

I observed the imposing double doors that stood before us, serving as the entrance to the pass. Their sheer size left us pondering how we could gain access. Ethan voiced our collective concern, questioning the feasibility of opening such massive doors.

I contemplated the situation, offering a glimmer of hope. "I believe we don't need to open both doors. We just need to create enough space to allow us to enter," I suggested, considering the practicality of our task.

"Why is this passage so much larger than the others?" Aria wondered aloud.

"Perhaps the reason behind its size will reveal itself once we gain access," I mused.

With renewed determination, the team collaborated, pooling their strength and ingenuity to unlock the passage. They experimented with various methods, exploring every avenue to open the doors. After many attempts, we made progress, budging one side ever so slightly.

Having deciphered the mechanics of the process, we synchronized our efforts, employing our combined strength to widen the gap. We applied force to the door, exerting ourselves until it yielded, revealing a narrow opening just large enough for us to squeeze through.

"Alright everyone, let's proceed and discover what lies within," I said. "Retrieve your luminescent rocks and prepare yourselves, for we venture into the unknown."

The team, armed with their glowing stones, squeezed through the opened passage, their hearts filled with a mix of excitement and trepidation. They emerged into a vast expanse that extended far beyond the reach of their feeble light. I, ever cautious, reminded the team to remain alert.

"Be prepared for anything," I cautioned. "In this expansive darkness, we cannot expect what dangers may lurk."

Undeterred, we pressed forward, our steps echoing through the vast space. As our eyes adjusted to the dim illumination, a peculiar sight greeted our gaze. We stood amidst what seemed to be the heart of an ancient army. Weapons of war, siege weapons, and even remnants of a cavalry lay scattered throughout the chamber.

I marveled at the sight; my voice filled with astonishment. "There must be at least twenty thousand stone statues of warriors here," I whispered, awestruck by the sheer magnitude of the spectacle.

"It's rather peculiar, isn't it? Who would invest so much time and effort to assemble this vast collection?" Lucas pondered aloud.

As we surveyed the awe-inspiring sight of the multitude of statues, our minds filled with wonder and curiosity. It was a scene that defied comprehension, and we felt compelled to explore further. I took charge, suggesting we split into teams to cover more ground and increase our chances of discovering something of significance.

With a rational plan in mind, Lucas, Ethan, and the remaining guard ventured off in one direction, while Arabella, Aria, Shadowfang, and I embarked on our own path. We weaved through the silent company of stone warriors, our eyes scanning every crevice and detail in search of clues that could aid our quest.

Time seemed to stretch as our teams roamed through the ancient statues, our footsteps echoing in the vast chamber. Each team pressed onward until we reached the outer walls, having traversed in opposite directions. We continued our exploration, moving away from the entrance until we encountered what appeared to be the farthest point within the chamber.

Standing at the back wall, we turned to face each other and started making our way back, our steps leading us towards one another. With each stride, we drew closer, our anticipation growing. Our paths converged at another passageway, beckoning us to venture even deeper into the depths of this mysterious place.

"Indeed, let's press on and discover what lies ahead," I commented, while taking the lead. Arabella nodded in agreement, and we proceeded down the winding passageway, our anticipation mounting with each step. We reached a room branching off from the hallway.

We entered the room, eager to unravel the secrets it held. Inside, we found shelves lined with ancient tomes and a table adorned with scattered parchments. My eyes gleamed with anticipation, realizing that we might have stumbled upon the very knowledge we sought.

"I believe we've found what we were searching for," I remarked. I wasted no time in immersing myself in the study of the parchments, determined to decipher their contents and glean valuable insights. The rest of us, however, continued exploring the pathway, ensuring that no lurking dangers awaited us further ahead.

"That's a wise plan. We'll venture down the path and keep a vigilant eye out," Lucas proposed.

I expressed my gratitude, acknowledging the importance of our shared responsibilities.

"I'll stay here with you, Valaric. Besides, a moment of respite will do me good," Aria offered.

I nodded, grateful for her presence and support.

While I immersed myself in the collection of parchments, my eyes fell upon a trove of battle plans and designs for the formidable weapons we had encountered during our journey. The room seemed to hold valuable insights into the military prowess of the past, shedding light on the origins of these powerful artifacts.

As I examined the parchments, my attention was drawn to a specific one placed next to a small, ornate box. Its contents hinted at something momentous—the very information we had embarked on this perilous quest to uncover. Excitement coursed through my veins as I realized the significance of my discovery.

"I believe I've found it," I exclaimed, a mixture of triumph and relief in my voice. The weight of our journey, the challenges we had overcome, now felt justified. Aria, by my side, couldn't contain her enthusiasm.

"Really? That's incredible! I'm glad our efforts weren't in vain," Aria exclaimed, a smile spreading across her face.

The prospect of uncovering the truth behind our mission reinvigorated our spirits, reaffirming our purpose.

As I delved deeper into the parchment next to the box, my eyes followed the ancient symbols that foretold of a pivotal moment when the armies of Thalondor would awaken, ready to defend the world against looming evils. The weight of the words sank in, igniting a mixture of curiosity and concern within me.

However, as I reached the latter part of the parchment, I made a disquieting discovery—several pages were missing, leaving gaps in the narrative. My brows furrowed in contemplation.

"Interesting," I mused aloud. The absence of those pages raised questions about what vital information might have been lost to time.

I turned my attention to the small box nearby, anticipating that it might hold further clues. To my surprise, when I opened the box, it revealed emptiness within its confines. Yet, the realization struck me like a lightning bolt. There, carved into the box's interior, was a rough cutout bearing an uncanny resemblance to the shape of the ornate dagger I had been carrying in my bag all along.

A mixture of astonishment and realization washed over me. Could it be possible that the dagger I had carried possessed a key role in unraveling this enigma? My mind raced as I connected the dots, considering the implications of this newfound revelation.

"Could I have been carrying the key to this entire puzzle all this time?" I muttered softly to myself.

"What was that? Did you say something?" asked Aria.

"Um, nothing," I replied. "Just lost in my thoughts for a moment."

Just then, Lucas, Arabella, and the guard arrived at our location. As if guided by an unspoken understanding, they uttered, "Guess what we found?"

"What did you discover further down the path?" I asked.

Ethan's eyes gleamed with excitement as he revealed, "Another egg, similar to the one you found."

A flicker of recognition flashed across my face, mingling with a tinge of astonishment. "Could it be?" I pondered aloud.

Arabella stepped forward, cradling the found egg. "That's what we thought, so we brought it with us," she explained, her voice tinged with wonder.

"And what did you stumble upon?" Lucas inquired.

"We found the parchment detailing the awakening of the ancient army," I began. "However, there are missing pages we believe hold crucial information. And right beside it, we discovered an empty box."

"Indeed, we have gathered all the artifacts to bring back to the elders," Lucas remarked. Contemplating the perilous journey through Serpents Pass during the night, he proposed, "It would be wise for us to remain here and take refuge until morning. Venturing in the darkness would pose too great a risk."

"That works well for me. I can use the time to explore this chamber and see if there are any other hidden secrets awaiting us," I said.

With our decision made, we settled down, making ourselves as comfortable as possible within the ancient chamber. We prepared a makeshift camp, ensuring our safety and keeping a vigilant watch. The mysteries of the chamber surrounded us, urging us to rest well and embrace the anticipation of the new day's discoveries.

As I prepared to rest for the night, a nagging thought consumed my mind. Could it be possible that the missing pages from the parchment I had discovered were nestled among the parchments I had been carrying all this time? Intrigued by the notion, I withdrew the parchments from my bag, inspecting them. To my astonishment, the torn edges of the parchments I held aligned with the missing portions of the original parchment.

Excitement coursed through my veins as I realized the significance of my discovery. With renewed vigor, I began delving into the ancient symbols inscribed on the parchments I had possessed. The words revealed a crucial revelation—the key to the awakening lay hidden within the depths of Thalondor, concealed beneath the very castle that was in ruins. Buried within the castle's labyrinthine dungeons, the answers I sought awaited.

Realizing the urgency of our situation, my determination soared. We couldn't afford to rest just yet, for the mysteries of Thalondor beckoned us. It was imperative to investigate the castle and uncover the secrets that lay dormant within its ancient walls before we could find respite.

## *Chapter 39 Glimmering Caverns Mishap*

As we stirred awake, our minds buzzed with anticipation of our return to the kingdom, bearing the valuable knowledge we had uncovered during our expedition.

Breaking the morning silence, I remarked, "There is an abundance of history hidden within these walls."

Arabella, sharing the sentiment, nodded in agreement. "Indeed, this journey has opened our eyes to a wealth of knowledge we were unaware of," she affirmed.

With a sense of purpose, we prepared to depart, making sure everything was packed and accounted for. A unanimous show of readiness resonated through the group, a clear signal they were eager to make their way back to the kingdom.

In a determined tone, I declared, "Let us set forth and make our return."

Leaving the chamber behind, we ventured through the expansive area adorned with the towering stone army, our eyes drifting over the intricate details of the statues. Step by step, we advanced, each footfall resonating with a newfound understanding of the history that surrounded us. The weight of our discoveries infused our movements with purpose.

With a mix of satisfaction and caution, we reached the familiar entrance we had squeezed through the previous day. As we bid farewell to the chamber that had unveiled its secrets to us, we knew it was crucial to conceal our discovery from prying eyes. Putting our combined efforts into action, we closed off the access point, leaving behind no obvious trace of the chamber's existence.

Despite our best attempts, a faint line on the stone wall remained, hinting at the concealed passageway. It served as a lingering reminder of the hidden realm we had traversed—a secret we hoped would remain elusive to those unaware of the mechanisms that opened its doors. We held our breath, relying on the hope that our concealment efforts would be enough to safeguard the chamber's mysteries.

Little did we know the events set in motion would soon overshadow any concerns about the chamber's discovery. Fate had its own plans, weaving a chain of events that would captivate our attention and redirect our focus. The impending tide of events loomed ahead, beckoning us to navigate uncharted waters and face unforeseen challenges.

As we continued our descent down Serpents Pass, we noticed that our progress was smoother and faster compared to our arduous climb.

"Let's hope that the harpies don't return," Ethan said.

"I have to agree. Those harpies did nothing but hinder our progress. We need to stay focused and catch up," Aria said.

"Alright, I know everyone is thinking about the other piece as well," Ethan began.

Curiosity sparked within Arabella, and she asked, "What's that?"

Ethan, with a thoughtful expression, responded, "I'm referring to whether or not we should enter Glimmering Caverns through the same entrance we exited from yesterday."

Considering our previous experience, Lucas voiced his opinion. "Well, for us, it worked out twice. So, I will try it again. Going through the moving cavern seems to cut down on the time to travel between locations."

Ethan continued, assuaging any doubts that might have arisen. "Even if it doesn't work out as we hope, we've noticed that we spend only about fifteen to twenty minutes inside the cavern. So, it won't be a significant loss if we give it another shot."

"Well, we may all be getting ahead of ourselves. The entrance may not even be in that location," I added.

Lucas, ever practical, asserted, "I guess there is only one way to find out. Let's continue to the bottom of the pass."

We marched onward as our anticipation built with each step. As fortune would have it, when we reached the bottom of the pass, we discovered that the entrance to Glimmering Caverns remained in the same location.

"Well, it is our lucky day," exclaimed Lucas. We stood at the entrance of Glimmering Caverns, still amazed it remained in the same spot.

Without hesitation or further debate, the group ventured into the depths of Glimmering Caverns. The air felt fresh, charged with anticipation, as we treaded the familiar path.

"You know what I've been wondering?" Aria began, her voice echoing in the cavern.

Lucas, always attentive, turned to her and asked, "What's that?"

She paused for a moment, collecting her thoughts. "When I first came in here, there were many little creatures scurrying about the cavern. But now, it seems like there are none. Even when we're not around, why don't any of them venture near the entrance?"

"You're right, Aria. We stumbled upon a few of those creatures when we came searching for you. It's curious why they seem absent now," Ethan mused.

Lucas took a moment to reflect before responding, "Perhaps that is yet another enigma we'll have to unravel on another day. For now, let's focus on our current journey and the mysteries that lie ahead."

As we continued down the winding paths of the cavern, we arrived at the site where the intense battle against the Gem Golem had taken place. Shimmering remnants of shattered gems adorned the floor, serving as a somber reminder of the formidable opponent we had faced.

"You should have seen it! Aria was over there, Lucas was over there, and I was sprawled out right over there," Ethan exclaimed, as he pointed to different spots. "If it weren't for you, Valaric, none of us would have made it."

I waved off his praise, trying to remain humble. "Come on, it was just a stroke of luck when I landed critical hit while blocking. If it weren't for that fortunate strike, I would have been defeated too," I explained.

Ethan's mischievous grin persisted as he added, "Luck or not, we can all laugh and talk about it today because of that moment," appreciating the shared bond forged through our ordeal.

Feeling satisfied with our exploration, I suggested it was time to begin our journey back to the kingdom. The distance ahead was considerable, and we needed to cover it before nightfall. The group nodded in agreement, ready to retrace our steps.

Just as we were about to turn and head back, my gaze caught a familiar statement etched on the cavern walls:

"Victor of Glimmering Caverns possesses mystical abilities within the caverns."

It struck a chord within me, and the pieces of the puzzle fell into place.

A profound realization dawned on me. I was the catalyst for the appearance of the entrance and the determination of our destination. Somehow, I possessed a unique connection to the caverns, explaining why no one else could find the entrance in my absence.

"Well, Princess, what did you think of all that?" Ethan asked.

"It was all quite exquisite," Arabella replied, choosing her words as she noticed my discomfort with the conversation.

"You know, it's okay to take some credit," Arabella said, sensing my humility. "It sounds like if it hadn't been for you, none of them would be here today."

I shrugged, still reluctant to accept the praise. "I understand, but again, it was more sheer luck than skill that aided the situation."

"Luck or not, the result remains the same," Arabella insisted. "You all walked out of the cavern alive and victorious."

I paused, considering Arabella's words. "I suppose you're right," I conceded, but to stop the conversation.

We pressed on; the sight of daylight beaming buoyed our spirits through the cavern entrance in the distance. I couldn't help but feel a surge of hope, wishing that the cavern had shifted once again, just like it had on our previous two journeys. The prospect of a shorter trip back to the kingdom, perhaps by at least a day, filled us with excitement and anticipation.

Fueled by the prospect of reaching the entrance, we quickened our pace. Each step brought us closer to the light, and our enthusiasm grew with every passing moment. We could almost taste the joy of returning to the kingdom, imagining the warm welcome that awaited us at the kingdom's edge.

But as we emerged from the cavern, our elation turned to bewilderment. The landscape before us was unfamiliar and far from the familiar surroundings of the kingdom. The truth became apparent: the cavern had indeed shifted locations, but not to our desired destination.

Staring out at the unfamiliar terrain, we felt a mix of disappointment and confusion. The reality of our situation sank in, dashing our hopes of a swift return. Our journey was far from over, and we would need to adapt and navigate this new, unexpected landscape.

## *Chapter 40 Lost*

Lost, we scanned our surroundings, trying to make sense of our new location. The sight before us was one of desolation and decay. Dilapidated structures stood as haunting reminders of a forgotten era, their crumbling walls whispering stories of a bygone time. Weathered statues, once grand and majestic, now stood as mere echoes of forgotten glory.

Puzzled and apprehensive, Aria broke the silence, voicing our shared confusion. "Does anyone recognize this place?" she asked with uncertainty.

We exchanged glances, our brows furrowed in deep thought. The eerie landscape seemed unfamiliar, a forsaken realm that none of us had ever encountered.

Ethan's voice trembled with a mix of awe and unease. "I've traveled around the kingdom, but I can say with certainty that this is no land I've ever set foot in," he stated, his words echoing the sentiments of the group.

As we continued to survey the desolate expanse, questions swirled in our minds, seeking answers that were absent.

"What could have caused the Glimmering Caverns to transport us to this forsaken place?" Aria questioned, her tone tinged with urgency.

Arabella, ever perceptive, offered her insight. "It seems we have stumbled upon an area that time itself has forgotten," she observed.

The decaying structures and weathered statues bore witness to pass countless years, their presence a testament to the abandonment and neglect that had befallen this desolate realm.

Lucas' revelation broke the veil of uncertainty that enveloped us, filling us with a mix of relief and curiosity. All eyes turned towards him, our anticipation palpable, as we yearned to understand the truth behind our current whereabouts.

"We are in the Ruins of Thalondor," Lucas declared. The words hung in the air, resonating with a mixture of awe and intrigue.

Aria's eyes widened in astonishment, her mind struggling to reconcile the ancient tales she had heard with the reality before her.

"The ruins," Aria exclaimed. "But how? Why would the Glimmering Caverns lead us here?" Her words echoed the bewilderment that gripped the entire group. We had never contemplated venturing into the forgotten remnants of Thalondor, yet fate had guided us to this place.

In silent contemplation, we exchanged glances, each member grappling with our own thoughts and questions. The puzzle pieces of our journey seemed to defy logical connections, leaving us yearning for answers that remained elusive.

Amidst the confusion and uncertainty, I broke my prolonged silence, my voice carrying an air of revelation. We turned their attention towards me, their eyes fixated on my every word, hoping for an explanation that would dispel their bewilderment.

"I may know why we are here. In fact, it's possible that I am the reason we find ourselves in this place," I declared. My words hung in the air, leaving my companions stunned and eager for further explanation.

"You? How could you be responsible for all of this?" Aria interjected. The others nodded in agreement, their gazes fixed on me, awaiting a coherent explanation for my cryptic claim.

I took a deep breath, gathering my thoughts before continuing. "Think about it," I began, my voice laced with conviction. "The entrance to Glimmering Caverns appeared in the same location we were at, or it led us to the exact places we intended to go. But what if it wasn't a collective decision? What if my presence alone influenced it?"

My words hung in the air, their weight sinking in as the team contemplated the implications. Confusion etched itself onto their faces as they struggled to comprehend my assertions.

Lucas, unable to contain his frustration, interjected, "Valaric, you're not making any sense of your rambling. How can you claim to be the sole influence behind our journey?"

"I believe it's because I delivered the final blow to the Gem Golem," I stated with conviction.

Confusion clouded Ethan's face as he questioned my assumption. "But how does that make you responsible?" he asked, seeking clarification.

I took a moment to collect my thoughts before responding. "Consider the facts we've encountered so far," I began. "The guards could not find the entrance, yet whenever we were present in an area, the entrance revealed itself. And each time we focused on a destination; the caverns guided us there."

Lucas, still skeptical, interjected, "But that doesn't explain how you alone led us to this destination. All those instances occurred when all four of us were together."

I nodded, acknowledging Lucas's point. "You're right, but think about the destination we all hoped the caverns would lead us to," I proposed. We pondered for a moment, then answered, "The Kingdom."

"Exactly," I affirmed. "I was the only one among us who desired to come to this specific location. I was the only one who could perceive the hidden message on the cavern wall."

"What message are you referring to?" Asked Aria.

I paused, then revealed the cryptic words etched on the cavern wall. "It said, 'Victor of Glimmering Caverns possesses mystical abilities within the caverns."

We fell silent, absorbing the weight of my revelation. The pieces of the puzzle were falling into place, unveiling a connection between my triumph over the Gem Golem, my unique perception of the hidden message, and the remarkable influence I seemed to wield within the caverns.

"But why would you choose to come here instead of returning to the kingdom to share the information we discovered in the hidden chambers?" Ethan inquired.

I sighed, contemplating my response. "Because, if we're honest, the information we've gathered during our journey is rather limited," I explained. "All we've accomplished is uncovering a few additional chambers by my ability to decipher the ancient symbols."

"We still lack a clear understanding of how much time remains before the impending evil resurfaces. Without that knowledge, it would be futile for the King to prepare the kingdom for a threat that he may not believe exists--especially when his faith in my ability to read the ancient symbols is questionable."

We absorbed my words, realizing the inherent challenges we faced. The urgency of our mission weighed upon us, yet without solid evidence and a comprehensive understanding of the impending danger, convincing the King to act would be hard.

I spoke, my voice carrying a mix of earnestness and apology as I addressed the team. "I understand that none of you are thrilled about our current situation, and you might harbor some resentment towards me," I began, acknowledging the potential tension in the air. "But I believe that investigating this area before returning to the kingdom is necessary."

I paused, giving my companions a chance to absorb my words. "Of course, if any of you decide that you'd rather head back, I won't stand in your way. The kingdom is a three to four-day journey east of here," I offered, providing an alternative for those who felt compelled to return.

Turning my attention to the guard, I continued, "You could share the story I've relayed to you based on the information I deciphered from the ancient symbols," I suggested, handing over the materials I had gathered from the chambers. "You know the kingdom, its people, and the King's trust better than anyone. Perhaps your firsthand account will have a greater impact."

The group exchanged glances, their thoughts swirling with a mixture of uncertainty and contemplation. My request carried weight, and they grappled with the implications of our next steps. As we deliberated, we recognized the importance of our mission, the need for solid evidence, and the potential consequences of returning without substantial information to support our claims.

Arabella's voice resonated with determination as she spoke up to support me. "You know what? He's right. My father won't heed the words of an outsider, but if I accompany you into the ruins, perhaps we can unravel this mystery together," she declared.

The group listened to Arabella's decision, and one by one, they echoed their agreement. Each member recognized the significance of gathering more information before making our way back to the kingdom. They understood that returning without concrete evidence or insights would do little to sway the King's judgment.

"Agreed. Let's make the most of the remaining daylight and continue our journey. Our starting point should be the castle," I replied. "According to the parchments, the answers we seek lie within the lower levels of the castle."

With the guard now in route back to the kingdom, we embarked on the path leading to the imposing castle. Determination fueled our steps as we navigated through the ruins, our anticipation growing with each passing moment. We were eager to uncover the secrets concealed within the ancient walls.

## *Chapter 41 The Awakening*

With our eyes fixed on the crumbling yet awe-inspiring architecture that surrounded us, we continued our journey toward the castle. As we traversed through the remnants of Thalondor, we couldn't help but marvel at the city's former grandeur, despite having fallen into ruin over a millennium.

The once bustling streets, now overgrown with weeds and tangled vines, gave glimpses of what Thalondor might have been--a vibrant hub of trade and commerce. Ethan's words echoed through the dilapidated marketplace, conjuring images of merchants and customers engaging in lively transactions. Aria's imagination painted a vivid picture of the bustling atmosphere, where the air would have been filled with the scents of exotic spices and the echoes of animated conversations.

As we continued our journey towards the castle, we couldn't help but feel a sense of reverence for the fallen Kingdom. Each step we took was a testament to the resilience of Thalondor's enduring spirit, even in its current state of decay.

After what felt like an arduous trek, the towering silhouette of the castle emerged on the horizon. With each step bringing us closer to our destination, our anticipation swelled, our minds brimming with questions that begged for answers. We had embarked on this journey with a singular purpose—to uncover the truth about the imminent threat looming over the forest.

We reached the majestic steps leading to the castle entrance, a mixture of hope and uncertainty filled our hearts. The weight of our quest pressed upon us, knowing that within those ancient walls lay the potential for enlightenment or disappointment. We stood at the threshold, poised to enter, our collective determination overriding any doubts that may have lingered.

I chuckled, breaking the tension with a light-hearted comment. "Well, this is your last chance to back out," I teased, glancing at my companions.

Lucas, with unwavering determination, spoke up. "We've come too far to turn back now. We owe it to ourselves to push forward and unravel this mystery."

His words resonated with the team, stirring a shared sense of purpose. Ethan nodded in agreement. "You're right, Lucas. There's no better time than the present. Let's forge ahead and discover the truth that awaits us."

Aria, though less enthused than the others, shrugged. "Well, I might not be as excited as you two, but I didn't come all this way just to stand still. Let's get moving," she said, determined to see our mission through.

I paused for a moment before addressing Arabella. "Princess..." I began, but was interrupted.

Arabella's voice carried a touch of assertiveness. "Valaric, please stop calling me Princess. My name is Arabella, and I didn't embark on this journey to be treated. Let's keep moving forward," she asserted.

I met Arabella's gaze, a flicker of admiration in my eyes. "Very well, Arabella. Your determination is inspiring. Everyone, follow Arabella's lead. It's time to continue our quest," I declared.

"Let's Boudreaux this," I exclaimed with a mischievous grin. Lucas and Ethan chimed in, echoing my words with excitement. However, Aria and Arabella exchanged confused glances, not understanding the reference.

"What does it mean to 'Boudreaux it'?" asked Aria?

Ethan took the lead in explaining. "Well, you see, it's like when people throw caution to the wind and approach things with reckless enthusiasm and gusto. It's about taking bold actions without holding back. That's what it means to 'Boudreaux it'."

Aria and Arabella exchanged another glance, considering Ethan's explanation. After a moment, they both shrugged and nodded in agreement. "Alright," Aria and Arabella said with a hint of amusement. "Let's Boudreaux it then."

With each step up the majestic staircase, my anticipation grew, my heart filled with a mix of trepidation and excitement. As we ascended to the pinnacle of the castle, we crossed the threshold into a realm frozen in time.

Despite passing a millennium, the castle's enduring beauty and architectural splendor remained visible, testaments to the craftsmanship of its builders. The worn stone walls whispered stories of a bygone era, while the ornate archways beckoned us further into the heart of the castle.

Sunlight filtered through narrow slits in the walls, casting ethereal beams that illuminated the space with a soft, golden glow. The air was heavy with the scent of age and decay, yet beneath the layers of neglect, hints of the castle's former magnificence emerged.

Intricate carvings adorned the walls, depicting scenes of heroic conquests and mythical creatures. Despite the ravages of time, the delicate details of each masterpiece still kept a semblance of their former grandeur. I marveled at the skillful artistry, my eyes tracing the contours of every sculpted figure.

As we ventured deeper into the castle, we discovered rooms adorned with faded tapestries, their threads worn thin by passaging centuries. Although their colors had faded, the remnants of vivid hues hinted at the vibrant stories they once told. Portraits, now cracked and discolored, hung on the walls, gazing down upon us with ghostly eyes. The castle held a haunting beauty, a testament to passaging time and the stories it had witnessed.

The echoes of our footsteps reverberated through the empty halls, a solemn reminder of the castle's past inhabitants. Time had taken its toll, yet the grandeur of the structure persisted, its regal presence refusing to yield to passaging years.

Amidst the decay and abandonment, glimpses of the castle's former glory emerged. We couldn't help but be captivated by the enduring beauty that lingered within these ancient walls. With each step, we became part of the castle's living history, compelled to unravel the mysteries that lay dormant within its chambers.

"Despite the abandonment, this place still holds a captivating beauty," Aria marveled.

"To think of all the stories and events that unfolded here," Ethan exclaimed.

"It's a testament to the craftsmanship and artistry of those who built it," Lucas remarked.

"That its beauty remains intact after all these years is remarkable," Arabella mused.

As we continued exploring the castle's chambers, we felt a deep connection to the past, a shared appreciation for the enduring legacy of this once magnificent place. Each room held secrets waiting to be unveiled, and the journey ahead promised to be both enlightening and enriching. With the weight of history upon our shoulders, we pressed on, eager to uncover the truths hidden within the castle's ancient walls.

"Indeed, we are fortunate to witness the enduring grandeur of this place," I acknowledged. However, my determination to uncover the castle's mysteries remained unyielding. "Let us continue our journey and descend into the depths of the dungeon."

As we made our way deeper into the castle, an eerie silence enveloped the air, broken only by the faint echoes of our own footsteps. A series of strange, unsettling noises reverberated from the lower levels, like a series of screeching moans, sending a shiver down our spines. We exchanged cautious glances, our senses heightened and hearts pounding.

"Did you hear that?" I whispered.

The others nodded in agreement, their expressions reflecting a mix of anticipation and unease. We knew we had to be prepared for whatever awaited us in the depths of the castle.

With determined resolve, we continued our descent, each step taken with caution. We approached each corner with stealth, peering around, straining our senses to catch any glimpse or sound of the mysterious presence lurking below. The dim light cast eerie shadows, adding a layer of tension to our already tense surroundings.

Sensing the imminent encounter, I tightened my grip on my sword, the cold metal reassuring in my hand. I shared a silent nod with the rest of the team, a silent agreement to stay vigilant and ready for any confrontation that awaited us.

As we ventured further down, the atmosphere grew heavier, as if an unseen force permeated the air. The anticipation built, and we could feel the weight of the unknown closing in on us. I broke the silence, my voice filled with determination. "Something is down there."

Lucas, mirroring my determination, spoke up, "Well, there's no point in hesitating. Let's face whatever lies ahead and handle business." His words sparked a renewed sense of bravery within the group, bolstering our resolve to confront the mysterious presence head-on.

As we descended deeper into the castle, the noises grew louder, resonating through the stone corridors. Our anticipation reached a crescendo, our hearts pounding in our chests. The source of the sounds lay just around the next corner, beckoning us forward.

Peeking around the corner, our eyes widened at the sight that greeted us. Standing before us were some colossal creatures, their towering form of commanding space. Covered from head to toe in a thick layer of moss and foliage, it seemed to meld with their surroundings. The creature's rough skin blended with the earthy tones of green and brown, camouflaging it amidst the vine-covered ruins that had reclaimed the castle.

The creatures possessed a hulking frame, muscles rippling beneath its mossy exterior. Their sheer presence exuded strength and primal ferocity, hinting at the power it held within. Their mossy appendages, like twisted branches, added to its imposing stature, while its piercing eyes glowed with an untamed intensity.

We stood frozen for a moment, mesmerized and wary of the mysterious beings before us. The creature's moss-covered form seemed to pulsate with ancient magic, a fusion of nature and arcane energy. It was a sight that spoke of creatures born from the depths of forgotten legends and the wild embrace of the natural world.

"Does anyone have any idea what those creatures could be?" I inquired, scanning the faces of my companions for answers.

Lucas shook his head, his eyes filled with bewilderment. "I've spent countless days in these forests, and I've never encountered a being like that," he admitted.

I turned to the rest of the group, hoping that someone might possess a shred of knowledge about the mysterious creature we faced. However, before anyone could respond, a sudden disruption shattered the silence. Without warning, a stone hurtled through the air, striking Lucas on the head.

Lucas staggered backward, clutching his injured temple. The impact had caught him off guard, leaving him disoriented and in pain. The team rallied around him, their expressions a mix of concern and determination.

With our cover blown, I wasted no time issuing the command. "We can't afford to hold back! Attack," I shouted.

Ethan and Arabella drew their bows, releasing a flurry of arrows toward the enormous creatures, their projectiles finding their marks with deadly accuracy. Meanwhile, Aria conjured a blazing inferno, unleashing a torrent of fire upon the towering beasts. The intense flames licked at their mossy forms, causing them to roar in agony and flail in distress.

I charged towards the nearest creature, my sword and shield at the ready. With each swing, I aimed to cleave through the thick layers of moss and strike the creature's vulnerable flesh beneath. My strikes were swift and precise, leaving deep gashes in the creature's mossy exterior. The clash of metal against moss filled the air as I fought with unwavering determination.

Lucas, shaken but resolute, recovered from the surprise attack. He joined the fray, his senses sharpened by the sting of his wound. With a grimace on his face, he engaged the second creature, his blade slashing and stabbing with desperate ferocity. Blood trickled down his face, mixing with his sweat, but he refused to yield. Every strike he landed on was a testament to his indomitable spirit and the will to protect his comrades.

As we pressed forward, the echoes of battle filled the air, signifying more creatures lurking in the shadows. Undeterred, we moved from one encounter to another, engaging in a series of intense clashes. Ethan and Arabella's arrows flew with precision, finding their mark on the monstrous foes. Each piercing hit weakened the creatures, chipping away at their formidable strength.

Aria's fire attacks continued to prove devastating, engulfing the enormous creatures in searing flames. The creatures writhed in agony, their moss-covered forms smoldering under the intense heat. Seizing the opportunity, Lucas and I closed in on the injured creatures, our weapons slashing and striking with lethal precision. With each strike, we dealt the decisive blows, delivering finality to our formidable adversaries.

The team's synergy was clear as we coordinated our efforts. Ethan, Arabella, and Aria provided cover and weakened the creatures from a distance, while Lucas and I capitalized on the chaos, delivering devastating close-range attacks. The combined forces of arrows, fire, and steel proved to be a formidable combination, allowing us to overcome the odds and emerge victorious in each encounter.

However, unbeknownst to us, our string of victories was about to come to an abrupt halt. As we pushed forward, focused on the immediate threats before us, we failed to notice the hidden presence of a few remaining creatures lurking in the shadows. These cunning large beings had blended in with the overgrown vines that entwined the castle's structure, camouflaging themselves until the perfect moment to strike.

Completely absorbed in the heat of battle, we pressed onward, slaying the enormous creatures that crossed our path. Our relentless determination and skill allowed us to eliminate each foe we encountered, unaware of the growing danger that lay in wait. But as we ventured deeper into the heart of the castle, we came across an unsettling sight—a peculiar crack in the floor, emitting an eerie, dark light. It was from this sinister opening that the enormous creatures materialized, emerging with malevolent intent.

"Can any of you see what I'm seeing?" I called out, my sword piercing through the flesh of a creature before me.

"We see it too," Lucas replied, his blade cutting down another foe.

"They're already here, emerging from that crack," Aria said.

"It seems we've arrived too late; the darkness has already taken hold."

"The rate at which these creatures are pouring out of the crack is overwhelming. We cannot hope to keep up," Ethan remarked.

"Perhaps this is not an isolated incident. What if this is happening in multiple locations throughout the land?" Arabella's voice rang out amidst the chaos of battle. The thought resonated within us, amplifying our urgency and the gravity of our mission.

Swinging my sword with determination, I deflected a creature's attack. The realization that our immediate battle was just a fraction of a much larger conflict weighed upon us. We fought, fending off the relentless onslaught of creatures emerging from the crack. But it became clear that our current strategy was inadequate. The relentless stream of darkness pouring forth threatened to overwhelm us.

"Perhaps we should retrace our steps, return to the Glimmering Caverns, and make our way back to the kingdom to inform the King. We have gathered enough information!" Lucas shouted.

Ethan agreed. "That sounds like a solid plan. However, our path of retreat was cut off as hidden creatures emerged from the shadows behind us. We're surrounded," Ethan exclaimed.

I assessed the situation. "Focus your attacks, push them back," I commanded, thrusting my sword into another creature.

Arabella unleashed a barrage of arrows in all directions, but the number of enemies seemed overwhelming. "There are too many to hold off," she said. The odds were stacking against us, and we needed to find a way out of this dire situation.

We found ourselves trapped, fighting to survive. The odds were stacked against us, and the realization of our dire situation sank in. Uncertainty clouded our thoughts as we wondered if we would make it out of this perilous encounter alive.

Despite our grim circumstances, we fought with unwavering determination. Each swing of our weapons and every well-aimed attack held the weight of our survival. Yet, the sheer onslaught of the creatures threatened to overwhelm our defenses.

As our energy waned and our injuries accumulated, our outlook appeared bleak. The hope of a successful escape dwindled, and we braced ourselves for the worst. But even in the face of imminent danger, we refused to surrender.

"I have an idea! Everyone, gather back-to-back and alternate between sword and bow," I commanded. "Aria, create two rings of fire around us—one close and the other further out. Maintain that pattern as the flames die down," I explained. Without hesitation, the team formed a tight circle, our weapons at the ready, while Aria conjured the fiery rings.

"This will slow them down and give us a chance to concentrate our attacks," I assured the group, hoping my plan would buy us enough time to strategize. As the creatures closed in, we executed the plan, and it seemed to work. Ethan and Lucas took advantage of the brief gaps in the fiery rings to launch their attacks.

But the creatures proved relentless, breaking through the flames one after another. Our hope waned as we fought to hold our ground.

Realizing that our current tactics were not enough, I knew we needed to take more drastic measures.

"Alright, new plan," I declared.

Lucas, ever vigilant, asked, "What are we doing now?"

I replied, "Just hold this front and stay alive." My intention was obvious as I braced myself for the risky move I was about to make.

Ignoring the protests and exclamations of my companions, I charged into the two fire rings, using the intense flames as a barrier between me and the encroaching horde of creatures.

Aria's panicked shout echoed in the air, reflecting the group's shared concern. "No!" she cried out, mirroring the worry etched on the faces of the others.

Ethan sought answers, questioning, "What is he doing?"

Lucas, frustrated and worried, muttered, "The idiot is going to get himself killed."

Yet amid the uncertainty and fear, Arabella's voice rang out with a mix of resignation and admiration as she exclaimed, "I guess he is going to Boudreaux it."

Their eyes widened in disbelief as they witnessed Valaric's daring act, sprinting through the protective fire rings that had been carefully set up to safeguard their lives. It was a moment that defied reason and comprehension, yet the immediate effect was undeniable. A sudden realization washed over them as they noticed that the horde of creatures that had breached the flames had halted their advance.

A mixture of awe, gratitude, and sorrow flooded their hearts. Valaric's selfless sacrifice had created a respite, a fleeting opportunity for them to regroup and make their escape from the treacherous depths of the dungeon. The weight of his sacrifice bore upon them, and their resolve to honor his bravery burned brighter than ever.

With heavy hearts and unwavering determination, the team pressed forward, pushing towards the exit of the accursed dungeon. Each step they took was infused with a bittersweet mix of sadness and regret. Valaric's absence was acutely felt, his presence lingering in their memories and driving them to persevere in his honor.

As the weary team members mustered their strength to ascend the staircase and escape the confines of the dark, oppressive dungeon, their hopes of a swift exit were shattered by a sudden, blinding flash of light. The intensity of the flash was accompanied by a deafening percussion, shaking the very foundations of the crumbling castle. In an instant, the world around them seemed to ripple and distort, and a sense of profound unease settled upon their souls.

The luminous burst that had enveloped the area would soon become legendary; its radiance witnessed by all who lived in the vicinity. It marked a pivotal moment during everyone's lives, for little did they know that the ancient slumbering forces of good and evil had been stirred from their age-old rest.

The celestial spectacle, like an ethereal key, had unlocked the dormant animosity that had lain dormant for a thousand years. Good and evil, forces that had once clashed in an epic struggle, were now stirred back to life, ready to engage in a titanic conflict that would shape the fate of the world itself.

## *Epilogue*

After the intense flash, I witnessed a vision of an overwhelming scene of both awe and terror that unfolded before me. From my elevated position, I beheld a colossal battlefield teeming with warriors, their ranks stretching as far as the eye could see. The clash of arms and the thunderous roar of war filled the air, creating a symphony of chaos in the desolate landscape that lay in the wake of this cataclysmic confrontation.

As my gaze swept across the desolate expanse surrounding the great armies, a profound sense of emptiness settled in my heart. The once-vibrant landscape now lay ravaged and lifeless, a haunting testament to the relentless march of time and the ceaseless conflicts that had consumed this land. Here, amidst the vast barren wasteland, not a trace of normalcy remained.

The canvas of the land was empty of vegetation. There were no trees stretching towards the sky, no verdant foliage dancing in the breeze. The land stood stripped and desolate, bearing the scars of relentless battles that had razed everything in their wake.

As I continued to survey the surroundings, my eyes were drawn to the central stage of this barren land. Two great armies stood poised for conflict, their banners fluttering in the wind. The clash of opposing colors, symbols of allegiance and defiance, painted a vivid scene against the backdrop of emptiness.

Silence hung heavy in the air, broken only by the distant murmurs of warriors preparing for the imminent clash. The tension was palpable, as if the very land held its breath, anticipating the eruption of violence that was about to unfold. The war cries, fierce and resonant, echoed through the barren expanse, intertwining with the eerie stillness that enveloped the battlefield.

My gaze shifted from one army to the other, captivated by the sheer magnitude of the impending conflict. Each side exuded a palpable sense of determination, their spirits aflame with unwavering resolve. The anticipation was tangible, a charged energy that crackled in the air, as warriors on both sides awaited the command to unleash their fury upon one another.

And in a pivotal moment, the resounding blast of horns pierced the stillness, signaling the commencement of battle. First from one side and then the other. My eyes remained fixed on the formidable armies before me, their presence dominating the desolate landscape. As if commanded by an invisible conductor, a synchronized dance unfolded before my eyes.

With fluid precision, the archers leaned back, their bows pointing skyward, drawing the tension in unison. Time seemed to suspend itself as I witnessed the release of thousands of arrows, a breathtaking spectacle unfolding in slow motion. The flight of each arrow traced a mesmerizing path through the air, like ebony silhouettes dancing against the backdrop of an infinite canvas.

As the arrows soared, their collective presence formed an ethereal figure, a dark specter gliding through the heavens. My gaze followed the graceful arcs of these lethal projectiles, their trajectories intertwined with the anticipation of the impending clash. The air itself seemed to hold its breath, enraptured by the imminent collision of forces.

In a swift and decisive instant, the arrows descended upon the opposing armies, finding their mark amidst the clash of shields and the flesh of warriors. The piercing screams of the wounded echoed across the desolate expanse, their haunting cries reaching far beyond the immediate battlefield. The collision of forces had ignited the flames of war, and the great armies now converged with relentless ferocity.

Barren landscape was transformed into a theater of carnage and strife. The dry earth, void of life and sustenance, would soon bear witness to a torrential flow of crimson. A battleground, now drenched in the blood of fallen warriors, painted a macabre tableau of sacrifice and despair.

With the resounding blast of horns, the battlefield erupted into a cacophony of chaos and violence. The archers, guided by the call of duty, let loose another volley of arrows, their deadly flight blotting out the sun. As the lethal rain of projectiles fell upon the advancing forces, it seemed as if fate itself had cast its judgment upon the battlefield.

A clash of armies, like two titanic forces hurtling towards one another, ignited a maelstrom of destruction. The ground beneath their feet quaked with the thunderous resonance of armored boots pounding the earth. The air crackled with tension as warriors, fueled by bravery and desperation, closed in on their adversaries. Each step they took was a testament to their unwavering resolve to defend their cause and emerge victorious, no matter the cost. The battlefield, now a chaotic symphony of clashing swords and war cries, held the fate of countless lives in its grasp. As the intensity of the battle intensified, I knew that only the strongest and most resilient would survive this trial of blood and steel.

In an eerie display of symmetry, the two opposing masses moved as one, their momentum building with each step, like two unstoppable tides destined to collide. The sight was both awe-inspiring and terrifying, as the fate of countless lives hung in the balance.

And then, with a bone-chilling crescendo, the clash of steel reverberated through the land. Swords met with swords, unleashing a symphony of metal upon metal. The clash resounded in my ears, a haunting reminder of the grim reality that engulfed me. Each clash sent shivers down my spine, as if the very essence of battle had seeped into my soul.

Amidst the chaos, the battlefield became a swirling vortex of sweat, blood, and unyielding determination. Warriors locked in deadly duels, their faces etched with determination and grim resolve. The air was thick with the acrid scent of sweat and the metallic tang of blood, intermingling with the cries of pain and anguish.

Caught in the grip of this relentless tempest, I couldn't tear my eyes away from the devastating spectacle. I witnessed the clash of warriors, each one fighting for their cause, their beliefs, and their very survival. It was a sight that would forever be etched in my memory, a testament to the indomitable spirit of those who dared to face the horrors of war.

My eyes remained transfixed by the relentless carnage unfolding before me. From both sides of the battlefield, trebuchets launched volleys of fiery projectiles into the air. The sky became a canvas of destruction, adorned with flaming balls of death, hurtling through the air with terrifying velocity.

As each fireball found its mark, chaos erupted on the battlefield. Explosions of heat and flame engulfed the unfortunate souls caught within their deadly embrace. The ground trembled beneath my feet as the impact of the projectiles unleashed a wave of devastation, scattering warriors like leaves in a violent storm.

The acrid scent of smoke and burning flesh permeated the air, mingling with the anguished cries of the wounded and dying. Flames danced upon the earth, consuming everything in their path as they rolled across the battlefield. I watched in awe and horror as the infernal projectiles mowed down opponents, leaving behind a trail of destruction and despair.

The devastation wrought by these fiery spheres was too much for my senses to bear. My heart sank as I witnessed the relentless onslaught, the sheer magnitude of the destruction washing over me like a torrential wave. It was a scene of unbridled chaos, where hope and despair clashed in a symphony of destruction. Faced with such brutality, I could only hope that the indomitable spirit of the warriors would endure, for they were the ones destined to shape the outcome of this ruthless conflict.

The once pristine battlefield was now an apocalyptic landscape, scarred by fire and brimstone. I could fathom the magnitude of suffering that unfolded before me. Lives were lost in an instant, reduced to ashes by the merciless fury of the flames.

My gaze remained fixed on the relentless carnage unfolding before me. The clash of swords and the sickening sound of metal meeting flesh reverberated through the air. With every swing and thrust, warriors on both sides fought tooth and nail, hacking away at their adversaries with unwavering determination.

As the battle raged on, the ground became a gruesome tapestry of fallen bodies, strewn weapons, and splatters of blood. I observed with a mix of horror and awe as the combatants pressed forward, their resolve undeterred by the grim reality that surrounded them.

However, amidst the chaos, a glimmer of hope emerged. My sharp eyes discerned a subtle shift in the tide of battle. One army, with each passing moment, seemed to bear the weight of greater losses. Their lines wavered, and their ranks thinned as the opposing force gained ground.

Amidst the relentless chaos of the battlefield, the toll of significant losses manifested on one side. Their ranks dwindled, their formation weakened, and a sense of desperation permeated the air. The opposing army, fueled by their earlier momentum, surged forward with renewed vigor, their victory seeming more certain with each passing moment. The outcome of this cataclysmic conflict was now teetering on the precipice, and only time would reveal which side would emerge victorious from this harrowing ordeal.

Amidst the fury of the clash, I found myself consumed by confusion. The sight unfolding before my eyes was bewildering. Who were these two armies locked in such a brutal struggle? And how was I able to witness this momentous battle as if I had been transported across time?

As I surveyed the battleground, my mind swirled with unanswered questions. The air was heavy with the scent of blood and the echoes of war, yet the details of this conflict remained elusive. The banners of the warring factions offered no clue, their symbols unfamiliar to me. How had I stumbled upon this scene, and what role did I play in this enigmatic clash?

My thoughts raced, seeking answers amidst the chaos. Was I a mere observer, caught during a cosmic spectacle? Or did I have a more profound connection to this conflict, one that had yet to reveal itself? Uncertainty gnawed at my core, mingling with the awe and trepidation that the scene inspired.

As I redirected my gaze towards the waning battle, where the scales of victory seemed to tip in favor of one side, a peculiar sight unfolded amidst the chaos. Amidst the throngs of warriors engaged in combat, a luminous orb materialized, emanating a radiant glow that set it apart from the surrounding mayhem. The sight of this ethereal presence left me with an inexplicable sense of wonder and intrigue, adding yet another layer of mystery to the unfolding events.

The ethereal orb hung suspended above a select few individuals at the rear ranks of the losing side, captivating my unwavering attention. Their brilliance defied the grim backdrop of the battleground, casting a shimmering aura that stood out amidst the darkness of conflict.

My eyes widened with intrigue, and a hint of apprehension as I fixated on the expanding orb. Its radiant glow intensified, bathing the battlefield in an otherworldly hue. With each passing moment, the orb grew, surpassing the boundaries of its initial manifestation.

The chaotic clash of steel and the cries of combatants faded into the background as my attention became devoted to this captivating enigma. Victory or defeat on the battlefield lost significance, replaced by an insatiable curiosity to unravel the mystery that lay before me.

Drawn closer, I took hesitant steps towards the ever-expanding orb. Its brilliance shimmered, casting dancing shadows across my face, as if whispering secrets and possibilities. I couldn't help but wonder about its purpose, its significance in this grand tapestry of events.

Standing at the threshold of understanding, I voiced my thoughts aloud, my words lingering in the air like a silent prayer. "I wonder what that is for," I mused. The enigmatic nature of the orb stirred a myriad of questions within me, urging me to uncover its true essence.

In an instant, the serene existence of the orb shattered into a dazzling explosion of light, illuminating the entire battlefield in a blinding brilliance. I raised my arm to shield my eyes, but the radiance penetrated through my feeble defenses, leaving me disoriented and vulnerable. The intensity of the light engulfed everything, obscuring my vision, and plunging me into a realm of transient blindness.

Then, as the luminance waned, a pulsating wave rippled through the air, sending tremors coursing through the land. The ground beneath my feet quivered with each throb of the wave, as if the very fabric of reality itself had been shaken. The magnitude of the tremors reverberated through my body, awakening a primal instinct within me.

Struggling to maintain my balance amidst the tumultuous vibrations, I braced myself, my heart pounding in my chest. The land itself seemed to respond to the powerful surge, as if awakening from a long slumber. It was as though an ancient force had been unleashed, rippling through the earth with unyielding power.

As the luminous cascade receded, relinquishing its grip on the battlefield, my eyes adjusted to the residual glow that lingered in the air. Blinking away the remnants of luminosity, I surveyed the aftermath of the explosion, my surroundings obscured by the remnants of the ethereal display.

In the explosion's wake and the ensuing wave, a profound stillness settled over the battlefield. The once-ferocious clash of swords and the echoes of battle had been replaced by an eerie calm, a hushed anticipation that hung in the air. I could sense that something momentous had transpired, something beyond the realm of comprehension.

My gaze swept across the transformed landscape before me, and my eyes widened in awe and disbelief. The desolate battlefield, once littered with the remnants of a fierce clash, had undergone a miraculous metamorphosis. Where once there stood a barren wasteland tainted by the horrors of war, now flourished a vibrant, lush forest.

Gone were the traces of carnage and destruction, replaced by a breathtaking tapestry of towering trees, their branches adorned with verdant leaves that shimmered in the gentle breeze. The air, once heavy with the stench of blood and battle, now carried the sweet scent of blossoming flowers and the harmonious chorus of chirping birds.

I stood in awe, my mind reeling with questions and astonishment. The stark contrast between the recent battlefield and the blossoming forest before me left me speechless. I struggled to comprehend the magnitude of the transformation that had taken place, the vanishing armies, and the absence of death and devastation that had once permeated the area.

With a sense of wonder, I voiced my thoughts aloud, my words echoing in the newfound serenity. "What transpired here?" I pondered, my voice carrying a mix of disbelief and curiosity. "Where have the armies gone? Where has the cycle of violence vanished?" My questions hung in the air, unanswered and enigmatic.

As I took hesitant steps forward, my voice softened, a whisper. "Is this the birth of Eldoria Forest?" The words escaped my lips, filled with a sense of reverence for the miraculous emergence of nature's embrace amidst the chaos that had once reigned. The possibility that I had borne witness to the genesis of a legendary realm ignited a spark of excitement within me.